WEDDING DATE WITH THE BILLIONAIRE

ANDREA BOLTER

THE CHILD WHO CHANGED THEM

TARA TAYLOR QUINN

MILLS & BOON

First Published in Great Britain 2020
by Mills & Boon, an imprint of HarperCollinsPublishers,
1 London Bridge Street, London, SE1 9GF

Wedding Date with the Billionaire © 2020 Andrea Bolter
The Child Who Changed Them © 2020 TTQ Books LLC

ISBN: 978-0-263-29895-6

0121

WEDDING DATE WITH
THE BILLIONAIRE

ANDREA BOLTER

For Linda

CHAPTER ONE

"LADIES." KENTO YAMAMOTO stood on the boat dock and bowed his head to one then the other of the overly perfumed females who had just flanked him, a blonde on one side and a brunette on the other.

"How are you, Kento?" the blonde asked in a high-pitched tone.

"We've missed you," cooed the brunette.

He'd met the two years ago but, for the life of him, couldn't remember their names. It was hard to fathom that they'd *missed* him when he barely knew who they were.

"Isn't it exciting, Christy and Lucas's wedding?" The brunette stated the obvious. "And you're going to be the best man!"

"You came all the way from Tokyo to stand up for Lucas," the blonde chimed in, as if he was unaware of where he lived. "You're such a good friend!"

"Yeah, he's lucky to have a good friend like you."

"Yeah."

"Yeah."

Kento responded with a tight-lipped smile, already

done with this superficial chitchat. He'd been about to board the small private yacht he'd chartered for the ride across Seattle's Puget Sound to Willminson Island for the wedding weekend of his oldest friend. Then the two bubbly girls, friends of the bride's, if he recalled correctly, recognized him and came clamoring toward him, clomping down the wooden dock on their high heels even in Seattle's misty weather.

"We were just about to take the state ferry." The brunette pointed to the next dock over, where the enormous vessel that transported tourists and residents the quick half hour to the island was loading. "And then Mac-Kenzie spotted you, so we came running over to say hi."

Aha. The blonde's name was MacKenzie. One down.

"Amber said we just *had* to!"

"Had to." MacKenzie giggled.

Blonde, MacKenzie. Brunette was Amber. Noted. Kento didn't wonder why they just *had* to rush over to say hi. It wasn't because they were actually old friends gathering to celebrate the nuptials of two of their inner circle. No, it was because women like these two were professional money sniffers and had no doubt heard that Kento Yamamoto, the Seattle-born Japanese American billionaire who made his fortune in Tokyo, would be in attendance.

"How have you been?" MacKenzie asked through her awful bright orange lipstick.

"What's Japan like?" came Amber's probe with a sweep of her hair, as if there was a one-sentence answer to that question.

Kento knew their type. He'd encountered them all over the world.

As was usual for the breed, they were pretty. In a calculated way. They were both tall and statuesque and wore nylon windbreakers, one bloodred and the other as brash an orange as her lipstick, as if to be properly protected for the weather. But their jackets might have been a child's size, so snugly did they fit against their torsos. Surely there was no shield from the elements when those coverings were worn unzipped so low that Kento could make out the color of each of their bras. Jeans skimmed their long legs down to the spike-heeled boots that looked ready to catch in between the wooden planks of the boat dock.

Both had hair styled to perfection, which was almost pointless if someone was to spend any amount of time outdoors in Seattle. As if to illustrate the point, the mist in the air had turned to rain in the few minutes since they had been chatting, as often happened in the Pacific Northwest. They both wore heavy makeup, and individual raindrops began sticking to their false eyelashes, creating little bubbles.

"Mr. Yamamoto, ready when you are, sir." The yacht's captain appeared with his announcement.

Having just flown in on his private jet from Tokyo, Kento had a couple more legs to his long journey— a boat ride to the Willminson Island harbor and then a limo to the luxury lodge that had been reserved for the destination wedding. He'd spent most of the flight working and was tired, looking forward to a little rest before the numerous events of the extended weekend began to unfold. Plus, he'd learned that once a person was running a multibillion-yen software development empire, there was no such thing as a total escape and he'd be supervising operations from afar over the weekend. So he was ready to board and let the captain set off.

"Ladies, if you'll excuse me. I'll no doubt see you at the welcome reception tonight."

The smiles that had been glued onto their faces both dropped in unison. He didn't know what they were expecting, but their expressions read disappointed. They'd wanted something from him. Just as the rain turned heavy and a downpour began.

Cripes, Kento thought. He couldn't shoo them away and send them teetering in the rain with their heels and wheeled suitcases all the way over to the other dock to take the public ferry. He'd have to give them a ride.

"Come onto my boat. I'll take you," he said, stretching an arm out to help the first one of them onto the deck. They both grabbed hold of him at the same time.

"Thanks, Kento!" one exclaimed and clumsily hoisted herself on. He became part of a tangle of outstretched hands and luggage handles while the rain whipped around, so he didn't notice which of them had thanked him.

"You're a hero," came the other's voice.

"Our knight in shining armor."

It was going to be an endless ride across the Sound if they continued with their sucking-up routines. Did men actually fall for that sort of thing? Not men like him, he affirmed. When just about every human encounter of his formative years had been a verdict on what his financial and social standings were and weren't, Kento had developed a healthy skepticism for people's motivations in wanting to get close to him.

In fact, he'd soon be face-to-face with some of the very people who had ingrained that distrust into him, who'd seared it into him like a hot iron's brand that he still wore like a tattoo. An attitude that he was proud of at this point. While the upcoming weekend was meant to send Lucas and Christy into what would hopefully be a lifetime of wedded bliss, Kento had some less idyllic business of his own to take care of.

After he ushered the two women into the shelter of the boat's cabin, Kento returned to the open air of the stern as it pulled away from the dock. He would no doubt get soaked, but he didn't care. From his vantage point at the back of the yacht, he kept his eyes fixed on the mainland as they pulled away, the sights of the Seattle skyline that he hadn't taken in for years. The Ferris wheel. The renowned food stalls of Pike Place Market. The office skyscrapers. There were the mountains in the distance, dwarfed by Mount Rainier, the tallest in Washington, the stratovolcano that hadn't erupted since the late 1800s.

Kento felt a special nostalgia to once again see the most famous of the city's landmarks, the six-hundred-foot-tall Space Needle observation tower that instantly identified Seattle. As it had since its construction for the 1962 World's Fair, the structure with its flying saucer design watched over the storied city with a parent's caring eye.

Seattle used to be home. It was where he'd grown up and gone to university. After his software design corporation, NIRE, continued to grow and grow, Kento moved his parents to Japan to be with him. His sister now lived in Connecticut, so he no longer had cause to return. Breathing in the wet mist of the Sound, he was reminded that there was nowhere quite like Seattle, the Emerald City, so named for the year-round greenery in and around the metropolis.

It was a city filled with memories for Kento, some good, some not so. In particular, there was one recollection that he needed to bring into the present so that he could put it in the past. A remembrance with dusty blond hair the color of pure sand and eyes so light a brown they were almost transparent. With skin that smelled like sweet cream. The scent that still lingered in his nose, all these years later.

"I hear you and Erin Barclay used to date," MacKenzie blurted after Kento returned to the cabin and instructed the first mate to serve him and his guests a quick coffee for the short journey.

Kento looked her in the eyes but, really, peered right through her. "We did," he answered barely above a whisper. "A long, long time ago."

"And now you're best man and maid of honor at the wedding. That is *so* cute." Amber's voice entered from his side.

"Is it?" Kento raked his fingers through his thick, now soaked hair.

Of course, he'd been honored when his oldest friend asked him to stand beside him as he said his vows to his bride. Especially as the two men no longer saw much of each other. Kento had accepted, though not without trepidation, predicting that Christy would tap her cousin Erin to be the maid of honor. It had been seven years since he'd seen Erin and zero days that he hadn't thought about her. As maid of honor and best man, he knew there'd be expectations that the two would spend a lot of time together, giving speeches, dancing for photographers and fostering a general camaraderie among the wedding party throughout the activities of the weekend.

As he'd thought about it over and over again sitting in his luxury penthouse overlooking kinetic, buzzy Tokyo, Kento began to believe that returning to Seattle for the wedding was perfect for the reckoning that he so desperately needed. Maybe that time spent working closely together would help him finally exorcise Erin from his brain and his soul. Hopefully, he could break free from the hold that his memories still had on him. "Cute." He hypnotically repeated Amber's stupid comment.

"I hope you'll save a dance for me," MacKenzie chirped. "We're bridesmaids, you know."

"Do you want to sit together at the welcome dinner tonight?" Amber asked. Kento found the question annoyingly pushy and didn't respond.

Luckily, neither of them wanted to leave the cabin to go with him to the boat's bow as they neared the island's shoreline. Lush fir trees appeared to cover every inch of earth, tall, full and close together, creating a dense forest. It was an unspoiled and pristine spot that would make for an unforgettable wedding.

Kento felt the tiniest kick of sadness in his gut.

When his boat docked in the harbor, he helped

Amber and MacKenzie disembark, refusing their offer that he join them. The public ferry arrived at the same time, delivering other wedding attendees. He recognized a few, scrutinizing the group and looking for that familiar sandy hair but not seeing it.

A covered walkway had been erected to shelter guests from the ferry dock as they loaded into the van that would shuttle them to the lodge. Amber and MacKenzie joined the group. A waiter was there to greet everyone with a tray of champagne in flutes. Continuing to observe the scene from afar, Kento could hear MacKenzie's shrill giggle.

There was a banner hung to welcome their party. It read, Christy and Lucas. Forever Begins Now.

Kento knew that transportation from the harbor to the lodge had been prearranged. But he'd booked his own, guessing that he wouldn't want to be part of the festivities until he'd settled in. He waited for the van full of wedding guests to leave. A second, empty van pulled into position for the arrivals from the next ferry. The waiter set more flutes on his tray and filled them with bubbly.

Only then, in the solitude, did Kento make his way up the gangplank and slip into the black limo that awaited him.

"Did you hear? Harris Denby drained her bank accounts before he vanished."

Erin Barclay entered the lounge adjacent to the lobby of the upscale Locklear Lodge on Willminson Island, where her cousin Christy was marrying longtime boyfriend Lucas. Erin had arrived just in time to overhear a group of wedding guests talking about her.

"Where did his parents finally track him down?"

"Partying in Greece with some European actresses."

"He just left Erin? Without a word?"

She turned away from their view so that she could listen in without yet being spotted.

"What kind of man does that?"

"The kind who lives off his trust fund with nothing expected of him and too much time on his hands. Apparently, his own family's wealth wasn't enough. He went after *Barclay* wealth."

"The passed-down-from-generations, too-much-to-even-count kind of money." A few high-pitched giggles erupted. "Our favorite kind of people."

Bridesmaids and daddy's little rich girls Amber Dutton and MacKenzie VanBurton seemed to know an awful lot about her. They were friends of Christy's that Erin had socialized with a few times over the years. The two stood in a cluster with the three groomsmen, who listened dutifully to the girls as they all sipped something warm-looking from heavy brown mugs.

Was this how the weekend was going to go? Erin wondered, with gossip swirling about her being freshly dumped by Harris T. Denby III? Who had left her at the town house they'd shared in Spokane, where her parents had created a job for her at one of their offices there. Harris had simply disappeared in the middle of one night. Once he was located and word got out, the media that followed high society jumped on the story and, thereby, made sure that everyone Erin knew had heard about it.

"Christy said she never trusted Harris from the beginning," MacKenzie prattled on.

"Not from the start," Amber echoed.

Erin knew that Christy must have been defending her by telling them that she had never liked Harris. If only she had heeded that warning!

Subtly peering around the lounge, she was still trying to avoid being noticed just yet. The lodge was as rustic glam as she'd remembered when she accompanied Christy and Aunt Olivia to tour it as a possible wedding venue. Everything was done in the finest materials. A fire in the huge stone hearth gave the room a comfortable warmth and smell. Thick rugs covered large areas of the tiled floor. Overstuffed leather furniture and tree-trunk tables were arranged into clusters. Paintings of nature, featuring flora and fauna native to the area, decorated the walls. A buffet table held a selection of coffees and teas as well as small sandwiches, fruit and cookies, all artfully displayed on raised platters.

Erin was hungry. She hadn't eaten since before she left the town house in Spokane to head to the airport for her short flight to Seattle. But she wasn't sure she was ready to face the bridesmaid firing squad and their potential interrogation. As the quintet still had their backs to her, she was able to continue listening for the two words she knew she'd hear. They came immediately.

"You know she used to date Kento Yamamoto?" One of the men spoke the only name that had ever made Erin's heartbeat sputter. Of all the things she was likely to have to face this weekend, seeing Kento again was the scariest.

Amber exclaimed, "We know! He gave us a ride here on his boat."

"On his boat."

"He's a major player in the software sector, isn't he?" another other man in the group asked.

"Major."

"He's *so* gorgeous," MacKenzie threw in.

He was at that. Erin knew that the seven years they'd been apart looked good on him because she'd seen articles in magazines about the young, unmarried billionaire. From the photos she could see that nothing had changed about him being six foot three with hair that was too long for a businessman. Nor the dark, probing eyes and slim hips. Although she'd noticed that his face had matured from that of university student to twenty-eight-year-old CEO.

"And he's megarich," Amber continued to blab.

"Mega."

Kento had brought them to the island on his own boat. Erin wondered how that came about. Unless things had changed, it wasn't like him to go for the gold digger types. In fact, that was what she had always suspected was one of the things that drove him away years ago, this elite Seattle crowd's obsession with money and success. Back then, just like Harris more recently, Kento had disappeared. She hadn't known why, but he'd vanished just the same, leaving Erin abandoned. Decidedly different was that Harris leaving didn't matter to her all that much. Kento's departure had been another thing entirely. One that, in fact, had altered her life.

As to the bridesmaids, back in the day Kento had loathed people like Amber and MacKenzie, judging men based on their bank accounts or status. Although what would Erin know about Kento's likes and dislikes anymore? She hadn't seen him since he'd gone from a have-not to a most definite have.

"Is he single?"

"Doesn't he live in Japan?"

"Was he born in Seattle?"

"Does he know Harris broke up with Erin?"

"He didn't have a date with him on the boat."

"Is he bringing someone to the wedding?"

"Look him up online."

"Whoosh." One of the guys finally put the kibosh on the gossip. Erin almost let out a chuckle, so laser-focused were these big-haired opportunists. "All I said was that he used to date Erin. I have no further intelligence. Shall we call in the FBI?"

If the two bridesmaids rode across the Sound with Kento, that meant he was already on the property. A pulse dashed through Erin's body at the thought. She glanced behind her as if she might see him suddenly standing right there, eavesdropping on her eavesdropping.

Instead, when she turned around she saw Bettina "Bunny" Marchand Barclay, her mother, coming toward her. Bunny Barclay was probably Seattle's most visible socialite, constantly appearing in the news at a gala fundraiser for a new museum or a mayor's luncheon or the like. Upper crust to a fault, Bunny wore pearls to breakfast. The Barclay fortune belonged to Erin's father, Ingram, the fifth generation of land and property owners who were in possession of a good percentage of Washington state. Her father wouldn't be in attendance for the wedding weekend, as he had important business in Walla Walla.

"You look absolutely gaunt," Bunny trilled as she air-kissed her daughter on each cheek. "I hope there's a makeup artist coming, and immediately."

Erin wasn't aware that she didn't look right. She'd scarcely checked a mirror today. Since Harris had fled three weeks ago, the days had been a blur spent mostly in the gloomy and overdecorated Spokane town house that she'd never liked, anyway. After Harris's departure, her parents had decided that Erin would move back into their palatial home in Seattle, with the intention of finding her a suitable husband, of course. Because breeding was to be Erin's most important purpose in life. After several disappointments, they'd thought they'd made a perfect match in Harris. How wrong they were. Hair and makeup had been the last thing on Erin's mind lately.

Having already checked into her room, she was certainly planning to shower, dress and groom appropriately for the welcome dinner later that would kick off the wedding festivities. It quickly crossed her mind that she hoped Kento wouldn't be coming down to the lounge now for the afternoon snack, not wanting to see him until after she'd pulled herself together. Not that it should matter, as it was far too late for anything between the two of them. He'd made that abundantly clear when he deserted her without even saying goodbye. Kento, a few others that never developed, then Harris, the aging party boy. Was there anyone on earth who had worse luck with men than she did?

"Erin," Bunny continued, "there are a number of eligible men coming to the wedding I want you to meet."

"It's only been three weeks since Harris left me." Erin sized her mother up like she was crazy. "Isn't a mourning period in order?"

"You do not tell people that Harris *left* you. You say that you found you weren't compatible."

"Mother, do you remember that I mentioned to you a 1902 property in Queen Anne I saw? Now that I'm going to be moving back to Seattle, I'd like to look at buying that for the company."

"You know we have an acquisitions department to handle new purchases. Let's concentrate on finding you a proper match so that the next generation of Barclays is insured."

"That's my purpose in life? I'm just a pedigreed racehorse?"

Erin didn't hide her cynicism. Really, though, what difference did it make? Let her parents choose a mate for her, sure. Her own attempts had ended with love jetting five thousand miles across the Pacific Ocean to build a future that didn't include her.

"And no, at your age we don't waste time licking our wounds."

"Yes, at twenty-eight, I'm an ancient sack of bones."

"The clock is ticking. Let me tell you about someone. Humphrey Colder."

"Kento Yamamoto is here, Mother. Now that he has money, maybe you'd like him better." The words fell out of Erin's mouth before she had a chance to censor herself. He'd devastated her by leaving, but he didn't deserve to be part of a sarcastic joke. Yet she'd always had a suspicion that her parents had had something to do with Kento walking out of her life.

Bunny bristled. Her small mouth pursed. "We deal in traditional wealth, Erin. Established families from the Northwest. Landowners. Not fly-by-night tech billionaires. The Kento Yamamotos of the world aren't our kind of people. They never were and they never will be. Have I made myself clear on that?"

You're not the one who should have been spending your life with him, Erin thought but didn't bother to say, as it was a lost cause.

Kento surveyed the view from the front porch of the second most deluxe cabin on the Locklear Lodge grounds. He'd reserved the largest for Christy and Lucas, his wedding gift to them. His was expansive and constructed in a rich red wood, the porch large enough to house a hammock and a sofa swing. He noted that the enclosed side deck offered complete privacy and was equipped with a sauna, hot tub and outdoor shower. It wistfully occurred to him what a romantic setting this would be for a couple in love.

The vistas were magnificent. Beyond the large stretch of lawn that the cabin opened onto, the dense grove of fir trees so plentiful in the Pacific Northwest stood proud and strong. Their bracing, earthy scent was like no other. It would do Kento some good to take a walk in the forest there, the moist earth under his feet. He couldn't have been farther from his ultramodern office suite in Tokyo.

He heard them before he saw them. Loud voices interrupting the hush of nature. Squishing sounds in the ground.

"Hi, Kento!"

"Hi, Kento! We didn't see you in the lounge."

It was Amber and MacKenzie trotting the footpath that crossed in front of his cabin en route from the lodge's main buildings.

"Hi, Kento." A third voice poked out from between the two. Kento's stomach lunged at the possibility that it might be Erin, whom he hadn't yet seen since he arrived. He'd skipped the revelry at the ferry dock and opted out of the afternoon tea. Was this the moment they'd lay eyes on each other again for the first time this weekend? Would she be happy to see him? He knew what hurt he still carried. What might she?

The clearing between the bridesmaids opened to reveal a short woman with large breasts. She was definitely not Erin. "I'm Divya Nadu, and I've been wanting to meet you." All three of them giggled. Kento wasn't sure if he was disappointed or relieved that he wasn't face-to-face with Erin yet. Although that would be coming soon enough, as everyone was expected at the welcome dinner.

"*Prosperity Magazine* named you one of the top five billionaires under thirty," Divya squealed.

"Did they? What's the criteria for that?" Kento snickered and folded his arms across his chest. "How did I get into the top five?"

"Oh, good question. I think it was that they predicted your fortunes would continue to grow."

"Based on what?" How familiar this was. All of Kento's life it seemed that within minutes of meeting someone, there was some inquisition as to his positioning and station. He was right to have left this toxicity behind him when he moved to Tokyo after earning his university degree. There were plenty of opportunists there, too, especially as he became more and more successful. But he'd learned how to better detect and fend them off.

It still nagged in his craw, though, how he'd left Erin, the only woman who saw him for who he was not what he had. Clearly she'd wanted him to go. After all, she had participated in his ousting. But he should have said goodbye. What they'd had together was important, and they'd owed each other a final farewell. All these years later and his business with her was still unfinished.

He'd met plenty of women in that time, Ayaka being the only one he'd gotten serious with. Which turned out no better than things did with Erin. The memory of Erin had never left him, though. In a way, it was holding him back. Maybe if he didn't still have foggy dreams of her eyes sparkling in the moonlight, or remember her smiles in the sunshine, he could be free from desiring something he knew he'd never have.

Billionaire bachelor. Ha. Always would be.

"I guess they think your company will get bigger and bigger," Divya continued. "I mean, it's so huge already."

"Huge."

"Enormous."

As these women babbled on, Kento figured it was going to be a long, long weekend.

MacKenzie said, "Let's have a drink at the bar before dinner."

"A little cocktail kickoff."

"And sit with us at dinner, Kento." Hadn't one of them already asked him that earlier? These women didn't know a thing about him other than what they'd read in a magazine. Yet they wanted him to sit with them. Was it any wonder he felt constantly measured?

"Sit with us." Amber was beginning to sound like a pouty little girl. Which, in fact, she was. Divya's smile was as forced and wide as a jack-o'-lantern's. How could he get them to move on?

"If you'll excuse me, ladies," Kento said politely, "I'm going to go inside to get unpacked and dress for dinner. I'll see you there."

"Okay," MacKenzie sang, "but you better at least dance with me."

"Me, too."

"Me, three."

He bowed his head at each of them. Thankfully, they skirted off after a chorus of goodbyes.

Swiping his key card, he stepped into the cabin and took off his shoes. Inside, it was thankfully quiet. The living room contained large furniture that faced the view through the windows. A dining table and chairs could accommodate a private meal for eight should that be desired. The kitchen area was stocked with local brands of gourmet snacks and a basket of fresh fruit.

Wines, sodas, waters and a coffee setup stood ready on the counter. A state-of-the-art media center allowed as much connectivity as a guest could want.

The bedroom was furnished with a king-size bed framed by a redwood headboard and posts, made up with plush green plaid bedding and a dozen pillows. A small sofa and coffee table faced the wood-burning fireplace as well as a second wall-mounted TV, giving the bedroom options for more than sleeping.

An extravagant bathroom was anchored by a claw-foot bathtub. There was a walk-in shower with glass walls. Shelves held stacks of fluffy towels and baskets of toiletries. Kento unbuttoned his shirt and threw it onto a vanity table. He quickly stripped off all his clothes, ready for a shower to reinvigorate him after a long journey and the grating encounter with the grinning bridesmaids.

Before stepping into the shower, though, he had a change of heart. The weather had cleared and there was even some end-of-the-afternoon sun, so he decided to make use of the outdoor shower.

Knowing the area was fully secluded thanks to its own cluster of trees, he grabbed a couple of towels and strode naked out the door to the side deck. The shower wasn't enclosed in any way. Its wide rain-forest faucet was embedded in a stone wall, leaving everything around it open. He turned the knobs until the spray produced a strong flow. When he stepped under the showerhead, the hot water pouring down onto him in conjunction with the soft breeze across his skin was a sublime combination. He let the water slide down his body, swirling to the drain at his feet. Breathing in, he took his time and allowed the sensations to envelop him. It was truly relaxing.

His nakedness outdoors felt so primal. As if an ancient drum was beating somewhere low within him, marching him toward something unseen. A hunger and virility inside him woke up, breaking out of hibernation. Spreading his arms wide-open like an eagle's wings, he presented his manhood to the blue skies. The water cascaded over his head, down his neck, his shoulders, his chest, his erection. Receiving the downpour, he stood like that, arms outstretched for the longest time. The only thing that kept him from roaring out loud was not knowing how far his voice might carry.

Eventually reaching for the bar of sandalwood-scented soap that had been provided, he began lathering his entire body, scrubbing it into his skin with his hands. Erin was somewhere on the lodge's property, and he'd be seeing her soon. Had she come into his mind so often over the years because she'd wounded him so badly with her betrayal? Was it because he was torn up by regret for running away, never even confronting her about what she'd been part of? Or was it because no woman had ever compared to her and until he saw her again she'd always have a hold on him? That was what he intended to settle this weekend. He'd return to Japan with no more unanswered questions.

In any case, Kento could smell change in the crisp Washington air.

CHAPTER TWO

"No, the maid of honor. She's the one Harris Denby dumped."

Erin pretended she didn't hear people talking about her from, literally, behind her back, although she didn't miss a word. She was like a dog that could hear high-pitched sounds that didn't register with humans. It was as if the whole room was talking about her. Again. Her head started to spin. She'd only been on the island for a couple of hours, but it already seemed like a month.

The weekend was full of planned events. Tonight was the welcome dinner. Tomorrow would be the rehearsal and the rehearsal dinner. The day after was the afternoon wedding ceremony, followed by the reception. And the weekend was to conclude with a gift-opening brunch the following morning. Erin didn't know how she was going to make it through with people pointing at her and her mother lining up men for her to meet.

Waiters passed glasses of wine, sparkling water and hors d'oeuvres on trays. There were teeny-tiny apples stuffed with creamy cheese. Cornmeal-fried oysters.

Prosciutto-wrapped asparagus. Erin grabbed at every-thing she could as it was carried past. She hadn't eaten at the afternoon tea once she was commandeered by her mother, who sent her back to her room until her appoint-ment with the makeup artist and hairstylist, deeming Erin unfit for public consumption until then.

The stylist did work wonders, she had to admit. Since Harris had left her, she'd been in a funk and didn't give a hoot about her appearance. So a haircut had indeed been in order, and the nice blowout would look good for the many photos Erin would have to stand for as maid of honor. Her makeup was flattering but not overdone. And the long burgundy, three-quarter-sleeved sheath dress worn with brown lace-up boots seemed spot-on for the evening.

Erin hoped the outfits for each of the weekend's occa-sions that she and her mother had shopped for conveyed maid of honor status without defying Erin's understated personal style. Unlike the credo that less is more, her mother was always telling her that more is more, that sparkly objects garnered the most attention. But some-thing in Erin's very being had always been repelled by her mother's constant flaunting of their wealth. Some-thing very few people in her life had ever understood. Definitely no one at this wedding, the crème de la crème of Seattle. No one except...

Her eyes inventoried the room with its enormous picture windows showing off the twilight and its bright blue skies over the trees. Erin's scan wasn't to admire the vista outside, though. She was looking for some-one inside. A certain tall, dark-haired someone whom she was both desperately dreading and breathlessly excited to see.

"You look absolutely radiant," Erin managed when she hugged her cousin Christy Barclay, soon-to-be Mrs. Lucas Collins. Erin's compliment was a stretch, because she thought the bride was a bit overdone with her ruffled yellow dress. But Erin knew Christy had to be camera-ready the entire weekend.

"Lucas has some great friends I want to introduce you to," Christy whispered in her ear before someone called her away. "Let's get that Harris mess behind you."

First her mother, now Christy! Was every person here determined to either gab about her being ditched or to fix her up with someone? It was embarrassing that everyone in the free world seemed to know about her breakup, and how that was apparently the best topic of conversation they could come up with. Right on cue, Erin's mother approached.

"Thank heavens they gave you a manicure," Bunny quipped, strangely focusing on Erin's nails, which had been polished in a bright violet shade that was similar to her maid of honor gown. Her mother offered another vague insult. "This afternoon you looked like a wild child who climbed out of the Olympic Mountains."

"Thank you, Mother. That's a lovely image."

"Now, where's that Mr. Colder?" Bunny said as she looked for a man different from the one Erin searched to find. "A very interesting prospect for you to talk to."

"After it went so well with Harris," Erin chortled sarcastically, "we know your matchmaking skills are top-notch."

"Don't be rude, Erin. Had you been able to get Harris to settle down, you would have been perfectly stationed for life."

"Oh, I see. It's my fault I wasn't able to turn his cheating, lying ways?"

She knew that she was being snippy when, in reality, she'd all but resigned herself to letting her parents make the match they wanted. One of the arranged Pacific Northwest society marriages that her father insisted made just as much sense now as they had throughout history. Left to her own devices, she'd die a spinster. She'd thought she'd once known what a true union was. What love was. But it stole her heart and flew far away, leaving only a hole that would never be filled.

Fine, she could procreate, carry on the family genes. As long as she didn't have to fall in love. That would be a fate worse than death. The most she could hope for was that she'd end up with someone with whom she'd have some things in common and they could serve their offspring-producing callings with an amiable companionship.

"I forgot something in my room," Erin lied. She followed the waiter with the fried oysters, just needing a break from her mother.

"I've got someone fabulous to introduce you to," Christy sang as she skidded past Erin while she was being led across the room by her husband-to-be. "He coaches basketball with Lucas." The groom was a big and tall man with a ruddy complexion, a high-ranking stockbroker at one of Seattle's top firms. As was his father. As was his father's father. *Old money,* as Bunny loved to point out.

Noticing two couples gesturing to her, Erin was getting dizzy from everyone's attention. The room seemed to be closing in. How could she get everyone to just leave her be?

She was a dutiful daughter. Yet for all of her cynicism about not caring with whom she produced heirs, in the secret, most hidden recesses of her soul, she was screaming for something else. She was starving for adventure. For risk. For passion.

At that exact instant, the moon outside rose and cast a powerful beam down through the window toward the opposite end of the party room. It was white and tapered open like a spotlight positioned on an empty stage. Erin's eyes followed it and she turned in its direction, wondering how moon glow could be streaming so intensely at that one spot and no other. She couldn't see what was over there because too many people were in the way. Without telling them to do so, her feet began moving toward the direction of the light.

The closer she got, the more the clusters of guests moved to the left or to the right, opening a path for her. Her steps became faster. Until she froze when she reached the other side of the room, where a solitary figure stood at the arched entrance to the party. He was observing the scene, almost as if deciding whether to enter. And he was indeed bathed in a moonbeam, or at least that's how it appeared to Erin.

The familiar handsomeness sent shivers racking through her. The high cheekbones, full lips and his imposing height reminding her, as they always had, of drawings of potent Japanese emperors with long swords from centuries gone by. Especially in the shadow profile of the light shining down on him, he commanded all he surveyed. His dark hair still fell in a thick, youthful tousle downward from his forehead, hinting at a rebelliousness despite the fine navy suit perfectly tailored to his lean muscular body.

As if knowing she'd be there, he turned his head. His gleaming almost-black eyes bored into hers the instant they made contact, causing her breath to shorten, and she went from a casual pose to standing at attention.

Slowly, the seriousness in his face melted to something gentler, where it lingered for a moment. Then the gaze quickly corrected itself, as if the previous move had been a swiftly caught error. He returned to his piercing stare. Kento Yamamoto bowed his head and said only, "It's good to see you again, Erin."

She was a real human. Flesh and blood. Not the almost otherworldly character that inhabited his midnights with snapshot remembrances of hopes long gone. After seven years, more than long enough to shed a skin, Erin Nancy Barclay was in front of him once again. The mixture of emotions Kento felt was like one of those cake beaters that whirled ingredients, wet and dry, salty and sweet, smooth and chewy, until they were too intermingled to separate. He wanted to reach out and hug her in almost equal measure to his desire to turn around and bolt away.

"Did you just get here?" she asked, the tones of her voice like an old song he hadn't heard in ages.

"A couple of hours ago. I checked in on some work."

"You skipped the welcome tea."

"How was it?"

"I didn't end up staying."

"Why?"

"I got waylaid by my mother."

The corner of his lip tipped up. Some things never changed. "Hmm."

"It's a really long flight for you from Tokyo, isn't it?"

"And oh, yes, we're getting some nice afternoons this time of year."

She looked at him questioningly. "What does that mean?"

"That commenting on banalities is the best we can do after all this time?"

"What would you like to talk about?"

They were off to a rocky start. She was right—he couldn't yet ask what he wanted to. About how she could have participated in the despicable forcing out of him that her parents had enacted. He'd come for those answers, but this wasn't the time or place. Outwardly, they needed to be pleasant exes who were attentive to their best man and maid of honor duties. To lead the bridal party and serve the bride and groom with whatever they needed.

"Did you write your speech?" he asked.

"I drafted out some ideas. Wishing people a happily-ever-after ride into the sunset is a little hard to write when you've just been broken up with."

Broken up with? His jaw locked. He'd heard from Lucas that Erin was living in Spokane with someone and that it was serious. He hadn't talked to Lucas in a couple of weeks other than some emails, in which the groom hadn't mentioned that Erin and her man split up. Kento had assumed that she'd have him in tow for the weekend. He guessed that the boyfriend was certainly someone Erin's parents had sanctioned, as approval was always one of the key tenets in the Barclay family.

Did that mean that she was here on her own for the wedding weekend? Kento's mind began to spin. He'd wanted to see her again, to finally emancipate himself from the shackles their past kept him in. But he needed to do that from a safe distance, with her unavailability serving as an impenetrable barrier that would prevent him from considering things that couldn't be. Erin single and unbound was too risky.

"Someone recently broke up with you?" He decided to play it cool, to pretend like he didn't even know she'd been in a relationship. Meanwhile, at seeing her again, the hurt he'd brought along with him spilled out of his pockets, breathed out of his nose, blinked in his eyes. At the same time, she was so exquisitely beautiful a wail fought to make itself known.

"You mean you haven't heard? It's all anyone seems to be talking about this weekend."

"Did your parents like him?" He couldn't resist the dig. After all, if it weren't for Bunny and Ingram, and Erin's allegiance to the way her parents thought, the two of them might have had a future together. Who knew what could have happened? She could have moved to Japan with him. Or perhaps he wouldn't have gone. They might be married. Have children. For that matter, they could be divorced. There were so many could-have-beens. He wondered if this ex-boyfriend suffered the same fate.

"Indeed. My parents fixed me up with Harris."

Ah, so nothing at all like Kento. "He was the right sort, then?"

Erin blinked a few times. He realized he was being cruel. After not seeing her for so long, his emotions had had a chance to compound. He needed to take it slow. Watch what he said. She'd just been broken up with. Even though he didn't know the circumstances, he was never one to kick someone when they were down. In spite of how many times that had been done to him.

"He looked great on paper, as they say. In reality, it didn't work out that way."

"I'm sorry to hear that." Was he? Whether or not she was with someone should have no effect on him.

"It's another cliché, but better to find out sooner rather than later."

She didn't look exactly the same as she did in the mental photo album he flipped through far too often. From a ponytailed girl with designer jeans and purses, her wealth something that had always been visible, she'd ripened into a striking woman who wore her wine-colored dress with style. The close fit outlined her slim body, the one he'd known every inch of in days gone by. His belly tightened at the recollection.

Her eyes were a little drawn, perhaps revealing her

recent romantic failure. He found himself wondering about the details, why he'd broken up with her. But those unusually light brown eyes of hers were still her most arresting feature. He remembered peering into them for hours on end, trying to count the little gold flecks in her irises. He was glad that tonight her lips were covered in only a natural-looking gloss. It was easier that way to imagine…

They stood contemplating each other, perhaps melting into the same remembrances, perhaps opposite ones. Kento's body was so alert and on edge that he wondered if his nerve endings could take much more. He felt almost out of control, something he wasn't accustomed to.

"What about you?" Fortunately, Erin recircuited his brain. "Single, married, divorced, gay?"

"Married," he tittered. Did something register in those eyes of hers in response to his answer? "To a billion-yen software development company." Then, did he sense her relief after his explanation?

"I've heard. So, after graduation when you left…to work with your uncle in Tokyo, you never came back?"

"At first I'd come to see my parents now and then." He'd never attempted to see Erin on those trips. Her parents had made their lack of welcome infinitely clear. And she'd proved that she wasn't capable of defying them. "I moved them to Japan a couple of years ago, and I haven't been back here since."

Kento's parents. Who couldn't be more different from Erin's. Who didn't have money in the bank but labored so hard to pay for their two children to go to good schools and top universities. Because they wanted them to have options. His sister had become a lawyer. And Kento had found his niche in software.

Ultimately, what his parents wished for him proved to be a double-edged blade. The exclusive schools with the high academic reputations certainly taught him well. But being the charity case among the upper crust, one of the few who had to apply for every scholarship and dollar of financial assistance available, set him up for constant embarrassment and ridicule. Rich kids showed no mercy for the übersmart boy who received help with his tuition. Kento bore those scars silently for his parents, though, who were so proud of every good exam score and achievement of their son's.

"How are they?" She'd only met them a few times, as they were always busy working at their small grocery store in the nearby city of Tacoma.

"I was so glad when I could give them the word a couple of years ago that they should retire because I could easily provide for them. Typical for them, they were too modest to let me buy them a spacious home. Instead, they chose an apartment in a retirement living community just big enough to suit their needs." Unlike Erin's parents, who wore their wealth on their sleeves, their cars and their mansions. And, most especially, with the people they surrounded themselves with, whom they picked and chose as if selecting only the shiniest unbruised apples from the farmer's basket.

"Kento, Erin, will you kick off the evening with an impromptu toast?" Lucas yelled over to them from the gaggle he was standing with. The reminder of the reason they were there startled them both, with Kento lost in days past.

"I guess it's showtime." Kento shrugged. He gestured with an outstretched arm that they should enter the thick of the group.

After doing so, when they were surrounded by partygoers, a waiter appeared with a microphone. Erin took it and began. "It's great to see everybody here. On behalf of Christy and Lucas and their parents, welcome to Locklear Lodge."

Kento reached to tip the mic toward him, noting the tingly contact his fingers made with Erin's. "Or to be known this weekend as the Forever Begins Now Inn," he said, repeating the sentiment printed on the banner that had greeted guests getting off the ferry earlier. "We wish you all the health and joy in the world."

"And children," a male voice in the crowd added.

"And money," another yelled, earning a laugh from everyone.

Erin finished with, "Let's enjoy our dinner as we begin to celebrate the nuptials of these two very special people."

Fortunately, that appeared to be sufficient for the moment, because people clapped and then began making their way to the dining area of long tables set up with a campfire theme.

The best man and maid of honor presided over the guests as they took seats.

"Kento!"

"Kento!"

"Kento!"

The three voices he'd already come to know charged toward him like a battle army. He caught Erin mashing her lips together as if to stifle a laugh.

"Hi, Erin."

"Hi, MacKenzie, Amber and Divya," she answered.

Ah, so she knew the three barracudas.

"Kento, we're sitting together, aren't we? You promised!"

"You did!"

He'd done nothing of the kind and might rather starve than have to endure dinner conversation that would no doubt pertain to his holdings in the Tokyo Stock Exchange.

Thinking quickly to help him out, Erin broke in with, "I'm sorry. We're obligated to sit with the bride and groom."

The three mouths that again wore the most unfortunate bright shades of lipstick drooped into mopes.

"Okay…" Divya whined. "But you'd better at least dance with us this weekend."

"Yeah."

"Yeah."

With that, the three clip-clopped away on their high heels.

Kento could have almost kissed Erin for getting him out of their clutches. Absolutely almost kissed her.

"Oh. Kento. Yes, hmm…how nice to see you again." Erin's mother was one of the last to enter the party. Bunny stumbled over her words. "I hear your company is doing fabulously."

"Mrs. Barclay." Kento bowed his head, the Japanese custom that must be second nature to him now. Without warmth or familiarity, he moved no closer to Erin's mother than where he was standing. He certainly wasn't going to give her a hug. Bunny and Ingram had made no attempt to hide their disapproval of him back when he and Erin were dating, and there was no reason to think they would warm up to each other now. It was far too late for that.

It hadn't been of interest to her parents that Erin was her happiest when she was with Kento. They'd had a connection unlike anything she'd ever known. When they were alone together, the outside world disappeared. Her family's wealth and his family's lack of it meant nothing. What was important was smiling into each other's eyes and the passionate kisses that fortified her like nutrition. Looking back, she knew it was a cocoon they'd existed in, university students excited to exchange ideas, share insights, make love. With him, she was alive. Inspired. Involved.

"I think you're sitting over there." Erin pointed to a few of Bunny's contemporaries in an effort to get her away from Kento as quickly as possible. Her mother seized the opportunity and immediately joined her friends.

They made their way to the long, narrow table, where they sat opposite each other. Set chuck wagon–style in keeping with the woodsy lodge, it was a chic and expensive fantasy of roughing it, of course. Sterling silver utensils were styled flat and plain, looking like they were meant for campfire eating. The dinner plates were also metal, and the water glasses were short and solid. Colorful bandannas served as napkins at each setting. Instead of floral centerpieces, groupings of small logs and pine cones were stacked as if they were ready to be kindled.

Erin took her seat with her uncle, the father of the bride, Vernon, to her left and Christy on her right. On the other side of the table, Kento was seated between the bride's and groom's mothers. Servers brought baskets of warm sourdough bread and pots of soft butter wrapped in more bandannas. Private reserve wine was poured into tin cups as the first course, cioppino, was served in bowls with handles, continuing the homespun theme. The tomato broth was deep red, and the stew was packed with plump shellfish. Erin spooned a bite into her mouth. A guitar player in the corner of the room strummed country songs.

"Kento sure looks good after all this time," Christy whispered in Erin's ear. "Is he seeing anyone in Japan?"

"I have no idea," Erin said in return, even though she thought whispering in each other's ears was rather childish.

"I told you," Christy continued, "you should talk to Demarcus Hall, sitting next to Amber." She gestured with her head as if Erin wouldn't know where to look otherwise. Erin had recognized him as one of the group listening to the giggle girls' gossip earlier at the afternoon tea. She'd certainly noticed that Demarcus was a nice-looking man in a tan suit politely listening to Amber, whose mouth never stopped moving.

Sure that Kento wouldn't have heard the exchange

between her and Christy, her eyes nonetheless darted across the table, over the mini log centerpiece, to check on him as he chatted with Lucas's mother. His eyes shot briefly to her and then back to his conversation.

It was nothing less than surreal to be in his presence again. His invisible pull was so powerful it was as if there was only an inch between them rather than a table. As if she could feel his breath on her. No wonder that a few minutes ago it had seemed to her that the moon was shining down on him. The moon existed only for him.

She sneaked another peek while he was bringing a spoonful of stew to his mouth, reacquainting herself with his big hands and their long fingers. She could almost sense them on her skin as if it was yesterday, not years, since they'd last touched her. The cioppino had no idea how lucky it was to be crossing his lips.

Erin herself was almost too nervous to eat, though she nibbled small spoonfuls for the activity it provided. How different this moment would have been if Harris had waited until after the wedding to desert her. With his extroverted personality, he would have sucked up all of the oxygen in the room and demanded her full attention. Not leaving her alone like this, inside her mind, to reminisce about Kento and days long ago.

On a day shortly after their university graduation, they were to meet at their favorite bakery café in the city's Belltown neighborhood. The day before, Kento had been with her at her parents' house, and when Erin was coming back into the room after a phone call, she'd observed something suspicious. Her parents were in a heated discussion with him. He kept snapping his head back at what they were saying, as if he was surprised by it, almost as if they were delivering blows. His body had been taut with tension. All Erin had been able to catch when she reentered the room was her father saying to him, "Just so we understand each other."

She'd been looking forward to the coffee date so that she could ask him about the conversation. Especially as, when she asked them, her parents had denied that anything strange occurred. Kento would provide the truth. Arriving at the bakery ahead of him, Erin ordered a tea latte and a dill-and-goat-cheese scone.

Little did she know when she snagged the window table to look out on a rainy afternoon that she'd be sitting there alone until after dark. Picking at the scone and bitty sips of her latte ended up as a clean plate and empty cup. After Kento was past a reasonable amount of late, phone calls to inquire went straight to his voice mailbox. Finally, Erin acknowledged that he wasn't coming, and she left.

Could something have happened to him, she fretted? He could have been lying in a hospital somewhere, or worse. After a horrific night of worry, it wasn't until the next day that she was finally able to reach his roommate and hear the news that Kento had boarded a flight for Tokyo. Taking the offer of a job from his uncle Riku that Erin had thought he was going to turn down. She must have read the situation between them very wrongly indeed.

The welcome dinner progressed with Erin and Kento stealing glances at each other over their plates of cowboy pepper steak, jacket potatoes and sautéed green beans. Bunny sauntered by and whispered in Erin's ear for her to sit up straight as, unforgivably, she must have been slouching. "Eleven o'clock." Bunny did one of her nonobvious-obvious finger points. "Jack Piccadilly. Accounting firm in Pioneer Square, keeps the books on everyone who's anyone in Seattle finance."

"Is he the one with the three hairs on his head doing a comb-over?" Had all of Seattle's best sons under thirty been taken, and now Bunny was looking within the available crop of *older* gentlemen?

"We're going to find you an appropriate match, Erin. Weddings are a wonderful place to get things started."

Kento made Lucas's mother smile with something he said. She dropped her bandanna napkin, and he instantly reached down to the floor to retrieve it for her. She smiled in recognition like a schoolgirl. Bunny's voice sounded like an insect in Erin's ear that she swatted away. Thankfully, her mother moved on.

She stood up, telling Christy, "Excuse me." Out of the corner of her eye, she could see Kento watching her go.

Working her way through the narrow channel between the tables, she overheard someone she didn't know say to their dinner companion, "That's the one Harris Denby dropped like a hot potato."

Glancing behind her, she saw MacKenzie, Amber and Divya had wasted no time in surrounding Kento after Erin left the table. Not to mention a few other overtly flirty women. The look on his face told her that they all grated on his nerves. She hadn't known whether he was with someone or was going to bring a date to the wedding. Even if his money wasn't good enough for Ingram and Bunny, the sheer volume of it was attractive to the bounty hunters. It seemed as if the both of them were going to be driven crazy this weekend by matchmakers, gossipers and hangers-on. If only there was a way to get everyone off their backs!

Instead of going to the ladies' room, Erin darted through the lobby and out the lodge's front doors. The sky was pitch-black and a constellation of stars filled the sky.

The evening air was nippy, and she hadn't brought along a sweater or wrap. But as she moved farther and farther away from the lodge, the darkness and quiet were welcoming. She continued into the night, reassuring herself she'd get through this. Although if one more person made reference to Harris leaving her, she thought she might blow a fuse.

Honestly, she also need to process seeing Kento again. Unlike Harris's flashy personality, Kento's magnetism was grounded and solid, like one of the majestic trees in front of her, with unseen roots and a firm standing on the earth. No one else had ever reached down right into her soul like he had.

A cold breeze swept under her dress and chilled her to the bone. She wrapped her arms around herself as she shivered. Behind her, she heard a rustling and figured the wind was kicking up. The night was wild, untamed, making her wish she could emulate it. But it was time to go back inside and be civilized for dessert. She'd make an effort to get to know some of the guests she'd never met and smile for every photo.

As she was about to turn around and go back, she heard leaves crunching again. Suddenly, she felt a presence behind her. Her body startled as a low voice hummed into her ear, "Are you cold?" just as Kento put his suit jacket around her shoulders. It felt like a long-lost blanket that she had been searching for everywhere. She pulled it tightly around her. Involuntarily, her cheek rubbed itself against it, and she inhaled its scent. Kento's scent. "The stars are beautiful, aren't they?"

CHAPTER THREE

"WHAT ARE YOU doing out here?" Erin turned around to face Kento after he'd slipped his jacket around her slender shoulders in an impulse that managed to feel affectionately familiar and crackling new at the same time. With the moon and stars above them, Erin was luminous. A harsh intake of the night air barely hid his reaction.

"Same as you, I'd imagine. I could use a break from the crowd." It was true that Kento had been looking for a reason to get out of the party room. Besides the bridesmaids, it seemed like every unmarried woman on the island for the wedding had been trying to make his acquaintance. The wealthy class of the Northwest was an insular bunch. A person practically had to have made their money during the Klondike Gold Rush to be legitimate in their books.

Now that Kento had amassed a fortune, his new *foreign money*, as some of them regarded it, was apparently good enough for some of them to try to get near, even if it wasn't respected. And so the women here were marching their cosmetically altered assets in a parade for him. It was no different in Japan—prospectors came in every race, creed and color. He had bitter memories from Tokyo as well, though not as many.

He supposed there were men who would take advantage of the situation. They wouldn't care about ulterior motives when receiving attention from these glittery objects. Kento understood. These women used their wiles as currency. Everything was a bargaining chip. A commodity. Everything had its price. Erin's family thought quite literally in that way.

As if money and accomplishment were the only ways to define a person. He'd never encountered anyone who really saw him. Not growing up poor here and not staggeringly wealthy in Japan. Not Ayaka. He'd originally thought that Erin was the exception to the rule. That he'd found his soul mate. Until he learned the hard, burning way that he'd been very wrong. Erin was, and always would be, an heiress to not only a financial portfolio but to a way of thinking.

Still, watching her hold the lapels of his jacket around her after all this time stirred him inside. *His* jacket. Once he'd gotten over the squeeze to the gut from seeing her after so long, he was grateful. He required this. To be with her here in the States, no longer the ghostly mystery still haunting him from across a gigantic ocean.

"We have to be *on* this weekend," she said. "How are we going to survive it?"

"I was expecting you to be huddled with your boyfriend when I saw you again." A boyfriend whose jacket she'd already have over her shoulders, signaling that Kento's was unwanted and that she belonged to someone else.

"So was I."

"What went awry?"

"My parents."

"What do you mean? I thought you told me they liked him." Kento didn't allow his smirk to grow wide. The conversation never veered far from Bunny and Ingram.

"They chose him for me. A founding family in the Pacific Northwest—they own fleets of cargo ships and whatnot. Could have been a great merging of families."

"Right, that sounds like a business transaction that would make your parents ecstatic." The sarcasm poured off his tongue. Her eyes looked glassy in the moonlight, almost as if she was going to cry. He hadn't meant to upset her with his tone. Even though she was at the top of the list of people who had instilled the cynicism he lugged like a ball and chain.

"What my parents hadn't spent any time on was figuring out if Harris and I were compatible past our family coffers. You have to at least like a person a little bit, even if it was an arranged union, don't you?"

"I wouldn't know." More quips in his voice.

"If my parents had investigated a little better, they'd have heard the common knowledge—he was a cliché bon vivant with the yachts and the models in bikinis and all of that bling. He had no interest in settling down in Spokane, or anywhere else. Or with me."

"You found out after you were already together?"

"I was willing to give it a try. I'm not expecting to find love after…" Her voice trailed off, making Kento wonder what she wasn't saying. "But they could at least try to find me someone who actually wants to be in a relationship."

Kento snickered. Which finally made a small smile appear on Erin's face. That was part of what had made them work as a couple, their ability to laugh even when the going was at its toughest. He was glad to bring her some relief from what was obviously a painful recollection. "So what happened?"

"We dated for a while, attending charity functions and the like, as good heirs do, and then our parents pushed us to move in together. We played at the domestic routine. Within a month Harris began disappearing, first for long weekends and then for weeks at a time."

"Where did he go?" Even though Kento was bitter about what had happened between them, he wouldn't have wished her the disappointment or shame she was describing. After all, he had left her, too. He hated that he'd hurt her, that he'd never said goodbye. In fact, the guilt of that decision tortured him still. To hear that another man had left her without an explanation tore at his heart.

Forces opposed within him. On one hand he'd never forgive her for being complicit in her family's doings against him. Yet on the more mature other, he felt sorry for her inability to break away from their hold. He respected family loyalty, so he couldn't blame her. It just made no sense that this beautiful and dynamic woman wasn't making her own decisions.

"Martha's Vineyard. Rome. Rio. You name it. When

I asked Harris if I could go with him, he'd say it was for business and that there was no place for me there."

"You knew he was lying?"

"He had no business to take care of. And even if I didn't know he was lying at first, it wasn't long before my gossipy so-called friends—" she gestured her head toward the lodge, where the snooty party guests were probably forking into their desserts "—sent me photos and videos they saw online. Harris was either too uncaring or too stupid to even try to keep his image clean for his parents' sake, let alone mine."

"I hate the internet."

Erin belly-laughed at his joke, as obviously his multi-billion-yen business was dependent on the high-tech world. She was so infectious that he laughed, too, until the sound of their laughter permeated the silent darkness that surrounded them.

She had wounded him deeply, the most profound cut he'd ever received, a knife stab that would impair his breathing for the rest of his life. Yet he felt relief to be near her again. Finally. She'd never know the torment she had caused him. The replaying in his mind of the times they shared. They were only together for a year, but it shaped him. She didn't assess him, unlike everyone else. He could just *be* around her, relaxed, with nothing to prove. He'd learned who he was through her.

Their coupling was unlikely, the well-to-do white girl and the son of a Japanese grocery store owner. Yet they created something genuine together. They were natural around each other, just as their laughter was now. It was as if they were the only one in the other's life who saw through to their insides, laying their souls bare. They'd met in the early fall of a university class and by graduation had dreamed of a future together. She spent more time in the cramped apartment he shared with a roommate than she did in the mansion where she grew up. Until Ingram and Bunny squelched everything.

The recollections of those days and nights together still called out to him, randomly in the middle of a conference or looking at a flower. Confusing his conviction that avoiding relationships altogether was the solution. He'd never met, or believed he'd ever meet, anyone like Erin. He'd never experienced that closeness with Ayaka or anyone else he'd dated. He'd been given one chance at the real thing, or at least he'd thought he had, before Erin and her family snatched the dream away from him. That was the result of taking a chance on trust, of opening his heart. That's why he so desperately wanted to see Erin one last time, to liberate himself from the hold she had on him.

Because although he'd never love again, he did need some companionship and fun. As he approached thirty, the lone-wolf life was unsatisfying. He had sexual encounters with women here and there, after which he couldn't get away fast enough. Even that was growing tiresome. He knew he'd never genuinely partner again, but maybe some kind of casual understanding with a woman was possible. After Erin and then Ayaka, he'd closed himself off. It wasn't healthy. Except how could he hope to have anything when he compared every woman to Erin and found them lacking? He had to find a way this weekend to let go of her once and for all.

"This is good," Erin said as she pulled his jacket to her tighter in a way that made him feel like his arms were wrapping around her instead of the garment. "A moment's tranquility from being fed to the sharks."

"I know what you mean."

"Our wedding party jobs will keep us busy, although they haven't stopped me from being the most gossiped-about maid of honor in Washington State history. And everyone has someone new for me to meet."

"A destination wedding without a date. The pressure is already killing me. Get me back to Japan." They laughed again. Kento had been working especially hard lately to launch a new accounting software program. It was a huge hit in the marketplace, his biggest yet, and the stress had left him drained. Howling into the star-filled Seattle sky with Erin Barclay was about the best remedy he could possibly imagine.

"Actually, I was thinking something kind of outrageous," she said.

"I already like the sound of that."

"If I was here at the wedding with a date, that would show everyone that I'm not just Harris Denby's old cast-off. And get the matchmakers and my mother off my back at least for the weekend."

"So you're going to call someone and ask them to come to the island?"

"Oh, no, I wouldn't have anyone to call." He was surprised that she said that so matter-of-factly. She must know dozens of men who would jump at the chance to be with her, even without her family's name. "No one I could trust, anyway. It was just a crazy thought."

With the moon and stars as their only light, Kento could make out Erin's outline as they walked the outskirts of the lodge's property, beyond the courtesy lamps stationed to keep guests on their path. The two of them alone together again at last. Unexpectedly, he pulsed with the urge to pull Erin from the perimeter into the tempestuous unknown of the adjacent forest. He could imagine pinning her up against one of the enormous tree trunks, pressing his body against hers, into hers, as he took her lips without restraint. He could only shake his head in amazement of his own thoughts.

"These people are your family and friends, yet you want to pretend to be romantically involved with someone even though you're not?"

"I just want a break from being talked about, you know?"

"Oh, do I. Don't forget I've been a great source of amusement and ridicule for your crowd ever since I was a kid."

"Look, Kento has the same ratty backpack as he did last year."

"Maybe we should all chip in and buy him a new one."

"Can you believe no one picks him up from school? He takes the bus."

"The bus? Ew."

He'd had to endure the teases and taunts. As a boy, he wasn't invited to the extravagant birthday parties with the clowns and the pony rides. When he was a young teen, pretty girls snubbed their pert noses at him in the school hallways.

"That wasn't my crowd, as you say," Erin defended herself. "That was my family's."

"In any case, I was thrown into the center of it."

"Did you ever tell your parents what you went through?"

"No, of course not. It was out of the love my parents had for my sister and me that they insisted we go to the best private schools in Seattle. We'd sit at our kitchen table, the four of us, year after year filling out the financial assistance and scholarship forms that could make it possible."

"I remember your parents as very kind."

"I did everything I could to help them. I studied hard to excel in my academic subjects. Played sports and the violin. Volunteered my time at hospitals and interned at tech companies. Everything I could to be a desirable candidate for whatever tuition aid we could apply for."

"I don't think back then I really considered just how different our home lives were. We'd kind of created our own little world, you and me, right?"

Yes, they had been more an oasis for each other than they'd ever realized.

"In one respect, it all paid off. I graduated high school with many honors and received acceptance at high-ranking universities. You know at Rainier U, I was invited into prestigious fraternities and social clubs."

"I remember you said you never felt truly welcomed."

"The positive outcome of all of that negativity was that I got tough and worked even harder."

"If it's any consolation, when I was with you was the first time I'd ever really chosen the company I kept. I'd never connected with anyone like we did."

Her words echoed in his chest. Perhaps she was saying something he'd always wanted to hear. Although her lament didn't make him forget what had happened between them. Kento was not a person who was capable of forgetting. Indeed, it was remembering that drove him. Motivated him. And it would continue to do so.

"That wasn't enough for you to stand up to your parents, though, was it? Instead, you stayed behind their shield." There. He'd said it.

"What are you talking about? You're the one who left. Without even a word."

Kento hadn't meant to get into a rehash of the past. He supposed he was just incapable of bull. Her saying that when she was with him was the only time she'd chosen her own companion had sent fire up his spine.

There was nothing to reconsider. Or process. His intention was merely to see Erin again, to be near her, so that his soul and mind could say a formal goodbye. Her nonplace in his life was like a sickness. All he wanted was the cure.

What are you talking about? You're the one who left. Indeed he was, but she knew why.

Kento had a strange niggling. Was it possible that he remembered things differently than what had actually transpired? Digging into historic record wasn't what he'd come to do, yet it itched like a bug bite begging to be scratched.

He turned his head toward her, the moonlight glistening off her hair like her locks held tiny sparkles that only he could see. He'd forgotten many things about her. Like her exact height, which he could see was perfect to lay her head against his shoulder. He'd forgotten those graceful fingers that now held his jacket around her shoulders. The fingers that she'd thread through his when they walked down the street. Bags too heavy with books and electronics, sometimes he'd show off for her by carrying both of theirs. More glorious than he remembered were her pillowy lips, which under the stars looked especially ripe for the claiming. If there was any chance of him surviving the weekend, he'd have to get thoughts like kissing her against a tree out of his mind.

When the funky beat of a popular song crashed sound into the hush of their walk, they realized they'd been outside for a long time.

"Deejay," they said in unison.

"We'd better go back in."

Several heads turned when Kento and Erin returned to the welcome dinner together. If she'd thought of it, she'd have gone to the ladies' room to stall so that Kento could have walked in alone with her arriving a few minutes later. As it was, she felt the scrutiny of many eyeballs. One thing she did know was that when he flattened his palm against her back as he guided her back to the party, she had to fight to keep her facial expression neutral because her body sizzled from head to toe.

Darn him for being able to cause that response in her after all this time! Outside, in the dark, when he'd startled her by coming up from behind and placing his jacket around her shoulders, her body's sense memory instantly took her back. How much she'd always craved his touch when they were together. After they'd part to go to classes or some other business, she couldn't wait to get back into his arms. His close embrace became quite simply her favorite place to be. He'd always held her tightly, possessively. Even at twenty-one he was sure and solid, a take-charge person who had the fortitude to persevere no matter the obstacles. She hadn't envisioned his future career at the time, but creating and helming a massive corporation was not hard to picture, even then.

"How dare you make me miss dessert," he joshed. He was right; waiters were already clearing the empty dessert plates. The remnants of a milk chocolate tart with salted caramel sauce looked delicious.

"Hey, you came outside on your own volition. I just happened to be out there," she shot back to him with a smile.

"You ensnared me with your shivering shoulders. What kind of best man would I be if I didn't give you my jacket?" Although she'd returned said jacket to him once they got back inside, Erin could still sense it on her, around her, as distinctly his. Intoxicating.

"Can you forgive my shoulders?"

"I'll consider it. If they get me cake."

Bridesmaid Divya, who was jumping up and down for no explainable reason while waving frantically at Kento, called out, "When's my dance?"

He leaned to get very close to Erin's ear, so near that she could feel the warm stream of his exhale as he whispered ever so lightly, "Cake."

His voice coated her, sweet and thick as the caramel sauce. Not missing a beat, as a waiter walked by with an untouched slice of the tart on a plate, Erin relieved him of it and handed it to Kento.

"That's my girl" was his response. Erin's jaw dropped at his word choice as she watched Divya continue to bounce up and down like she was on a spring.

His girl.

She was his girl. Until she wasn't. Five thousand miles away kind of wasn't. She could never forget the desertion. Especially when he'd never explained why he went. Outside, he'd made reference to her hiding behind her parents, but he hadn't explained specifically what he meant.

"Can I get a shot of you two?" the photographer, Billy, gestured to bring Erin and Kento together for a photo. As he posed them, Kento took hearty bites from his tart, making *mmm* sounds that were ridiculously sexy. Once they were in position, Erin took the plate from him, which was met with a frown that made her grin.

"Do I have cake on my face?"

She inspected the area around his exquisite, sensual mouth. Had there been even the slightest crumb, she would have had the opportunity to brush it away with her fingers, an activity that sounded delightful. She'd almost melted into liquid when he'd merely wrapped his jacket around her.

Billy requested, "Look at me, please." The best man and maid of honor conceded and smiled their brightest and best. The photographer shifted them again for the shot he wanted. He then brought over Lucas and Christy for some photos of the foursome.

When they were done, Lucas took Erin's hand and said, "May I dance with the maid of honor?" As she accompanied the groom to the dance floor, she saw the three bridesmaids lunge toward Kento. Fortunately, he quickly took Christy's hand to follow Lucas's lead. The four of them began to dance to an upbeat song. At the deejay's urging, other guests joined.

"Dumped her like a sack of laundry from what I was told. Sent her running right back to Mommy and Daddy Barclay."

Erin overheard a couple dancing near them and could hardly believe the glee in their voices at her misfortune. Kento heard it, too, and shot them a scowl. This was why she had come up with the pretend-boyfriend idea. If people were going to gossip, let them marvel at how fast she'd found another man so soon after her breakup rather than continue to make fun of her about Harris.

A romantic ballad began. Lucas brought Erin a respectable distance to him and they began their dance. Within a verse or two, though, the photographer appeared and wanted to do some shots of the bride and groom dancing together. That left Erin and Kento standing on the dance floor. He raised his palms up in surrender as if there was only one option.

With a cute bow from the waist, he asked, "May I?" Not waiting for an answer, he swept his arm around her waist and pulled her to him.

Her body met his, a divine joining from a muddled dream she'd had so many years ago. Docile, she got lost in his muscular chest, his shoulder span so broad and arms so long she felt completely enveloped. It was almost as if in his embrace she could finally breathe again. Being so close together, as their maid of honor and best man roles were going to necessitate, she'd need to gird herself against his allure, to remember that moments like this were fake. He'd already broken her heart once before, and he would be jetting off forever in just a few days.

After they'd danced a little, she replayed the conversation they'd had outside. She tilted her head back to ask him, "What did you mean before when you said that I stayed behind my parents' shield?"

"When your parents decided that the way to get me out of the picture was by making it worth my while, you went along with it."

"Get you out of the picture? Worth your while? You're the one who left for Tokyo without a trace."

"I was angry. And frightened. I think my feelings were justified. There was nothing to say."

"You were angry about what?" She was getting tired of this cryptic conversation. Here she was in Kento Yamamoto's arms after seven long years, and he was making references to things she didn't understand. She glanced away from him and spotted her mother at the edge of the dance floor. Erin noticed how rigidly her teeth were clenched. Her fists were balled. Even though it was perfectly legitimate for the two of them to be dancing together, Bunny was absolutely livid at the sight.

"We can be honest at this point, Erin." He brought

her attention back as he swayed them in dance. "I know you knew about it. They told me they had discussed it with you and that you were in agreement it was for the best. It made sense. Your parents' social stratum has entrance criteria that I was never going to meet. They were right."

"What are you talking about?" What on earth had happened that day before he'd stood her up at the bakery? Despite repeated questioning, her parents had denied that anything unusual had transpired, so she never got any further insight into what happened.

Just so we understand each other.

She'd only heard the last of it, what her father said. What had there been to *understand*? Her parents probably assumed she and Kento would separate after graduation. He wasn't *their kind*, as they always categorized people. They were going to uphold their moneyed little Seattle orbit. But Kento was ambitious and hardworking, and she'd hoped her parents respected that she cared for him. She had been sure that *he* at least had *known* that she did.

"You walked in on the conversation. And must have known what it was about. You certainly didn't ask any searching questions about it."

"You never gave me the chance," Erin snapped back. Although nagging in the back of her mind, suddenly, was the same question. Why *hadn't* she asked more questions? Tried harder to get to the truth? "I do remember that when I came back into the room, you were rigid and eager to leave. The air was thick enough to cut with a knife."

She'd sensed that something was wrong. Kento had always had little patience for her parents and she rarely left him alone with them, so it wouldn't have been surprising if they'd said something that offended him. They'd probably made some kind of elitist statement that went against his grain. She hadn't read that much into his bad mood at the time. Just as she'd decided not to be concerned that the kiss he gave her at the door wasn't his typical, full of decisiveness and heat. It was distant, perfunctory, impersonal. She didn't know it then, but it wasn't a good-night kiss—it was a goodbye.

"Afterward," she continued her account, "I asked my parents what you three had been talking about, but I never got a direct answer."

"So you let it go at that. You didn't fight for me."

"I didn't know I needed to. You never explained, either."

"They told me you knew."

While they continued to dance and hold up appearances, both were becoming palpably upset.

"Knew what, Kento?"

"About your parents' proposition."

"Huh?"

"They wanted to make sure I fully comprehended that I was just a college fling for you. Now that we'd graduated, you'd be beginning your adult life, and that didn't include me. To make sure I got the point, they offered me a very large sum of money to go away and never contact you again."

"They did what?"

"You heard me." Erin's eyes opened wide. Her heart

pounded a thousand beats a minute. Snippets of that day flooded her brain. What her parents had told her was not the truth.

"They twisted it all around to make you look like the bad guy," she eked out in a constricted voice. "When I found out you'd left, they had a *told you so* attitude." Saying that he was just the sort to flee without an explanation. Exactly the person they worried he'd be. They'd lied to their dumb, trusting daughter. And they must have told different lies to him.

Offered him money! And told him she was in agreement about it! Erin was sickened at what her parents had done. She glared back to where her mother had been standing, but Bunny was no longer there. Erin's head spun like a top. Her arms fell from around Kento's neck. She had to get away again, couldn't stand being in the fishbowl of the dance floor. She needed to be alone to absorb the shocking news he had just delivered. "I need to go to my room," she muttered and bolted off, leaving him standing alone. Behind her she heard three loud voices rise above the music.

"Kento!"

"Kento!"

"Kento!"

CHAPTER FOUR

"GOOD MORNING." KENTO waved when he saw Erin walking toward him in the lodge's lobby the next morning.

"Good morning." Erin shot back a wan, tired smile. "I got your message. You're right, we do need to talk."

With a few hours until their wedding party duties began for the day, he'd hired a car to pick them up to take them to island's harbor, where he'd arranged to have a boat waiting for them.

In her jeans, athletic shoes and waterproof jacket, she was dressed appropriately for the boat ride. Last night she'd been an elegant maid of honor in that burgundy-colored dress. She was just as pretty in her casual gear. He hadn't forgotten how lovely her face was in the early-morning light, yet it was even more striking than he had remembered. Her skin looked as smooth as velvet, and although those translucent eyes hadn't had enough sleep, they were still mesmerizing in their honeyed, crystalline uniqueness.

"Are you ready?"

She nodded.

After the car ride to the harbor, he helped her onto

the boat. Once they made their way into the cabin, the first mate presented a breakfast of omelets, toast and sliced fresh fruit, all served on fine china with a silver pot of coffee. "Please signal if you need anything further, sir."

"This is nice," Erin said as she speared a wedge of cantaloupe from her plate.

"After everything we talked about last night, I thought it was a good idea for us to get some privacy. None of that was anybody's business but ours." With emotions flying, he'd worried that one of the gossip hounds would perceive the tension between them and start some kind of rumor. They both had enough eyes on them already. Especially as Erin had left the party with a sudden need to be alone. And not to mention the state of near swoon he'd been in dancing with her. Confirming that she still smelled like cream and the two of them melding into the single unit they used to be.

But now in the safety of the boat's cabin, Kento wanted to get it all cleared up and out in the open. At last. "So, last night, discussing your parents'...offer to me..."

"I know my parents are ruthless," she jumped in. "I've seen how they conduct business dealings. But I can't believe they'd sink so low as to offer you money to get you out of the picture."

"All this time, I thought you knew. They told me the three of you had talked it over and that you'd concurred it was for the best." Worse than Ingram and Bunny's cut-and-dried bribe, a disgusting bargain to affect two young hearts, was that they'd lied and told him Erin was in agreement. "How naive I was to take them at their word." As a matter of fact, it was only yesterday, upon finally seeing Erin again, that he'd flashed on the possibility that there was more than one version of what had transpired. His hunch had been right.

"If I was in cahoots with them, why wouldn't I have just broken up with you? Do you really think I would have agreed to a plan to buy you off?"

"I believed what they told me. I was a twenty-one-year-old kid," Kento said, all of it still sinking in. "They said you didn't love me."

Anguish changed her face. "How could you have taken that as truth?" Her voice cracked. "Hadn't you noticed? What we had was real for me. I never would have betrayed you. Give me a little more credit than that." Kento had no idea what lengths Erin would have gone to at her parents' behest. All he knew was that Ingram and Bunny had tight control over their daughter. And he hadn't even told her all that was said that day with her parents.

"Let's get some air." Erin got up and mounted the four steps to the boat's deck. Kento followed her as she made her way to the starboard side, wrapping her two hands around the railing and peering out into the distance. Kento took a stand right next to her. He'd been scorned and devastated, yet his gut was twisting that he had upset her. All this time, she'd thought he'd left her for reasons of his own. Because he didn't love her. In fact, the Barclays had bent things around so much he never knew that Erin was unaware of their horrible plot to get rid of him.

The boat moved in between two smaller islands on the Sound, dense with trees. Erin started to speak and then stopped herself. He didn't let it slide. "What were you going to say?"

She took in a slow inhale and let out an even slower exhale. Whatever she wanted to share wasn't coming easy. "All of the time we were together, my parents tried to brainwash me into distrusting you. They told me that people like you were looking for connections. For the opportunities that aligning with a family like mine might bring. I told them you'd never do anything like that, but they tried to get me to doubt your sincerity in even being with me."

As he took in her words, blood came to a boil through his veins. "How dare they tell you those kind of lies!" In another repeat from seven years ago, Kento was stunned at the lengths the Barclays would go to in order to maintain their private bubble. He'd never met people like that, who thought nothing of lying to and manipulating their own daughter. Kento slapped his hand against the railing, compelled to bang his anger out somewhere. Smacked it a second time.

"When you left for Tokyo, they assured me how right they were, that you only cared about me because I was a Barclay. And that once you figured out they weren't going to usher you into their life of standing and privilege, you left. Further proof that you'd never loved me in the first place."

Erin searched him, as confused as he was by all that had been said. Contemplating, trying to piece it together. Until she gasped. What had been teary eyes began to weep in earnest. Her cries carried off the boat deck, and the wails merged with the crashing of waves in the Sound.

"What is it?" he finally asked. "Why are you crying so hard?"

"I just *got it*," she sobbed. "You took the bribe. That's how you had the money to start your software company. No wonder you never reached out to me again after you got to Japan. NIRE was founded on my family's money."

Everything Erin had held on to for the past seven years turned to dust and scattered off the boat deck and into the waters of Puget Sound. This was Kento Yamamoto, a man so forthcoming and fair that he wouldn't even accept the meal assistance some of his university scholarships included, letting the aid committees know that his parents could provide food for him. How could that same person pocket a payoff from her parents to get out of their lives, all the while knowing it would break her heart in the process?

Which was the real man and which was the facade? Anything was possible. Maybe she'd glorified him too much and never saw who he really was. Could her parents have been right? After all, he didn't come to her, didn't meet her at that bakery to demand an explanation.

"Erin!"

She didn't turn her head, instead focusing her eyes on the waves.

"For heaven's sake, Erin!" he exclaimed until he

shocked her out of her trance. "I didn't accept their attempted payout! Is that how little you think of me?"

"Oh, my gosh." Erin put her hand over her mouth to muffle her tears.

"Do you really think I'd have taken it?"

"Look at it from my point of view. Someone who flees without a goodbye has surely done something wrong." Even though she tried to sync her eyes to his, now it was he who wouldn't look *her* in the face. He could be lying, but something deep in her soul assured her he wasn't. And he was certainly more likely to be honest than her parents were. "But no. You wouldn't have been part of a dirty deal like that. The possibility just popped into my mind. I shouldn't have voiced it."

"I built NIRE on nothing! My uncle Riku gave me an entry-level job after graduation. I started designing software at night and on the weekends, using every moment of my spare time to learn and develop. I'll tell you anything you want to know about my company, but I'll ask you not to make any assumptions."

Erin noticed the boat turning to begin its return to the harbor. They had to get back to their duties at Christy and Lucas's wedding. There was the ceremony rehearsal and then a rehearsal dinner. They had to get ready.

What a mess they'd unearthed in less than twenty-four hours. Thanks to her parents, she'd spent seven years thinking it was so easy for Kento to leave. In turn, he'd spent that time believing she hadn't loved him. It was a tragedy of misunderstanding. More tears began to form, ready to spill from her eyes. After the disaster with Harris, she was starting to genuinely realize that her parents' prescription for her life wasn't working out. She hadn't married, hadn't bred. They had failed at creating the next-gen socialite they wanted her to be. Hearing about their foul behavior years earlier was the icing on the cake.

And now she'd greatly offended Kento with her guess that he'd taken her parents' dirty money. They needed a way to put this all behind them and get on with the day. She eked out, "Forgive me for even acknowledging the possibility."

He was silent, and they both watched as the boat approached the dock.

"I think you might have to earn that forgiveness," he answered finally. Why did the way he'd said that sound more flirty than angry?

"How would I do that?" she flicked back, grateful he was lightening the mood.

With one of his long fingers, he tapped his cheek, indicating that he wanted Erin to kiss it right there. The gesture was both silly and thrilling, making Erin's spirit brighten, not to mention causing her stomach to tingle. Holding fast to his demand, he leaned down a bit, bringing his cheek closer to her. She lifted up on tiptoes and placed a prolonged but gentle kiss onto his cheek. His satisfied grin would have irked her if it wasn't so adorable.

Back at the lodge after their breakfast cruise, Kento and Erin parted to get ready for the rehearsal. Trying to pull all the pieces of the morning together, she showered and put on her outfit for the day. A silky, fitted silver T-shirt went nicely with the full skirt, also silver, that came together with a black belt and black ballet flats. As she was slipping on some bangle bracelets, Christy called and asked her to come to the dressing room in the main lodge, because she was having second thoughts about her own ensemble.

Erin helped her sort through some options, all in the vivid colors the bride gravitated toward. She settled on the blinding pink shantung dress originally bought for the occasion. Christy had just been having jitters.

The bridal party had been instructed to meet outside at the wedding canopy for the rehearsal. The weather was dreary but not raining as staff members arranged rows of cushioned white chairs for the ceremony. Erin and Christy arrived last, and Lucas called out, "Oh, wow," at the sight of his intended in her bright pink dress. That it was the color of stomach medication didn't stop him from bending his head to one side as he gazed adoringly at his bride. It was cute how smitten he was. Erin sincerely hoped their affection would last a lifetime.

Christy donned the practice veil she'd been handed, and Billy, the photographer, snapped some candid shots. Kento stood beside Lucas. The best man wore a fine charcoal suit with a white shirt and no tie, his hair in its sexy tangle. He looked so tall and stylish, Erin had a moment's jealousy that it wasn't her wedding to him that everyone had gathered for. A wish that the past hadn't played out as it had. That, for once, her relationship was going right and the man she loved stood ready to declare his intention of eternal partnership, of staying rather than going.

True love was never going to happen for her—she wasn't even open to it. Most especially not with Kento and all of the bad blood that had been spilled. He was the very person who had destroyed her hope of devotion. Even though she hadn't known about her parents' horrible behavior, she'd learned that he was capable of leaving her in a blink. If he could just disappear once, she could never trust him not to do it again. As their prickly boat ride this morning proved, there was still so much hurt and misunderstanding between them.

Although, for the first time she could ever recall, Erin pictured herself as a happy bride, mired in flower selections and reception menus, excited to begin matrimony with her groom. Seeing Kento again reminded her of all of the whimsical little daydreams she used to have about him. Imagining them as an already-married couple. Participating in all of the tiny moments that added up to a lifetime together. The stylish but unfussy house they'd live in. Trips they'd take. She'd gone as far as envisioning beautiful children who were not only bequeathed with their father's good looks but with his brains and hardworking determination. No, she cautioned herself again. Those hallucinations were part of her history, and she needed to leave them there. What-ifs had no place between the two of them anymore. She was glad they'd cleared up some of her questions about the past, but there really didn't need to be anything more than that.

"Mother of the bride—" Suni, the wedding planner, began organizing the decided-upon processional "—you'll be the first to walk down the aisle and then take your seat. Mother and father of the groom will already be seated in the front row. Next are the bridesmaids and groomsmen in pairs down the aisle, and then the maid of honor and best man."

Who would all part at the altar. Next was the flower girl. And last would be Uncle Vernon and Christy walking to the head of the aisle, where Lucas waited to meet his bride. As was traditional, Erin would hold Christy's bouquet as needed during the ceremony. Kento would be in charge of the rings, as Christy had opted not to have a bearer. "Everyone will run through the ceremony twice with me to make sure the placements are correct."

When it was their turn, Kento presented the crook of his arm for Erin to take as they began their promenade according to instructions. While they did, his revelations on the boat this morning came flooding back, angering her to the point of distraction. But the best man and maid of honor strolled in the slow step of a formal processional—one foot forward, the other one meeting it. *Step, together, step, together.*

They'd explained so much to each other, yet she was still tormented. All of this happily-ever-after wedding business was just making her more and more incensed about her parents' inconceivable bribe. About her falling for their cover-up. At Kento for not having enough confidence in her to know that there was a limit to her condoning of her parents' behavior. That she wasn't a monster like they were. She would never have participated in a plot so evil as to let them buy off Kento.

But was that true? While they'd never done anything quite so reprehensible, she'd had no record of standing up to them.

In reality, she desperately wanted to break away from them, to go her own way. Kento was the one who had planted that seed in her long ago, encouraged her to think for herself. To question whether the attitudes held by her insulated parents, who'd never known toil and struggle, were accurate, fair, real. It was only now, being reunited with him, that brought those feelings back to the surface. Because when Kento left, it was as if he took the key to her cage with him, as if the gumption and fight he gave her flew out the door along with him. Not even realizing what she was doing, without Kento she'd walked right back into the prison of her parents' life.

"You still haven't explained why you didn't come to me after my parents tried to pay you to go," she blurted into his ear as they walked down the aisle, not censoring herself. "You believed them, believed that I would have gone along with their sickening scheme to get rid of you. Without even asking me. That's what you thought of me?"

"A bit slower, please," Suni called out. Kento adjusted his pace, and Erin followed suit.

"Is this really the time and place?"

"I don't care anymore, Kento." At this point, she didn't.

"If you hadn't known about what I've already told you, then you surely don't know the rest of it," he whispered.

"What are you talking about?" *Step. Together. Step. Together. Smile.*

"Your parents also informed me that I was lucky they were even offering me money. That if I didn't take their generous graduation present and immediately go away and never contact you again, they had some other actions they were prepared to take."

Erin's head whipped to look at him while he managed to keep them at the processional pace. "They threatened you?"

"Your father said they had been looking at a property on 4934 Spruce Street in Tacoma."

"Why would he say that?"

"You've been there. The address is the building where my parents' grocery store occupied the ground floor. The shop they'd owned and operated for thirty years. Your father told me he was thinking of buying the building for a teardown. To build condos." *Step. Together. Step. Together.* "After all that time there, my parents wouldn't have been able to start over somewhere else."

Erin felt light-headed, nauseous.

After a few breaths to collect her wits, she said, "I wish you'd never met me in that philosophy class." *Step. Together. Step. Together.*

"I don't feel that way. The year we had together was…"

"I mean," she interjected, "if we had never met, my parents couldn't have treated you so horribly."

She was shocked, mortified. Embarrassed to even be the offspring of thugs who would go to such lengths.

They thought it was all for her own good, for the good of the family. With their own laws to answer to. But it sickened her nonetheless, that they would have terrified this upstanding young man who'd already had doors slammed in his face, who'd been said no to countless times. How people so fortunate could be so heartless was baffling.

He tilted his head in resignation. "I suppose I should thank you for that sentiment?"

"Can you understand how much you destroyed me by leaving rather than coming to me with all of this?" *Step. Together.*

"I was just a kid!" His voice rose and then he corrected it. "I was being crushed myself. Regardless of how you felt about me, I assumed it wasn't enough to make you defy them."

Erin used her pinkie finger to dab at the corners of her eyes. *Smile.*

"Are you all right?" Billy inquired.

"Everything is just so beautiful," Erin quickly fibbed. "I always cry at weddings."

Billy snaked left, right and sideways.

Once the maid of honor and best man reached the altar, they parted. Erin joined the bridesmaids on Christy's side of the aisle. It was agonizing to leave Kento's side, Amber and the girls looking on. Kento slapping a fake smile across his face reminded Erin to do the same. He took his place beside the groomsmen, with Lucas standing proud as he watched his bride in her pink dress walk toward him on her father's arm.

Of all the merciless and cutthroat things Erin knew

her parents did in their business dealings, what they
had done to Kento took the prize. The Barclays did as
the Barclays saw fit. They were afraid of no one; their
cold hearts kowtowed to no one.

Bunny and Ingram had decided their daughter's future, and Kento had no place in it. That was that. A
mutually beneficial marriage was key. A merging of dy-
nasties, another business agreement. They hadn't even
given her a real place in the company. She'd thought she
had a knack for finding interesting historic properties
for sale and wished she could direct her energies toward
that, but they had never allowed her in. It had already
been formally documented that while she would eventually inherit Barclay Properties, she would not be put
in charge of its operations. Gender roles still prevailed,
even in her mother's mind. Male cousins were being
groomed for the key positions when the time came.

After Christy and Lucas took their places, everyone
participated in a practice of the ceremony. Erin pretended to help the bride with the imaginary train of her
gown. She took Christy's bouquet to hold for her, today
made of plastic flowers provided by the wedding planner. Suni stood in for the officiant and ad-libbed some
vows. Kento mimed handing Lucas the wedding rings.

Once the rehearsal had been completed twice, the
wedding party did their second recessional back down
the aisle. Kento and Erin joined arms again. During the
short intervals, she'd missed resting her hand around
his rock-solid bicep.

Billy was at the end of the aisle, shooting everyone

on their return walk. "Let's have a cheek-to-cheek photo of the maid of honor and the best man."

MacKenzie, Amber and Divya craned to get a good view.

"I can't stop thinking about what you must have gone through, with me disappearing into thin air and you not knowing why," he said, resuming the conversation Erin thought was over. She brought her cheek against his, which was warm and clean shaven. "You asked me to forgive you for thinking that I might have accepted your parents' money. Now it's my turn to ask you for forgiveness. For not coming to you back then, for choosing to silently run away."

Erin was dumbstruck by the simplicity and humility in his request. Given all of the circumstances, she thought she could forgive. Although she'd never forget.

After the rehearsal, the wedding party joined other guests, who mulled about on the lawn and on the large patio with its firepits. Some people made s'mores with the fixings provided, toasting the marshmallows over the open fires with long sticks. Others enjoyed green appletini cocktails from the bartender's station. Kento got called into conversation by some flashy women. Erin saw Bunny coming toward her. Her mother was just plain fortunate that there were a lot of people around, or else she might have started a shouting match. As it was, she shot her mother a vicious glower.

"Erin, there's someone I want you to meet." Bunny charged in, obviously not reading her daughter's mood. Or, more accurately, not caring.

"I had a little chat with Kento this morning," Erin

spat in staccato. "It seems there were some events from the past I had no knowledge of."

"Mmm, yes, well, your father and I made some choices at the time that we thought were in everyone's best interest."

"Yeah, I heard. You threatened and intimidated a twenty-one-year-old whose only crime was loving me. Great decision."

"Do you see that gentleman over there?" Bunny ignored Erin's words and pointed one spindly finger in an indiscreetly discreet way to a small man in a black suit standing with a group of suited men. Erin estimated him to be fifteen or so years older than her. His upper lip curled under as he rapidly shook his head in agreement at what someone was saying, making him look like an eager mouse. "That's who I was telling you about. Humphrey Colder. Big oil money. His family worked with the Alaskan pipeline and all that implies. They own half of Fairbanks."

"Mother, do you hear me? I am livid, not to mention heartbroken, about what you did to Kento after graduation, and that you lied to me about it."

"And don't you understand me, dear? Humphrey Colder is the type of match we need to make. You and Kento had your college fling, fine. But we certainly weren't going to let you continue to associate with a young man unsuitable as a marriage prospect. It just wasn't prudent."

"Prudent! Good heavens, can you hear yourself? Are you heartless?"

"Barclays look forward, not back. Go introduce yourself to Humphrey." Bunny put her brittle hand between Erin's shoulder blades to give her a push in the man's direction. Out of the corner of her eye, she saw Kento watching the entire exchange, too far away to hear them but seething nonetheless. Surrounding him were several women trying to get his attention, but his eyes were on her.

"Didn't she know his reputation? He never stays with any woman for too long."

"I heard they lasted six months. That must have been a record for him."

Kento overheard two of the wedding guests talking about Erin as she walked by. This crowd certainly loved gossip. He'd been overhearing comments left and right about poor Bunny, whose daughter hadn't been able to find a husband. And when he watched Bunny steer Erin toward a man who was clearly too old and stodgy for her, Kento snarled in disgust.

Not that he was faring much better. As soon as the rehearsal was over and the bridal party joined other guests, the glamazons surrounded him in a swarm. The discussion seemed to center on how many carats Christy's diamond ring had and did he know where Lucas had bought it? Once he saw Erin break from the man her mother insisted she meet, Kento pulled away and toward her, along the way grabbing a couple of the pretty green appletinis in stemmed glasses.

"Fed to the lions?" he asked as he handed her the drink.

"My mother simply could not wait another moment to introduce me to a bore who smells like garlic."

"Helpful to ward off vampires?"

"Very funny." She took a sip of the sweet and tart drink. "This is good."

"In everything we've said to each other, I don't know if I've stated clearly enough how sorry I am that I didn't confront you seven years ago about what your parents did. It's something that has haunted me for years, even without all of the new information. If I had, then neither of us would have spent all of this time with hurts and resentments based on falsehoods."

"That's for sure."

He was startled by her bluntness but almost proud of her for it. "How can I make it up to you?"

"You can't. It's too late." She was right, yet her words cut like a knife. Another thought occurred to him. How much had his leaving influenced the way she related to men in general? Was she expecting to be disappointed by any man she might date, therefore creating a self-fulfilling prophecy? Had his own actions not only held him back from developing any meaningful relationships but done the same to her? Guilt racked through him. Bad enough that Erin had merciless parents who controlled her, but Kento had come along and made everything worse with his desertion. What could he do for her that would be a gesture of repentance, some way he could be of service to her?

Christy swooped in and said into Erin's ear loud enough for Kento to hear, "Do you see that man making the s'more over there?" She gestured to a beefy bald guy who was frustrated when he set his marshmallow on fire so badly it turned to black ash. "He's another excellent prospect. Scooter Markinson. Of the Markinson department stores! Go talk to him."

Erin looked at Christy with wide eyes to try to indicate she didn't want this conversation to be happening in front of Kento, which he could understand. It would be humiliating to have people trying to matchmake right in front of someone important from your past. Didn't these people have any tact? That was something he could say about Japan—people were for the most part polite in front of each other regardless of what they might be thinking inside. In any case, the marshmallow torcher was nowhere near good enough for Erin—he could tell that from first glance.

An idea popped into his head. It might not have been a smart one, in fact, it probably wasn't, but it was a notion nonetheless.

"I can't undo the past, but I just thought of a way I could help you out now," he said after Christy moved on.

"With what?" She took a sip of her drink and then licked her lips. Instant proof that what he was thinking wasn't a good plan, because it would involve not wanting to kiss the drops of appletini right off her. And he wasn't sure he was capable of that if she insisted on having such a sexy mouth all the time.

"Remember you had said you wished you had a date to the wedding so that the marriage brokers and gossip mongers would see that Harris didn't trample you? That you're still a catch?" *To say the least.*

"Yeah."

"What about me? What if you and I pretended to be back together? That would get everyone off your back, wouldn't it?"

"You and I?" Her eyebrows furrowed. "That would be too weird, wouldn't it?"

"It would just be pretend, right? Only when we were around people. We could pull it off."

"I don't know."

"Almost everyone here knows we have a past together. And they must assume we've remained friendly, or else how could we stand as maid of honor and best man? And…"

"Slow down a minute, will you?" She was trying to grasp the concept even as Kento reeled at his own crazy suggestion. The two of them posing as a couple was a terrible prospect. Unless it wasn't. What if it even benefited him in his initial quest for this weekend? To get over her, once and for all. Maybe the proximity of pretending to be a couple would be the final capstone on feelings that had lingered for too long. Playacting for a short time could help him find the closure he was seeking.

"It would get the leeches off me for the weekend as well, right?"

"I suppose so," she pondered. "What, we'd just tell people that we'd gotten back together?"

"Yeah. Things like that happen to people all the time at weddings. The romance brings it out in them."

He sounded like he was reading from a promotional brochure.

"I see."

"Then what? After the weekend is over?"

"We'll leave telling everyone that we'll be traveling back and forth to see each other as much as possible."

"I'm not sure pretending like that would be a good plan."

"What about your parents? They would be vehemently against you and I getting back together. The mere idea of that would infuriate them."

A cat that swallowed the canary's smile slowly widened across Erin's face. "Now, that it would."

CHAPTER FIVE

JUST AS KENTO'S proposition was starting to sink into Erin's brain, the photographer sidled up to them. "I need to test some light at the wedding altar. Christy and Lucas are visiting with some family that has just arrived. Can I get you to come with me and stand in for the bride and groom?" Naturally, they obliged. As they walked across the lawn to the site, she contemplated the proposal.

"Harris Denby. The crazy one who drinks champagne from the bottle." She watched a less than subtle couple point at her with no shame whatsoever.

Although Erin appreciated Kento's offer, especially as he meant it as a peace offering, she was very skeptical. While it might make the weekend outwardly easier, it was already a lot to see him again, let alone act as if they were back together.

A number of guests looked on while Billy positioned them as bride and groom for the ceremony. Grabbing the practice veil that Christy had rehearsed with earlier, he placed it on Erin's head with the top layer cloaking her face. He also handed her the plastic bouquet, which she held in both hands like a proper bride. "Great. Gaze lovingly at each other and I can check for shadows."

Gaze lovingly was not a hard command to fulfill. What took concentration was how hard she had to work at not picturing the moment differently. Billy was looking for shadows. She knew exactly where they were. It was as if all the secrets and lies that had just come forward had served to bring her and Kento closer to each other than they'd ever been, even more than seven years ago. With the maturity of adults, they could analyze the damage that had been done to both themselves and each other. The disappointment and melancholy were all the more profound when shared by two people who were too shattered to ever stand at an altar in wedding clothes.

"Kento, can you lift Erin's veil as if you were the groom?"

But what if this was real? That she'd get to have Kento, to have and to hold, for the rest of her life? Something that was never going to happen. He dutifully raised the tulle and smoothed it behind her head with a tenderness that was almost tragic.

What about his offer, though? If she took him up on it, presumably she wouldn't have to be galloped around like a thoroughbred for the rest of her time on the island. Nor be pitied by the snobs who laughed at her gullibility in partnering with Harris. It would help Kento keep the gold miners away, too. And most importantly, it would incense her mother, and a little revenge would taste sweet in Erin's mouth right about now. All short-lived, but what did she have to lose?

Except for one thing. How on earth would she act as if she was with Kento without conjuring up the longing for something decidedly unphony? Embarking on this could be a cruel make-believe. Looking into his luminous, captivating eyes, she knew she'd have to take care not to be destroyed by him for the second time when this was over and he went back to Japan alone.

Billy took her bouquet and adjusted the two of them a little closer. "Blah, blah. Blah, blah, you may now kiss the bride."

Erin noticed Bunny standing farther back on the lawn with her friends but turning her head toward the altar. The bridesmaids and groomsmen watched in a gaggle, all holding their appletinis. The mousy garlic man, the bald s'mores maker and just about every guest clustered around turned their attention to the scene.

Kiss the bride.

Kento took her face in his hands. She reached her arms around his neck. Was she about to playact as Billy had asked them to? Or were they embarking on the more complex charade that Kento had suggested? If they made this kiss convincing, it could kick off the ruse he was suggesting. With so many people's eyes on them, it could serve as the announcement that the maid of honor and best man were once again a real-life couple.

If so, it should be a kiss that looked passionate, yet the two of them would know it was only for show. She'd watched enough movie smooching that she could imitate how to press her whole mouth against his and rotate her head a little as if he was rubbing the kiss in. That way it would look like he was giving her a deeply romantic kiss. He'd understand what she was doing and follow along. As a matter of fact, they should remember how they did it, because it was a tool they'd be utilizing throughout the wedding weekend. Okay. This could work, she told herself.

Unfortunately, though, that's not how it went.

In fact, he urged his mouth against hers with a force that made her instantly lose concentration on the task at hand. His lips found hers, certain where to go, as if no time had passed. A two-piece puzzle that easily fit together into a groove. His mouth was even more persuasive than she had remembered, and her resolve to control the kiss was obliterated. His lips insisted hers open, and he circled his tongue around hers. Her knees buckled. She was in big trouble.

There was no level of pretend going on, no matter which game they were playing. Her body jutted into his, unable to contain her physical reaction. And in pressing herself against him she could feel his firm physique beneath his clothes, reminding her, all but taunting her mind to replay the days and nights of intense, inexhaustible heat that they had once shared.

She hadn't had a chance to truly consider how much she would still respond to him. It was too late now, though, as the kiss, in front of everybody to boot, effectively answered the question as to whether or not they were going to enact the charade. In fact, the kiss swirled on far too long, their bodies becoming one being. The world all but disappeared until finally the sound of voices slowly reached her ears.

"Kento?"

"Kento?"

"Kento!"

"So the two of you are a real-life couple," a man said to Kento with a wink to Erin as he entered the rehearsal dinner. The best man and maid of honor greeted guests as they filed in for the evening, which was to include a show.

Kento had barely recovered from what transpired on the lawn a few hours ago. Since then, he and Erin had been busy with helping Lucas and Christy rework the table arrangements, as one couple unexpectedly brought their children, who hadn't been included in the head count. Also, Christy wasn't happy with the hors d'oeuvres samples, so they met with the chef to modify them to her satisfaction.

All that hadn't left him with much time to review his moves. Erin had never even answered him about whether she wanted to playact that they were a couple. He'd decided for them. At the altar, standing in for the bride and groom as they were pronounced husband and wife, he'd intended to give her a kiss that *did* let everyone know they were back together, but one that would assure the two of them it was only masquerade.

Instead, reuniting with her lips was more intoxicating than he could handle. Blood and arousal had coursed through him in equal measure. The challenge to pulling off the fake-boyfriend act would rest on his ability to be immune to her charms. He was going to need to protect himself at every step. Because Erin was dynamite and could blow right through his plan to keep this phony. Worse still, he could easily envision her doing so. On top of it, he couldn't get the honeyed taste of her soft mouth off his tongue.

"I hope we'll hear wedding bells ringing in your future, too, someday," an elderly lady said to them.

"Do you know who she is?" Erin asked after the woman passed by.

"Not a clue."

"There are always a lot of the parents' friends in attendance," she whispered out of the side of her mouth. "Weddings are really for the moms."

"Don't tell that to my mine," Kento shot back as he greeted another stranger. "It's driving her nuts that I don't have a woman in my life. She's itching for grandchildren."

"Nice to see you. Take a seat anywhere," Erin continued her hellos.

"There's not a bad seat in the house," Kento followed along.

He'd never thought of himself as part of a married couple. After Erin and then, to a lesser extent, Ayaka, he figured trusting someone was out of the question. So what would be the point in marrying if not to have wholehearted faith in the other person? All of these revelations since he'd arrived on the island were making his head throb to the point that he could actually imagine himself taking wedding vows. Maybe it was no wonder why he chose that exact moment at the altar to initiate their supposedly fake union. He really needed to keep his facts separate from fiction.

Being Erin's husband would make Bunny Barclay his mother-in-law. Which was never going to happen. There would be nothing that woman would hate more than seeing her daughter married to him. To *new tech money*, as if those were forbidden words. As if there was something dirty or wrongly gained about his fortune.

There was some measure of comfort in confirming that Erin hadn't known about her father's threat to him, to undermine and ruin the life Kento's parents had worked for so long to create. He'd always suspected that she didn't know that part of what had occurred. It turns out she knew none of it. But even if she had, it wouldn't have been enough to have turned her against them. The Barclays were ruthlessly clever in convincing her that Kento didn't love her. That was their best strategy. Telling her that he was only out to use her for what her family could do for him. Now it was far too late to put the broken pieces back together. Genuine sorrow washed over him.

"You still haven't told me," Erin inquired as more guests filed into the dinner theater, "in all these years, have you been dating?"

"I've met a few women who wanted to get close." He knew that sounded harsh, but it was the truth. "I've learned to spot insincerity."

"Hello. Welcome."

"Good evening."

Once most of the crowd had taken seats at the tables that surrounded the stage, Kento and Erin slipped in and stood against the wall near the back doors in case they were needed. They surveyed the room while waiters delivered blue mugs filled with steaming broth made from locally caught clams to each table as a toasty welcome. A server handed two to Erin. She gave one to Kento, and they both had a sip of the salty, savory liquid.

"I suppose I've done a fair amount of dating," Kento continued as the mug warmed his hands. "There was a woman I was with for eight months."

"Not someone you thought of staying with, though?"

"No, and after Ayaka, I made it my policy not to let anyone near."

"She betrayed you?"

"Ayaka is a corporate executive, busy and driven. I thought we were more or less leading the same lives and would be compatible." Indeed, when he was introduced to Ayaka Sato at a business party three years ago, he'd thought maybe he'd met someone he could share his existence with. Although the connection he'd had with Erin still lingered on him like a perfume that overtook him and transported him back to Seattle, he'd needed to step out, and Ayaka seemed to come along at the right time. In his heart, he knew that his solitary life had led him to loneliness. That casual encounters with women here and there were completely unsatisfying. That it would be ultimately unhealthy for him, and for his empire, if he continued in isolation.

So when Ayaka's quick mind and high energy appealed to him, he began dating her. At first only once every couple of weeks, because he'd never been dependent on anyone besides Erin, and he wasn't ready to risk being hurt again. But when the companionship proved pleasant, and Ayaka was more than willing, he increased their get-togethers to once a week. "We're dating, and then she announces to me at dinner, out of the blue, that she wants to become pregnant with my child within the next three months."

"Wow." Erin's voice rose. "Just like that?"

"Yes. She said this was an optimal time in her career for her to have children. That she and her family had considered my lack of pedigree but given that I had built NIRE into such a prominent company, I must have genes that would be desirable for coparenting."

"Desirable genes… That's intense."

"It always turns out that every woman I meet wants something from me, is thinking of how she can benefit from me. I don't mean to sound arrogant, but do I read as desperate? Where did Ayaka get the impression that because she'd come to a verdict about having children it was a done deal?"

A jagged breath reminded him how angry that situation had made him. The years of judgment he'd endured growing up had only led to more, in subtle adult ways that were even more insulting than school hallway taunts. "After eight months," he went on, "I'd thought that maybe she and I had come to understand each other, that we'd opened up enough to show each other our real selves." Like what he'd had with Erin.

"But you were mistaken?"

"Yes. We'd only gotten as far as discovering we liked the same ice-cream flavor and political candidates. That wasn't really getting to know someone. And in the meantime, she, along with her parents, had been busy selecting me as a breeder."

"Well, I know all about having decisions made for me," Erin mused.

"Yes, you do."

She was forcing him into thoughts he hadn't had in a while. Before and after his time with Ayaka, he'd made sure to let any women he'd spent time with know up front that nothing serious would grow between them. Still, he had no trouble finding dates. In his world, filled with young people in the big city, there was an endless stream of attractive women charging toward him. He could hardly dismiss them fast enough. Everyone was measuring and trading and leveraging assets at all times, even if they didn't consciously realize that's what they were doing.

It had never felt like that with Erin, except when he'd left Seattle convinced that she was in on her parents' plans to get rid of him. Before that, and now during this weekend, she brought out the parts of him that rarely saw the light of day. With her, he felt he could be natural and instinctive, almost innocent. Like the wholly inappropriate way he'd kissed her for the photographer. He could have easily given her the fake smooch he'd meant to. The savage, ravenous beast inside him had had other ideas. He knew he'd surprised her with the insistence of his lips. And all he could think about was wanting more. Craving it. Needing it.

However, practice would make perfect. How many times did he have to go over and over one of his new software programs until it ran like clockwork? This was the same. Soon enough, he'd be immune to Erin's kisses and they'd be able to play their roles to perfection. Once he got used to her again, she'd no longer have such an effect on him. It would be no problem to act like lovers for the weekend and then be out of each other's lives forever. No problem. At all.

Perhaps it was maturity that advised him, something innate that told him that he had magic with her, the kind that only comes around once in a lifetime. So he needed to watch out. Even standing next to her against the wall in the middle of this wedding fanfare, she made him feel connected. Almost daring to think that all the destruction of their past wouldn't matter an iota if he had her.

Lucas and Christy entered the theater, followed by the groomsmen and bridesmaids. Kento and Erin would sit with them once their greeter duties were done. He'd made sure to confirm to Demarcus that he and Erin had rekindled their romance, knowing word would continue to spread to the all of the guests.

"Ladies and gentleman..." A voice broke in over the loudspeaker. "Welcome to Locklear Lodge's *Song of the Golden Eagle*, a celebration of the Native American peoples who first populated the Pacific Northwest. In a few minutes, you will be enjoying our presentation of welcome dances. That will be followed by our buffet dinner, with a menu inspired by foods that might have been eaten by the first inhabitants of the island. Prepare to feast on fresh salmon cooked on cedar planks over an open fire, grilled squash, our corn and lima bean succotash, and molasses bread. After that, our resident storyteller will share tales of his ancestors, to be followed by our performers, who will dance, drum and chant wearing native dress and masks."

They both watched as Bunny sat down at a table with her friends.

"Will you talk to your mother about what you've unearthed?"

Erin's sarcastic resignation of them was a front, but to his knowledge she'd never taken any real steps toward freedom. Which pained him greatly. Even if he wasn't going to spend the rest of his life with her, he'd wish her one of independence. An existence without it was slavery.

"I already did, at the marshmallow roast." She shrugged. "It was in my best interest, and to protect our holdings and all that. Which I need to respect. Nothing will ever change with them," she added with a chin-up gesture that was somehow excruciating.

"As expected."

"I don't really care what she thinks anymore."

Kento knew that wasn't accurate, but he liked the sound of it.

When her mother glanced over to them, Erin went up on her tiptoes and brought her lips to his, continuing what they had started a few hours earlier on the lawn. Kento squinted out of the corner of his eye to watch as Bunny's expression turned enraged.

But then he stopped noticing Bunny and got lost in the fervor of Erin's kiss, which sent hot lava bubbling up through his body.

The guests enjoyed their dinner. For dessert they were served Native American fry bread, discs of dough that had been browned in oil and topped with jams and honey. At each place setting was a party favor to take home. It was a dream catcher, a small wooden hoop made into a net with fibrous crisscrossing threads and adorned with beads and feathers. The storyteller explained that dream catchers resemble a web, and that spiders are considered symbols of protection and comfort in some cultures. They are sometimes hung over a baby's crib while they sleep, as they were believed to keep bad dreams away and let good ones in.

During the show, Erin found herself stroking the dream catcher with her thumb. All of what had gone on with Kento and her parents was like a nightmare that kept repeating in her head. Maybe the party favor could help put the past to rest.

After the performance guests began to retreat to their lodgings, anticipating the wedding day ahead. Kento and Erin spent some time with the bride and groom, making sure everything was in order and that they weren't suffering from anything other than typical wedding butterflies. Both seemed happy, excited, nervous and tired all at once, and they were looking forward to a good night's sleep. Erin advised, "Hang the dream catcher on your bedpost tonight." She figured it couldn't hurt.

"I'll walk you to your room," Kento said as the two of them left. A floor of suites in the main lodge was being used by the bridal party, although she knew that he had instead booked one of the luxury private cabins for himself.

"Should we take a little walk first?"

"Sure."

She wasn't ready to part company with him just yet. All of what had gone on today was tangled in her head. One fact she was having trouble grappling with was that in spite of hearing about all of the atrocious actions she'd never known about, her heart had begun to sing again.

As they strolled the footpath that surrounded the lodge's main buildings, the night was quiet and Erin had more to say. "I'd always considered you leaving after graduation an absolute rejection."

Kento mashed his lips together in distress at her words. "Of course, when you hadn't known that there were bribes and threats."

"That's more than a young man could have been expected to combat."

"Your parents, in their own twisted way, subscribe to family loyalty and realized I did as well. So they figured out how to leverage that to overtake me and send me packing."

"It made sense that you fled to Tokyo when you had the chance. In addition to being outright scared by the menacing threat to destroy your parents' life, you probably left, in part, to protect me."

"I can't say it didn't occur to me. I was afraid that if you defied your parents and persisted in being with me, you'd have to break from them completely. That's a big decision that might never, ever have been reversed."

"You mean, if I turned my back on them, all their wealth and property and standing, what if it hadn't worked out between you and me?" He had no way of knowing at the time that he'd become the success he did. Which didn't guarantee happiness, anyway. "What if I regretted it later? What if I was left with nothing? And what if that was in Japan, where I'd be completely alone?"

"And your parents were just merciless enough to let that happen."

By vanishing, Kento had been thinking ahead, covering every possibility in what he thought was best and safest for her.

Something that had come right back between them was how they cut to the quick of their feelings. "This reminds me of the old days. I was more honest with you than I've ever been with anyone before or since."

"I was my most real with you, too," he agreed. "Except when it mattered most."

"There's the ultimate irony."

In a way she would never act on, she wished for more from him. As if by his side, she could conquer the world. All these years later, she would be ready for his wisdom and strength to help her escape her jail, escape from living like a half woman, half child, prized only if she produced heirs. Facing how truly brutal her parents were, she didn't know how she was going to be able to return to their Seattle mansion after she'd packed up the remains of the Harris Denby disaster in Spokane. She'd have to ask her dream catcher tonight to bring her an entirely new life.

As they strolled, she was certainly in no hurry to get back to her room. Who in their right mind wouldn't want to spend as much time as possible with this warm-blooded, smart, sexy, soulful man? Kissing him was electrifying, and she couldn't resist doing it again in the theater. With her mother watching, no less. She was bothered, aroused, alive, in his presence. Her assumption that they could play at this for the weekend and that it would mean nothing afterward was fading away.

"Where on the grounds are the cabins?" she asked as they rounded a corner. She knew that Kento had booked the biggest one for the bride and groom, although for tradition's sake Christy would sleep there alone tonight with Lucas in a suite in the lodge.

"Come on, I'll show you." He gestured down a walkway that led away from the main buildings.

They reached the dozen or so cabins, built far apart from each other for privacy on the expansive grounds.

"This is a lovely and secluded setting. What are the cabins like inside?"

"Country charm meets highbrow—what else would you expect? There's an outdoor shower."

Erin was most definitely not thinking about Kento naked under the outdoor tap when she asked, "Have you used it?"

"As a matter of fact, I have," he answered with a hint of a smile that made her curious. A moment's silence fell between them under the dark night sky. After what seemed like a contemplation, he finally asked, "Do you want to see my cabin?"

Trepidation prickled her body. They both knew that if she visited his cabin, there was every possibility that the shell of their masquerade would become even further cracked than it had been by the unfake kisses they'd already shared. In a couple of days, Kento would board his private jet and she would probably never see him again as long as she lived. Would taking their intimacy further be the crescendo of goodbye to the only man that had she ever cared about, or would it make the pain of their saga even more profound and unlivable?

"Yes," she answered in almost inaudible whisper. Yes, physical connection with Kento again would be worth the heartache it would surely cause. It was past an option for her. It had become inevitability.

He took her hand as they walked, which felt only too good. When they reached his cabin, he helped her up the porch steps and released her hand while he fished in his pocket for the key card to swipe open the front door. Once inside, he used one foot to help the other out of its shoe and then reversed it to take off the second. Erin remembered that he'd always observed the Japanese custom of removing shoes when inside his home. With a chew to her lip and her body a bundle of nerves, she took off her shoes as well and placed them next to his just inside the doorway. How they looked together! His big black dress shoes next to her much smaller black ballet flats.

She hoped he'd make small talk, although that wasn't his style. He was well aware that she wasn't in his cabin for a nightcap. Nor to see the paintings on the wall. She could still read him enough to know that he was leaving this up to her. He wasn't going to throw himself on her. But she also registered the lust in his eyes. Telling her he wouldn't refuse her tonight.

"Kento."

That's all she wanted to say. Wanted to hear the

sound of his name out loud, hanging in the air. He bent down so that she could bring her lips to his. Caution rang in her, begging her to reconsider. This could be a mistake that she'd be burdened with forever. His life was five thousand miles away. What about the loneliness she'd feel when he left again, just to have shared their bodies one last time? Yet she couldn't stop herself. Being with him was the best thing she'd ever known. No one could blame her for craving a small taste of it again.

His hands traced down her spine as he finally pulled her tight, reassuring her that she was as desired as he was. He urged himself against her and she molded to him, their bodies together forming a perfect seal. His mouth moved from her lips to her jaw and then to her neck, where his teeth caught a bit of her skin, causing her to moan. Prompting him to continue as a quiet stream of pleasure vibrated low in her throat. His lips made their way just under the neckline of her silky T-shirt, and he flicked his tongue all the way around the scoop.

Becoming urgent, his hands lifted the bottom of her shirt out from its tuck into her skirt so that he could have her bare skin. His palms flattened against her back and then circled around to her rib cage. Which wasn't enough, and so he skimmed the shirt over her head and off her, tossing it to a nearby chair. And quickly removed her bra so that her entire upper body was without barrier. His wide hands completely covered her breasts, making tingles dance all over her.

He looked her in the eyes, arousal hooding his, to ask, "Do you want to see the outdoor shower?" Her smile answered the question.

Leading her toward the door to the side porch, he grabbed a stack of towels from the bathroom along the way. Once outside, he flicked on the standing heaters, which immediately began their task of metering the chilly night.

Face-to-face again, Erin unbuttoned his white dress shirt and slipped it off his shoulders. Her hands lingered on his bare, smooth chest, not the same as it had felt years ago. He was somehow both more muscular yet leaner than he used to be. Rediscovering him was thrilling. As they kissed again, she felt him work at the belt of her skirt, which he then carefully unzipped and helped her step out of. She slid off her underwear as he removed everything else he had on. With only a few lights to illuminate the area near the shower, his body glowed, alert and potent.

Turning on the tap, he eased her under the faucet so that the hot water flowed down her body. His wet hands felt her all over, as if they were committing her every curve and crevice to memory. Her body yielded to his every move, silently begging him not to stop even for a second. She'd never had a sexual experience with anyone that was even close to what she'd had with him at such a young age, intense and united and uninhibited. Both were each other's first lovers. How shocking it was that here they were revisiting that joining like a favorite travel destination they had to see again.

She wondered if she seemed different to him after all this time, as he did to her. He slid his hand between her legs, fingers exploring. Her center clutched down on him, dying for this, dying for him. They thrummed together like musicians playing the same tune. Just when she thought she might not be able to take any more without exploding, he dropped down to his knees so that his mouth and tongue could cover her very womanhood. And there he gloried with the spray of the water raining down on them, the heavy drops rolling along his dripping hair to his taut body and glinting skin. As soon as he found the right groove, he stayed put until she threw her head back and her torso rollicked over and over again with blinding pleasure. After which she could barely stand.

Once the tremble passed through and she steadied, he wrapped her in two big, fluffy, white towels and lifted her into his arms. He carried her back into the cabin, into the bedroom, where he placed her down on his king-size bed with its many plush pillows. Admiring her like she was the most beautiful sight he'd ever seen, he reached in his travel bag for a condom, unrolled it onto himself and laid his body on top of hers.

CHAPTER SIX

IN THE MORNING, Kento opened the front door of his cabin to find the breakfast tray he'd called for. He carried it into the bedroom, where Erin was just stirring, looking so sleepy and pretty it tugged at his heartstrings. It was really almost too much to grasp that she had been in his bed again after all this time, which sent his mind back to all-night erotic encounters when they couldn't get enough of each other and he could scarcely grant her a minute's rest after lovemaking until they were at it again, hungry for more.

This was stuff that belonged in fairy tales. Things like long-lost loves didn't happen in real life. Although there she was, no longer merely the mythological siren who'd inhabited his visions. What had happened so far this weekend had truly brought him face-to-face with the reality of her. Not the milky recollections he'd traveled to Seattle to revisit so that he could leave them behind. Because making love with her didn't feel like something he was going to want to leave in the past.

He worried that the result would be the reverse of what he intended, which was to forget her.

He snatched the single pink rose from its vase that had graced the room service tray. Sitting at the edge of the bed, he brushed the velvety bloom across Erin's cheek as a wake-up call. She smiled but squirmed away. He chased after her with the flower, this time using it to stroke the shoulder that peeked out from the blankets. "Maid of honor, it's wedding day."

Her eyes clicked wide-open like a cartoon character's. "Oh, my gosh. Are we late?"

"We're due in the main lodge for the morning get-together." The bridal party had been instructed to meet for some kind of shared activity to begin the big day on the right footing. Kento hoped it wasn't some kind of guided meditation where he was going to have to listen to his breath for half an hour or something like that. After the night he'd just shared in carnal ecstasy with Erin—which a hunch told him he shouldn't have—the last thing he wanted to do was check into his thoughts. "Do you know what this is all about?"

"Nope."

"Up and going, missy." He pulled back the blanket both to shock her awake and also because he wanted to see her naked body again.

"You are sneaky," she shrieked.

"I am. Do you want to shower?" At that, they smirked, remembering the erotic encounter under the outdoor shower last night.

"I'll go back to my room, because I have to change into casual clothes. After the mystery activity, the girls have hair and makeup, and you have a final tux fitting."

They downed a quick breakfast, and Erin departed.

As agreed, an hour later he knocked on her door to accompany her to the lodge's lounge, where they entered arm in arm as the couple everyone thought they were. It turned out the group was to participate in a nature drawing class, designed to *destress*, as explained by Suni, the wedding planner.

Kento didn't hate the plan. After Erin left to get changed and he showered, this time indoors and alone, a muddle of emotions had brought confusion to his usually organized brain. He'd just made shattering love with her after years of hurt feelings on both of their parts. They were both closed off to love because of each other. What a paradox that the only person he'd ever wanted to be committed to was the very one who'd killed his belief in the practice. Tomorrow he'd go back to Japan with no reason to return to Seattle. Erin and he were supposed to be posing as a couple, not becoming one! All together, he was in the middle of one hot mess. A drawing class, with a break from words, sounded like as good an idea as any.

As soon as they walked in, he and Erin sprang into action as maid of honor and best man, making sure that everyone received an apron to wear and was ushered to a place. Easels were set up for each person, along with sketch paper, pencils and erasers.

An art teacher, her apron pockets overflowing with extra supplies, circled around, introducing herself as Natasha. "Lucas and Christy, up here." Erin pointed to two easels front and center facing the glass wall.

While Erin was directing traffic, Kento took it upon himself to help her into her apron. He slung the strap

over her head. She quickly glanced his way to acknowledge his doings and then continued, "Mother of the
bride, let's have you over here." She gestured to her
aunt Olivia.

Carefully lifting Erin's hair out from under the apron's
strap, he appreciated probably far too much the way her
shoulders rose at his slightest touch. Tugging on the waist
strings, he enjoyed even more the feeling of circling them
around her, giving a few extra pulls for emphasis.

Yes, he was ready to tie her up like a bundle, carry
her back to his cabin and lay her down on his bed, just
as he had last night with the towels after their outdoor
shower. He'd like her all to himself, and for as long as he
wanted. Obviously there'd be none of that on wedding
day—not to mention the fact that, if he was smart, he'd
keep himself in check for the rest of the weekend. Running an enormous corporation, Kento well knew that it
was the long game that was important, that no moves
should ever be made that only benefited the short run.

"Mother of the groom. You come and sit up front,
too."

He was glad that only the bridal party was in attendance and he wouldn't have to see Bunny's unfriendly
face this morning. Maybe drawing could distract him
from the bona fide anger toward her and her absent husband that slowly burned like acid in his throat. Having learned that what he'd held to be gospel all of these
years wasn't exactly as he'd remembered it, there was
a lot of new information to manage.

How he wished they could turn back time and try
again. Maybe things would have ended up the same,

but maybe not. As it stood, what had happened had left an indelible mark on both of them. It had convinced him he'd never marry, would never be able to count on someone or be sure what their motives were. Attitudes born from what he'd grown up around. For Erin, he'd become the first in a series of abandonments that left her permanently fractured, a guilt he'd have to live with.

Once everyone was settled in, Kento brought Erin to a couple of side-by-side easels. "Welcome to this very special morning," Natasha began with a gesture to Christy and Lucas, who beamed. Kento could hardly imagine what the excitement of a wedding morning would feel like to a groom. It wasn't a thought he'd ever entertained. He'd attended weddings in Japan, those of employees and business acquaintances. Some were Western-style. Others were traditionally Japanese, with the bride wearing a special white wedding kimono and headdress and the groom in a dark kimono adorned with his family crest. The wedding custom of san-san-kudo struck him as quite romantic, the ritual exchanging of cups of sake in a binding ceremony, a symbol of their union. Yet he'd never pictured himself in either that kimono or tux.

"Don't feel like you have to sit at your easel the whole time," Natasha continued and pointed to a side table with refreshments. "There's coffee and mimosas. We're just here to relax, have fun and learn a little bit about sketching nature. And no worries about the results, absolutely no judgments allowed," she said with a kind smile.

"Today we'll focus on drawing one of the trees that

we see out our beautiful glass wall," Natasha said, continuing with the lesson, an easel beside her facing the students. "So pick out a single tree or a cluster of them. We have many specimens to choose from. Zero in on something that strikes your fancy. There are no rights or wrongs."

Strikes your fancy. Erin struck his fancy.

"Let's lift up our pencils now and create the trunk of the tree with two vertical lines. You can decide on the thickness of the trunk and on its height," Natasha instructed and demonstrated.

"I'm drawing a tree, but it's not as big and tall as my future husband," Christy exclaimed, loud enough for people around her to hear. Lucas's size was his most distinguishing feature. Everyone cooed. Kento side-eyed Erin. It occurred to him how hard this wedding must be for her, having just been left by a guy who was surely the world's biggest idiot for not appreciating her. Kento picked up his pencil and began to sketch.

Natasha walked around, counseling anyone who signaled for help with their drawing. "Take a close look at the tree you've selected. Every tree is special, very different from the one next to it. Take note of how the branches extend from your tree trunk. Vary the sizes and the tapers of those branches. They are all individuals."

Several people looked up for assistance, and Natasha acknowledged each of them. Kento enjoyed the work, not obeying the teacher's instructions but instead letting his pencil take him wherever it wanted to. It was indeed relaxing to sketch. As his pencil danced, he kept glancing over to Erin, who was involved at her easel as well, his eyes only willing to go a minute or two without peering at her again.

"And when you're ready, you can begin adding the foliage to your branches," Natasha said. "Hold your pencil flat against the paper and shade some of your leaves dark and some of them light to imitate sun and shadow."

Drawing, drawing, Kento's pencil moved fast, easily knowing where to use shade and what to emphasize.

"Now let's blend the base of the tree into its surroundings. How does the tree take root in the ground? Is there dirt or grass surrounding it?"

When time was up, Natasha asked if anyone would like to show their drawing to the group. MacKenzie, Amber and Divya all three raised their arms high, shaking their hands to get noticed. Natasha held up Divya's first, and everyone clapped politely. Kento didn't think the drawing was in a realistic scale. But Natasha found something to praise in each drawing. As she returned to the front of the class, she stopped at Kento's easel and took in what he'd created.

"Here's someone who took the idea of individualism to heart." Before he could stop her, Natasha lifted Kento's drawing for the class to see. There were oohs and aahs in response.

His sketch was not of a tree, or even a branch or leaf.

No, his was a finely drawn rendering of Erin's magnificent face.

* * *

"I'm *so* nervous," Christy shrieked as the stylist rolled a curling iron on her hair. "What if I trip? What if Lucas flubs his vows?"

"It'll be fine. Everybody here is on your side." Erin was having her hair fussed at beside Christy at the lodge's salon, its walls made of brick with brushed-nickel appointments. Studded silver-framed mirrors hung were hung in front of each styling chair, which were light blue leather. Erin reached sideways to give a reassuring squeeze to the bride's hand.

Thinking about the words she'd just spewed, Erin knew she didn't have anyone on *her* side. Sure, her parents would try to shield her from, let's say, an untimely death. But support her in what she might want? Only if it was in line with their own wishes. And Kento? Here today and then, literally, gone tomorrow, regardless of the intensity they'd shared since arriving on the island. She tried not to dwell on that. The party line they circulated was that they'd fallen back in love and would be visiting each other as much as possible. The rest would be figured out later.

Amber, Divya and MacKenzie had already had their hair blown, set and poufed and were being ministered to by the makeup artist. "When did all of this happen with you and Kento?" Christy asked. "You never even told me you were in touch with him."

Yikes. Erin knew the scrutiny was going to get complicated. She wouldn't confide in her cousin about the fake-out. Christy was a Barclay through and through, about to wed her stockbroker with family hopes that she'd soon give birth to the next generation of opulence. Erin didn't trust her not to report to her mother or aunt with any inside information. Boiled down, Erin had never been especially close with her cousin, and she wasn't about to start now.

"Oh, we started talking when he found out I was going to be your maid of honor," she bluffed. "I guess the old feelings resurfaced."

"Erin, that was so cute how Kento drew that picture of you instead of the trees," MacKenzie said as the makeup artist tested different shades of lipstick on the back of her hand. "You are so lucky."

Erin smiled, more to herself than anyone. If they only knew.

"Are there any *good* single guys at this wedding?" Divya bubbled.

"Demarcus Hall is nice," Amber piped up. "What do we know about him?"

"Christy," MacKenzie asked, "does he work with Lucas?"

"No. They coach kids' basketball together."

"Aw."

"Aw."

"Aw."

"Is he unattached?"

"I think so. We told him he was welcome to bring a date to the weekend."

"But he didn't!"

"He didn't."

"Didn't!"

The modern world. Someone found someone else attractive and then tried to suss out as much as possible about the other without directly asking. It was a surprise that these bridesmaids hadn't already cybersearched groomsman Demarcus to the point that they knew his income, the value of his home and where he went to school. Still, it was all probably better than the archaic arranged-marriage routine Erin's parents adhered to. Obviously, they should have better researched Harris and not relied on his parents' sales pitch for their son.

Kento had mentioned yesterday that he figured this wedding weekend was especially hard on her only a few weeks after her breakup. It really wasn't, as far as the subject of weddings, since she certainly didn't love Harris and hadn't pictured marrying him. It was the humiliation of being broken up with that hurt. Which was why playacting that she was back together with Kento was proving to be a successful distraction. People were still nosy enough to talk about the two of them as a couple, but at least the focus was off Harris, everyone in seeming agreement that new-world Kento was at least better for Erin than the reckless playboy. This charade was a really good idea.

Or was it?

It might have been if they'd stuck to the pretend part instead of writing a symphony with their bodies during the most divine lovemaking Erin had ever known. Things had always been exciting between her and Kento in that department. But what they'd shared last night was a mature eroticism that was so poignant and complete, it made their young adult eagerness of the past an unfair contrast. The rush she felt in her solar plexus was escalating. What they'd been sharing this weekend together, through all of their walks and talks and the uncovering of horrors, had burrowed deep into Erin's soul. The sheer rawness of it was terrifying.

It was far easier to imagine a loveless coupling, formed to carry on family names and fortunes, where emotions weren't ventured and, therefore, couldn't be lost. With Kento it was the opposite—to be with him was to live powerfully, as if every day counted. She was almost exhausted by all the feeling she'd done since arriving at this wedding.

What was on Kento's mind at this very moment as he had his tux fitting with the guys? She wondered if he was thinking about her as much as she was about him.

"So, Erin," Divya broke into her musings, "do you think you'll move to Tokyo?"

Which prompted a barrage of inquiries as everyone was being primped and prettied and polished and perfumed. "Would you live at Kento's or find somewhere new together?"

"Does he live in one of those high-rise apartments with all the lights on the buildings?"

"Do you speak Japanese?"

"Does he work 24/7?"

"Does he want kids?"

Eek! Erin didn't know how to respond to all that probing. She locked eyes with her own reflection in the mirror facing her salon chair. She knew better than to be wishing those questions really were hers to answer, but she couldn't stop herself.

"Bridal party, please help yourself to an energy-boosting light lunch," wedding planner Suni sang out as she entered the salon along with a food server wheeling a cart. All of which happened at the perfect time to divert everyone from their interrogation. At least for now. "Green tea to sip. There's spinach salad with avocados, walnuts and dried goji berries. Grilled chicken breast. And we've got some dark chocolate to snack on. All chosen for their health benefits. After hair and makeup, you'll be dressing for the ceremony."

"My dress is a little loose in the chest. Can I get an alteration?" Amber asked Suni. The bridesmaids' gowns were short-sleeved V-neck style on top, leading to a bias-cut skirt. Erin's was embellished with pearl piping to differentiate her maid of honor status. She'd been relieved that with Christy's tendency to dress over the top, the gowns weren't too gaudy. Although the neon-violet fabric wouldn't have been Erin's choice.

"Yes, we'll have someone here to do a final check on everybody."

As the bridesmaids moved toward the food, Erin gave herself one more stare down in the mirror. She'd continue to try to elude those difficult questions the girls had asked since she'd likely never see Kento again after this weekend. And she'd have no real reason to go to Japan. The thought of that was so profoundly somber it turned her perfectly made-up face to ash.

"Here comes the groom!" Kento and the groomsmen sang to the tune of "Here Comes the Bride" as Lucas exited the changing room in his tuxedo. The men's dressing room was a large space with tan-colored carpeting and comfortable furniture upholstered in several shades of brown. A central area was surrounded by tall mirrors arranged in a semicircle so that ensembles could be inspected from every angle. With three groomsmen, one best man, one groom and six mirrors, there was a lot of male energy in the space.

Lucas looked every bit the proper groom in his black tux with its violet cummerbund and tie, the color chosen by Christy to match her bridal party's dresses. The tailor checked Lucas's fitting and pinned a few alterations here and there. The rest of the men had been checked over in their tuxes that echoed the violet tie but sans the cummerbund. They were back in jeans and T-shirts for the time being. Their boutonnieres were laid out on a table, a pale purple rose surrounded by lilac tied with a plaid bow, a nod to the rustic surroundings. Kento's had two roses to denote him as the best man.

The groom's hair had been styled stiff from the multitude of products no doubt employed, but it would stay put for the many photos in the outdoor elements. Kento had allowed the hairdresser to add a bit of hold to his mane. He didn't know Lucas's attendants prior to this weekend, although they were a jovial enough bunch. Demarcus Hall was a buddy from basketball coaching, Hart Westlake was a work colleague and Griffin Meyer a family friend. The latter two were married, their wives in attendance.

Kento attended to some work via his phone. Numbers were just coming in on the Fastracc revenues, and they were even better than he expected. The staff had worked hard on the project, and he authorized a salary bonus to the team.

"What's with the rabbit food?" Hart chided when Suni brought in their lunch.

"These are foods for high energy. Here at Locklear Lodge, we want to do everything we can to foster the participants' well-being on wedding day. There's a spinach salad with avocado, walnuts and dried goji berries. And grilled chicken breast. All energy-boosters."

"Hey, Suni," Demarcus chimed in, "how about some double bacon cheeseburgers? That'll give us plenty of pep."

She raised her eyebrows at him in a good-natured way. "Dark chocolate to finish with and green tea to drink."

Hart pitched, "How about some cold beers?"

Even mild-mannered Griffin joined the fun with, "And a nap. A nice long nap would give us loads of vim and vigor."

"I can't promise a nap—" Suni shrugged "—but you can have whatever you want to eat and drink after the ceremony."

Kento smiled at their carrying on, but his mind was elsewhere.

"What's up?" Lucas noticed Kento's pensiveness as the others helped themselves to the food. The two had formed a strong bond in high school and university years and kept in touch, but with calls and texts that became less frequent as time went on. It was an honor that Lucas had asked him to stand at his side when he married his beloved. "Everything right with you and

Erin? You hadn't even told me that you two were in communication."

"Absolutely right." He forced a bright answer.

Things were actually a little *too* right with her. That was the problem. He didn't like how the combination of blazing lovemaking and the *forever after* sentiments of this wedding were making him feel. They were causing him to second-guess. And that was not something he did. Kento was a man of conviction. That's how he built his empire. He never put out a product before it was ready. Never made a miscalculation. Never regretted hiring or firing an employee. Just the same, he'd gotten on the plane to Seattle with the certainty that relationships, and definitely marriage, would never, ever be in his future.

Finding that Erin hadn't betrayed him in the way he'd always assumed she had, his brain short-circuited while it tried to sort true from false, impossibility from opportunity, head from heart. While the tailor attended to Lucas's tux, Kento stared at himself in one of the full-length mirrors. What was on Erin's mind right now while she got glammed up with the girls? Was she thinking about him?

This time Mr. Sure of Himself was anything but.

The best man and maid of honor strode toward the altar. While doing so, Erin forgot for the tiniest moment again that she was wearing a shocking violet gown and not a white one. That the guests assembled had not brought the toasters and china place settings for her. That the breathtaking man whose arm she was holding wasn't about to become her mate. *Husband* suddenly sounded like the sweetest word she had ever heard, and yearning flooded through her.

As they had rehearsed, they moved in measured increments. Instead of a fabric runner, the aisle they walked down was delineated by a carpet of moss that was pretty but actually not that easy to navigate. Erin's heels kept getting tangled every few steps, and Kento had to disguise his little tugs that helped her from falling and being ensnared by the greenery. They moved on pace toward the archway altar that was now completely covered in cascading wisteria. She'd figured that with Seattle's frequent rain they'd use a marquee tent for shelter, but instead it was a dry day and it had been decided that the ceremony could be held in the open air. There were clouds, but sunlight peeked through them. A flutist played from a nearby bench. Guests sat on both sides of the aisle, on rows of white chairs dressed with white cushions in the center of the extensive lawn, the lodge's forest of trees behind the altar framing the space.

When they reached the arch, Kento and Erin parted toward their respective sides. An involuntary wince shot through her after separating herself from him. It was wrong that she was starting to like being with him more than being without him, and she knew it. Those inclinations could only lead to more agony, and hadn't the two of them suffered enough by each other's doings?

The bride and her enormous dress, with a skirt full enough to house four small children under it, minced slowly up the aisle, accompanied by her father. Now standing next to the three bridesmaids, Erin reflected as she watched Christy approach. All that had happened with Kento still felt unresolved—many misunderstandings, many mistakes made. And most significantly, both of them wore so many scars from the past they'd been completely disfigured by them. Even if she thought she could open up to something ongoing with him again, to try to heal, he'd made it abundantly clear that he couldn't. Glancing over, she noticed her mother seated in one of the rows of chairs, talking to someone Erin couldn't see due to the tall woman with a big hat who sat in front of her.

With Lucas beaming, Christy detached from her father and joined her groom to face the wedding officiant. Erin took the bride's bouquet as had been rehearsed.

They were just not meant to be, her and Kento. She had to accept it. Maybe in another lifetime, not this one. She knew that she should take charge of the situation by not making it any worse, not getting any closer. Under no circumstances should she make love with him again. It had been too perfect, too moving, too life-affirming. The least she could do is spare them getting any further invested in each other, which would make tomorrow's separation even more harrowing.

"Ladies and gentlemen, we are gathered here today to celebrate the union of Christy and Lucas," the officiant began.

The ceremony progressed quickly. Or was it that Erin's focus drifted in and out from the long rhyming poem written and read by an older uncle of Lucas's?

This day begins our start, in the waters we shall chart
Holding hands we now depart, as I keep you in my heart
You are my work of art, sharing wisdom we impart
If we fight we will restart, we must be smart, for life is sweet but sometimes tart
May we never be apart, for you are my...counterpart.

Christy dabbed away a tear.

Erin glanced over to Kento, who closed his eyes and mimicked his head dropping sideways as if he had fallen asleep, making it hard for her not to laugh.

The conventional vows were spoken, and soon enough Erin was reunited with Kento's arm, firm and strong, and they receded down the aisle.

Guests were directed to the grand ballroom inside the lodge for the reception. There was a photo call for the bridal party, as Christy had gone the traditional route of not letting Lucas see her in her dress until she walked down the aisle. They were sequestered in an area prepared for the task, with all sorts of flower arrangements on pedestals set against the backdrop of tall green trees.

Suni assisted the photographer with his groupings.

"When do we get to eat?" Kento whispered into Erin's ear. "Did you have those salads when you were getting dressed? Nice, but I'm starved."

"I can't eat until the photos are done. It might muss up my lipstick."

"*I'd* like to muss up your lipstick," Kento let fly. The electric thrill that shot through Erin's body was a charge that could have lit up Seattle. He needed to stop being so unrelentingly sexy. A girl could only take so much.

She forced out what she wanted to say, though with limited conviction. "I don't think we should do any more…mussing, if you know what I mean. You're leaving tomorrow, and we've gone far past the playacting we agreed to participate in."

"Oh, that's right, we were supposed to be pretending, weren't we?" he responded with a bitter sort of undertone she didn't exactly understand.

"I mean, we've both made it clear we have no interest in relationships. Especially after our past together. But my plan may have backfired." She saw no reason not to be honest with him again. "The more time we spend with each other, the more I question…"

"Okay, I'll need everyone lined up for a group shot," the photographer called.

Wasn't Kento feeling the same thing—that every second they were together was going to make it harder and harder for him to board that plane? She was willing to state that out loud. How would withholding words serve her at this point? She might have thought she could pull off this charade, but she'd underestimated the influence Kento still had over her. And it had become impossible to distinguish what was real and what was fantasy. She was dreading having to say goodbye so soon tomorrow. Although it was for the best.

With the photos finally completed, everyone except the bride and groom, who would be formally announced as a married couple, was seen into the ballroom.

With smiles left and right, the best man and maid

of honor said hello to many of the guests in the large ballroom. Hors d'oeuvres were passed on trays held by waiters in white jackets. Erin had one of each of the chicken satay skewers with peanut sauce, spinach and feta cheese meatballs, and crostini with olive tapenade that had been refined yesterday to the bride's satisfaction. All were delicious. Marionberry spritzers were pretty and frosty cold.

The ballroom was done up to Christy and Aunt Olivia's exact specifications. Tables were dressed in dark green linen. Lavender-colored napkins were rolled and tied with twine into which a sprig of wisteria was slipped. The china was copper-rimmed. Centerpieces were enormous on tall pedestals, with larkspur, lilac and hydrangea selections dotted with long strands of fairy lights.

Out of the corner of her eye, Erin spotted her mother in conversation with a man she could only see from the back. Recognizing immediately who it was, apprehension darkened over her like a raincloud. Without drawing Kento's attention, she said to a woman she was chatting with, "Excuse me for a minute."

While he continued his conversation with some of the guests, she beelined across the room toward her mother, where her suspicion was confirmed. Important business in Walla Walla was supposed to have been so critical it was going to keep Ingram Barclay from attending the wedding. Yet there he was in a tuxedo and tailcoat. "Father, why are you here?"

"Your mother called me, and rightly so. I flew into town and chartered a ferry to the island." Erin glared at

Bunny, whose face pinched as she listened to her husband. "Surely you don't think we're going to allow you to get involved again with Kento Yamamoto."

With the band having taken the stage, the reception was in full swing. Oldies dance songs had many revelers up and boogying in the grand ballroom, another event space on the lodge's property with walls built mainly from glass to display the lush flora outside, a formal garden filled with fountains, birdbaths and colorful flowers. Bridesmaid Amber caught Kento's eye as he watched her literally drag groomsman Demarcus onto the dance floor, the poor guy popping the crostini he held in his hand right into his mouth to keep up. She wore that same brash violet color as Erin and the other bridesmaids. He didn't know where the maid of honor had gone, but he was ready for her return. This whole wedding biz was much easier to take with her on his arm.

In his bed, too, but that was another matter entirely. In fact, he'd been thinking during the ceremony that as magnificent as it was to make glorious love with Erin last night, the long-dormant passion in him set aflame, she was right to say up front that she didn't think they should do it again. Even with the past hurts from the Barclays explained, the calculated ambitions of Ayaka behind him and the childhood of rejection now history, Kento made it his policy to keep his guard up at all times. His armor was always on. He wasn't a man who was ever going to rely on anyone. But instead of confirming those edicts, as was his intention this weekend,

Erin made him question them. Things were becoming too dangerous—*she* was too dangerous. What he felt around her could explode his plan into a million pieces.

He wholeheartedly alleged that trust was what fed an intimate relationship, which would shrivel and dry up without it. Good for Lucas and Christy, he'd thought as they promised each other love and loyalty at the altar. Of course, the *for richer or for poorer* part of the vows sounded silly coming out of the mouths of Seattle's bluebloods, where daughters were still bargained off along like land and holdings. Erin would walk down the wedding aisle to her approved future someday, and it wasn't going to be Kento. A part of him wished he could steal her away to be his, to take her back to Japan where she could leave this life that wasn't making her happy, anyway.

After the band finished the song they were playing, the ballroom lights flashed and then went slightly dim. The bandleader, a stocky man whose limbs strained against his tuxedo, boomed through his microphone, "Introducing for the first time as husband and wife, Mr. and Mrs. Lucas Collins."

A purple-tinged spotlight was aimed at the ballroom's entrance as Lucas and Christy burst in holding hands. At the same time, Erin arrived at Kento's side. The band began the song that would be the couple's first dance. As they took to the dance floor, the videographer and photographer snaked in a circle around them, capturing the moment.

Kento noticed there was a stress in Erin's eyes, her brows slightly bunched, that hadn't been there before.

While they watched the newlyweds, he asked, "Is everything okay?"

He could tell she was making a decision before she told him, "My father is here."

"And that bothers you?"

"He wasn't expected to come. My mother called to tell him you and I had resparked our romance."

Understanding why she was upset, his own blood pressure rose. He'd hoped not to get involved in any conversation with either of Erin's parents other than to exchange pleasantries. No longer the intimidated twenty-one-year-old, Kento saw no benefit in cutting loose the fury he'd held for the Barclays. It was of no importance now—he just wanted to get through the weekend and get back home. There was nothing to be gained by any kind of confrontation with them. That was Erin's fight, should she ever suit up and make it to the battle line.

After the bride danced with her father and then father-in-law, the groom with his mother-in-law and then with his own mother, the bandleader announced, "We now call for the best man and maid of honor."

Kento firmly grasped Erin's hand and led her to the center of the dance floor. He pulled her close and they began to sway. Once they'd reached a rhythm, he asked into her ear, "Did your father have anything new to say on the topic?"

"I told him that I had maid of honor responsibilities and that we needed to discuss it later."

"What is there to talk about?"

"I'll have to explain that us getting back together is a hoax."

The sequence of lies and exposures had gotten complicated, just as he'd suspected it might. "Which means you'll have to tell your parents that one of the main reasons you embarked on this charade is because of your mother trying to fix you up with every society billionaire in Seattle. Even though ending up with one of them is, actually, the destiny you're allowing them to choose for you."

They whirled to the music, photos and video capturing every move. Kento felt himself becoming more and more agitated. For her, but maybe for himself as well. Because perhaps he had to admit that he secretly did want to see where this weekend with Erin might lead. Could it be that she'd hammered cracks into his stone wall? Was it possible that he might he be able to open his heart after all? He'd become a man who got what he wanted. What was it he wanted this time? In any case, he wished that the options were not her parents' but his and Erin's.

"I suppose a few years from now I'll hear through Lucas that you produced a couple of heirs to the throne," he egged her on. He felt her body freeze in response. She stopped dancing, forcing him to stop as well. With a smile so fake she could be a model in a toothpaste commercial, she moved to leave the dance floor.

His jaw pulsed, him exasperated by his own lack of diplomacy, conceding that this was further proof that he was not meant to get close to someone. She must have already been upset that her father found it necessary to fly in to intercede. Kento had made it worse by not controlling his own reaction. He grabbed her hand before she could scoot away. "I'm sorry. I shouldn't have said that."

"It's what you think."

"That may be true, but what kind of bully am I? I'm as bad as your parents." His strong impulses toward her were making him desperate. How could he argue with her family allegiance when that was a value he respected? "It's not right that I made you feel judged. That's something I know far too much about myself."

"We sure spend a lot of time apologizing to each other, don't we?" she asked with a half smile.

"Let's eat."

As they sat down to dinner, the first course was served: Alaskan king crab cakes. With Erin sitting at Christy's side and Kento next to Lucas, they didn't talk after that sharp exchange on the dance floor. He spotted Ingram and Bunny a few tables away. If either of them cared to engage in a stare down, he was more than ready. But, of course, they were too cowardly to give him more than an occasional glance.

In accepting Lucas's request for him to stand as best man, Kento had figured he'd be encountering both of Erin's parents. What he hadn't expected was discovering all of the new information that brought the musing about Erin he'd been haunted by in Tokyo into a different light. Which made her predicament a frustration he himself experienced along with her, for her. At this point, getting back on that plane to the place that was now home couldn't come soon enough. Although his suitcase full of thoughts about Erin was going to be heavier, not lighter.

After the entrée of beef Wellington and crispy brussels sprouts, the time for the maid of honor and best man's most important task of the night arrived. She was to speak first, and then his speech would be a champagne toast as wedding cake was served.

Erin stood and was handed a mic. She spoke of the serene location and how nice the ceremony was. Wished the couple every happiness and then looked over to Kento, whom she hadn't spoken with during the meal. "Earlier, I was reviewing my speech and decided I wanted to find a quotation that was meaningful to me personally, as a gift I could give to Christy and Lucas." The bride and groom kissed, and the guests applauded them doing so. Erin focused her eyes on Kento's and kept them there as she finished. "Sophocles tells us that 'one word frees us of all the weight and pain of life. That word is *love*.'"

The message bulleted into Kento, making his Adam's apple twitch. He couldn't help thinking those were words she'd picked for him, not the newlyweds. He'd heard sentiments to that effect before, yet they'd never sounded as poignant. Could love set them free?

The mic was passed. It was his turn. He began, "As some of you know, I live in Tokyo. So I thought I'd bring along some age-old wisdom from Japanese proverbs. The first is 'Eat before falling in love.'" Laughter came from various directions. "I presume what the ancients meant by that is that love is all-encompassing and can command your full attention. Love is hard work. It's not for the weak." More chuckles came as a response. As the champagne was poured, he offered his well wishes to the happy couple.

As Kento lifted his glass high, the guests followed suit. His eyes met Erin's; she hadn't taken hers off him. In fact, her stare bored into him. "And I'll conclude with another Japanese proverb that says simply, 'No road is too long in the company of a friend.'"

Erin bit her lip as her eyes became glassy.

Kento sat down.

The cake was wheeled across the dance floor. It was a three-tiered white affair with green frosting trees decorating the sides. No doubt a tribute to the Pacific Northwest but a bit tacky, in his opinion. Slices were soon delivered to each place setting, and coffee service followed immediately after.

At a discreet moment, Kento got up and moved behind Christy and Lucas to Erin's chair. He leaned down and hushed into her ear, "We've done our job. Let's get out of here."

She turned her head toward him in question. "What do you mean?"

"It's early. Let's go into the city. I've got a boat for us."

CHAPTER SEVEN

"WHEN DID YOU arrange this?" Erin asked as Kento helped her into the limousine waiting at the lodge's main entrance. He took a seat beside her, allowing the driver to then close the door.

"During the beef Wellington. After I was such a jerk to you on the dance floor." Being teased about her station in life and fidelity to her parents—as she viewed it, anyway—was no joking matter. He'd become aggravated at Ingram's arrival as well. And wished he could do something to protect her. From her own parents? That was family drama he had no place in. Making a joke about sometime down the line hearing from Lucas that Erin had produced the heirs everyone was waiting for was a low blow he wished hadn't snapped out of his mouth.

"What's this?" she asked as he slid over a large gift bag from the floor of the limo. It was gold with two handles, and the contents were hidden by bunches of shimmery tissue paper.

"Just something I had the driver pick up from a personal shopper."

After a quizzical look, she yanked at the tissue, throwing it left and right, which gave him a grin. As intended, the item she pulled out was a tan-colored woolen coat.

"I stole you away from the wedding. The least I could do is keep you warm."

"Just as you gave me your jacket when we walked together after the welcome dinner." She shook her head in charmed disbelief, her smile filling him with delight. "Where are we headed?"

There was a double meaning to that question.

"Let's revisit somewhere we used to go."

The limo delivered them to the island harbor. Kento ushered her into a private ferry he'd ordered online from his phone, which he'd cleverly hidden under the table during dinner. He'd guessed her size closely enough that the coat fit her well. After the short ride to the city dock, another limo met them there. Once they were ensconced inside, he pulled a bottle of champagne from the silver ice bucket it rested in and poured some into the crystal flutes provided on a tray.

"To history." He lifted his glass.

"One word frees us of all the weight and pain of life. That word is love.*"*

He didn't know why he was toasting their sometimes painful past, only that it was something they were bound by. Shared. Together. It was genuine. Before extortions, bent realities and inevitability tore them apart, they'd passed far more good times together than bad. She was still the only woman who had affected his soul.

With that, after they clinked glasses and sipped, he

leaned right over and planted a deep kiss onto her sweet lips. Their tongues met in an intermingling that sent pleasure down his entire body. His fingers threaded through the silk of her hair as he held her head to him. One kiss led to another in a dreamy haze that he couldn't break away from.

"Excuse me, sir," the voice of the limo driver came in through the speaker. "Would you like me to continue driving without a destination?"

Erin giggled, and then so did Kento. "We weren't supposed to do that anymore," he scolded her, wagging his finger like a disapproving schoolteacher. "You are too alluring!" Her sly smile in return made his chest swell.

"Do you want to do something goofy like go to the Space Needle?" she suggested.

Raising his glass to tap hers again, he instructed the driver to take them there.

Memories flooded him when they reached the Seattle Center, where several of the city's tourist attractions were located. He recalled countless times that he and Erin would lie on a blanket on one of the many patches of lawn that surrounded the Needle. The driver let them out at the entrance base. Both of them tilted their heads back to look upward at the impressive height of the tower from this vantage point.

"We going up?"

"Absolutely," she answered. "I never do tourist things."

"And I feel like a visitor in my hometown."

He bought tickets, and they were soon in the elevator rocketing them over six hundred feet upward to the observation decks.

Since the last time Kento had visited, much had been changed at the top of the Needle, including a revolving glass floor. "It's always been an unbeatable view," he mused aloud as he and Erin made their way around the circular deck that afforded vistas from all angles. At one point they stopped to stare silently at the cityscape, sparkling in the night sky. Without knowing if his hand reached for hers or hers for his, suddenly her velvety palm was in his grasp.

Kento had seen the world's sights from the sky, from atop the Empire State Building to the Eiffel Tower to Dubai's Burj Khalifa. Yet there was nothing like this. Because Erin was next to him. "Did you know that the initial design for the Space Needle was sketched on a napkin by a hotelier?" she asked.

"Yeah. That story was always inspiring to me. Remember how many times we used to hang out here lying on the lawn?"

They'd come to study, to relax, to kiss, to talk.

"I used to bring one of those blankets with the university logo printed all over it." After spreading it open, she'd stretch out on her back, body flat to the ground. And he'd lie down as well, perpendicular, with his head on her stomach, where he'd stare idly at this space-age architectural marvel, the flying saucer in the sky.

During those quiet times, when she'd rhythmically comb her fingers through his hair seemingly for hours on end, he'd felt completely accepted. All of the negative talk and ridicule, and sometimes humiliation, of his upbringing would disappear. The worn shoes on his feet when everybody else had a new pair each season didn't matter. All the sneers of Erin's sorority sisters and her parents held nothing over him in those moments.

"In a way, those afternoons here with you were when I had the inklings of what would be my first software design." Which launched his empire. It occurred to him, for the first time, how much he owed her for that approval. For that safe space. Without it, he wasn't sure he'd be in the position he was. The enemies might have beaten him down after all. "We had something pretty great once, didn't we?" he asked wistfully, both of them still looking out at the city.

"When I was with you, I almost believed I could have anything I wanted."

"What would you want if there was nothing holding you back?"

"Are you really asking?"

"I don't pose questions if I'm not interested in the answer."

"I'll show you when we're done here."

After the elevator delivered them back to terra firma, they returned to the limo. Erin called up an address on her phone and instructed the driver. Kento was intrigued.

A bit later, the driver pulled to the curb of a mansion in the city's Queen Anne neighborhood.

"What are we looking at?"

"You asked what I'd do if I could do anything. I'd buy this mansion. That's what I'd like to pursue, acquiring historic properties. Find the really special ones. Faithfully restore them if they need it. Research chandeliers and woodwork and all the details."

"That's what Barclay Properties does. Your parents and your paternal grandparents."

"Yes, but they give me reports to check, a bunch of numbers our accountants have already prepared. Or an office task, such as pricing new computers for employees. They're just marking time until they can marry me off."

"Erin, this isn't the olden days. You can have a meaningful career and still produce children."

"Tell that to them."

"Have *you*?"

"Yes. They don't listen."

"Do you ever think of just…breaking away?"

"Of course. But where would I go? Alone." His heart cracked for her. At how little choice she perceived herself to have. "You were the only taste of independence I've ever had. You encouraged me to think and say anything I wanted to."

"We gave each other more than we realized at the time."

"I wish it wasn't too late."

"Is it?" What was he thinking? That there was some scenario that saw the two of them together after tomorrow? It was impossible, yet he couldn't conceive of walking away from her again. Was it too much to dream of more? He owned a private jet and had every resource money could buy at his disposal. Perhaps he could start by returning to Seattle again in a few weeks.

Maybe every few weeks. Alternately, he could fly her to him if she'd come.

While he'd been so convinced an ongoing union wasn't for him, spending time with Erin had made him doubt those conclusions. Could he leave the hurt behind and start a future with her? And even if he could, what about her? She was resigned to her lot, considered it her destiny. But maybe they could start slowly and get more acquainted with the adults they'd become rather than just debriefing on the past. Perhaps, in time, he could help her see her options in a new light.

"What do you like about this property?" He decided to start getting to know her better right now.

"I've toured it. Built in 1902. Ten thousand square feet. What I love—" she gestured as she spoke "—is the wraparound terraces with marble tile flooring and fantastic views. And look at those double entrance doors."

"Do you know a lot about real estate?"

"Not formally. But it's in my blood, I guess. Is it interesting to you?"

"What's interesting to *you* is what's interesting to me. Tell me more."

"It's three stories with curved wooden staircases. A massive party lounge with a built-in wooden bar. A full catering kitchen. Twenty-three original chandeliers."

Her enthusiasm was infectious. He couldn't help but lean in and swoop a kiss to her cheek. The chuckle he got in return was enchanting. After she'd shown him another property she liked in Ballard, the limo driver asked through the speaker where they wanted to go next. "Just go ahead and circle the city," Kento answered. With the privacy glass separating them from the driver and the blackout windows of the limo allowing them to look out but no one to see in, Kento knew exactly the sights he wanted to take in next.

Leaning over, he brought a hand to Erin's face and then kissed her other cheek with its creamy softness. His mouth found hers, and he kissed her intensely, a ravenous kiss that felt like a man's daily bread, like something he couldn't live without. When he'd had enough to survive for a minute, he moved down to her throat. The catch of desire he heard in her breath encouraged him on. Warm enough in the heated limo, he slid the coat he'd bought her off, first one silken shoulder and then the other.

To think, it had only been a few hours ago when she marched down the wedding aisle in that violet gown she still wore. The one he was reaching behind her to unzip. He shimmied it down her body and off her and made short work of the lingerie underneath. Likewise, he slipped off her shoes. There she was for him, completely naked, gorgeous, excitement evident in her eyes. He sat back and pulled her onto his lap, him still in his tuxedo because he wanted to slowly caress and savor every inch of her before undressing.

He poured a fresh flute of champagne and brought it to her lips for a sip. And took one himself from the exact same spot her mouth had touched. Just to provoke her response, he brought the cold flute to the skin of her neck. The tip of her tongue darted out to flick her upper lip in arousal. His teeth bared with pleasure, his loins bracing under his trousers. He drizzled a bit of the champagne onto her exposed throat only so that he could quickly lick it off. Her head fell back at the same time her spine arched to allow him even greater access.

Eventually, with an occasional glance through the blackout windows to the downtown office buildings, he laid Erin down on the limo seat. After removing a condom from his wallet, he stripped off his tuxedo and got on top of her. The elevation to which they brought each other was far higher than the top of the Space Needle they'd just come down from.

"Where to now?" After the urgent merging of body and soul that Erin and Kento had just shared in the limo, she wasn't ready to return to the wedding across the Sound at the lodge. No doubt a group of drunken revelers were still dancing, now to recorded music once the band finished. She most certainly didn't want to encounter her parents. That could wait until tomorrow. Her mother calling her father in from out of town was yet another indignity Erin would have to add to her already full mental tote bag of similar behavior.

No, she didn't want to think about any of that at the moment. All she could see, breathe, feel or hear was the naked man sprawled right next to her, who was stroking her cheek with the backs of his fingers. After the fiasco with Harris, she thought she'd arrive at the wedding with a hardened heart and not susceptible to any new, or revisited, emotions. She'd greatly underestimated the magical powers of Kento Yamamoto to make her care, to make her hope, to make her imagine.

"Are any of those nightclubs we used to go to still

around?" he suggested. With Seattle the birthplace of many great musicians, the city's live music scene was a mecca. There had been countless nights that she and Kento spent nursing a long-necked beer bottle and listening to a rock-and-roll band, some good, some simply loud.

"That's not something I ever do anymore, either, but let's look it up." With a few swipes on her phone, she located a club that sounded promising and gave the driver the address. They crawled back into their clothes, Kento in his tux again but skipping the tie. Despite their agreement that they shouldn't further complicate the weekend with more physical intimacy, their pull toward each other had trampled over any common sense.

People milled about outside the Emerald Bar. Dressed in jeans, flannel and leather, it looked to be a crowd of university students. Just as they once were. Which made her so aware of how much time had moved on. All heads shot toward them when the limo pulled up to the curb. Eschewing the driver's offer to open the door for them, Kento exited and extended his arm to Erin to help her out.

"I just thought of the fact that tuxedo and gown isn't quite the dress code for places like this," she said, hearing the thumping music spilling out from the club's doors.

"I suppose not," he replied with a chuckle.

They were eyed up and down by the people outside, where there was nothing for Erin and Kento to do but shrug their shoulders. A girl with arms covered in tattoos called good-naturedly, "How was the wedding?"

"Pretty good," Kento answered for them, "but our personal after-party was even better."

Erin sparkled recalling the drive around Seattle they'd just taken, the limo serving as more than just a mode of transportation. She forked a hand through her hair, wondering if it had become messy, although not really caring if she looked wanton. On the arm of the most appealing man she had ever known and after what they just did, she felt confident in her own sexuality in a way she never had before as they traipsed into the club.

Finding seats to the side of the stage, he pulled out the chair for her to sit and then arranged his own to be right next to it. The small table was wood and people had carved their initials or slogans into it. "Beer?" he asked above the beat of the band as he perused the sticky laminated menu card, noting that even in a dive like this the brews were artisanal with lofty descriptions. That was Seattle. "How about notes of pine, herbs and orange peel with a bitter crispy finish?"

Which struck them both as funny. "How can beer be crispy?" she inquired.

He mimicked taking a big bite and ordered two when the waitress came.

Soon they were sipping from long-necked bottles, just like the old days, as they both pumped their shoulders in rhythm with the bass-heavy foursome on stage. All skinny in torn jeans, two with bushy beards, the band blasted out rapid-fire songs one after the next.

Erin surely couldn't remember the last time she'd had this much fun. Why couldn't have things gone differently for them? her mind lamented. All these years when she'd thought of him, it was with the sting of loss, of being walked out on. Knowing now that he thought she was part of the militia mustered to force him out only slightly assuaged that mixed-up ache.

What if he had told her about the bribes and threats? Would she have stayed with him, taken a side? If she was being brutally honest, probably not. She would have been too afraid back then. But in her imagination, what if she had chosen him over her parents? Might they have gone forward as young adults together in Seattle? Would he have stayed here, or would he have pursued the opportunity with his uncle in Tokyo, anyway?

The central question that had arisen time and time again lit up in her mind like it was written in neon lights. If he'd asked her to move to Japan with him, would she have? Might not that have been her only chance at a true break from the preplanned life her parents had already drafted for her?

Five thousand miles could have been far enough away, on a continent they had no connection to, for them to give up on running her life. Would they have let her be out of spite, daring her to turn her back on their money and the safety it brought? Or would they have chased after her, employing surveillance, making her life unpleasant and still controlled? She was only beginning to understand the depths of their cold-bloodedness, so maybe it was a naive fantasy to think she could have jetted away with Kento from everything she knew, to start fresh. But it was a dream she'd allowed herself for seven long years.

After two sets from the band and two crispy beers, they were hungry. Returning to the still-in-business twenty-four-hour diner they used to go to for late-night eats, they sauntered in with their violet satin and black tux. The decor had been spruced up, but the vibe was the same. Night-crawling hipsters, workers who'd just finished shifts, lovers who only had eyes for each other, even big family groups all munched from massive, heavy white plates. Kento and Erin ordered breakfast food of bacon and eggs, served with potatoes, toast and coffee. They dug in as soon as it was served.

She returned to the thoughts of what could have been that she'd had at the club. And the far recess of her mind was screaming, *What about now?* She didn't know whether to give that voice any credence, yet it kept popping up. With fork in hand, she asked, "Tell me more about your life in Tokyo. How did you go from working for your uncle to creating NIRE?"

"It's a fast pace there in general, but I have to admit I ascended quickly. I was just ahead of the curve on what people wanted programs to do for them. I seem to have a knack for coming up with what the market will respond to."

"So, as soon as you got there, you started working at your uncle's office?"

"Yeah, at first I lived with some other cousins on the outskirts of town and had to commute into the city every day. Uncle Riku had a small development company, and I did coding for him and whatever work he needed done. I started designing apps in my spare time. After I sold the first few, I got on to the big software projects I had in mind, and I had enough money to open my own office."

Erin tried to picture that. Going to look at empty office space to lease in the modern high-rise buildings of the business districts. Attending to all of the details of running a business. She was amazed at his bravery, still only in his midtwenties when this was taking shape. Opening his own company had to have been a big risk to take. "Did you hire employees right away?"

"We started with a·small staff in a space that had one office and a half dozen workstations. Within a couple of years, we took over the entire floor. Now we have six floors and a think tank outside the city."

"Was it ever an obstacle for you, being an American?" What she was really asking was how it would have been for *her* had she gone with him. Which, of course, wasn't a true comparison, as he was of Japanese descent and spoke the language.

"The culture is more formal and modest there than it is here. People don't express how they feel as much. And they don't touch as casually. They bow. Social hierarchies are important."

How would she have fared as a stranger in a strange land? Learning any language was a challenge, but Japanese, with its character sets and writing systems, would have been especially difficult. Not looking like the majority, when walking down the street she'd have been instantly identified as a foreigner. In addition to language, there were those social norms to learn. Could she have made a life there, created a home for the two of them?

"Where do you live?"

"Now that's just like it would be anywhere in the world for a bachelor billionaire. I have a sleek penthouse on the forty-third floor. Glass walls, black and chrome furniture, extra rooms I never use. Food delivered. A housekeeper who takes care of everything. I'm a cliché." Erin tried to picture what he was describing—an elevator like the Space Needle's shooting him up to his apartment. He abruptly put down his fork and reached across the table to take both of Erin's hands in his. "Why don't you come visit me sometime and let me show you?"

After their explosive encounter under the shower and in his cabin last night, they'd agreed not to make love again, that they'd stop playing with fire. Which was supposed to help keep her internal volcano from erupting. But they hadn't held themselves back. Tonight, being in the city with him again had switched the light inside her to the on position. From this evening forward, she was forever changed. In fact, she knew in a blink that she was going to see that penthouse, lie down on his bed in the sky. No matter what it took.

"I don't speak a word of Japanese."

"You could learn."

"Teach me how to say something. Right now."

"Okay." He hesitated then said, looking into her waiting eyes, *"Aishiteru."*

"What does that mean?"

"It means 'I love you.'"

After the ferry whisked Erin and Kento back across the Sound in the wee hours, they returned to his cabin. Due in the morning at the gift-opening brunch, in a few hours they would be thrown right back into the throng of the wedding party. It had been a long day, and after a dozen or so tender kisses good-night in bed, beautiful Erin fell quickly to sleep in his arms.

Slumber didn't come as easily for him as he watched the night shadows play against the skylight in the bedroom.

Aishiteru.

I love you.

He'd said it aloud. In two languages. The crazy thing was, it was true. It had always been true. Maybe the stars had been in his favor when Erin had the idea of a fake boyfriend for the weekend. Without that, they wouldn't have spent so much time together, helping him to realize that it wasn't the past with her he planned to forget that mattered. It was the future they were going to create.

He stroked her arm ever so gently so as not to wake her, the mild movement in contrast to the giddiness inside him. He'd declared his love to a woman. To *the* woman that he'd been in love with all along. How distorted a mind could get five thousand miles away from the person who owned his heart. Pain had removed the longings of his soul.

When he'd uttered those important words in two different tongues, she didn't return them. For a moment, sitting in the diner's orange plastic booth, their plates of American breakfast in front of them, he'd felt slapped by her lack of response. Fortunately, the practicality and patience that had enabled him to build his company to where it was today served him in this facet of life also.

He'd wounded her so critically years ago. Even though he was only a frightened kid, he'd always been tormented by guilt that he'd deserted her in the process. And learning this weekend about how little she knew of what went on made him guiltier still. After him, she'd had a series of disappointments in dating. Then she was abandoned, another dismissal, by Harris. She was quite smart not to bark out a forced and cursory *I love you, too.*

The moon shining in from the skylight above his bed shifted to give a glow to her face. He could wait for her. In a way, he'd been waiting for her all along. They'd go at her pace. He had to earn her trust again, and that was okay with him. The main thing was that they'd made a plan at the diner. He'd return to Seattle in a few weeks. After that, she'd agreed to come to Japan. She'd even expressed interest in learning about the customs that she would be unfamiliar with. It wouldn't be easy there as a white woman without knowing the language. They'd start by getting a tutor here. Optimism tingled through him. He wouldn't just show her Tokyo, but he'd take her outside the city, to see stunning Mount Fuji. Like Mount Rainier here in Washington, Fuji was the tallest volcano in the area. There were so many places he wanted to show her in the beautiful country he called home.

Above all else, Erin was finally determined to chart her own path. That would be far harder for her than learning a new language. The break she'd have to make from her parents might be absolute. That they could hate

Kento enough to turn their back on their daughter was in and of itself an illustration of their character, one that should make it easier for her to walk away. He could support her as much as possible, but that turning point would be hers alone. Dotting her peaceful-looking face with wispy kisses, he knew she could tackle whatever lay ahead. It was her time.

His eyes moved to the dream catcher party favor the guests had been given at the rehearsal dinner. He lifted it from the nightstand and hooked it onto the bedpost. It must be working, he thought with a smile that no one saw. Holding Erin, he finally drifted into a contented sleep.

At daybreak, Erin left his embrace to go prepare for the morning. They'd meet at the brunch. But when Kento arrived to the lodge's lounge, he couldn't spot her anywhere. Christy and Lucas were front and center, with the guests seated at small tables arranged in a semicircle around them. People nibbled from their brunch plates—baked French toast, a fruit and yogurt bar, and coffee and tea were set up as a buffet. Lucas held up the latest kitchen mixer, eliciting oohs and wows from the group. Christy tore the silver wrapping paper from a set of luxury bedsheets.

He spotted Amber and Demarcus sitting together, his arm around the bridesmaid. *Good*, Kento thought, suddenly soppy about people finding their significant other. As a matter of fact, on closer survey, he also saw MacKenzie and Divya each sitting with a man. Bunny and Ingram were nowhere to be found.

Kento was beginning to get worried about Erin

and stepped out of the lounge to call her. Until his eye caught sight of Ingram in a small side salon across the lobby. Kento made his way over there, wondering if Erin was with him.

Careful not to be seen, as she needed to deal with her parents herself, he got close enough to see that Bunny and Erin were in the room as well, huddled close. All three of their faces were strained. Still moving sideways to avoid notice, Kento couldn't help but listen in when he heard the harsh tones coming from their mouths.

"It started out fake, but it's become real. Realer than anything I've ever felt."

"We won't stand for it."

"You should like Kento now, Father," Erin hissed. "He has both fame and fortune. Lots and lots of money. Let's order the criteria of what's important to you. Is there anything besides pedigree and wealth?"

"Erin, are we to have a repeat of seven years ago?" Ingram asked sternly.

Bunny followed suit. "He's not one of our kind."

"What on earth does that even mean anymore? Isn't rich and successful *our* kind of people? I found someone rich."

Kento winced. She'd *found* someone rich. He didn't like the sound of that. Why didn't she say that she'd *found* someone she loved? Oh, that's right, she'd never told him that she loved him. Last night during the fun and exhilaration of the limo and the nightclub, she'd confided a change, but not one she was honestly going to be able to make. Maybe it was something that sounded doable in theory but, when push came to shove, she couldn't put it into practice.

"For heaven's sake, Erin," her father scolded. "You know what your mother means. Established families. Multigenerational wealth. You have a duty to marry strategically and produce the next generation of the Barclay legacy."

Erin glared at both of them but had no retort. Here it was. In the time it took for the wedding guests to spoon blueberry yogurt into their mouths, Kento's dream come true had morphed into the recurring nightmare from the past. She wasn't going to stand up to them. Ever. He recognized the body language. Her shoulders slumped. Her eyes deadened. Once again, she'd been defeated.

Unable to witness any longer, Kento dashed away. As he rushed toward his cabin, cries of disappointment stifled in his throat. How ridiculous of him to allow the thoughts he'd had while lying in bed a few dark hours ago with Erin warm against his chest. He should have been the wiser one at the diner, where they talked like they had as young adults about great plans and bright days ahead.

He burst into his cabin and slammed the door shut. Furious with himself. Why didn't he protect her from fighting a futile war she was never going to win? She was no match for Ingram and Bunny and never would be. That's who she was and she was entitled to that much, at least. He wished he hadn't tempted her, prompted her. Subjected her to more frustration, more loss. One thing was for sure—he wouldn't do it again.

The best thing he could do was to leave before it got

even worse. And again go without a trace. That way he could be the bad guy. Let her hate him. Let him take the blame. Let the naysayers be right. Love stretched the limits of what a person would do for another. He'd do that for his love. He'd go home, lick his wounds and then move forward. Like he always did. Alone. This brush with could-have-been would be the final one. Yes, a new set of memories would forever vie for his attention. Memories he'd secretly treasure like jewels for the rest of his days. Just there to remind him of what was almost possible. They'd be enough.

They'd have to be.

He tossed everything he'd brought for the trip into suitcases and called for a car and ferryboat. On the table, he noticed the drawing he'd done of Erin when everybody else was sketching trees. How much he'd enjoyed putting her likeness down on paper, the curve of her jaw, every strand of her shiny hair. But he wouldn't take it back to Tokyo with him. He'd leave his drawing, along with the love he felt for her, here in the States. As it had always been. Tucked away. Where it belonged.

Grabbing a piece of the lodge's stationery, he dashed off a short note. And folded it, plus the drawing, into an envelope. He exited his cabin, went to Erin's room and slipped it under the door, figuring she was still at the brunch. Then, making sure not to be seen, he walked out the lobby doors and slid into a limo. Just as he had slid out of one a few days before.

CHAPTER EIGHT

"Isn't rich and successful our kind of people? I found someone rich."

"For heaven's sake, Erin. You know what your mother means. Established families. Multigenerational wealth. You have a duty to marry strategically and produce the next generation of the Barclay legacy."

Erin's shoulders slumped. Her eyes deadened. Once again, her parents were taking the reins away from her. They'd summoned her to a private meeting room, irate that they hadn't been able to find her last night after the wedding. She hadn't returned their calls or texts. *No, Mother and Father*, she wanted to yell. *I was too busy making love with Kento Yamamoto in a limo to check my phone!*

Bile crept up her esophagus. Almost as if she was going to vomit. But it was words instead that spilled out of her with ferocity. "I love Kento!" she exclaimed. Last night, she hadn't been able to repeat those words back to him. Too afraid to say them out loud, of what admitting them might mean. But they came bursting out of her now—she couldn't shy away from them. "I love Kento. I love him! Doesn't that mean anything?"

The tone in her voice shocked all three of them. Bunny leaned back, like she was physically threatened. *Good*, she thought, let her mother be scared. Because Erin wasn't going to be anymore. She examined them. They looked older this morning than they ever had, stuffier and completely out of touch. Ingram in a stiff shirt buttoned to the neck and Italian loafers that cost more than some people earned in a month. Bunny in a tweed jacket with coordinating slacks and a gaudy necklace.

All her mother had been concerned about when she first saw Erin at the lodge a couple of days ago was that her nails weren't done. Not her grief about her failures in relationships and the breakup with Harris. No, her mother had intimated that Erin herself was to blame for his philandering, that she had failed to hold his interest.

Her parents kept a strategically curated and orderly life. All that mattered to them were bloodlines and insulation from anything outside their bubble. Her mind flashed forwarded. Probably with a few more tries, it would be her in the tweed jacket soon, spending her days with women just like her for overpriced salad lunches picked at while passing judgment on others. Who was married to whom and who was having whose children, as if they were all merely purebred animals.

A wry, knowing smile crossed her lips. When she'd taken Kento to see those properties she liked, he was genuinely interested. Asked her questions and was impressed with her answers. Didn't think what she was saying was trivial. He made her feel like she could do anything she wanted. And didn't understand why she wasn't.

Flying up in the Space Needle with him like the sky really was theirs to navigate, that's what she was going to have. Rocking out to a band in a club if she wanted, sharing plans and schemes at a greasy-spoon diner in the middle of the night, making magnificent love with him under a shower—it was all hers if she would only take it. Kento lived and breathed freedom. And the time had finally come. Erin was going to do the same.

"You will put this to a stop right now, Erin," Ingram admonished, her mother echoing the ruling by pointing her gangly finger. "It is nothing short of ridiculous that we are repeating business that was settled years ago."

"You're right, Father," she snapped back, "it is ridiculous. Through your disgusting, unconscionable behavior, I lost him once. I'm not going to lose him again."

Strength continued to rise in her. As if she was undergoing metamorphosis into someone else. Determination swelled, unstoppable.

"Be reasonable," Ingram implored.

"Was it reasonable how you tried to pay Kento off to leave me? And was it reasonable that when he didn't take your obscene bribe, you terrorized him? Have you no humanity? A boy who grew up being teased and shamed because his parents didn't have *wealth* and *status* as defined by you and your crowd?" Her heartbeat pounded against her chest, pure and clear.

"We did what we thought was right," Bunny said feebly.

"What about the *status* of decency? The *wealth* of

hope Kento's parents had, daring to place him in schools with families like ours? And it turns out you two were bullies far more evil than those in the schoolyard."

"Enough," Ingram said with a tightly furrowed brow.

Again, Erin's parents looked so old and brittle to her. This life was all they knew. Actually, she felt sorry for them. She had never contemplated whether or not they were happy, whether they were in love. They weren't affectionate with each other or with her. She'd grown up in a mansion with an elevator where the three inhabitants hardly saw each other. That mansion was a jail. She was going to break out. They never would.

"You're right, Father, this is enough. I don't know if you ever had hopes or dreams, because, if you did, you never told me about them. But I'm going to take a chance on mine."

"We won't have it, Erin," Bunny yapped.

"Well, then, you won't have *me*."

"Is that a decision you're ready to make?" Ingram clicked his tongue against the roof of his mouth.

"When I tell you that I love him, that I want to spend the rest of my life with him, that means nothing to you?"

"It sounds like you have a choice to make." Ingram's face was as rigid as stone.

The reckoning had come. All the anger expunged out of her, it was with nothing but genuine sadness that she said quietly, ultimately, "The decision isn't mine. It's yours."

Just a few tears stung Erin's eyes after the confrontation with her parents. She dabbed at them in the lobby ladies' room before heading into the lounge where the gift-opening brunch was still in session. Christy was regaling guests with the design plan for her and Lucas's dining room as she showed off the new tablecloths and napkins they'd received. An enormous array of gifts awaited placement in their new home.

Erin knew she'd been remiss in her maid of honor duties during the brunch, having been called away from Christy's side by her fuming parents. Returning to the lounge, she expected to find Kento there. She had something to tell him. Something important. Yet she scanned past the buffet tables that were now empty, past the guests who were still huddled around the newlyweds, and she couldn't spot him.

Catching Christy's eye, Erin put her hand to her heart as a gesture of apology. To which her cousin saluted and went back to swooning over her new crystal stemware and china gravy boat. It seemed as if she hadn't even noticed Erin's absence. MacKenzie sat next to the bride, filling in for the maid of honor's job of disposing of the wrapping paper and making note of which guests brought which gift.

The conversation with Erin's parents had concluded abruptly, with them telling her that if she opted to be with Kento, they would cut ties with her. She'd again reminded them that no matter how they later explained their split from their daughter, the three of them would always know that it was their choice and not hers.

Hopefulness mixed with terror mixed with confidence. Naturally, she felt uncertain. She'd allowed her parents to lord over her for twenty-eight years. It would be a whole new world for her, one where nothing was guaranteed. Well, maybe one thing was. That's what she needed to tell Kento.

As she rushed to her room to get her phone, which she'd forgotten, her enthusiasm swirled. While no one would want it to be necessary to separate from their parents in order to fully realize their own life, in her case, she had to. The emancipation was already a relief. There was no predicting what would happen with her and Kento, but the thrill of anticipation had her flying down the lodge corridor so fast her feet weren't touching the ground. She wasn't able to say the three crucial words last night, still too repressed to utter what she knew was true and always had been. Nothing would stop her now.

After swiping the key card and opening the door, the first thing she saw was an envelope bearing the lodge's logo that had been slipped under the door. Perhaps it was checkout instructions, as the wedding party would be leaving the island in a few hours, either heading for homes in the Seattle area or boarding airplanes to their destinations. Erin bent down to pick up the envelope and used a fingernail to tear it open.

Inside was a short note along with the drawing of her that Kento had done yesterday morning for their destressing activity. While the others were sketching trees, he was depicting her. When he'd allowed the art teacher to look at it, which she turned to show to everyone, an erotic charge had sizzled through Erin. That he had been staring at her, scrutinizing her to put her likeness down on paper made her feel desirable and desired. This time, unfolding the two creases that divided the piece of paper into three sections, the air around her turned gray.

Likewise it was with dread that she then unfolded the letter. On the lodge's stationery, a precise and even handwriting she remembered from years gone by filled her with alarm.

Dear Erin,
It was fun to dream with you again after all this time. But I think we both know that wishes can't always come true.
    I'll cherish what we had until my dying day.
Farewell,
Kento

Both the note and the drawing slipped from her hands and fluttered down to the carpet. Feeling faint and unable to take a complete breath, she made it a few steps backward so that she could sit down on the edge of the bed. The discarded pieces of paper demanded her attention, and she glared at them. As if the words could magically be erased and replaced with better ones, as if the pencil sketch was merely of a tree branch after all.

Had he deserted her again? She reached over to the nightstand and picked up the lodge's phone to ring the front desk. "Kento Yamamoto's cabin, please." Her voice was so tight and strained she didn't even recognize it.

"Mr. Yamamoto has already checked out and left the property," came a reply that sounded like a robot, tinny and faraway. "Is there anything else I can help you with?"

"No." She wasn't sure if the word came out or if she had only mouthed it. She set the receiver down.

We both know that wishes can't always come true.

Of course. This hadn't been real for him. After all he'd suffered here in Seattle, much of it at her parents' hands, he'd come back for a redo fantasy. To clear his own mind. As a purge. A catharsis. A vindication. He'd reached a point in his life where he needed to set the record straight. She understood that he'd had to use her for that. There was no other way. As they tripped down memory lane, it was important to reckon, at last together, with what they had lost.

What of his declaration of love? He was only human and had gotten carried away by the romance of the island, of the wedding, of the city. Would this have ended differently if she'd told him she loved him last night? That was something she'd never know the answer to. An opportunity she'd never get back. Regret pounded through her.

Despite their flighty talk about him returning to Seattle and her traveling to Japan, the morning dawn must have enlightened him that none of that was ever going to happen. That he'd told her he loved her only in the unreal wee-hours hush that going backward in time had brought. The daylight convinced him Erin would still, as always, submit to her parents' rule that would never include him. She hadn't had a chance to explain to him the epiphanies she'd come to, conclusions made. Because of him.

Collecting the pieces of paper from the carpet, she ran her index finger slowly across the words he'd written. As if touching the letters brought her closer to him. Made him able to hear her silent plea for him to come back. To grasp that he'd been mistaken.

Only when a tear dripped onto the note did she realize that she was crying.

Maybe it was he who needed change. He'd arrived at the wedding sure that he'd never be in a serious relationship ever again. Trust was not for him, neither to give nor receive. Perhaps letting go of that was more than he could manage. It was he who was in jail. He'd proven once already that goodbyes were not his style. The message was easy to understand. *Farewell*, he'd written. She didn't know if she could *fare well* without him now that he'd returned and shown her that what might have been could still be. She held the note and sketch at arm's length so that the flowing teardrops didn't mar them. Those pieces of paper would get tucked away somewhere, but she'd hold them in her heart forever.

After lying facedown on the bed pillow until it was drenched and heavy with her sobs, she rose up to pack her luggage. Moving sluggishly, like a zombie, she carried out the motions. The original plan was that she'd return home with her parents to the Tudor monstrosity where she'd lived her lonely childhood, eating her meals in the kitchen with servants. The fiasco with Harris in Spokane still needed to be mopped up, but that was to come later. Even if she wasn't going to be granted the gift of a life with Kento, she would not go running back to her parents. She was done with them, done with the people that wouldn't sanction love and happiness.

Harris had withdrawn most of her personal savings to finance his jet-setting. Fortunately, Erin still had a little bit of protected money to keep her afloat until she figured out her next move. So instead of Seattle, she'd head to Spokane to collect her belongings there. After that, she didn't know what was around the corner. But she vowed to embrace the new beginning because Kento would have wanted her to.

Downstairs, she said her goodbyes to the wedding party. Her lip hitched up when she noticed bridesmaid Amber and groomsman Demarcus holding hands. MacKenzie and Divya were both chatting with men.

Amber saw her and winked. "'By-ee."

"'By-ee," MacKenzie echoed.

"'By-ee," Divya rang in.

"Did Kento say anything to you when he left?" she whispered into Christy's ear as she kissed her cheek.

"Only that he had an early flight scheduled. Now that I think of it, he seemed upset. Is something going on?"

"It was a beautiful wedding, cousin." Lucas grabbed her for a bear hug.

Then she stepped into the shuttle van that would take her to the ferry. Rain distorted the view out the window as they left. Chugging down the road away from the lodge, the weekend became further and further away.

Christy had said Kento was *upset* when he left. It wasn't possible that he'd overheard some of Erin's conversation with her parents, was it? How could he have? What did it matter, though? He hadn't come to her to discuss it. Once again, he'd left. He'd soon be five thousand miles from her heart, never knowing that he actually held it in the palm of his strong hand.

Once Kento boarded the boat he'd hired to ferry him across the Sound, his mind was already halfway home. As a matter of fact, he kept his eyes forward and refused to look back toward the island to what he was leaving behind. He zipped his jacket and pulled on his hood in the rain, wondering whether Erin had seen his note yet. He'd hardly known what to write, only that, this time, he *should* just leave and not linger around trying to hash things out any further. Every second, every word spoken, was just prolonging the inevitable, and he'd hate to make anything harder on Erin than it already was. There was nothing left to talk about.

The first mate handed Kento a cappuccino, for which he nodded numbly in recognition. He sipped, taking in the Seattle skyline from the bow as the boat rushed him through the waves toward the city. Proud Mount Rainier stood noble. Pike Place Market was no doubt filled with tourists enjoying how the fishmongers called out the types of their fish and then threw them across the displays to entertain the crowds. And he took a final gaze at his favorite landmark of them all, the Space Needle, whose elevators were lifting visitors up to that spectacle in the sky. He drank his cappuccino just as he drank in the city, savored it. Wished it well, knowing he might never see it again.

When he reached land, he transferred to yet another limo to take him to his jet. The opulent plane was equipped with everything a fine home would have. Once they were at a safe altitude to move around, Kento decided to take a shower. Afterward, he'd put on comfortable clothes for the long flight and concentrate on getting some work done.

A wistful sigh let loose once he was under the water. While it was quite dramatic to be flying across the Pacific as he showered, with a window looking out to the clouds and blue skies, he couldn't help but remember the two times he'd used the outdoor shower at the lodge over the weekend. The first time, he'd been alone and felt keenly aware of himself sexually, as a carnal, primitive being, spreading his arms wide and offering his body to the open elements. That's how Erin made him feel. And the second time exploring her body under the luscious gush of water until she shuddered.

He cursed himself for allowing what he'd feared would happen, that he'd return to Tokyo not having unchained himself from her. Worse still, he'd realized that he loved her, then and now, and he was ready to let go of the skepticism he'd worn as a collar for most of his life. Loving her had not been in his plans. And, as it turned out, nor was it in her parents'. So the love he'd been willing to risk himself for was not even his to have and hold.

After a couple of hours' worth of work that had piled up, he ate a meal without gusto or any sense of flavor. He systematically chewed while he stared out the window, his heart flying somewhere outside his body, too far away to grab it back. The empty thud of his torso ached. Would it always? Afterward, as he paced the cabin, the flight had never seemed longer. Attendants offered him chocolates, a cocktail, a magazine. Nothing interested him. Eventually, he put on a mindless movie that would lull him to sleep and help break up the travel time.

Another limo ride after landing and, finally, he used his key fob to open his apartment's door and slipped off his shoes. He'd returned home alone from faraway journeys many an instance but, this time, the clang of loneliness in his apartment was deafening. The verve of Tokyo made its way in through the floor-to-ceiling windows of his penthouse flat. But that didn't energize him like it had before. Instead it was a mockery of the city's promise while he stayed above it all, alone.

As he sorted through the mail that the housekeeper had neatly stacked for him, the desolation was like a prolonged scream that almost drove him mad. The kitchen had been stocked with all of the groceries he typically ordered, yet they seemed unfamiliar now; he had no connection to them. He searched online and was able to find someone's low-quality video, no doubt shot on a phone, of the rock band he and Erin had gone to see after the wedding. After they'd made wild love in the limo and before they'd eaten middle-of-the-night breakfast. The guitar chords and persistent drumbeats were the only thing that kept him from breaking down to sob, which was what he felt like doing.

The next day passed in a fog. Kento visited his parents, who were ensconced at a retirement community just outside the city. They'd eschewed his offer of a deluxe apartment in the city center like his, and it was some measure of comfort to see them well and content. Within the grounds of the facility were walking paths with colorful year-round gardens. He strolled with his mother, Hina, and his father, Matsu, who wanted to hear about the wedding.

"It was nice to see old friends," he mused.

"Did you spend time with Erin?" Hina asked, getting to the center of the matter as mothers had a knack for. He'd never told them what had happened when he first came to Tokyo to work for Uncle Riku, only explaining that he and Erin had parted after realizing they were on different paths. He didn't want them to know the disappointment he'd suffered. And caused.

"Yes, we worked well together as best man and maid of honor."

"You've never forgotten her, have you?"

"Water under the bridge, as they say."

"I don't think so, son. I can see it in your eyes."

To that, his father smiled. "Your mother is a wise woman."

"You'll be thirty soon. We couldn't be prouder of your accomplishments. But something has always told me—" Hina brought her fist to her chest and tapped "—that Erin is why you've never met a woman to settle down with."

"What's the point of anything without love?" Matsu added.

After their walk he prolonged the hugs goodbye, taking that extra moment to cherish them.

Later at the office, marketing for the Fastracc program was on schedule. But Kento wasn't, and he knew it. That night he walked aimlessly through Roppongi, where the streets were filled with an international crowd. But he couldn't dodge his own shadow.

At home, he stared at the dream catcher he'd brought back from the wedding. Holding it this way or that to observe the shadows beaming through the weblike threads. Questioning if shards of light, of energy, really had any power to affect dreams. And, if they did, begging them to stop tormenting him with sweet visions of him and Erin, hand in hand, walking through the blooming of Japan's celebrated cherry blossom trees, in a bliss that had become their reality. Had Erin taken her dream catcher home from Willminson Island, or discarded it as a disposable party favor that held no meaning? He knew he'd keep his forever.

Every minute that went by, he missed Erin more, not less. The next morning he rode his motorcycle to the hiking trails and natural beauty of peaceful Okutama, one of his favorite places outside the city. A destination he'd hoped to show Erin, because he thought she would appreciate it. Although today, he could hardly notice the sights around him because his senses were filled to the brim. With Erin. How much they laughed. That fragrant sandy-colored hair that he could bury his face in. The arch of her spine when he thrust closer and closer to her as their bodies joined in divine mating. The way they could just be together, sometimes quiet, bonding one another to the earth and to each other.

How could he have done the same thing to her a second time? Leave without confronting her, asking her, begging her, to choose him. After agreeing that they'd see each other again soon, maybe this time with him by her side she might have been able to stand up for what was fair. Instead he'd bolted again, convincing himself that was in her best interest. What if he was wrong, and he'd stolen from both of them the chance they had to start from here?

His parents were right. What was the point of anything without love? Somehow he had to right all of the wrongs. This couldn't be how things ended—with him sitting alone on his empty black leather sofa way up in the sky.

CHAPTER NINE

ONCE SHE AND her luggage were inside the Spokane town house, Erin shut the door behind her. Eyes panning left to right, it was as if she'd never been there before. Blech. It was as ugly as could be, ornamental and overdone, a ridiculously large staircase with wrought-iron railing and a carpet runner eating up the space. In a historic property, the rail would have been done in a fine wood, with the stairs made of marble. The town house was built a mere five years ago, in a supposedly traditional style that managed to be only drab.

With that staircase it was no wonder that Harris left her, she thought, knowing she was being sarcastic even to herself. Kento would have laughed at that. He might have been the only one who would have. That was one of the things she loved about him, that they could share a dark humor. The anguish of the morning replayed itself over and over again as she contemplated the antique Victorian vases that adorned the foyer table, again like this was the first time she was seeing them. The whole room was a bore. The Barclay empire could do with hiring some new decorators. Not that anything to do with her family was a concern of hers anymore. The tiny twinkling in her gut that wanted to rejoice in the fact that she'd finally set herself loose from them was squashed, because without Kento the turn of events was more bitter than sweet.

Exhausted from the journey—the van to the ferry to the car service to the airport to the taxi home after the flight—she was hungry and thirsty. Making her way to the gourmet kitchen that she and Harris had rarely used, she opened the fridge to find that the housekeeper had stocked it with food and beverages. For some reason that annoyed her, maybe because Erin hadn't asked her to. She was quite capable of going to a market and buying her own food. Something she was looking forward to doing for the rest of her life.

Nonetheless, she needed to eat before she could just go upstairs to bed and wake up to her new and uncertain life tomorrow. While the microwave heated up the pasta and vegetables she selected, she flicked on the television for company. And barely glanced at it as she chomped the meal just to be done with it.

In her bedroom, she opened her luggage. Spotting the violet maid of honor gown, she sniggered. The dress had been through a lot. Not just the wedding ceremony and reception. That piece of purple satin had ridden up the elevator of the Space Needle. Had happily spent time on the floor of the limo while she and Kento were engaged in an activity that required a different dress code—an undress code. Then the gown arrived overdressed to hear a rock band. And finally to eat a predawn breakfast before it finally got a few hours' sleep on the chair beside the bed in Kento's cabin.

Inspecting it now, she saw the hem had become soiled and frayed, no doubt from getting in and out of the limo on the wet city curbs. There was a stain on the bodice. Erin vaguely recalled spilling some coffee at the diner. And there was a bit of a tear on the side under the arm. Had Kento been overeager when he took it off her in the black-windowed privacy of the limo ride? It thrilled her to think so. What would she do, have the gown cleaned and mended? That seemed absurd. It wasn't as if she'd ever wear it again. One thing was for sure, though. She was not going to throw it away.

As she shuffled through her toiletries to get ready for bed, another reminder she'd brought home caught her eye. It was from the rehearsal dinner when they'd seen the show about Native American history. She held the dream catcher up by the loop that the guests were told could be used to hang it above their beds. The beads were weighty and the feathers smooth. Had Kento taken his back to Japan with him, or thrown it out as a meaningless party favor?

What dreams would that catcher bring now? What was to become of her? Not sorry that she'd walked out of her cruel parents' grip, the fact remained that she was a single twenty-eight-year-old with no sure future. Once she packed up here, there was nothing for her in Spokane. Would she return to Seattle? The wedding crowd and their lives there had been hers, the overprivileged offspring their families raised them to be. Without her parents, she didn't belong in that world anymore. She was no longer *their kind* of people. There was nowhere Erin could call home.

Adding self-pity to the mash-up of emotions that swirled within her, she knew she had to do this alone. Reinventing herself would be not just easier with support, but this weekend she'd come to realize that everything was so much more fulfilling when shared with someone, partnered with someone. In life and in love. Not just anyone, she corrected herself. *The* someone. Two go-rounds, and yet she still ended up without him!

Kento, Kento, Kento, Kento, her brain chanted.

Please, she begged the dream catcher she clutched like her life depended on it as she crawled into bed. *Let me at least dream about him.*

Waking up in the morning after a fitful but dreamless sleep, Erin showered, dressed and had breakfast. In the clear light of day, she made a list of what she needed to do. Moving out of this awful town house was the first order of business. Someone else could deal with Harris's things; she didn't care who. She'd carry the love and loss of Kento with her for the rest of her days on earth. But not of party boy Harris, or of the other Mr. Wrongs she'd dated. They'd be easy to put behind her.

In the basement looking for boxes to pack up with, she found one that she'd stashed away because it was filled with private mementos from her university years. Carrying it up to the living room, she placed it beside one of the ornate wooden-framed sofas on the Persian rug. Not remembering where anything was kept, she riffled through a couple of drawers in the desk before she found a pair of scissors to cut through the tape seal-ing the box. Sitting down, she began sorting through its contents.

A couple of old sports uniforms padded the top. Followed by some trophies and certificates. Framed photos of club events. Nothing of great recognition or importance to her. In fact, she had no idea why she'd saved them. But as soon as her eyes made contact with the next item, the hairs on her arms stood on end. It was an album of photos she'd printed back then. Of her and Kento.

Tears quickly filled her eyes as she turned back the cover to see the first page. With arms around each other, they both had smiles on their faces. Kento wore shirtsleeves but with a tie, and she had on a lot of makeup. Without thinking twice, her fingertips trailed across Kento's thick hair and then his full lips.

Alternating between turning the pages and hugging the album to her chest, sobs erupted from her. The two of them barefoot at the beach. Dressed as superheroes for a Halloween party, a sneaky, sexy smile on his face. In caps and gowns on graduation day. The clarity was as bright as a sunny day. She loved Kento with all of her heart and always had. Always. Had. Since the very first day when they met in that philosophy class.

They'd been named partners, assigned to a project that required meeting several evenings at one of the campus libraries. He'd bring tangerines from his parents' store that they'd eat sitting on the stone ledge outside once they'd finished their work for the night. Conversation flowed easily—they finished each other's sentences. He wasn't like the people she'd been surrounded by, closed-minded and always measuring what others thought. Kento had big opinions and even bigger ideas, never censoring himself. And once he sneaked a kiss under the lamppost after a stimulating night of exchanging theories, they became inseparable. As they should be.

In an instant, agony turned angry. How could he have walked out on her again? He'd professed his love but hadn't given her the time to make her move. He refused to have faith in her. For the second time! Of course, she understood that he assumed her parents would get what they wanted in the end—after all, he didn't yet know she was ready to leave holding his hand. Did he think he was doing her some kind of favor by simply abandoning her again? How could he have not comprehended that was the last thing she needed?

Oh, was she going to give him a piece of her mind! Read him the riot act! And not over the phone or text or email, either. If she had to be the one to step up, fine. So be it. This was life or death as far as she was concerned. Nothing could be more worth fighting for. And so much time had already been wasted. He'd soon see what she was made of. The marching orders had come.

She knew what she needed to do and sprang into action. Swapping out the maid of honor outfits, soiled gown included, Erin repacked her suitcase with clean clothes and called for a driver.

Narita Airport was bright and bustling when Erin deplaned after the long flight from Seattle. It stunned her to step foot on solid ground after arrival, to believe that she was really here. Without talking herself out of it, she'd simply booked and boarded a flight to Tokyo. Unfinished business at the wedding weekend had prompted her to go, even when phone calls to discuss her plan went unanswered. In the boldest move she had ever made, she traveled alone to this mighty city across the Pacific on a mission to get what she could no longer live without.

She'd spent the flight studying the Japanese language lessons she'd downloaded before leaving. Sure, she'd only remember a couple of basic words, but at least it was a start. Airport signs for the baggage claim and ground transportation were written in Japanese and in English, some in Chinese and Korean as well. With their help, she was easily able to locate her luggage and get a taxi.

A mixture of exhilaration and fear greeted her when the cab dropped her off in front of the hotel she'd reserved in the busy Shibuya ward. She stood for a moment on the street, hardly able to comprehend the scene. The crowds at Shibuya Crossing were massive, the intersection far bigger than Times Square in New York. Tens of thousands of people trod through every day. It was nicknamed the Scramble, and she understood why. Businesses were bustling. Building exteriors were stacked with flickering ads, giant video screens and so many lights—more than the eye could even take in. The pulse of the entire area was pounding. Erin had never seen anything like it.

Entering her hotel, she was greeted with bows by the welcome desk staff. Erin knew there were specific rituals regarding the practice of bowing she'd need to learn, but a tourist could get away with a nod of the head and still be considered polite. "*Konnichiwa*. Hello," one of the staff members said to her as she handed over her identification and credit card.

Her room was decorated with tasteful earth tones. Recessed lighting on a dimmer gave options, and the minimalist room had been nicely divided into work and sleep space. It was afternoon, and Erin planned to spend the day getting acclimated before beginning her business in the morning. That business being taking her place next to the man she loved.

But knowing she was in the same city as him now, she couldn't wait any longer. When she tapped into her phone, the call to Kento went straight to voice mail, as had the two she'd tried before leaving Washington. It was disappointing and alarming that there was no reply. Maybe he hadn't received the messages. The phone number he'd given her had a Seattle area code— perhaps he was only using that one for the wedding and didn't check the voice mail. She'd hoped not to have to get anyone in Seattle involved, but she'd call Lucas tomorrow if she had to. Another very logical consideration dawned on her. He could have heard her messages and decided not to respond. When he made up his mind about something, he acted on it. Conviction—yet another thing she loved about him.

She'd known what she was doing by getting on that plane. He'd told her that he loved her and she hadn't assured him that she did, too, in return. She needed to say it in person. There was nothing to lose now except him, and she wasn't going to let that piece of her past repeat itself. He might not be good at goodbye, but Erin was going to give him one heck of a hello. As many hellos as it took, as a matter of fact.

Restless, she left her hotel to explore the busy streets. Shops, restaurants, nightclubs and bars took up every bit of space. She wandered a bit away from the commercial blocks thronged with humans, curious to see where residents lived and to begin to envision a life in this city. Weaving this way and that, she found a city park, tranquil green space that was a quiet oasis from the throb. The small park was rimmed by private homes, single-family residences as opposed to the many highrises and apartment buildings.

The For Sale sign written in several languages in front of one of the properties caught her eye. Punching the Realtor's code that was provided into her phone, she learned that the two-story wooden home had been built in 1924. At twenty-five hundred square feet, it would be considered large for the populated inner-city neighborhood. The architecture of the simple home was beautiful, and the adjacent park was a huge asset. Erin wondered if the little germ of interest she'd always had in historic properties could grow here—a possibility she'd never considered.

After wandering for hours, she was hungry. Near her hotel were many restaurants that offered menus in English or with photos of the food so that a visitor need only point to what they wanted. She had the freshest assortment of sushi she'd ever tasted and watched from a window table as the city went by.

This was already the riskiest thing she'd ever done, flying halfway across the world toward complete uncertainty. But this was her now, one way or another. Although she refused to acknowledge a future without Kento, her life was finally starting. It was scary. She accepted that.

Following a hot shower in the smooth stone of the hotel bathroom, she checked her phone. No messages. Okay, she promised herself. Tomorrow would be a brand-new day.

Naturally, the first thing Erin did when she woke up for the first time in Tokyo was check her messages. Still none. Since it was a business day, she assumed that Kento would be going in to work, so she would head to NIRE. Showing up to his office was going to be a shock. She hoped it would be a good one.

NIRE occupied six floors of a green glass–windowed building in Akihabara, a high-tech mecca with shops that served fandom cultures—entire stores dedicated to fictional characters, video games and electronics. After Erin rode a lightning-fast elevator to the NIRE offices, the doors opened to a reception area, which Erin stepped into. A beautiful woman in a blue suit bowed from behind a check-in desk, where a sign in a signature font read *NIRE*. Erin had meant to ask Kento over the weekend what NIRE stood for, but she hadn't had the chance.

"I'm here to see Kento Yamamoto," Erin stated after bowing her head in return.

"I'm sorry," the receptionist answered quickly, "Mr. Yamamoto's schedule is only by appointment. He is very busy." It made sense that he had a gatekeeper. Perhaps more than one. Erin began to worry how she was going to make her way into Kento's inner chamber, where he was no doubt protected from unwanted interruption.

"Could you get a message to him for me, please? We are old friends." That was the best and most important description she could think of. An old friend who came to see him, if she could get through the barriers. A half dozen glass doors led to different corridors.

"I can relay a message to his assistant." The blue-suited receptionist stretched out her hand as if to receive an actual paper message. "Mr. Yamamoto will let us know if he wishes us to contact you."

Erin hadn't conceived of being refused access like this, although she should have. Obviously as the CEO of a huge corporation, Kento's time and security were carefully guarded. Her face got hot. Nerves began to get the best of her as she searched through her purse for a piece of paper or something to handwrite a note on. What she found seemed only too appropriate.

It was Kento's drawing of her from Lucas and Christy's wedding morning. She wanted to be up front and not waste another precious moment, so she wrote on the back.

I've come to tell you *aishiteru*.
I love you.

As soon as the drawing was handed to him, and not arriving through the postal mail, he'd realize that she was here. At least she'd know right away where she stood. Hopefully he'd burst through one of the doors and into her arms.

"Thank you." The receptionist offered another bow after receiving the folded drawing with two hands. They both stood still. Finally she asked Erin, "Is there anything further?"

"No. I'll wait for Mr. Yamamoto's response."

"I'm sorry. This is a waiting area for people who have appointments today."

Erin knew that there could be hackers, spies and all sorts of unwelcome visitors to a company like Kento's, so she understood the need for regulations. Still, though, tears burned behind her eyes as she nodded once again to the receptionist before returning to the elevator and pressing its call button.

"Thank you." The words came out of Kento's mouth in slow motion as he unfolded the piece of paper Emiko had just handed him after she relayed that someone claiming to be a friend had stopped by the office. When he unfolded the note, he couldn't believe his eyes. "How did this get here?" he demanded. How on earth could the drawing of Erin that he'd slipped under her door on Willminson Island be in his hands right now? His pulse sped, wanting more information.

Emiko confirmed the conclusion that was taking shape in his head. "Ms. Barclay delivered it herself."

He wanted to be angry at his staff for not letting the special guest in, but they'd have no way of knowing that Erin Barclay was, and would always be, more than welcome wherever he was. Emiko bowed deeply from the waist in her boss's presence and then turned to leave.

Erin was in Tokyo? How could that be? Over the course of his years here, there had to have been hundreds of times when Kento saw something on a Tokyo street or saw a scene in a movie or ate a food that he wanted to share with her. The distance to Seattle never seemed greater than it did when he was missing her, which he'd done so much of. He stared again at the note she'd written on the back of the drawing.

I've come to tell you *aishiteru*.
I love you.

She loved him. He took more air in one breath than he had in the past hundred. All of a sudden his lungs were completely open, the inhale and exhale flowing unforced and natural. Erin was in Japan and she loved him! That changed everything. Guesses popped into his mind about how she'd gotten herself here. A far cry from what he'd overheard of her conversation with her parents at the gift-opening brunch that sent him packing, deciding for both of them how best to finally end the cycle they'd been on for far too long.

In his desk drawer, he found the burner phone with the Seattle number that he'd tossed aside after he got back from the wedding. There were three messages on the voice mail, all from Erin. She explained only that she had something to say to him in person so she was getting on a plane, each message sounding a little more desperate than the one before. It hadn't occurred to him to check the phone once he got back.

As it happened, he'd reached a decision of his own. That in a couple of days, after some high-level meetings he needed to stay in town for, he was going to fly back to Seattle. Because he'd never rest until he looked Erin in the eye and apologized for deserting her not once, but twice. Begging on his knees if he had to in order to make her see that her parents couldn't deny her love and happiness. That the life she and he could have together would be worth the cost. The note and the fact that she was here had him churning with optimism that she'd already made her choice.

Where was she now? Perhaps worried that she hadn't been able to see him. When he tapped the phone number he had for her, the call went to a mailbox, where her lush voice instructed him to leave a message. "My staff just told me you'd come by. I am so sorry you weren't let in. Meet me at the Hachikō statue at noon."

After having a driver rush him to his destination, Kento couldn't get out of the car fast enough. He didn't know if or when Erin would retrieve his phone message, but he wanted to get to the meeting spot as soon as possible. As usual, many people were gathered near the statue, taking photos with Japan's most famous dog depicted in bronze.

Those clear breaths that had given him such certainty after seeing Erin's note were spiky now. He wouldn't exhale easily again until he saw her. He didn't want to get too far ahead of himself, but the fact that she was in his city made him speculate that she had gone against her parents' wishes, and that alone filled him with pride. He could hardly imagine how difficult that must have been for her, if that's what had come to pass.

Finally, the head of dusty-colored hair he'd known for so long became visible. "Erin," he yelled as he ran toward her, darting around people this way and that to get closer. "Erin!"

Once she turned her head and spotted him, a huge smile swept across her face, letting him know that the woman he loved was going to be his in the end. When he reached her, he kissed her face over and over again, her cheeks, her lips, her forehead, her eyelids.

"Kento."

"How can this be? How is that you're here?"

"Why did you leave me at the wedding?"

Wow, she wasn't mincing words.

"I saw you talking to your parents and knew…"

"Knew what? Did you hear us?"

"Only a little bit. What I heard was that you and I were still the impossibility we always were."

"Well, then, you didn't hear everything I said to them. Why didn't you wait?"

"I was trying to make it easier for us to say goodbye."

"Hey, Yamamoto. I'm not saying goodbye. You got that? I'm never saying goodbye. I made a big enough mistake after the wedding not telling you I loved you. I'm never going to let a day go by that I don't say it again."

He took her hand in his and kissed her palm. "That's the best thing I've ever heard in my life. Come here." A big, long hug in the center of the fast-moving city brought his breath back to sure and even. He positioned them so that they could take a selfie with the famous Akita statue.

"What's the story of the dog, anyway?"

"Hachikō used to wait here every day for his owner to come up from the railway station after work. Even after the owner died, the dog still came every day. For nine more years. Every day for nine years. Until he himself died."

"A symbol of loyalty."

"Of not giving up."

Kento ducked them into a café, where he ordered tea. They explained to each other what had happened after the wedding. Erin told him that her parents would have nothing to do with her anymore. That she was going to create her own path, one alongside his. "I want you to see this home I found for sale. I think I want to buy it."

That was his woman. Someone who was ready to embrace chance, to find her destiny, to look herself in the mirror. "I can't wait."

More kisses and excitement followed as Kento told her ten places in Asia he wanted to take her to see, followed by ten more.

"Hey, I never asked you something."

"What, my love?" he responded with a brush to her hair.

"You've never told me, what does the name of your company mean? Is NIRE some kind of acronym?"

Pulling a pen from his jacket pocket, he wrote the four letters big and bold on a napkin. And then held the napkin up toward the window so that she could see them written backward in the reflection.

"*E-R-I-N*," she read aloud, and then her mouth dropped open. "What? After all this time I'm finding out that I've lived in Tokyo all along?"

"You see? Even when we were apart, we were together."

"And we always will be." She reached her hand to his face and brought him close. "*Aishiteru*, Kento."

"*Aishiteru*...my heart."

* * * * *

THE CHILD WHO
CHANGED THEM

TARA TAYLOR QUINN

For Chum. I hope you don't blame me.

Chapter One

This is only a preliminary exam. It's not like you're fully committing to anything yet.

The words replayed themselves in Elaina Alexander's head as she sat, dressed again in the dark blue scrubs she'd worn to work. The physical exam she'd just had was the last piece of the preparatory testing, counseling and paperwork she'd been through on her way to starting a family of her own that afternoon. Now she was waiting for a consultation with Dr. Cheryl Miller, the ob-gyn at The Parent Portal fertility clinic.

This is only a preliminary exam. It's not like you're fully committing to anything yet.

She was nervous. Apprehensive on some levels.

But she was most definitely fully committed. Cassie, her sister-in-law of almost a year, had only been trying to assuage Elaina's qualms; she'd made the statement to comfort Elaina in an early morning phone call. Cassie's words hadn't quieted her inner turmoil any, but they'd proved to her how very much she needed to know that she'd passed all the initial steps and could be scheduled for her insemination, should she choose to fully commit to something.

She and the team at The Parent Portal had talked about in vitro—about combining her egg and Peter's sperm outside her womb, creating an embryo and then implanting it—but she'd opted to have Peter's sperm injected. To have their baby created *inside* her body.

After months of thought, talking with Peter's brother, Wood, and Cassie, and after counseling, research and more thought, the doctor part of her, the analytical part had only one question left.

How soon could she start monitoring her system for ovulation so that she could get her deceased husband's sperm inside her? At thirty-four, she was far too conscious of time passing.

As a woman who ached with the need to have her own family, and to honor the husband who'd died when she'd lived, she couldn't get pregnant fast enough.

The sun had been shining when she'd come into the clinic half an hour before, with a forecast of blue skies and sixty-five degrees in Marie Cove that

March Thursday. The sterile, mostly white room in which she sat had a bit of a chill. Or she did.

Refixing her long dark hair into a ponytail, she glanced for a time at her blunt-cut but perfectly healthy-looking fingernails.

Ten minutes had passed since Dr. Miller's PA had completed her exam and Elaina had been told the doctor would be with her shortly. A quick glance at her smartwatch told her what she already knew—though she had nothing specifically scheduled, her shift at the hospital started in an hour. Having recently finished her last year of residency, she'd taken on a full-time nuclear radiologist position at Marie Cove's prestigious Oceanfront Hospital—something she'd been working toward for more than a decade. Being late wasn't an option.

Another five minutes passed. Elaina got up to pace the small room. Checked her watch. Her phone. Saw a work email indicating that Dr. Greg Adams, in the ER, needed her to do some imaging as soon as possible. He had an eight-year-old repeat patient who'd come in again that morning with symptoms that didn't make sense with the medication she was on, and he wasn't going to release her until he knew more. He was specifically requesting Elaina's opinion.

Quickly thumbing off a reply, scheduling the appointment as soon as her shift started, she thought about the child—a young girl with whom she was familiar from a chain of somewhat perplexing previous visits. But she didn't spend any mental power on the doctor who'd sent the request. She and Greg, though they'd been friends with benefits for a time, had a good working relationship and that was all that mattered right now.

The door opened and Elaina spun from her nonperusal of an impregnated uterine diagram to face Cheryl. And she knew the pronounced lines at the corners of the doctor's eyes didn't foreshadow the go-ahead Elaina wanted to hear.

"What?" she pretty much blurted. And quickly followed it with "What did you find?"

She'd deal with it. Yes, thirty-five was the first cutoff date for healthy delivery, and risk grew exponentially in women over thirty-five carrying children. But she had time, at least statistically, to fix whatever had to be fixed...

"Have a seat," Dr. Miller said, sitting at a black pad-topped stool in front of the monitor mounted on a wall by the door. Elaina didn't want to sit.

She wanted to read the screen, which she couldn't see without standing over the doctor's shoulder. But she trained her eyes on the doctor instead as she reclaimed the chair she'd vacated minutes before. They were both medical doctors. Professionals trained to maintain boundaries, no matter the news being delivered.

Cheryl didn't look at the monitor. Elaina's per-

sonal information probably wasn't even up there.
The PA had clicked out of it when she'd left the room.

And did it really matter, other than to distract
Elaina's immediate emotions from flooding all over
her and onto the floor?

"What we found, and what I've just confirmed—"
Dr. Miller's tone was measured "—is that you aren't
a candidate for fertilization."

Moving back a few inches, as though she could
distance herself from the news, Elaina studied the
woman who'd been a doctor twenty years longer than
she had. Needing to know that she was wrong in her
assessment.

"Not a candidate?" she asked. What did that
mean? They wanted her to just go away? Be done
with the rest of her life's plan?

Dr. Miller shook her head. "There's no..."

"Wait," Elaina interrupted, not ready to hear the
medical proof that backed up the doctor's claim.
She had to be fully braced and ready to believe that
Cheryl could be wrong first. That medical science
did get things wrong sometimes, if for no other reason than because of the human error involved in
procuring that information.

Dr. Miller watched her, as though she had all day
to sit and wait.

"I'm sorry," she said as she snapped back to herself, appalled that she was wasting the busy woman's

time. "I...can you tell me, first, is it permanent? Are you telling me I can't ever get pregnant?"

When Cheryl Miller's brows drew together, Elaina's heart sank. Her stomach sank. "I know how badly you wanted to have Peter's child," the doctor said. "And only Peter's child." Dr. Miller had been at The Parent Portal back when Peter, and everyone he could talk into it, had donated sperm for the then fledging supply in the portal's "bank."

At the mention of her dead husband in that moment—her *first* husband—tears sprang to Elaina's eyes. He hadn't been perfect, but Peter had been a good man. Dedicated to giving his all to the medical community.

Dr. Miller had been present at one of Elaina's initial visits, when they hadn't been certain that Peter's sperm was even still viable; her use of another donation had been discussed—and summarily dismissed. If Peter's sperm wasn't usable, she'd rethink the plan.

"That's why it's a bit difficult for me to tell you that the reason you aren't a candidate for fertilization is because you're already pregnant."

Elaina knew she was not. "The lab mixed up samples," she blurted out, too flummoxed to keep the thought to herself.

"Your internal exam showed changes in the cervix and uterus that we see within the first few weeks, so we ran the urine test right away to be certain, which is why I'm a bit late getting in to see you. It'll be another couple of hours before the blood test is back, but…"

"So there's a chance… Urine tests aren't the most accurate. Blood tests are. Urine tests are known to be wrong sometimes…" Elaina could hardly believe she was the one babbling. She had never been prone to do anything that didn't have her exhibiting at least a modicum of control.

"Your cervix is soft and has changed color. Your uterus is already enlarging. You're pregnant, Elaina."

She couldn't be.

That wasn't the plan.

And it wasn't fair.

Not to the baby.

Not to the baby's father…

Oh, God.

Oh, God. Oh, God.

"Are you in a relationship with the father?"

A quaint way of handling the hugely awkward situation, she supposed. Peter, as a resident, had worked with Cheryl. Not that anyone would blame her for getting on with her life. Peter had been gone a long time.

"I'm not in a relationship with anyone," Elaina quickly blurted.

What?

Oh, God. It wasn't happening.

Wasn't supposed to happen that way.

The whole plan…the self-realizations…the move

from being reliant to self-reliant…from using a man for her own emotional security—even at the risk of that man's happiness—to standing on her own and giving back to those who'd given to her.

To Wood.

Cassie's husband.

Elaina's own *ex*-husband.

Dr. Miller was studying her with a look of concern. Not that Elaina blamed her. She'd be doing the same if she were on the doctor's stool rather than the chair she occupied. Hell, she was doing it even in the chair she occupied. Watching herself fall apart.

"I had relations…a friends-with-benefits thing… but I broke that off…"

"Does he know about your plans to be inseminated with Peter's sperm?"

She shook her head. "He doesn't even know I want to have a baby. We weren't…that kind of close…"

Greg had made her laugh out loud. Something Elaina wasn't prone to doing. He'd given her moments of freedom from everything she expected of herself. Freedom from grief.

She'd used him. Just like she'd used Wood for emotional companionship after Peter's death.

Unintentionally. Unknowingly. Until he'd met Cassie and she'd slowly begun to see the truth about herself.

But that didn't change the facts.

"He... I didn't really talk about Peter...we weren't..." *That kind of close.* "He knew about him," she hastened to add to the tail end of her unfinished previous sentence. "Knew that Peter had just gotten his license to practice, and that he was killed by a drunk driver. He knew that I was in the car...and seriously hurt...but about his sperm being frozen..." She shook her head.

They weren't that kind of close.

The words just kept repeating themselves in Elaina's head, as though their truth could put a stop to the madness.

To turn events back to the way they were supposed to go.

She couldn't be pregnant. Most certainly not with Greg Adams's baby. He wasn't even a permanent hire—would probably be leaving town as soon as he found a job at a bigger hospital.

"Forgive me for asking, but is he married?"

"No!" Horrified at the picture that made of her, of her friendship with Greg, she clamped down on her tongue.

"Do you know his feelings on having a family?"

As Elaina stared at the doctor, humiliated to admit that she did not know, it occurred to her that Cheryl was spending far more time with her than her job stipulated. It was up to the doctor to just deliver the news, then let Elaina find a counselor who could help her sort out the horrid mess she'd made of things.

"I broke up with him after I'd made the final decision to proceed here," she said, heat inflaming her face as she told another god-awful truth. She'd been sleeping with a man, intermittently, no strings attached, while meeting with a counselor and going through preliminary paperwork to have her husband's child.

It was all so…mixed up.

"Peter's been gone for so many years…"

Cheryl shook her head. "It's not wrong for you to have a man, or even men, in your life, Elaina. You have your whole life ahead of you."

A life she'd promised herself wouldn't include a man propping her up anymore.

"I didn't intend to live celibately," she said then, honesty pouring out of her as though she could somehow redeem herself. As though she needed redeeming.

"I just… I mean I was intending to be celibate for a while—until the baby was old enough that I'd feel comfortable going out on a date now and then. Maybe longer." She'd figured that she could cross that bridge when she came to it.

Everyone at the clinic had seemed to take a personal interest in her quest to have Peter's baby. Most of them had known him. Known how much she'd loved him. Known how much he'd loved her, too. Almost as much as he'd loved medicine.

She'd let them all down.

Let his memory down.

Shaking her head, she stopped her thoughts before they took such a melodramatic turn that she made more of a fool of herself. She hadn't been having Peter's baby for him—she didn't owe it to him. Or if she did, it was only in small part.

If she hadn't raised her voice to his raised voice… maybe he'd have seen the car driving in the wrong lane sooner…could have reacted in a timelier fashion…

Still, a baby didn't change any of that.

No, it just changed her life. Gave her a family to love. To raise. To watch grow into a contributing member of society. To be happy and find joy with… as a single parent.

Peter's baby wouldn't have come with the added complication of a living father.

And yet, he or she would have had Wood as a father figure…a very willing biological uncle who came with an equally willing aunt. Cassie and Wood had been thrilled when she'd told them she wanted to have a family. Had offered to help her in any way they could.

Said they'd babysit, that the cousins—their new baby and Elaina's soon-to-be—would be pals for life. Go through school together. Celebrate holidays together.

Even before they'd found out that she intended to do it alone. With Peter's sperm.

She glanced at the doctor. "You're sure?"

Dr. Miller nodded.

And Elaina watched her whole future change course once again.

Chapter Two

Greg had to admit he was curious to see Elaina's home. In a train-wreck kind of way. His own emotional equilibrium train wreck. In all the time they'd been involved, he'd yearned for and never received an invitation. Going there after the breakup was more a slap in the face than anything.

He was driving from the hospital to her place for a private meeting she'd requested—to tell him, he felt sure, that she suspected, as he did, that there'd been a mistake with drug administration going on at work. Greg allowed himself a small bit of anticipation at the prospect of finally seeing where she lived.

Six weeks before, he'd have been all over an invitation to the sprawling home with the built-in pool.

He'd been mildly intrigued about the place when he'd first met her more than a year ago and she'd told him she shared the home with her ex-husband. Wood had since married and moved out, but…how did a divorced couple coexist happily and separately under one roof? Greg hadn't asked. She and Greg had just been coworkers on the same charting committee at that point.

And he'd been brand-new to town.

Once he'd become her lover, he'd had a little more reason to need to understand just how the situation worked. But they'd been drawn to each other because of their shared resistance to a committed relationship, having both come off divorces, and they'd kept any really personal questions off the table.

Then Wood had remarried, moved out, and Greg still had not received an invitation to her place. They always liaised at his rented apartment near the hospital. He'd actually been hoping to change that. As months passed, and they still enjoyed each other's company, he'd found Elaina on his mind from the moment he awoke in the morning. He'd been thinking he wanted her beside him in bed in the morning, rather than just her image in his mind, and that maybe they should live together—had even been considering accepting the permanent ED position Oceanfront had offered him six weeks before—when Elaina had abruptly broken things off with him.

Having had time to reflect on the matter since,

he realized that the breakup was not only inevitable but in good timing. He'd been about to embark on a path and make past mistakes again, push for something before it could get away from him, and end up with another life mess to clean up.

Much better that he focus his efforts on eight-year-old Brooklyn George, the patient whom he'd had Elaina test that afternoon. A recent meeting of a special hospital charting committee to which they'd both been assigned, had led to a suspicion that some in the hospital weren't following protocol as carefully as necessary. The committee of four had been established to spot-check charting in all departments for compliance. They'd discovered some discrepancies in chain of command for medication distribution. He and Elaina had had a specific conversation, just the two of them, one night over dinner when they'd still been seeing each other, regarding the possibility of problems in drug administration. They'd brought up a particular nurse, but hadn't mentioned her to their colleagues, not wanting to hurt this woman's reputation if they'd been wrong. They had reported her to hospital personnel, and while they had no knowledge of the outcome of the issue, the nurse was still on staff. And was the nurse who'd been responsible for administering medication to Brooklyn the last time the child had been in the hospital.

While his personal life, in terms of relationships, was pretty much a disaster, he tended to get it right professionally. Probably came from all those years of nerd-dom as a kid. For him, observing others, as opposed to interacting with them, had been the norm. He'd honed an ability to read people with whom he wasn't personally involved.

Maybe, if he found a way to take a step back, he'd master the ability in nonprofessional relationships, as well. One could always hope.

He turned onto Elaina's street, slowing as he took in the landscaped spaces and well-maintained homes. He wanted a large yard, as well.

Wanted a home of his own. Maybe something like the white two-story with black shutters he was passing. At the moment, though, he was on the brink of accepting a position in LA, with the promise to himself that once he made that final choice, once he'd found his permanent professional home, he was going to buy a house.

He'd always thought marriage would come first. Discussion of how big a family would follow so he'd know what size house to purchase.

Then he'd found out he couldn't father children, and the shadowy little figures in his design had faded off the page.

And since his marriage had failed, in large part because of his infertility, he'd changed the course of his life plan.

He was back on track, though. Ready to stay the

course. His career was his life and he wanted to own a home.

No more quests for his happily-ever-after.

Finding the address she'd given him, he turned into the long drive. While it was nice, it seemed... pretty much like the rest of them on the street. And on many other upper-middle-class streets all across the nation.

Like his relationships with women, he'd made it into more than it was.

Thank God he was done with all that.

To meet Greg, Elaina had changed out of her scrubs into a pair of black leggings and a longish beige sweater with short sleeves, and black suede bootlets. Slicking her long, dark hair back in a fresh ponytail, she'd put in a pair of small, plain gold ball earrings Wood had purchased for her on the day their divorce had become final.

He'd said they were a symbol of the bond they'd always have.

It was only later that she'd begun to wonder if they'd been a sign that he intended to remain devoted only to her for as long as she needed him. A sign she hadn't wanted to see.

Because she'd needed to believe that he felt free to leave anytime he wanted to do so.

And she'd put them on specifically in preparation for her meeting with Greg because she wasn't going to fall into her old habits. She would not use Greg Adams to ease any of the burden of single parenting as she birthed and raised his child.

She would not let herself become more enamored of him. She would make herself remember that she'd chosen to break up with him, and she most definitely would not let herself build a fantasy world where they became one big happy family.

Beyond that, she would give him as much contact with his child as he wanted. And be completely supportive if he wanted no contact at all.

She'd had several hours to figure it all out and stood firm on her resolutions.

So much so that she barely registered that he'd evidently come straight from work, was still in the light blue scrub pants and white T-shirt that he generally wore to and from the hospital. He kept in his office the scrub shirts and the white coats he wore for work, and changed them as necessary throughout the day.

She'd been in his office, seen the closet full of them…

His slightly curly sandy hair was mussed, as it generally was at the end of a shift, and the bit of stubble shading his jaw was normal after a day's work, too. Nothing she'd have had to go to bed with him to know.

The expanse of soft hair on his chest…

No reason for her to be thinking about that. So she

turned from the door before either of them had even said hello and led the way out to the big backyard.

Retro's yard, though Wood's dog didn't live there anymore. Wood had put in the kiva fireplace that flanked one end of the pool and the outdoor kitchen space off to the left of that, too. He'd planted rose-bushes for her, and when she'd suggested it, had built his workshop in the back corner of the yard so it didn't spoil the naturally landscaped view. She liked the rugged look.

In the yard, not necessarily on her man—though Wood had never really been that. Her man. Their supportive bond had been mostly platonic.

"Elaina?"

She'd heard the front door shut behind him. The sound of footsteps following behind her was rare.

And not just since Wood had married Cassie. Their lives had settled into a routine of her mostly remaining alone in her suite when she was home. She'd been satisfied enough with the arrangement that she'd probably have continued it indefinitely if Wood hadn't found out Cassie's baby—his, biologi-cally, from a sperm donation years earlier—required a bone marrow donation. If the two hadn't had to meet and fallen in love.

She'd like to believe her yearnings and needs, her coming back to full emotional life, needing a child of her own, was all Cassie's fault for rocking their very stationary boat. But of course, she couldn't, and it wasn't.

Turning, she faced Greg, so caught up in memories that she completely forgot the words she'd planned to say.

He held up a folder he'd carried in with him. "I've made a spreadsheet of all instances where Martha charted on Brooklyn," he said. Standing at the table as he opened the folder, he pulled out a piece of paper and laid it down in her direction.

What?

She looked at the paper, glad for the chance it gave her not to meet his gaze. How was she going to tell him that they were going to have a baby?

She couldn't do it. How did she look at this man who she'd chosen not to be with, and tell him that she was pregnant with his child? And how could she focus on a patient right now?

"You'll notice that each time Brooklyn was in, Martha scanned medication out for her, and there was no matching scan from Brooklyn's wristband signifying administration. It's exactly what we've talked about…"

Wait. *What?* She glanced over at him without considering that she'd be looking him in the eye—an occasion she'd decided it was best to try to avoid. Just until they got through this difficult first step.

The intensity in those golden green orbs stabbed

her for a second. Until she took a breath. And a step back from the table between them.

"I…um…didn't call you here to discuss Brooklyn," she told him. She'd done the scans he'd requested. Found nothing to warrant a meeting between them. Had charted the lack of change from previous tests.

"Oh." His blink gave her the chance to look away. She took it. Desperately.

Gratefully.

And wished she'd left them talking about Brooklyn.

"Look, if you're feeling bad about breaking things off, I'm fine with it. I told you that at the time. I hope my reaching out to you today didn't make you feel like I was expecting anything."

"Of course not!" Her gaze darted back to him. "The thought never even crossed my mind! I'm glad you reached out. And was happy to work the scans in first thing…"

He nodded, and she glanced away.

"So…" He moved closer as his voice softened. "What is this then? You want to get dinner or something?"

He was not hitting on her. He couldn't be. But her lower body flooded with reaction, anyway. For a second there she went with it. Dinner would be so much easier than the item on her agenda.

"Really?" she asked him. If she'd wanted food,

she'd have asked for it. Or offered it. He knew her well enough to know that.

But she couldn't blame Greg for scrambling. In all the months she'd known him, she'd never invited him to her place. And then, out of the blue, she suddenly had, a month after breaking up with him.

"I'm pregnant, Greg."

Both of his hands slid quietly to the table. He made no other movement. Just stood there. Looking at her.

"I don't know how it happened. I mean...well...of course...we know *how* it happened...but how it happened when we...when I...the only thing I can figure is that my device moved before that last time... you know...when we were done and then did it once more..."

And she called herself a doctor? Had a license to practice medicine?

"We?" His expression, the frown, showed confusion more than blame, but...

"I didn't get this way by myself," she said, kind of perplexed herself. She'd been prepared for disbelief. For him to be upset, even. But she wasn't sure how to deal with this one-word reaction. Like he wasn't part of the situation.

"Well, you certainly didn't get there with my help, if that's what you're trying to tell me," he said. As he spoke, he stood upright and then crossed his arms across the chest she'd been imagining naked moments before, as though for emphasis.

Or to shut her out.

Either way, she was shocked. In all of the numbers of ways she'd imagined him reacting, denial hadn't been one of them.

"You need to get with whoever else you've been with," he continued, his tone calm, assured. "Because I can tell you for sure it wasn't me."

What? A thousand times, *what*? "You're the only man I've slept with in a couple of years."

He shook his head. Was his gaze one of *compassion*? He felt sorry for her? "Give it up, Elaina. I'm not going to fall for this one."

Fall for... She started shaking her head, too. It was like she'd been transported into some kind of twilight zone. A nightmare where things got all twisted up and didn't make sense, but you couldn't get out.

That was it. She just had to wake up.

"I'm not trying to get you to fall for anything," she said, clearly, calmly, feeling as though she was outside her own body, watching the nightmare. Waiting for it to end. "I'm asking nothing from you. I planned to tell you that you have no obligation here. I'll leave your name off the birth certificate so that you have no financial obligation. I just felt that, morally, you had a right to know."

His frown grew until every inch of his face bore a portion of it. "Why are you doing this?"

How could she have thought she'd liked him so much? How could she have been friends with benefits with him, worked with him, for over a year and not have seen this jerk side of him? He was doubting her integrity?

"I'd like you to leave now," she said. Pushing him out was the only thing left to her. She was too stunned, too hurt, to deal with him.

He shook his head again, dropping his arms, but otherwise making no movement—certainly not doing anything to get himself any closer to the front door. "I'm not the father, Elaina."

"I'm not going to argue with you, and since I'm not asking anything of you, this conversation is over. I've done what I felt was the right thing to do. I've told you. Now I'd like to be left alone to get on with my life."

Whether he noted her tone, a look in her eye, or was just plain ready to be done with her, she didn't know, but when Greg gave her one last nod, and a long, somewhat searching look, then turned and let himself back out of her house, she was relieved to see him go.

And to lock her door behind him.

She and her baby would be just fine on their own.

Chapter Three

Greg didn't get it. What possible reason could Elaina have for naming him the father of her child, but only in conversation with him...with no intention of getting something out of him?

The answer was none. Her actually being pregnant by him was a medical impossibility, and she apparently wasn't after his money, so what reason could she have for making such a claim?

The irony was almost too much to bear.

Elaina was pregnant?

Shaking his head as he drove the fifteen minutes from her neighborhood to his apartment, Greg couldn't get his short time at Elaina's home out of his mind.

Couldn't wrap his mind around it, either.

Elaina was drop-dead gorgeous. She didn't need to snare a man. And he knew she just wasn't the type to do so. To the contrary, she'd been adamant about going it alone when she'd broken up with him. Something about having been blind to a neediness within her, with which she'd unknowingly prevented men from finding their own happiness.

Even minutes before, when she'd been telling him about his supposed baby she'd been all about going it alone. Asking for nothing from him.

Her reputation at Oceanfront was stellar. She was compassionate, yet completely able to get any job done, no matter how emotionally difficult it could be. She stayed late, came in early. Served on committees with such meaningful contribution that she was one of the first picks among staff when a new committee was formed.

She'd even been a dream in bed.

His gut clenched on that one, another jab of the familiar pang of having lost her, and he passed by his street, continuing on to a beach parking lot. He didn't get out. The March air, while balmy, still carried a bit of a chill after dark. But he rolled down his window a couple of inches. Enough that, if he concentrated, he could hear a hint of the soothing sound of waves moving along the shore.

At one point in his life, he'd been certain he wanted nothing more than to have a child. He'd been married to a woman he'd thought he loved. He'd finished his residency. Completing two of his major life goals; the third was becoming a father.

You're the only man I've slept with in a couple of years. If only Elaina knew how badly he'd like to believe that statement.

Especially considering the timing of the pregnancy. She'd said she was breaking up with him because she needed to be alone—without a man in her life. She had to have met someone else to be pregnant now.

For the next five or so minutes, he contemplated who that someone else might be. He considered her ex-husband, Wood, as a possibility.

There'd been something really tight between them.

But in all the time Greg had been sleeping with Elaina, he'd never had a sense that she and Wood had ever had that hot-for-each-other kind of relationship. She'd been so amazed by the fire between her and Greg.

Her connection with Wood had always seemed like an emotional one, a close friendship more than a traditional marriage.

Greg found that bond more of a threat than sex would have been. She'd never let him get even near the door of her deepest heart.

So how could he have felt that he really knew Elaina, even from way outside that door?

Because he was who he was, which meant he went all in with a woman way too soon, being too eager to share his life with a permanent companion. Because he really wanted a partner in his life.

He'd always been the nerd who'd spent his high school and most of his college years on the outside looking in at the popular kids.

Rather than getting drunk—he hadn't liked giving up his mental autonomy—he'd liked to watch movies that ended well. To read. To analyze and figure things out.

Sometimes his observations had been too on point for the comfort of others. His own mother had once told him he intimidated the heck out of her. She'd meant it in the best possible way, but like some inadvertent words do, those had stung. And stuck.

Staring out into the darkness of the ocean in the distance, his car being the only one in the lot, Greg grabbed the steering wheel tight.

Elaina was pregnant.

He might not have any candidates for the identity of the father, but he knew it couldn't be him.

He'd been tested by three different facilities, and all three confirmed his condition. He had a not completely uncommon condition of antisperm antibodies, where his antibodies attacked his own sperm, and with extremely low motility, he had a count so low he was unable to impregnate a woman.

And Elaina had no idea. Other than his ex-wife,

no one knew. It wasn't the type of thing a guy went around bragging about.

Elaina had just seemed so absolutely convinced it was him. Which told him that she firmly believed there was no other possibility.

Because the other guy had used a condom? They were only effective 98 percent of the time. Maybe the father of her child had told her he'd had a vasectomy.

Whatever the reason, she was pregnant, thought him the only possible father, and would go on thinking it unless he proved her wrong.

And if she wasn't at all the woman he thought her to be, if instead she was like Heather Baine, the girl he'd dated the summer before leaving for college, and knew, as Heather had known, that he wasn't the father of her baby as she'd claimed, then he had a right to clear his name. Heather had burned him bad. He'd turned over his first semester tuition before he'd found out that she'd been lying to him all along. A guy didn't forget that, either. He wasn't going to be burned, be used, a second time because the real father wouldn't stand up. He couldn't believe Elaina would do such a thing. The idea of it pissed him off a whole lot more even than Heather's duplicity had done. But he also couldn't be the father of her child. Grabbing his phone from the breast pocket in his scrubs, Greg hit the speed dial he hadn't yet bothered to erase, half expecting her not to pick up.

"Hello?" She sounded...tentative. Not unfriendly, but not sure she wanted to speak with him, either.

"Hey." He wanted, first and foremost, to reassure her. Because when it came out that he wasn't the father, Elaina might need a friend.

The line was silent then. He'd made the call. The onus was on him.

Glancing out at the sand that was barely visible as it faded into the darkness, he hung his free hand over the steering wheel. Remaining calm. He had proof.

"I want a paternity test done." Greg had never thought to be having this conversation again in his life. And certainly not with Elaina. The whole thing made him feel slightly sick.

"Excuse me?"

"They can be done in vitro now. At seven weeks. With no risk to the baby." Helped having a head filled with medical knowledge.

"You're seriously requiring a paternity test?" Her voice rose at the end of the sentence. He'd offended her.

Or at least she was pretending to be affronted. He didn't see that type of deceptiveness in her. And he'd been wrong before.

He let his silence answer the question for him.

"I can't believe this," Elaina finally said, her tone low. Defeated. "You know how insulting this is?"

How embarrassing would it be for her to get the

test done in Marie Cove, where the medical community was relatively small?

"You can go to LA," he said.

"I have no need to go to LA," she shot back. "Cheryl Miller's my ob-gyn. I'll go to her. At seven weeks." With that, and the sound of tears in her voice, she hung up.

Greg would have liked to feel bad for her, but he didn't.

Well, he did. But not for asking for the paternity test.

She'd left him no option but to prove to her that she was wrong.

He most definitely was not the father of her baby.

Elaina didn't sleep well that night. Past grief and the need to wall herself off to do her job had taught her to get herself to sleep. But she couldn't turn off the restlessness in her mind. There were no concrete dreams, just a jumble of nonsense situations that she couldn't remember, but that left her feeling powerless. Upset. And tired.

Not in a good frame of mind to be in the next morning, either. She arrived at work early as always, to find a message. Greg was already there and needed a consult. He'd made the request through the online hospital portal, meaning there'd be an official record of it, and her response to it would be recorded into infinity, as well.

Curbing her first instinct to tell him to go to hell, taking a deep breath against the tears that suddenly sprang to her eyes, she took a sip of her decaffeinated coffee. Then another, before typing her affirmative response. The words were coming out fine. She'd just pretend he was a different doctor she dealt with regularly.

But an hour later, when she presented herself at Greg's office door, she really just wanted to turn around and go home. Or stop at the dog shelter, adopt a housemate and then go home. She knocked, instead.

The guy was an ass. She was lucky she'd already broken things off with him. Was glad she had. She'd never been so insulted in her life.

What were they? High school students? Like she'd insist she knew the identity of her baby's father if she didn't?

When Greg answered his door, standing there in scrubs and his white coat, his hair mussed and striking green-gold eyes loaded with compassion as he assessed her, she forgot how much she disliked him.

And felt like crying instead.

Which was ridiculous.

They'd been friends with benefits. Lovers and workmates. There'd never ever been a hint of anything emotional between them. Not only had there been no commitment, but not even any conversation that could lead to emotional closeness. She'd made sure of it.

So how was it possible for her to feel so…hurt… by his insistence on a paternity test, like there'd been some kind of trust between them?

"How are you feeling?" His question put her hackles up.

"You said you needed a consult?" Standing in the hallway, she made no move to enter his office. As far as Elaina was concerned, they could take care of whatever it was right there. They were in a secure hallway. No one else was around. No need to be concerned about patient confidentiality issues, about being overheard.

"Can you come in?" he asked, stepping back.

Because any other time she would have entered, because for any other peer she would have done as he'd asked, she let herself walk into his space and stood there, doing nothing, as the door closed behind her. Shutting her in alone with him.

Her first instinct was to walk into his arms, lay her head on his chest and let the strangeness between them evaporate. And she fought that instinct with all her might.

She didn't need to lay her head on anyone's chest. She wasn't going to spend her life using other people for her own emotional satisfaction. Even if a miracle happened and she someday fell in love again, she would not allow herself to be dependent on the person she loved. She'd done it with Peter. With Wood. She wasn't going to spend the rest of her life being that woman.

The boatload of counseling she'd had, some as recently as the previous week, had given her a clear vision of her future plan. Her relationships were to be interdependent. Not codependent.

"I need your take on Brooklyn," Greg said, and she blinked, blindsided by the sudden change in conversation. And then, realizing there'd really *been* no conversation; she'd been a fool for thinking his call for consult had to do with the two of them.

"I wrote my report."

He nodded. "I read it. I just wanted to talk to you about it."

"I put everything in there. I found nothing different."

"But after we gave her that medication four days ago, there should have been a difference since, shouldn't there?"

The little girl had multiple health issues, including a neurological disorder that, when she was stressed, created higher levels of hormones resulting in aggressive behavior. Brooklyn had a gastrological situation that also came on when she was upset. Born to a drug addict, she'd been in the system most of her life, but because her mother wouldn't sign adoption papers, she wasn't able to find a permanent home anywhere. Four days ago, a police car had brought in the girl, her foster mother following behind to say that Brooklyn was making up symptoms, and asking for the doctor on call to have a talk with her daughter. She felt that Brooklyn was using nebulous maladies as an excuse to throw fits anytime she didn't get her way.

"She's got a new sibling at home," Elaina pointed out. "Her stress levels will be higher, even with the medication."

She listened while he talked about the little girl complaining that her stomach had never quit hurting since her last hospital visit. All the while her mother was pointing out times at home that Brooklyn appeared to be pain-free, making it sound as though she only was in pain when she wasn't getting what she wanted.

And yet, it was clear that Brooklyn's foster mother loved her. Clear that she believed Brooklyn could get better. In Elaina's opinion, the woman was feeling powerless, frustrated, with her inability to help the child.

"Althea was right there, holding Brooklyn's hand, the whole time I was with her," Greg said.

"You know that her neurological condition can bring on psychosomatic symptoms," Elaina reminded him.

"And with the medication I gave her Monday, she should have been pretty calm for a few days, at least. I couldn't prescribe another dose today," Greg said, "but I sent her home with a prescription..." He named it. A drug with similar capabilities of the much stronger one he'd had administered by IV before he let Brooklyn go at the beginning of the week. But this was one that could actually be purchased at the pharmacy. "I asked that she be brought back in, through the ER, on Sunday," he told her. "I'd like you to do another set of scans at that time, paying close attention to the brain waves, and see if you notice any change at all."

"You think she didn't get the meds on Monday?"

"I think it's possible."

"But why…"

"Martha was on again."

She was a good RN, and one who'd tried to get her nurse practitioner license and failed the exam. Someone who thought she knew more than the doctors sometimes about what patients really needed. She was the one who was with patients for hours a day, who tended to their every need, while the doctors saw them for a couple of minutes and were gone.

This was a possible conclusion Elaina and Greg had drawn when they'd noticed some discrepancies in the charting the nurse had done per doctors' orders.

Nothing that they'd proven. Certainly, no patients had suffered ill effects under Martha's care.

It could also just be that Martha needed a refresher course on protocol before she found herself being written up. Not a call for Greg or Elaina or the chart-ing committee to make.

The administrator they reported to would be the one to make those kinds of decisions or determine if any action was needed.

"And if there's no change at all, I'm leaning to-ward the idea that Mom isn't giving her the meds at home, either. Some parents don't like the risk of side effects or determine that the child is better off without medication. Like the whole vaccine debate. Maybe she watches Brooklyn's behavior, finds her more agreeable without the drugs, and thinks she can help Brooklyn holistically, or by teaching her better behavior. And when symptoms get too bad, she fears the child's gastrological problems are rearing up and brings her to us to make sure she's okay."

Greg settled his backside against his desk, draw-ing her gaze to his thighs. And between them.

A familiar heat touched her privately for the sec-ond it took her to snap her gaze away. She sat down in one of the two chairs in front of his desk but then wished she hadn't. She'd just forced herself to have to look up to him.

This man who was demanding a paternity test on the child that was, even then, growing inside her. *Oh my God.*

She was pregnant.

Like it was just then hitting her, she sat there,

looking at Greg, wanting to break out in laughter. And break down in tears.

She'd gone straight to work from the clinic the day before. And had allowed herself to be consumed by the father problem.

Failing to let the rest of the news take root.

She was going to be a mother...sooner than she'd thought.

"So will you do the scans for me?"

"Of course." Sunday. On Brooklyn. "I'll do anything to help that little girl, you know that."

At least, he should know it. But then, he should also know that if she said he was the father of her child, then he was. "Are you thinking Martha didn't administer the medication you prescribed on Monday?"

"She scanned it out of inventory, but there's no scan of Brooklyn's wristband documenting that she actually got it."

"She probably got distracted and didn't do the scan. Maybe another emergency going on," Elaina said, though she was concerned by the lack of attention to a critical technical procedure. "She's great with the kids, gentle, patient. She gets along with all of the other disciplines, child life, radiology, she's always willing to work overtime, and she knows medicine. Knows when to call a doctor, knows what we're looking for when she does."

"So maybe she gave the medication to someone

else to administer and it didn't get done for whatever reason."

"I have to admit, I ran the scans you ordered yesterday, but I didn't read all of the charting." Her duties
didn't require her to know, or follow, a patient's total
care. Only that she know everything about her part
in it. She read scans. She didn't treat. "I'm assuming
you ordered blood and urine samples?"

He nodded.

"And they came back with no sign of the medication in her system?"

Another nod.

Based on the type of medication he'd prescribed...
"It should have been there for five days."

"And we were only at the end of the third day,"
he told her.

"Of course, systems process differently, but with
no change of neurotransmitters on the brain scan,
and no trace of medication in her system..." She
paused for a few seconds.

"What do you want to do?" she asked him, worried for Brooklyn, for Martha, for the hospital, but
also relieved to be able to be side by side with Greg
on the matter, to have something to share with him.

"We're going to have to report the discrepancy,
but I'd like the result of Sunday's scans before we
do. We'll then have comparisons with Brooklyn's
body three days post-medication. And I'd like your
help, as a fellow member of the charting commit-

tee, going over any charts Martha's had access to in the last month, as well as taking a look at any charting that others who worked in the ED on Monday may have done. It's within the scope of our committee work. But I'd like to limit it to just you and me for now. So we can keep this small, and reputations won't need to be damaged, until we know what we're dealing with."

As the head of the committee, he could make that call.

He was giving Martha the benefit of the doubt, without letting the matter go. Exactly what she would have done. "Of course, I'll help," she told him. "In this case, Brooklyn's going to be okay, but it could have been so much worse."

He opened his mouth as though to say something to her, but then turned away. And that quickly she was hurting again. Wanting to know what he'd held back. That didn't sit well with her. She knew they'd based their entire relationship on withholding the most emotionally personal parts of themselves, so why should his not telling her something bother her now?

How could she hurt over something she'd never had?

And how could she still be glad that there was a need for her to work with him over the weekend? How could she be clinging to the opportunity?

It wasn't logical.

She should be resenting the fact that she was pregnant with Greg's child when the baby should have been Peter's. Or at least feel sad that she wasn't carrying Peter's baby. Maybe that would come. As soon as she had time to process.

She was pregnant!

It still wasn't sinking in. Not fully. Maybe in bits and pieces. Like big, fluffy snowflakes falling softly around her and melting as soon as they touched the warm earth.

She agreed to see Greg later that afternoon, to split up charting detail, and as she was heading back down to Imaging, a thought occurred to her.

It was possible that she was romanticizing Greg, attaching to him emotionally, because she was pregnant with his child. She wanted to deny the assertion. To know in her heart that she was done being that woman. That it wasn't happening again.

But she couldn't.

Chapter Four

By Friday after their morning meeting, Greg was fully convinced that she truly believed he was the father of her child.

And while he wished wholeheartedly that the possibility existed for him to be a father, he knew that them having a child together wasn't the reality.

He knew he was in the clear. For her…he ached a bit. The fact that she so badly needed him to be the father that she couldn't even entertain another option told him that whoever had fathered her child wasn't someone she could fathom, or allow, as the father.

And also strictly for her, he worried a bit, too. What would the ramifications be for her when she realized that what she'd apparently mentally denied as impossible had become reality?

It was none of his business. He was perfectly clear on that point.

They were work associates, members of the charting committee, past lovers—only. They'd never been intimate friends, the kind you told your problems to, or turned to when you were at one of life's low points. He'd never really had—or been—one of those. He knew a lot of people. Hung with various groups of people—his golf buddies who were mostly financiers and lived in Nevada. He'd lived and practiced there before accepting the temporary position at Marie Cove as he made the move from internist to full-time ER doctor. And he was still in touch with a group of doctors he'd known since med school—male and female—who usually got together in Vegas at least once a year. And in Marie Cove, there was a newer group of younger guys who were teaching him to surf.

For emotional intimacies, there'd been Heather, the summer after he'd graduated high school. At least he'd been emotionally intimate in that one.

And his ex-wife, Wendy…for a time it had felt as though they'd merged two sets of wants and needs, goals, and hearts and souls into one life. It wasn't until after the relationship ended, and he saw how little of his private self he left behind with her, that he realized how much of an emotional loner he'd become.

And then there was Elaina. *Had* been Elaina… though he'd never really been emotionally intimate with her.

He'd been ready to make a life with her, though. Wow, had he been off on that one. Thankfully, she'd said her piece first, breaking up with him before he'd suggested furthering their intimacy. Saved him a load of embarrassment.

Not that it mattered in his current world at all. He'd already given up the lease on his apartment. Had turned down the full-time ER appointment at Marie Cove and sent his letter of acceptance for the position in LA—all that morning.

While he was in his office that afternoon after his shift, waiting for Elaina to arrive, he did an internet search on Dr. Cheryl Miller, the doctor Elaina had mentioned. Dr. Miller would know that he'd been involved with Elaina, that she was claiming him as the father of her child. And he wanted to know a bit more about the woman who'd have that information.

The medical world, while huge, was also small when it came to people who knew people.

And what he found—that Dr. Miller worked full-time at The Parent Portal, a renowned fertility clinic right there in Marie Cove—gave him pause for concern. Why would Elaina be seeing a fertility specialist?

Was it actually possible that she'd been accidentally fertilized by mistake, thinking she'd only been undergoing a preliminary exam?

The idea was ludicrous. Something for a TV show.

But stranger things had happened, too.

Medical mistakes happened.

He knew that firsthand. Had almost lost his license to practice medicine because of one. Not his own, but in the moment, that hadn't mattered. He'd been suspected at first, had even doubted himself. Could have even been looking at jail. At the time, though, when his patient—a woman close to his own age—had died, a prison sentence had been the least of his concerns.

Now his concern was in ensuring that if something had gone awry with Brooklyn's medication on Monday, they found out what and who was responsible. He was not going to lose another patient due to a medical mistake.

And he wasn't leaving Marie Cove until the mystery was solved. He'd given a month's notice to both hospitals. That gave him thirty days to wrap up the threads of the brief life he'd led in the quaint, upscale beach town.

The knock at that precise moment seemed purposeful to him. As though someone was trying to tell him that Elaina was one of those threads that needed wrapping.

She entered, looking as exquisitely beautiful as always, carrying her tablet with her. Anytime he'd ever been out with her, he'd noticed other men's heads turn as she passed. She didn't ask for it, didn't seem to even be aware, it just happened. The ponytail she always wore at work was as pristine as it had been that morning, and incurred visions of that long dark luxurious hair spread over him, and under him, too, splayed across the pillow. Her features, cheekbones that were unique and yet softly rounded, eyes that seemed to entice him into their pool-like depths and lips that were full and sweet and could do the most incredibly seductive things to a man's body...

"I've been over admissions from Monday and have a listing of all personnel who charted in the ED..." They were privy to these records as part of their commission on the charting committee. He wasn't surprised she'd done work ahead of their meeting. Elaina always came prepared. And carried more than her share of the load.

Taking her cue—and appreciative of it—he resolved to get right to work. He sat beside her with his own tablet as they designed a plan for divvying up patients and charts based on types of procedures, figured out the easiest way to seek out the data and designed a shareable spreadsheet for the two of them to use for documentation.

And in less than an hour they'd completed their work.

"Can you have your part done by tomorrow afternoon?" he asked as they both stood, pushing their chairs back underneath the table simultaneously.

Whether on the dance floor, in bed or at a worktable, they'd always been perfectly in sync. The thought crossed his mind and he batted it out of the ballpark.

"I can." Holding her tablet to the chest of her blue scrubs, she headed to the door before glancing over her shoulder to ask, "You want to meet here again then? Same time?"

He wanted to take her in his arms. Hold her while her life was imploding.

Recognizing that he did her an injustice with the assumption that it *would* implode. But he knew he couldn't possibly be the father of her child, and her adamant insistence that he was set her up for a shock that would rock her, at the very least.

"I'm infertile." He blurted the words. Like the nerd he'd once been.

Turning, one slow step at a time, she stared at him, mouth open.

Yeah. He watched her expression, trying to figure out what she was thinking, what way she was going to go, to help her deal with the ramifications if he could. A farewell gesture between coworkers with fringe benefits.

When she didn't say anything, he stepped up to fill the gap. "I looked up your ob-gyn and saw that she works at The Parent Portal."

She continued to stare at him.

"A fertility clinic," he added, as though speaking to someone who might not be following his conversation.

"*I'm* infertile," he repeated. He'd never just outed his infertility before. And there he'd done it twice.

Based on the wide-eyed look she still wore, she couldn't seem to grasp the information—not even the second time.

"Don't lie to me, Greg," she finally said. "Say you don't want a child, or don't want one with me. Tell me you don't ever want to be a father, fine. I already told you I'm fine to not even name you on the certificate. Just, please, don't lie to me." With that she turned and headed toward the door.

He could let her go. He'd done enough. And had his own demons to deal with.

"You want me to have the reports from the three separate fertility clinics I visited in Nevada sent to Cheryl Miller?" The question came anyway.

Even more slowly than before, she turned back to him, sliding around rather than stepping, her black foam-padded shoes seeming to stick on the carpet. Funny of him to notice the innocuous when he was forcing a woman to see something she most certainly could not seem to comprehend.

She appeared to be at a loss for words. At least she wasn't hurling insults, calling him names.

"Why were you visiting The Parent Portal?" he asked then, gently.

He could not possibly be the biological father of her child, not after having held on to hope as long as he could. For more years than his marriage had lasted. After the third round of tests in six years, he'd finally accepted that which wasn't going to change.

No way he could let her problem send him backward to revisit something he'd already dealt with.

"How many visits have you made there?" he asked. His first question had received no response, but she was still standing there, facing him, not the door. If yesterday's visit had been the first, he could definitively rule out wrongful fertilization.

Maybe, if he hadn't been through a nightmare of his own where a wrongful act had impacted one of his patients, he wouldn't be so quick to think it could happen.

"Have you been seeing Dr. Miller long?" He phrased his question a third way.

"Six months."

Six months. She'd been visiting a fertility clinic while they'd still been lovers?

He'd had no idea.

How did a woman sleep with a guy and not tell him that she was investigating her options for having a baby?

He felt his own mouth drop open now, as he

stared. Completely…he wasn't even sure what. Angry, now, for sure.

Had he known her at all?

"We didn't talk about such things, Greg."

Her pragmatic tone, filled with a bit of…warmth, brought him back to his senses. She was right. They'd been coworkers with benefits. He'd once considered them friends with benefits. Before he'd realized that they'd never even shared details of their lives.

"You've been planning to have a child."

So much for his sympathy for finding herself unexpectedly pregnant. She *wanted* to be pregnant.

He'd been having sex with her and he hadn't known that she wanted to be.

Had he not been sterile, would she have…

"Were you using me to get pregnant?" The words flew up and out of him before he'd thought them through.

She didn't flinch. Didn't even frown. Looking him straight in the eye, she said, "No." And then followed it up with another kick in the pants. "I've been preparing to have myself fertilized with Peter's sperm. He did his residency at the clinic, and like many of his peers back then, had donated sperm. I'm supposed to be having *his* baby. Yesterday's exam was the final check before insemination."

Tears came to her eyes as the words trailed off and Greg felt sick. Stunned. Hurt. And sad for her all at the same time.

She'd been sleeping with him, and while he was preparing to ask her to take their relationship to another level, she'd been actively pursuing having another man's baby.

Not just another man. She'd been planning to have a baby by the man who'd been the love of her life.

Not that she'd ever talked to him about Peter. But others had. They'd been the golden couple of Oceanfront.

Either way, Elaina had been happily married to a man who'd died tragically. And was still trying, all these years later, to have his baby.

If that didn't say "love of your life," nothing did.

He was nothing to her. Owed her nothing. How she got pregnant wasn't his concern. He knew it wasn't by him.

Greg moved to the door of his office, opening it like an automaton. "Is tomorrow afternoon, same time, good for you to go over my results?" he asked as though they'd just stood up from the table and hadn't already decided the point.

They'd made an unfortunate detour off their professional courses. A mistake he wouldn't be making again.

"Of course," she said, heading to the door.

But before it closed behind her, she poked her head back inside. "You're the only man I've slept with in a couple of years, Greg. This baby is yours."

It wasn't. But arguing the point with her was useless.

Instead, Greg waited to give Elaina a head start, and then walked out of his office, out of the hospital, and drove out of town. He drove for anonymity. To clear his head. And to stop in the first semilarge town between Marie Cove and LA—Mission Viejo—to pick up a home male fertility test.

He knew the results before he left the drugstore. Before he got back to his apartment. Before he did what he had to do to produce semen for the test.

And when those results came back exactly as he'd known they would, he felt tears prick the backs of his eyes, too.

They didn't fall. He wouldn't let them fall.

A guy couldn't cry for something he'd already lost.

Chapter Five

Elaina wasn't on call that weekend and spent a good bit of Saturday at her office on the hospital campus, filling out portions of the spreadsheet she and Greg had made the day before. Earlier, she'd called Cassie, telling her that she didn't want to go to the comedy club they'd planned to attend.

She assured her sister-in-law that she was fine, just that she had a situation at work—something Wood and now Cassie were very used to from her. Her work came first. Always.

Well…until eight months from now. For the first time since Peter died, she'd have a person in her life who would come before work.

When Wood called just as she was heading to

Greg's office on Saturday afternoon, she told him the same thing.

"I'm fine, Wood. You know me." And maybe he was the only person on earth who really did know her.

"Cassie says you haven't said a word about Thursday's appointment."

"It went fine," she said, slowing her steps to a standstill in an empty alcove off the mostly deserted Imaging hallway. "I'm definitely a candidate to be a mother. In every way."

She couldn't tell him she was pregnant yet. She hadn't accepted the news herself, though when she did actually think about it, she felt an elation she didn't recognize.

Even more than the burst of wonderful feeling and kind of ownership love she felt every single time she was around Wood and Cassie's little Alan. Her godson. The eleven-month-old owned her heart like no one ever had before.

"So...that's good, right?" Wood asked. That was so...him. Taking things at face value. Drawing no nuances or reading between lines.

"Yes, it's fabulous," she said, smiling as she placed a hand on her stomach. And it would be something she could talk about once the baby's father understood that he'd produced a child.

It just didn't seem right to bring the situation to light until Greg had a chance to assimilate the truth.

"You're sure you want to do this, Elaina? You don't want to wait a bit? See if you meet someone, fall in love again…"

Wood had been hesitant about her using Peter's sperm from the beginning.

"Absolutely sure."

Even if the clinic had made a mistake and injected her by accident—though the chances of that were so slim she couldn't seriously consider the possibility—she was still in shock over Greg's announcement, but had to believe that his tests were wrong. Maybe another reason she was reticent to tell Cassie and Wood what she'd found out the day before. When Greg had first demanded a paternity test, she'd hated that he was the father of her baby.

By that morning, she'd had to admit that she didn't hate him as the father, though she hated the circumstances they were in. Not that she wanted to start something up with him. She did not. Something else that would be hard to get Wood to understand. She had to do this alone.

But Greg was a good man. A great doctor and, really, a wonderful person. And didn't deserve to be sterile.

Any child would be lucky to carry his genes. Her heart ached for the pain he'd tried so hard not to show, pretending that he was okay with his situation, that he'd adjusted. She'd seen the shadows in his eyes and had known that he one hundred percent believed what he'd told her. And that he suffered from the knowledge.

"So...you're okay?" Wood asked.

"Yes."

"And you're going to do this? You're going to have a baby?"

"Yes, I am." She couldn't help the bit of elation that came out in her tone. She might not yet fully comprehend everything that had changed in her life, might not be ready to start thinking about actually being pregnant, but the fact was slowly finding a home within her.

After offering her his and Cassie's support in whatever way she needed it, Wood rang off. The best brother a girl could ever hope to have—even if he was really just an ex-brother-in-law, husband in name only, and then "adopted" brother.

She had to double-time it to make it to Greg's office on time, so she did. Thinking about the man with every quick step. As she'd been doing since the afternoon before.

Greg wasn't asking for a paternity test because he didn't trust her. He was asking because he'd been put in a position where he had no choice.

The man actually believed himself to be infertile! How could she not have known that? All those months they'd been lovers...

But then, she'd never talked to him about Peter. Or much about Wood, either, for that matter. She'd shrugged and said nothing. Not even the day Wood had come to see her at the hospital and found her having lunch with Greg in the cafeteria.

She should have introduced them that day.

And she'd been afraid that Wood would make more of her friendship with Greg than was there, that he'd think she didn't need or want him anymore, then move out. It was all so convoluted and mattered not at all at the moment.

How was it going to affect Greg, once he eventually realized that he was going to be a father? That was all she needed to be focused on where he was concerned in terms of her pregnancy. Had he wanted children before he found out he was infertile? The fact that he'd taken fertility tests three times indicated he'd wanted badly to be a father.

Most men didn't know they were infertile until they took a test, and that was generally done only when they'd tried and failed to impregnate someone.

Whom had Greg tried to impregnate?

And if he'd wanted a child badly enough to go through testing—three times, apparently—would he then be ecstatic to know he was finally going to have one?

Or would he be disappointed that the child was growing inside her instead of the woman he'd been trying to impregnate?

Either way, whatever way, her task was to think of him. Keep his needs in mind at all times.

Hurt feelings on her part were not necessary and not welcome, either. As a doctor, she certainly didn't fault him for believing the results. He'd done everything right. Tested multiple times, multiple places. She'd believe them, too, if she wasn't carrying the evidence of his false results inside her.

She knew it was much more likely that he'd had failed test results than that she'd been injected with sperm when she'd been in for a completely different procedure.

Firmly resolved, she knocked on his door, tablet in hand, ready to talk about charting issues. Nurse Martha. And Brooklyn George.

The door opened and the first thing she saw was Greg holding something: a piece of white plastic, a home sperm test, with a *C* underlined—the control line indicating that he'd done the test correctly. Greg's fingers, ones that had moved artistically over her body for months, were shaking. Reaching into his pocket with his free hand, he took out another test, also marked very clearly with a *C* result. Putting both in one hand, he then pulled several sheets of paper, each folded in half lengthwise, out of his back pocket, and handed them to her.

She took them because they were there; it was an instinctive move. She read them because she wanted to see what kind of testing he'd had, by whom, and compile the results. As another doctor would.

Her thoughts, though, were not on test results.

There was a chart, showing all of the efforts he'd made, followed by test results that showed no change at all. She looked up from the paper and saw a man who'd not only been tested, but done everything he could to change his results.

Over a period of six years.

She saw a man with resolution in his gaze.

Greg was a doctor. He knew what those results meant, and yet he'd kept trying. And trying. He'd wanted a child that badly. And continued to be told he wasn't capable of fathering one.

She could only imagine the level of pain that had to have brought him. Tears pricked at her eyes and she bent her head until her own emotions were under control.

Could he allow himself to be happy that he'd finally succeeded?

If he'd succeeded.

The magnitude of that *if* weighed heavily on her with his results in hand.

"These two—" he held up the testing devices with which he'd greeted her "—were last night and this morning," he told her. "I didn't bring the third one I did in between."

He'd ejaculated three times in twelve hours. That knowledge didn't surprise her. The man was as virile as they came. The sudden heat between her legs, accompanied by a wave of disappointment for not having been there, were completely unexpected.

And brought a new wave of shame in herself. The man was dealing with what he believed to be incredibly difficult news and she stood there getting turned on by him?

Because it was all about her, in her world, apparently. Her husband's death, Wood's sacrifices, all pointed to it.

How could she have slid so far into herself? Yeah, the car accident had been rough. She'd lost her husband, nearly lost her own life. She'd been paralyzed for a time, believing she'd never walk again. But she was good as new. And living like some kind of victim, as though she had to have a man in her life having her back at all times. Even when it hurt his own.

His test results weren't good. The home sperm count test confirmed what the others had told him.

"I understand that you have low sperm count," she finally spoke, trying to choose her words carefully. "But it only takes one good one out of thousands…" And as often as he'd emptied himself in her, those odds weren't as impossible as they might seem. "And I must have a particularly hospitable environment."

Shaking his head, Greg turned his back, leaving his testing apparatuses on his desk before grabbing his tablet and heading to their work space—the round table they'd occupied the day before.

"I don't just have extremely low sperm count, Elaina. I have antibodies that kill off my sperm. Probably due to a prostate injury I had during an impromptu high school football game. My sperm are sparse and they don't make it out of my body."

Antisperm antibodies. She was familiar with the condition, even before she'd just read his test results.

He wasn't talking in medical terms, she could tell. He wasn't a doctor in the moment. He was a man with a condition that hurt him deeply. And the chances of overcoming it were slim to rare.

She hadn't meant to touch him. Forethought would have prevented her from doing so. But her hand was covering his before she'd had a chance to form a thought. "One did, Greg," she said softly. Tentatively.

Could he be glad that he was finally going to be a father? Could they share this child and maybe manage to be friends in the process?

Real friends?

Not lovers. She adamantly couldn't go back there—she was too emotionally dependent to allow that. But with a child between them…they'd…

Pulling his hand from beneath hers, he shook his head. "You're a doctor, Elaina. You read the test results. You know as well as I do that I'm not capable of fathering a child."

She did know that, medically speaking, he was right. But somehow it had happened.

"I haven't slept with anyone else."

She needed the seventh week to arrive so she could get the paternity test. She needed him to know. For more than just herself. The man was meant to be a father. She wanted it for him. Even though it messed up her idea of what her future family was going to look like.

She hadn't figured on a live father in the picture...

"And there could have been a mix-up at the clinic. Maybe a PA injected you as opposed to getting cultures when you were in for testing."

The thought had occurred to her—because it was the only other possibility for a pregnancy within her. No one else had been near her space. But he was a doctor. He knew the unlikelihood of such an unprofessional and disastrous mistake. Too many checks and balances were in place for a mistake like that to happen. He was really grasping at straws. To the point that she felt sorry for him. And a bit hurt again, too. Was the idea of even considering the possibility that she could be pregnant with his child so abhorrent to him?

Or had he just been disappointed one too many times?

"Did you watch the procedure?" he asked, his gaze serious, and completely clear, as he looked at her.

"No." She'd done what she always did when being examined—turned her head, stared at the wall and put her mind on something else. On the day he was referencing, five weeks before, that last argument with Peter had sprung to mind and she'd spent the entire time hoping that having Peter's baby would somehow add a bit of salve to the egregious wound she'd unknowingly helped create. The exam had been somewhat painful, as her uterus had to be manipulated, and...

Elaina stared at her tablet, at the still blank screen.

And something occurred to her, causing her heart to jump a beat. She'd had to switch exam rooms that morning. The computer in the room she'd been in hadn't been working.

And then the system had gone down for a short time.

Was it possible that someone had mistaken her for another patient? One who had a painful exam, thinking she was being fertilized, and ended up not pregnant on that try?

The ramifications blew up in her mind's eye as she felt herself flush, then shiver.

Looking at Greg, she didn't realize that she was silently asking for reassurance until he said, "I can't imagine what you're feeling right now, but I'm here if you need to talk."

What she needed was to stop scaring herself and get him to understand that he was the father of her baby.

To get away from the misplaced, warm compassion searing her from his gaze, she turned her head, saw the test results on his desk, and took a deep breath.

Clearly, she had to have a fetal paternity test. But...

"I know it's hard to accept, a clinic as renowned as The Parent Portal making a mistake, but they happen, Elaina."

She shook her head. Clearing it as best she could. She didn't want an unknown man's sperm in her body. She'd made that decision early on: it would have to be Peter's, or no insemination.

But she wanted the baby growing inside her. Right then and there, her pregnancy became completely real to her as she was hit with how badly she wanted that child.

How she'd already wrapped her heart around it.

She hadn't wanted the baby to be Greg's, but she'd been falling in love with it, knowing it was his. So shouldn't she be equally accepting of an anonymous donor? It wasn't like she'd been expecting anything from Greg.

Greg picked up his tablet, turned it on, swiped and poked until the spreadsheet they'd been working on came up. They'd used a yellow highlighter to show charting discrepancies. Meds ordered and meds taken didn't always gel. There was a handful of such instances, one during the time that Brooklyn should have been getting medication through an IV.

He motioned toward the chart and said, "This isn't my first time seeing something like this."

His tone had changed, and she looked over at him.

"I lost a patient in Las Vegas," he told her. She knew he'd come from a major hospital there. But she knew very little other than that he'd been an internist, had done a rotation in the ER and had liked it so much he'd changed his specialty.

"Many doctors do, if they stay in the business long enough," she said softly. One of the reasons she'd chosen nuclear medicine as her specialty was so that she didn't have her own patients, but rather, was able to help a much larger group of people. While she was fascinated by medicine and the way the human body worked, while she cared deeply about people and helping them, she just didn't see herself wanting to stand in a room and deliver a difficult diagnosis.

The world was made up of all kinds of people, with varying strengths and weaknesses, for a reason.

"This one was due to medical error. She was a young teacher who'd come in for a simple procedure and ended up in a coma."

Shocked, she stared at him. Horrified for his patient. For him. For the medical field in general. And back for Greg again. A doctor with something like that in his history...

That was something he carried with him forever. Like being somewhat responsible for a husband's death...

How could she not have known such a monumental thing about him? The question seemed to be becoming a regular in her repertoire where he was concerned. And yet, she knew the answer. He didn't know about Peter, either.

How could she have been so hurt by his initial paternity test request, hurt that he was doubting her, when she knew him so little?

How could she have been missing him these past weeks, when she'd never really known him?

"As it turned out, the mistake wasn't mine," he said. "A nurse hadn't followed my orders. Medications had been administered wrongly. But that didn't come to light until I'd almost lost my license. And there was talk of criminal negligence charges being filed."

"I'm guessing you didn't care about either of those things so much as you mourned for that woman and her family." The words flowed naturally out of her. Because there *was* something she knew about him.

His gaze joined hers, held on gently. As he nodded, her heart leaped toward him.

And it felt like their messed-up situation got a little messier.

Chapter Six

Sunday's scans on Brooklyn showed significant enough change to convince Greg that the child hadn't received her medication the previous Monday in the emergency department.

"You saw my notes?" Elaina asked the second he showed up on her mostly deserted floor late that afternoon, looking for her.

Alone in her lab, she'd been on the computer, and had spun on her stool to face him as he approached.

He liked having her watch him.

Even though she was pregnant with another man's child, starting a new life completely separate and different from his, he liked having her watch him.

She turned him on.

She had turned him on since the day he'd seen her come into the boardroom for the first meeting of the charting committee more than a year before. He'd shoved the feelings aside then. Immediately. Greg didn't manage the feat as quickly today, but he did succeed, after a while. He needed her to have the paternity test run so that she didn't keep looking at him with that sense of deep connection that he'd been imagining the last few times he'd seen her. He needed her to know that he wasn't the father of her child.

"I saw your notes." He repeated her words as his mind gained control over his body, focusing on his purpose for seeing her. Grabbing a stool from another countertop station, he pulled it over. "I've gone over Brooklyn's chart from the first time she was in and I'm thinking that, while that mishap on Monday is a critical hospital mistake that must be dealt with, it also pointed out something crucial."

Elaina's nod didn't surprise him. "She's not getting the prescribed medication at home," Elaina said. These words didn't surprise him, either. "I was really beginning to suspect the child's problems were purely psychological. But what we see this week is similar to weeks on home meds, and then there's the change when we know for sure she got the meds here in the hospital... You were right to suspect there's something going on with her parent."

Her praise pleased him. In a personal way. He

got over it. "Since we don't have enough proof to do anything but convince the two of us, we need to determine how we proceed from here. With Brooklyn *and* her mother. And we also need to bring the other issue—Martha's misconduct—to Bradshaw. Let's go at that as a charting error for now, from our standpoint. If administration takes it further, they do."

With him being the head of the committee, the call was his. Martha might lose her job. Probably should, though from what he could tell, the woman had been called on a triage emergency and had passed the meds to another nurse, who must've failed to administer them to Brooklyn. He'd been thankful to find they hadn't been given to another patient, by mistake, but this kind of transferring the responsibility to another employee just couldn't be allowed. Such activity alone, without proper chain of command charting, couldn't happen.

"We should report it to administration immediately," Elaina added as she nodded, squirming a bit in her seat and turning slightly away from him.

"I'll do it as soon as we're done here."

She seemed uncomfortable in his presence—a problem recently new to them—and he wanted it gone. Just as he wanted to step in and offer his support.

She had a challenging road ahead of her.

And he had the time. The energy.

But he had no desire to go that route again. He

desired her body. But he wasn't going to settle for being the stand-in.

Been there, done that, too. Giving up his first semester's tuition to help Heather. Putting off his own education for half a year.

"As far as Brooklyn goes, I'd like to have a consult with her pediatrician, with you there, as well. It will be up to him to order periodic scans and blood work to prove our theory. Althea will be told that we're monitoring progress. Nothing more. I can think of no other way to go about this in a timely fashion. It should only take about a month, testing once a week..."

"I read in the chart that the mother's into holistic medicine."

He'd seen that, too. Though he didn't on the whole disagree with the approach, Brooklyn needed more help than she was getting.

"I'd like to set up the meet for tomorrow, if that works for you, so we can get going on the weekly scans straight off this latest ER visit. And also..." he debated adding the next part and being there alone with her, looking into those deep dark eyes "...this will give me the chance to see this through to the end, to leave the hospital, knowing that Brooklyn's going to be okay."

He watched her face for a reaction, not sure what he'd expected—or hoped—to see. She blinked. Swallowed. And said, "I didn't know you were leaving," as though he'd mentioned he liked ranch dressing on his salad.

"Yep," he stood. "I accepted the position in LA and have given up the lease on my apartment." Pulling the bandage off quickly was still the best option, even with all of the medical marvels brought on by modern technology. Him leaving before her pregnancy was even showing—that was getting that Band-Aid off quickly.

Lest he become a permanent Band-Aid in her life. Or try to be.

Heather had taught him a hard lesson on that score. He'd known she was still half in love with the guy who dumped her. But he'd believed she'd had genuine feelings for him, too. When she'd told him she was pregnant, he'd believed her. Had said he'd stand by her even if the baby wasn't his. After he put off going to college, using part of his first semester's tuition to put a down payment on an apartment, she'd been honest with him. Told him there was no baby. She'd been trying to get her ex back, and had tearfully admitted she'd been wrong to do what she'd done. But she'd needed Greg. He'd loved her. And loved her needing him…

Yeah, never again.

"You're moving to LA." The words came across as mere clarification.

"I start there four weeks from tomorrow. I'd like

to get an apartment sooner than that, though, just a temporary landing place until I find a home to buy."

"I didn't know you wanted to be a homeowner." He couldn't read her. Didn't like that. And didn't remember a time when he'd felt that way in the past.

"We don't really know much of anything about each other," he reminded her. Funny how that hadn't stopped him from thinking he knew her well. Yes, ironies abounded.

Heather hadn't been the only woman with whom he'd jumped feet first into a relationship, but she was the one who'd hurt the most. Until Wendy, of course. His ex-wife had been as eager as he was to marry quickly, in spite of them only knowing each other a couple of months. They'd been living together after one. They were both professionals at that point. Had known what they wanted.

And when it turned out that he wasn't able to provide what she wanted most—a biological child of her own—she'd divorced him and found someone who could.

And here was Elaina—a woman who'd slipped past all of his hard-built defenses, in spite of them sticking to their "no friendship, only sex" rule. Breaking up with him. And then thinking she was pregnant with his child, but still not wanting to start anything with him.

The ironies were almost comical.

Except that no one was laughing.

* * *

On Monday, Elaina met with Dr. Morgan, Brooklyn's pediatrician, with Greg present. On Tuesday, she helped Greg present their charting concerns to administration. They wouldn't be privy to results. It was the way things worked. You did your job. You didn't become attached. Most particularly when you worked with patients who were not under your direct care. She managed it all without exchanging a single personal word with Greg. She was professional, gracious. And remained absent.

She went to Cassie and Wood's for dinner, spending almost the entire time on the floor with Alan, stacking blocks that he'd knock down and then, each time, look at her with surprise and laugh out loud.

She wasn't telling anyone she was pregnant. Not until she could explain how it happened.

And she wasn't looking at nursery furniture or doing anything in the unused guest room in her home, in terms of painting or even planning. Not until she knew who the father of her child was.

The baby was coming.

It was hers and she was already in love with it.

She just wanted to know the identity of its father before fully accepting her changed reality.

And as for Greg…he'd made his decision one way or the other. Yes, he'd convinced her there was a good chance the baby wasn't his. That there'd been a gross mistake made at The Parent Portal. But it was possible that he was wrong. There were many things medical science could not explain.

A sperm slipping past the aggressors out to kill it could be one of them.

He was moving, regardless, even though Los Angeles was not all that far. Had already quit his job in Marie Cove by giving his notice. Had given up his apartment.

The message couldn't be any clearer to her.

No matter what the coming paternity test had to say, he was going.

She had to be fine with that. Logically, she was completely good with his decision. She'd broken up with him for good reason, even if her traitorous emotions didn't always comply with logic.

It was those same needy emotions that had prompted her to rely on Wood for emotional support for so long, rob him of years of his life by holding on to him so tightly. By refusing to get out and live her own life. True, neither of them had had other family...so Wood had made it easy for her to lean on him.

She wasn't leaning anymore.

She might not have chosen to be impregnated by either Greg or some anonymous donor—pray God it wasn't a husband whose sperm had been meant for his wife only—but she *had* chosen to be impregnated. And to raise her family as a single parent.

* * *

Over the next two weeks, to keep her sanity as the unknown consumed any thought of her future plans, she picked up a couple of extra shifts. And worked on the continuing education requirements required of all doctors to maintain licensing, online at night. Having made it through Peter's death and her own paralysis, she was well versed on how to keep her mind occupied to hold the demons at bay.

And unless necessary for work, she stayed away from Greg. Missing him more than she had when she'd first broken up with him, promising herself it was just because of the baby, wanting to believe herself. Succeeding sporadically.

She cried a lot. Quietly. Alone in her suite at a house that she loved and needed to fill with love. At night, when she was done with her responsibilities, she gave herself half an hour before sleep to peruse rescue dog sites, reading about individual furry friends needing homes. But she hadn't landed on anything—mostly because she couldn't choose from among several that she wanted. Saying yes to one meant saying no to others, and she couldn't decide who to say no to.

When she called The Parent Portal to make her appointment for a paternity test, she spoke directly with Dr. Miller and asked that the clinic contact Greg and schedule his part in things with him. A quick cheek swab was all he had to provide. No reason for them to need to be at the clinic at the same time.

She didn't explain why she wanted the test. If Greg wasn't the father, she'd be all over the clinic to find out who was responsible for her current predicament—both medically and paternally. But unless Greg wasn't the father, there was no reason to do anything that could harm the reputation of the renowned clinic.

Two days after she went in for the blood test, she had a call from the clinic, letting her know that the results were in. She'd expected to hear them over the phone, but was told that Dr. Miller wanted to see her.

That struck fear in her heart.

She was a doctor, too. She knew that when a patient was asked to come in for consultation over test results, that usually meant there was something unexpected to discuss.

Was it possible that she wasn't pregnant after all?

The thought was quickly followed by a mental admonition to calm down. If she wasn't pregnant, then she would soon be injected with Peter's sperm, as planned, and hopefully get pregnant.

She waited out the strong current of disappointment that coursed through her in spite of her self-reproof. Two weeks of falling in love wasn't just going to be swept away as though it hadn't been.

So...had the clinic discovered, on their own, that there'd been a mistake on their part? Had she, like

Greg thought, been inseminated with sperm meant for another woman?

The Parent Portal was unique in that it required all sperm donors to sign legally filed documents stating that they were willing to have their identity known to their recipient or child if a request was put forth. They'd agree to allow continued contact with the child on a limited basis, if requested. In return, all recipients signed paperwork allowing the same rights to the donors. Therefore, if she had gotten pregnant by someone other than Greg, she'd know relatively quickly who the donor was. Panic wasn't going to change anything, so she fought it with all she had.

Driving to the clinic an hour later, still early on that Monday morning as she'd been at work doing a scan before seven, she recalled her paralysis recovery. She flashed back to working on a nonelectric treadmill, her hands clutching the rails, finally getting one foot to move inches forward, the focus it took making her sweat, the pain...

She'd come too far, had fought too hard, to give up. And Wood had sacrificed too many years of his life to see her through. She would live a life worthy of that sacrifice. Worthy of his and Cassie's love. Of Peter's memory.

The reminders gave her strength right up until she stepped into the clinic's reception area and saw Greg sitting there, watching the door.

As though looking for her. Her heart gave that

odd jump, a flip she could physically feel, as their eyes met. She didn't even check in before walking over to him.

"What are you doing here?" She managed to keep her voice down, in deference to another woman seated across the room, doing something on her phone.

"Cheryl Miller called." He was answering the question her mind had already sped past. "Said that she had the results." He wasn't in scrub pants. And looked…different…in jeans and a black, short-sleeved cotton pullover and black leather slip-ons. Different and…good. *Really* good.

He was about to find out whether or not he was infertile, as he believed. If he was, would it hurt him all over again? Or just confirm what he'd known all along? Did he hope, even a little bit that…

"I'm the patient. Why would she call you?" she asked, standing there looking down at him, wishing she could will her emotions into a tidy corner of her life so they didn't keep getting in her way. Sending her on nonproductive detours that distracted from her purpose.

"I asked her to do so when I met with her to get swabbed." He was so calm. And being nice, too. As though he was completely in control. Feeling no more than he would if he were the doctor meeting the patient, not the other way around. "However," he continued, "I didn't realize that she'd call us both in at the same time."

Bring them both in at once... Did that mean... that had to mean... Why else would Greg need to be there?

He must be the father of her child!

She had no idea how he'd feel about that. And was pretty sure she should have some misgivings about it, too.

"Dr. Alexander, Dr. Adams..." A medical technician she didn't know stood at the door leading back to the examination rooms, calling to them both.

Glancing over at the receptionist desk, she noticed Christine Elliott Howe, the clinic's founder, standing there, nodding to her. Peter's former employer during his residency, she had been a distant friend over the years, the kind she always knew she could call but never did, because it brought up memories that hurt too much.

Christine wasn't smiling. Two doctors...she supposed that was enough of a shift from normal routine in a medical facility to merit some notice. They were treating two of their own.

By the time Elaina was shaking her head over that one, she and Greg, who'd walked separated by the technician, were shown into Dr. Miller's office—a cluttered space with a big desk, some armchairs, a couch and a flat-screen TV. The lived-in feel gave the impression that the ob-gyn spent a great deal of time in the somewhat large room.

Dr. Miller stood from one of the armchairs as they were shown in, motioning toward the couch. Elaina sat on one end, Greg on the other.

They hadn't ever even talked about families and children, their own or anyone else's, before all of this had happened. They'd certainly never planned to have a family together. They weren't even a couple.

Suddenly the nights they'd spent in each other's arms seemed cheap. Wrong, somehow. As though they'd played with fire without thinking about getting burned.

It hadn't been that way. She knew that. But sitting there, like she was in the principal's office...panicky and bordering on frighteningly excited, too... Elaina didn't feel like herself at all. Her whole life had become a surreal incident in time.

"I wanted you both here together because I understand from my conversation with you, Greg, that you expected Elaina to need good care and understanding when she finds out that you aren't the father of her child. In fact—" Cheryl, who'd been addressing Greg, turned to Elaina "—you specifically requested that I see to it that Elaina got the *best* care."

Elaina glanced at him. He'd specified that?

A sudden warmth flooded the cold that had begun to seep through her. She shivered.

"Elaina, on the other hand, came in for blood work

without requesting any consultation," Dr. Miller looked at Greg now as she spoke.

"Because she's certain that the baby is mine," Greg explained, nodding.

"The baby *is* yours."

She'd known it! Yes! Oh, God, a thousand times yes! Elaina maintained an outer calm as inside she exploded with immediate joy. She wallowed in it. For the thirty seconds it took her to realize that she wasn't alone in the room. In her life.

To realize that, officially, now this child would never just be hers, as she'd originally planned it would be.

But she then looked at Greg and saw the shocked expression he wore. There was no joy there—no sorrow or anger, either. He seemed to be truly in shock and those waves reverberated through her, too.

"I thought it best that the three of us talk through this together, or at least to make the conversation possible if either of you'd like to have it."

Elaina glanced at Dr. Miller and then back at Greg.

The doctor was studying Greg. But he didn't seem to notice either one of them. Standing, he excused himself, and walked out the door, shutting it quietly behind him.

Chapter Seven

As soon as he'd stepped out into the hallway, Greg knew he'd made a fool of himself. Made a mistake. His fight-or-flight instinct had kicked in when he'd heard the news, and he'd flown.

Turning, reaching for the doorknob, thinking he'd go back, he'd had a flash vision of Elaina sitting on the couch, of Dr. Miller in her chair—both of them watching him, expecting things from him, expecting a rational doctor facing medical news, and he'd flown again, bolted for the door that would lead him out into the waiting room—and from there to the exit that would get him out into Monday morning's hustle and bustle out on the streets of Marie Cove, where he could breathe gulps of air, all of it that he wanted.

Yes, he could get in his car, drive to work, and…

Do what?

He wasn't on shift.

He'd figure that out when he got to it. First one door. Then the next.

Sunshine bore down upon him as he emerged outside. A hint of warmth in a breezy spring day. Blue skies and brightness eased the steel around his chest. Breath was a glorious thing. Passing a stone bench, he considered sitting for a sec. Strode on past, his body too filled with energy to slow long enough to allow him any other choice.

He could consider that there'd been a DNA mix-up. Medical mistakes happened! He knew. He'd learned that lesson. Was it coming back to remind him?

Or…perhaps…he needed to slow down a moment and listen.

Elaina had tried to tell him, multiple times.

He'd had to believe she'd been wrongfully fertilized. Which he should have seen as the incredible long shot it was.

Still, it would have been easy enough to investigate. Had there even been another woman being fertilized that day Elaina had been at the clinic seven weeks before? Was that person now pregnant?

As he was not a patient of the clinic he had no right to that information.

But Dr. Miller did. And if she had any suspicions at all, she'd have followed up. As would Christine

Elliott Howe. She'd been there that morning. Greeting him by name as he'd come in.

She'd known.

They'd *all* known.

Either there was some mind-exploding conspiracy going on, and a helluva lot of medical malpractice, including the addition of a botched DNA test, or...

He was going to be a father?

He'd been around the parking lot twice. Elaina still had not appeared.

Probably talking to Dr. Miller about being pregnant by the wrong man.

Maybe about being pregnant by a man who was losing his marbles.

He was going to be a father? *Him?*

He'd watched the chain of command on the swab himself, as far as he could go with it. That DNA had come from him.

Seriously, one tiny little swimmer, in an ocean of thousands, had managed to survive the massacre that went on daily in his body, swim upstream, get past a foreign device meant to prevent it from entering a no-trespassing zone, meet up with an egg, and get it on?

What were the odds?

What an incredible little fella. He should be proud of that one.

Standing by Elaina's car, a black, newer-model, high-end, small SUV, he still realized he was failing to grasp the magnitude of what he'd just been told. He heard the words in his mind. Repeated them. And then got lost.

Why would he have been able to do it for Elaina in that moment? She didn't even want him. He hadn't been able to do that for Wendy...

He knew Wendy had left him because of how their life goals began to diverge, but he also knew the root of those changes between them had grown from his infertility. Her need to have her own biological child had bloomed, as had his constant trying to make things better for her. He'd driven her nuts with his trying.

But if he'd been able to give her the child she'd wanted...

And now here was Elaina...breaking up with him and then getting his child?

His *child*?

His child?

He was going to be a father.

Good God. *He* was going to be a father.

Finding his own vehicle, Greg got in. Drove to the beach. Parked facing the ocean. And let the tears roll.

Elaina worked her shift later that day, focusing on the patients who needed her, consulting with doctors and nuclear med technicians who required her attention. On her lunch break, she went to the cafeteria where she and Greg had shared most of the meals they'd eaten together, chose from the four food groups, going heavy on the fruit and salad, and headed back upstairs.

She used to always pack her lunch, mostly made up of leftovers Wood had made for dinner the night before. Perhaps she should take up cooking again. She'd done all the cooking when she was married to Peter. Had actually enjoyed it sometimes.

And her baby was going to need to eat.

She wanted to sit together with her child at the table every night for the next eighteen years minimum, share a meal while they talked. About big things, little ones, nothing at all.

She wanted her baby. Did Greg?

Feeling as though her life was on hold—still, even after the revelation—she picked up her phone to call him, and put it back down without doing so. A repeat of an action she'd done half a dozen times since leaving The Parent Portal.

Because she hadn't been inseminated with the help of The Parent Portal, she no longer technically needed their services. But Dr. Miller had agreed to keep her on as a patient and birth the baby anyway. She and her little one had had an unusual start. And Dr. Miller understood the situation with Greg. Felt for him.

She'd told Elaina that morning that Greg would come around.

Elaina wasn't so sure.

Nor was she sure she wanted him to do so.

She was thrilled he was her baby's father, as opposed to an anonymous donor. Maybe even just thrilled that her baby would have his genes, period.

But they weren't a couple. Never really had been. Not in any facing-life-together sense. They'd had lunch and sex for over a year.

They'd never been on a date or even out together anywhere. They'd eaten in the cafeteria. And when they'd had sex, she'd always followed him to his place after work.

But she couldn't stop thinking about him. About how he was feeling. What he wanted.

She wanted to wrap her arms around Greg and just hold on. That scared her, too. She couldn't revert back to her old ways, letting a man prop her up. The fact that she hadn't known she was doing it was no excuse.

She'd seen the light.

She had to be strong. In body, spirit and mind. She truly wanted to be.

For herself. Her baby. And others in her life.

Holding it together that day because that was all she'd ever known how to do, she finished her shift and drove home. At almost eight weeks pregnant, she had to start making plans. Figuring out the nursery. Shopping. Painting.

Finding a pediatrician. Changing her insurance policies.

Starting a college fund.

Telling Wood and Cassie that they were going to be an aunt and uncle.

She wanted little Alan to know that she'd always love him specially, that she was bringing him a playmate. A family member who would be there for him for life.

She wanted to call her mom. That yearning had never quite left, even after more than fifteen years since the car accident that had taken both of her parents from her.

And then another one had taken Peter, too.

But she couldn't dwell on that. Couldn't be the needy woman who'd been so ripe to marry Peter, simply because he'd loved her. Who'd perhaps fallen in love with him, or thought herself in love with him, because of the power of his love for her. Who'd leaned so heavily on Wood for so long, for the same reason.

Her dependence on Peter had eventually led her to believe she couldn't exist without him. But there she was, still standing. Miraculously standing after being confined for months to a wheelchair.

She could have a baby on her own. Raise that child in a healthy, loving home.

She didn't need Greg.

Still, her mood shifted, became less rigid, when she pulled down her street and saw Greg's shiny blue sports car parked on the far side of her two-car drive. The side she didn't use.

Opening the garage with the button in her car, she

pulled into her usual spot, telling her heart to stop pounding so hard. Taking a deep breath to help herself where she could.

Greg met her at the bumper. "I owe you an apology," he said before she could even form her lips around a hello. "I'm sorry. I…needed some time to assimilate and I acted like an ass."

"No, you didn't." He'd walked out. He hadn't been brash or purposefully unkind.

"I handled the situation all wrong," Greg said, meeting her gaze. "Can you grant me a do-over?"

There were no do-overs in life. There was only going on from where she was, but still…

"You want to come inside?" she answered his question with one of her own.

Still in the jeans and black shirt he'd had on that morning, he looked…wonderful. His sandy hair was windblown, giving him a carefree appearance that she, at that moment, found so appealing.

"I'd like to talk," he said. "How about if we do something we've never done and go get some dinner?

It might be easier for us if we were in a generic place, with life going on around us." His tone was serious.

She knew he was right. With a nod, she headed back toward her car door.

"Elaina?"

"Yes?"

"I thought maybe we could drive together."

Oh. Well, it made sense. It wasn't like they were going to have sex. It was only dinner. Between parents.

With another nod, and an admonition to her emotions to mind their manners, she followed him out to climb into his highly efficient, but not parenting-practical, lovely blue car.

They decided together where they'd eat. Truth was, Greg didn't figure either of them for being all that hungry, but the location allowed for the fact that they could have private conversation without being easily overheard. The restaurant, set on a cliff overlooking the ocean, was pricey, with high booths set up against a wall of windows. There were tables, too, set far enough apart to allow for the private high-powered business conversations that took place there regularly.

It was early yet for the evening crowd and they were shown a corner booth, offering them the privacy they'd need.

He ordered a mineral water, though a shot of scotch would have been nice to go with it. And he wasn't a scotch drinker.

She opted for cranberry juice with a side of water.

"I've had the day to process and I want to say, first and foremost, that I respect how difficult this must be for you." He started to speak as soon as their waitress had left, their menus still lying unopened in front of them.

"It can't be easy for you, either." Her gaze was clear, if distant, and he wondered if maybe he should have given her time to go in and change out of her scrubs. If maybe the doctoring attire was like a shroud of distance in which she'd wrapped herself.

So much for the clear thinking he'd thought he'd reached.

Of course, she could have said she wanted to change.

Maybe neither one of them was thinking all that clearly.

Maybe that was okay.

But he had things to say, and now was the time to say them. "I appreciate that you planned to raise this child on your own," he said, pulling from the mental list he'd spent the day preparing. "And I understand that there's going to be emotional residual on your part due to the fact that your husband was supposed to be the father of the child…"

Yeah, he'd been processing the things he needed to say—and her probable responses—all day long. Over and over again.

"I'm glad you understand, Greg, but this…isn't what we need to talk about."

"What do we need to talk about?" he asked, partially just out of curiosity. He'd spent the entire day figuring everything out. She'd had an hour at most during lunch and on the drive home.

"What role, if any, you're going to play in this

baby's life, starting with the prenatal portion. How we work together to be the best parents possible, even if you aren't going to play a role after the child is born. We'll still need to figure out how we'd handle that for the best of the baby. How would I eventually tell a child that its conception wasn't planned?"

"We won't be telling this baby that." The words came out a little stronger than he'd have liked. The plan had been to have a calm, kind conversation where they acknowledged each other's positions and found a way to respect both. Assuming she understood that there was no way on this or any planet that he was going to walk away from his child. He'd never imagined he could have a child of his own— and he'd be there for every step of its life.

"We won't."

"No."

"What part of that won't we be telling it?"

"All of it." He heard his tone and thrummed his fingers against the expensive linen tablecloth. "I'm open to discuss the actual child's not being planned, if there's a need for it that I am not currently seeing, though I can't at the moment figure out why a child should need to know the details. However, as I've just stated, I'm open to discussion on that point. As to the rest of it…unless you plan to give up custody of the child to me, or one of us dies, it will have two parents for its entire life."

Her expression didn't change. The straight line

of her mouth remained firm. And yet, he sensed a lightening, maybe a relaxing in the chin. Or a glint in those big, expressive brown eyes. No way was any of the conversation going as planned. At the moment, the only thing he appeared to have gotten right was the need for them to be someplace public, where they were forced to keep some decorum between them.

"I told you two weeks ago that you would be welcome to be a part of this baby's life, Greg. Just as I told you that if you didn't want to be, I'd understand and leave your name off the birth certificate."

Right. She'd already established answers to the questions he'd spent the day thinking about.

"I wasn't listening with the ear of a father, then."

He hadn't really been listening at all, he admitted to himself.

"I won't do that again," he added, figuring she deserved the honesty and commitment to hearing what she needed.

Her gaze darkened. He resisted the urge to lean closer in. To take her hand. He was not going to jump into a relationship.

He was going to be a father.

Chapter Eight

As if by unspoken agreement, the conversation stayed neutral for the rest of the evening. They kept to work talk, and Elaina was grateful for the respite.

It felt good to be eating with Greg again. A little odd to be out in public, rather than the hospital cafeteria, but with the past couple of weeks she'd had, that little bit of odd barely fazed her. Brooklyn's testing was proving exactly what Greg had suspected. When the girl was at the hospital and administered a larger dose of drug that would stay in her system three to five days, her scans showed up markedly different, and her symptoms lessened accordingly. During the week she was at home, supposedly on prescribed medication, the lower, daily dose, the scans were as they'd always been: high in cortisol levels, indicating stress. It appeared that Brooklyn's mother wasn't medicating her at home as directed.

Out of the realm of Elaina or Greg's level of control, but if the next two scans showed the same results, they would have something concrete to send to Brooklyn's pediatrician and to report to Social Services, as was their duty. Martha's mistake had probably been a blessing in disguise, leading them to discover the child's real problem.

"It'll be cleared up before you go," Elaina said without thinking, and then, fork in hand, froze. He was leaving.

She'd miss him. Just as she'd been missing their meals—and more—since she'd broken things off with him, like she missed a good television series when the last episode aired. She didn't want him to go. He brightened her days.

But he was just that—a great series, not part of her real life.

And...

They had to discuss how they were going to handle long-distance, shared parenting. LA wasn't that far, only an hour, but it was far enough that their child couldn't go to the same day care or school from both homes.

"I don't want my child to live in two different homes," she said suddenly. They weren't there to enjoy a meal together like the olden days. It was time to sit up and be the single mom she'd devoted herself to becoming. "To be split between two bedrooms, two routines, two sets of boundaries..."

She knew it often happened successfully. She just didn't want to raise her child that way if she didn't have to.

"I don't want that, either," he said, and then clamped his lips together, as though he'd already had second thoughts. Frowning, he put his napkin on his plate and sat back. "I spent my day thinking about being a father," he said. "I didn't plan out the next eighteen years of my life or envision how they might look."

Her heart lurched again, as it had been doing with him on and off for a while. The feeling was both invigorating and off-putting, and she shied away from giving it focus. But she most definitely wanted to be aware of his emotions. His needs. To understand as best as she could. And make certain that their association wasn't all about only her.

"So let's start there," she said, smiling across at him. The muscles in her face thanked her for allowing them to relax and be natural. "How do you feel about all of this?"

Shaking his head, he raised his brows, shrugged, and then broke into a grin. "I'm thrilled, of course. Thankful. In shock. Amazed. Confused. Overwhelmed—that whole shock thing. And certain that I want to be a father."

Little arrows of *something* good shot off inside her.

"You aren't sorry?" Wanting to be a father, she got that. But what about the rest of it? Finding out he was a father with a woman he wasn't even in a relationship with? A woman he didn't love?

"Hell no! How could I be? I've just been given back something that I thought was lost to me forever. My biggest disappointment, a life sentence, has been miraculously overturned. I'm still in the process of believing it's real. I mean the chances of a healthy sperm getting past my army of haters…"

Smiling for a minute, she absorbed his pleasure. Happy with his happiness. And wished that they could stay just like that.

But life didn't work that way. No one got to just keep their happiness forever. Each moment brought another move. Some good. Some so horrible they stopped you in your tracks.

Some were just…perplexing. Like her finally having a plan, being ready to have Peter's baby, and getting pregnant by an infertile man.

Not quite infertile, as it turned out.

"How do you feel about the fact that I'm the mother?" she asked him.

Her question didn't change his expression much. She got another shrug. "I'm fine with you as the mother," he said, though she couldn't tell if he was being kind, practical or completely honest. "I do find it ironic that I couldn't impregnate my wife, and then manage to successfully plant my seed in a woman who just broke up with me…"

There it was—the truth, out in the open. And he was still kind of grinning.

"Just like I find it ironic that you were in the process of trying to have your deceased husband's child when you found out you were pregnant with mine."

She didn't grin but nodded. She couldn't refute the facts.

"So we go on from here," she said. Nothing had been resolved about their situation, and yet, it felt as though she was no longer frozen in place.

"We go on from here." He'd pushed his plate to the side but didn't reach for her hand. Instead, he folded his hands together on the table in front of him.

A prayer?

A blessing?

A sign that he had no intention of holding hands with her, even in the sense of a friend helping a friend across the street?

She could get to the other side just fine by herself. It was time she took pride in her own abilities.

"I'm not sure how we incôrporate you being a father who lives in LA with the baby not having two bedrooms, two sets of routines, two sets of boundaries…" How could she keep her mind on the future, how could she plan, if she had no end in mind? No final picture to envision?

Shaking his head, he threw up a hand. And she pushed aside what was left of the mammoth salad she'd been delivered.

"I'm not sure, either," he said. "Right now, I'm not sure about anything, in terms of practical planning where all of this is concerned. But I think I can't go to LA. At least not right now. Not while you're pregnant. I need to be here…to help where I can. That's my role, my duty and my right as that baby's father. I want to feel him kicking. To have him hear my voice. I want to carry your groceries when you're so big carrying our child that your back is aching. To do what I can to ease the burdens of everyday chores when pregnancy fatigue hits. Or if you suffer from morning sickness."

He paused, his eyes widening. "I haven't asked… You're almost eight weeks now…have you experienced any discomfort in that area? Nausea and such?"

She hadn't. Was feeling a bit warm…thankful… and simultaneously alarmed, by his invasiveness. "No."

"And if there's a problem, I need to be here, to do what I can to help you get our child through it," he was continuing. "I need to be here when you go into labor. To make the process as smooth for you as I possibly can."

She'd been thinking his fatherhood would start when there was a child in the world to father.

His take was completely different.

And didn't seem unfair. Or wrong. She was already being a mother—in her food choices, her need for rest, her lack of a glass of wine at dinner, wearing protective gear at work when she did her radiological scans. She knew no one would've known the difference or guessed the reason. She was already falling in love with the being inside her body. He had a right to be a father, too.

"What about your job in LA?"

"I'll call tomorrow. Tell them I've had a change of plans."

Shaking her head, she couldn't believe how quickly he was moving—changing his entire career plan.

"So, then what are you going to do?"

"Last I heard they hadn't found anyone for the permanent ED position at Oceanfront. If it's still open, I'll take it." He didn't sound all that concerned about it, though. And figured he probably didn't need to be. Assuming that...

"If the position has been filled, you may have to go back to internal medicine..." If he stayed. Emergency medicine had become a calling for him. That was something she did know.

They'd talked about work all the time.

That golden glint in his green eyes seemed to become luminescent as he met her gaze. "I'm a doctor," he told her. "Medicine completes me. Yes, I fit emergency medicine well. But I was a good internist. I enjoyed the work. And I'd sweep floors if that's what I have to do to be a part of my child's life."

So there was that.

And even more compellingly, she understood. Those years she'd been doing medical technician work while Peter was in medical school, the years she'd put off her own aspirations, she'd still been happy. Peter had spoiled her rotten. And she'd soaked up his adoration.

Delaying her own career goals hadn't become a problem until Peter had wanted to delay them more permanently... That was when he'd quit serving her needs. Had quit spoiling her. And she'd no longer felt adored...

"Where did you go just now?" Greg's odd, softly caring tone brought her back to him. His "bedside manner" was definitely well honed.

With a quick shake of her head, she grabbed her glass of water. Took a sip.

"What about your apartment?" She got them quickly back on track. "You said you gave notice."

"I did."

"You think you can take it back?"

"I know I can't. I've already made arrangements to be out so the next occupant can get in before she starts a new job."

"Do you think she'd be willing to find someplace else? Since she hasn't moved in yet?"

"I've never met the woman, but I don't think so. Her daughter lives in my complex, too, and they want to be close. My unit was the only one available. The leasing agent set it all up." He sounded as though he was only then coming into awareness of the problem. It wasn't as though luxury places were a dime a dozen in Marie Cove.

There were other local places to rent, maybe a beach cottage or something. He could look for a place to buy. But he should have his career situation figured out before making such a big investment. What if he ended up with an ED position in Mission Viejo? That would be close enough for them to work out some kind of commute for school and day care...

None of which was her concern right now.

But...she was supposed to be thinking about *his* needs. Making them an equal in her equation. Not because they were a couple, or even parents, but because that was the course for every relationship she had—work, personal, family...all of them. She'd spent too long in an insular world of coping with her own needs and they'd somehow superseded her awareness of others. Especially those closest to her.

Wood.

Her heart ached every time she thought about the years her brother-in-law had spent tending to her, when he should have been living his own life. The years she'd convinced herself that Wood was happy just living in the same house with her. Because they were family and needed each other.

And…she stared at Greg.

"Wood's suite…it's empty," she said. She and Wood had shared space, details of physical life that would definitely include pregnancy, without any intimate relationship. Elaina had been sleeping with Greg for months and Wood hadn't even known he existed. "Maybe…while we both adjust to a pregnancy neither of us expected or planned for…while you figure out the next steps in your career life…you could…stay there. It's not furnished, though. Wood made all of his furniture and took it with him…"

Was she insane?

Or worse, falling back into her old ways and crafting a way to have Greg step into Wood's shoes? Giving her someone to lean on, to use, while she faced the scary steps of finding her future once again?

"It would give us time to figure out how we co-exist in the real world, rather than in bed or at work. To figure out co-parenting plans. And give you the prenatal time with the baby that you need."

The plan was logical. Practical.

But she didn't have to like the idea quite so much.

"On one hand, it sounds perfect," Greg said, clearly hesitant, even while he didn't immediately negate the option she'd given him.

"And on the other?"

He sighed. Looked out at a room where patrons had come and gone.

She'd never seen such a deadly serious look in his eyes as she did when he trained them back on her. Her stomach knotted and she clutched the napkin in her lap into her fist.

"I cannot consider this option unless it is one hundred percent clear, openly and on the table, that I cannot be in a relationship with you."

Pain sliced through her. The emotional kind that made her suck in her breath and tighten her abdominal muscles against tears that needed release. And in the next breath, she nodded.

Started to think. And to relax.

His not wanting anything personal between them made the plan that much more doable. It also allowed Elaina to safeguard herself against her tendency to lean on a man in her life.

Before she could tell him so, he continued, "I have a history of jumping headfirst and way too soon into relationships with women who need me, or who I feel need me, and everyone ends up getting hurt. This situation is ripe for a history repeat and I just can't make that mistake another time. Especially not with a child involved who would continue to need both of us, even if we got together and then broke because we came together for the wrong reasons." His wry grin made a bit of an exaggeration of his words, brought her heart back out of hiding, and yet…she heard a truth that calmed her, too.

She wasn't the only one who had to fight weaknesses within.

It was nice. Knowing that.

It all made sense. Both of them on the same page. Probably why they'd worked as lovers with no strings attached for so long.

And so, to give back to him what he'd given to her, she said, "Not only do you have nothing to fear on that end, but I am as opposed to the two of us together as you are, for my own equally personal reasons.

"I…can't get into the specifics…but…I can tell you that I have a habit of leaning on men for my own emotional security, without realizing that I'm not meeting their needs."

"You're speaking of Wood."

Her brother-in-law's name sounded foreign on Greg's lips. Making her uncomfortable. As though she could no longer hide away from what she'd unknowingly become. Her gaze lowered, but she made herself look over at him, eye to eye.

"That man sacrificed years of his life to support me after the car accident that killed Peter. He married me, for practical reasons, but I didn't love him in that way. And knowing that, I still allowed him to give up any chance he had to have a loving partnership, so he could give me what *I* needed. I let myself believe this situation made him happy. That I was giving him what he wanted." She paused, teared up, but didn't try to hide that from Greg. "I truly believed it, Greg…"

"Maybe you were."

She shook her head. No. She was not letting herself off the hook again. Life was already too short for her to make up for the years she'd robbed him of. "We had an agreement, that if there ever came a time when our arrangement wasn't working for one or the other of us, we'd tell the other. But he didn't. He'd met the love of his life, was having a baby with her, and was still holding my hand."

"Maybe that was his choice."

"Of course it was his choice. He's a grown man. But if I'd really cared for him as much as he deserves to be loved, rather than just selfishly accepting his support, I'd have seen what I was doing to him. And I didn't."

Probably because she hadn't wanted to.

She'd wanted to hide out in Greg's arms instead.

"It sounds like maybe we're made for each other," Greg said, serious and yet with an odd, quiet smile, as well. "What other woman could I have a baby with and not instantly propose marriage to, except one who is adamantly opposed to making another mistake as I am? One who has her own personal issues to tend to. As I do."

That bedside manner again. Making everything sound like it was going to be okay.

And yet, he was right; in their own flawed ways, they were perfect for each other. Neither would threaten the other's emotional well-being. Their individual weaknesses wouldn't even get the chance to take control of them.

They both had personal battles to fight. And by staying apart, they were able to help each other fight their battles. Separateness put them in the same army.

She liked it.

"So you're going to move into Wood's suite? Just until everything gets figured out?"

"I should take a look at the space, see the rest of the house, and, assuming we both still think it's a good idea, I'd very much like to be there with the baby."

She smiled. Couldn't help it. Just sat there grinning at him.

Solidifying that she would absolutely not be in a relationship with the father of her child shouldn't have made her happy.

But there Elaina was. Unexpectedly, gloriously pregnant. And safely single.

Maybe life really was going to be good again.

Chapter Nine

Greg had done some stupid things in his time. Like staying with Heather even after knowing that she hadn't been pregnant at all. That she'd used a fake pregnancy to try to get her ex-boyfriend jealous. He'd thought, after said boyfriend hadn't cared about her plight, that he'd somehow step in and save the day, take care of her and earn her lifelong love, loyalty and fidelity for having done so.

He hoped to hell he wasn't repeating a different rendition of the same mistake.

On Tuesday, he found his thoughts wandering to Elaina's house. Seeing himself staying there. Admonishing himself to wait until he'd checked out the place before mentally moving in. And then thinking about what of his things would need to go in storage if all he was going to have was a bedroom.

He'd need a unit he could get to regularly, with belongings stored in an easily accessible manner. He could be at Elaina's for months.

What the hell was he doing? Rushing ahead, as usual.

On the other hand—he had to be out of his apartment in less than two weeks. And he had a baby coming.

This was a whole new world. The child was his. Proven scientifically. Biologically his. DNA the same.

He needed to see the space—then decide whether or not he was going to move into it. And he continued on that way for most of that day—one that was relatively slow in terms of emergencies. Not good for his peace of mind, as it left him far too much time for personal contemplation. But good for the population of Marie Cove, which mattered more.

An hour after he'd left the hospital that evening, he was showered, in jeans and a lighter blue short-sleeved pullover, pulling onto the far side of Elaina's driveway. Facing the closed garage door, he made a mental note to ask about programming the automatic opener button in his car. Bluebird, the name he'd given the possession he prized so heavily, needed covered parking.

Even as he had the thought, the garage door

opened and Elaina, in skinny black pants, a white, tapered button-down shirt with lace trim, and black flip-flops with silver embellishment along the straps, came walking out to meet him.

"You know you won't be able to drive a child around in that thing, don't you?" she asked, motioning toward his car.

Glancing at the vehicle, a purchase he took pride and pleasure in, he assessed the situation from her point of view.

Children had to be in car restraints in the back seat until they were eight, and in a rear-facing child restraint seat until they weighed forty pounds or were forty inches in height. He knew this California law because he sometimes had to release children from the ER. Nothing he'd ever given a second thought to when it came to his personal life. On the contrary, he'd purposely wiped all of that kind of thinking out of his mind once his divorce was final.

His back seat wasn't full-size.

"I'll get a new car." Problem solved. But… "Will it be possible for me to program the garage code so that I can park inside?" No matter what vehicle he bought, he'd want covered parking. And judging by the huge and pristine garage that wasn't even half filled with Elaina's vehicle, he figured it should be possible.

She nodded. "As long as you know how to do

it," she said. "Wood programmed mine." And then added, "No, wait. I'll figure it out."

He knew how to do it. But didn't say so. Elaina was one of the smartest, most capable and independent people he'd ever met, but if she needed a boost to her personal power, he certainly wasn't going to stand in her way.

"That's my entrance," she said, pointing toward one of two matching solid doors, as she led him through the other into the kitchen.

The galley kitchen was large enough for two people to work in without running into each other, and also pristinely clean. The cleanliness didn't surprise him—Elaina was a doctor who worked with nuclear materials, so she'd be a stickler.

And so was he.

Not all medical professionals were. But he was glad that she was. Wendy had been more of a free-fall type of decorator. Where it fell, it was free to lie. Not a problem, though. She hadn't minded when he picked up behind her. It used to drive his mother nuts.

His mother—he had to let his folks know that he was going to be a father…but only when he was ready to have his parents descend on him. Still in Nevada, in the small town where he'd grown up an only child, where they both had siblings with grown or nearly grown children, they usually preferred him to come to them, but for a grandchild…

Nevertheless, until he knew what exact role he

was going to be playing in the child's life—and where he was going to live on a permanent basis—best wait to make any announcements.

"I don't use that area much," Elaina was saying as they passed a dining table with seating for six and he could see a step-down living room off to his right. He noted the state-of-the-art entertainment center and a television with a massive screen before she pointed further to the right. "That door there leads into my suite," she said. Off the living room. Around the corner from the kitchen.

She started down the hall off the other end of the dining area. "This is the office," she said, indicating a half-empty room with a computer placed on an organized, oversize wood desk. "You're welcome to move a desk in here if you'd like." She waved toward the vacant portion of the room. "Wood built that partition so we could work without disturbing each other."

He'd never seen someone go to so much trouble to live with someone—and yet stay out of their way.

"This is the guest room," she said, taking him further down the hall. Furnished with a queen-size bed, dresser, nightstands and a small work desk, he figured the room for being as big as the whole living area in his apartment.

And wondered who usually visited the room. "How often is it occupied?" he asked. If he was going to be sharing a hallway—and presumably he was, as she was supposed to lead him to the suite she had available—he should know with whom and how often.

"What?" She glanced over her shoulder at him, saving him from having to work diligently to keep his gaze off the backside outlined so attractively in those tight pants.

"The guest room. How often is it occupied?"

"Oh, never," she said. "At least not in all the years Wood and I have been here."

Never.

A room that size, all decked out, and it wasn't used?

So why have it?.

He kept the question to himself. Barely.

As she pointed out the guest bathroom—presumably to go with the guest bedroom across the hall—a quote from an old movie came to him. A favorite of his father's about building a baseball diamond for a team. The line that stuck with him... "If you build it, they will come"...or some close rendition thereof.

Maybe Elaina didn't want to be as alone as she was.

But then, if that was the case, why *was* she? People flocked to her, as far as he could see at work. And he knew she hung out with some of them after hours sometimes. He'd just never been invited to accompany them.

"And here's your suite," she said, then quickly added, "if you choose to take it."

The room was easily as big as his current living space and bedroom combined, minus the walls that held furniture. He could easily fit his bedroom set along two of the walls. His recliner and an end table would fit in the corner with plenty of room to spare. The entertainment center would need to go into storage; his dressers would take up the remaining free wall space. Half of the third wall was taken up by the double doors leading into an equally large bathroom, with a separate jetted tub and tiled walk-in shower.

The walk-in closet was big for his needs, too. "This whole suite looks freshly painted," he said, telling himself not to like it so much he'd like to own one just like it.

He'd have his house. Sooner than expected, now that he had a child coming.

Just had to take things one step at a time. Figure out the career move, first. And thinking of which… "I talked to administration today and the ED position is still open and still mine if I want it."

"Are you going to take it?"

"I think so, yes." What was there to figure out? He was kidding himself if he thought he was actually going to consider going anywhere but Marie Cove. Not while his child was growing up there.

He couldn't tell whether his answer pleased her or not, or even whether she'd had any reaction at all.

She'd turned to the wall with drapes that went almost to the ceiling, pulled the cord. The sun was setting, and gave him a view of the gorgeous, naturally landscaped backyard with a shed way in the back.

"Are you using that shed?"

"No. It was Wood's. He continued to use it for a while, coming here to do what woodworking he did, but he finally got one built to the side of the house he and Cassie now own together."

Their relationship was a little complicated for him. Wood, her ex-husband, had continued to use the shed at his old house with Elaina, his ex-wife— even after he'd married Cassie? There were so many questions there.

He asked none of them. "So I could use the shed to store the rest of my things? Just while I'm staying here?" He could buy shelves...

"Of course."

Another problem solved.

None of these things, his job, his living arrangements, storage, were major issues. He and the woman he was standing with were bringing their child into the world. They were going to be parenting together.

And he knew so little about her.

And she, him.

"Does Wood know I'll be occupying his suite?" They had to start somewhere.

Leaning against the door frame, she shook her head. "I haven't told him and Cassie that I'm pregnant yet, and they'd need to know that to understand why you have to be here. But it's not his anymore. I bought the house from him when he and Cassie got married."

She looked relaxed, leaning there, even with her long dark ponytail as pristine as her house. He missed seeing her hair down.

Around him.

Not a place he could go. Absolutely not, if he accepted her invitation to live there.

And he had to do that. He couldn't lose the chance to be around his unborn child. To feel the baby move. Or be there if something went wrong...

He glanced around, picturing his furniture in the empty space. Seeing himself living there. Wanting to live there.

And still needing to know more.

"You do plan to tell Wood and his new wife about the baby, then?" What was he walking into?

"Of course. They're my family."

And about that...

"Have you told your parents?" She'd never mentioned them but had never asked about his, either. Had she even considered that her baby was going to have two sets of grandparents?

Of course, until the day before, they hadn't even known if the baby was his.

There he was, rushing into things again. Wanting it all done at once.

Elaina straightened then, arms crossed, leaned against the doorjamb again. "My parents are dead, Greg. I thought you knew that."

His heart stilled. And ached, too. "I'm so sorry. I...how would I have known that?" How couldn't he have known that? He'd been sleeping with her, exclusively, for more than a year, longer than any lover other than his ex-wife, and he didn't know she was an orphan?

"What happened? How long ago?"

"They were killed in a car accident when I was in college. My sophomore year. I was an only child and already dating Peter then, and he was wonderful to me. He and Wood...they took me into their home, their family, as though I'd always been a part of their world..."

Everything slowed. His thoughts. The air pulling into his lungs. The vacant room seemed too full. "Did you say...Wood?" He homed in on the one thing that he could grasp.

She nodded. "He was Peter's older brother. Their dad died when Peter was little, and then, when Wood was seventeen, their mom died, so Wood quit school to take care of Peter. He even put him through medical school."

She'd lost her parents in a car accident. And then lost her first husband the same way? The fact that the woman was standing there, owner of her own home, planning a life for herself...spoke volumes to him. She was a survivor. One who didn't give up. No matter what the cost.

And... "You married your husband's older brother." It was all coming at him so fast. He was both fascinated and horrified, feeling the need to get out of there and also wrap his arms around her, hold her and never let go.

She met his gaze, held it for what seemed like forever. He held hers, too. It was all the touching they could do. They weren't lovers anymore. And couldn't be anything else. Still, Greg had to know who she was, this woman he'd taken to his bed for so many months, and who was going to have his child.

"It was Wood's idea," she said, sounding as though she had to reassure him of that point. He wasn't sure why. "And we were never intimate—just emotionally connected. But I should have realized what it was going to cost him."

"Cost him?" He'd gotten Elaina. There was no price to be put on that...

"He'd given up so much of his life to raise Peter, to see his brother through medical school. And just when he was about to get his own chance to make a life for himself, there I was, needing him, and he started all over again with me."

Greg considered the man lucky. To have had Elaina needing him...

Forcing himself to focus on what she was trying to get him to see, he asked, "How did marrying you equate to raising a little brother and seeing him through school?"

"I was just starting medical school. He was my support system."

"What about insurance? Surely with the accident…"

"The driver wasn't insured. At least not enough to make a difference. And Peter only had the mini-mum underinsured policy."

"And he didn't have life insurance?"

She shook her head. "And I was on his health in-surance plan, which was only going to be good for another thirty days. By marrying Wood, I was able to get my hospital stay and treatments, on his insurance. Without that, I don't know what I would have done."

He frowned. It was like she was trying to get him to see someone else. As though she saw herself as weaker than the woman he knew her to be. If the plan were the only reason to marry, she would have purchased her own policy. Gone on a short-term in-terim plan. She was still holding his gaze. As though telling him things her mouth wasn't saying.

Was it about what she'd said the night before? About her leaning on men? Was the independent woman he knew only a small part of the person she was? Was that what she wanted him to believe? Be-cause he didn't see it. At work the woman had shoul-ders the size of a mountain. She took it all on.

"I sure wouldn't have been able to start my classes on schedule and then would have had to reapply to med school," she said. "And who knows if, by then, I'd have done so. Or made it in if I had. And yet… that wasn't Wood's problem."

"If he loved you, it was."

She nodded. And then said, "I loved him, too. He was my brother—still is. He was the only family I had left. I leaned too hard."

"You were his only family, too, then, right?"

She shrugged again. Nodded.

Something else was nagging at him. "You said you wouldn't have made it to school without insurance— and that was why you married Wood, so he could take care of you?"

He knew she'd been in the car when Peter had died. A nuclear med tech had mentioned it along the way, but when more information would have been forthcoming, he'd shut it down, figuring Elaina would tell him what she wanted him to know.

With his own truths to keep to himself, he had to respect the rights of others to do the same.

"You've seen the scars," she said. The allusion to him having her naked in his bed shot straight to his groin. Yes, he'd seen the silver lines along her lower spine. And the ones on her abdomen. He'd never asked much about them. She'd said only that they were from the car accident, had asked if they bothered him.

They hadn't. At all. He'd spent quite a lot of time

showing her how very much they didn't bother him, as he recalled.

When what he should maybe have done was ask her how much they bothered her.

"I knew you were hurt. I assumed you had stitches. Bruising. Maybe a surgery if there'd been internal damage. But…none of that would have prevented you from going to medical school."

"I…couldn't walk."

"What?" Greg was shocked. He strode toward her, not sure what he was going to do when he got there, but when he saw the blank look that came over her face as he reached for her, he stopped about a foot from her, his arms dropping to his sides.

"You couldn't walk…" he said. Years of medical training caused all kinds of horror scenarios to play in his mind, scaring him. Dealing with images of Elaina gravely injured was beyond anything his training had taught him. And he had to remind himself that she was fine. Standing right in front of him, healthy and perfect.

And pregnant with his child.

"I was paralyzed," she said, as though telling him she'd lost a tooth. "For a while there they thought it was permanent, but with surgeries and Wood's constant care, and a minor miracle or two thrown in, I recovered."

She made it sound like she'd managed to make a good dinner when she didn't know how to cook.

"You recovered," he said. He knew about spinal cord injuries. "You had to have gone through pure hell," he said. "Learning to walk again…and the pain…it had to have taken months of constant work…"

And more strength than he figured he possessed.

"Wood was there," she said.

And he was beginning to understand a bit more. At least he thought he was. Hoped he was. "You were all the family he had left."

Pressing her lips together, she nodded.

"He'd lost his parents, just as you had. You'd both lost Peter…"

She didn't say a word. Just kept standing there, as though awaiting a sentence to be passed upon her.

As though she didn't see her incredible strength. Her endurance. As though taking for granted those things that made her so incredibly unique and wonderful.

"You may have leaned on Wood, as you say," he told her, "but it was a reasonable choice, Elaina."

"Reasonable to take my recovery, my happiness, at his expense? And then to allow it to go on for years?"

"Or maybe you gave him something to hold on to while he recovered from his own grief. Maybe you gave him a reason to keep going."

Her shrug, then, was a little slower. A little less self-deprecating.

And he was glad.

Chapter Ten

There were other things Greg was going to have to know. Despite them having shared some important memories with one another, Elaina knew they were virtual strangers responsible for the physical health, emotional health and happiness of a new person on the earth. Still hardly able to wrap her mind around it all—seemingly so different from her original plan to raise a child on her own—she led Greg back out to the kitchen, through the French doors and out to the backyard. He'd been there once before, but hadn't had a chance to explore it.

The air was a little cool as the sun set, but felt nice.

"This is something else," he said, looking impressed as he glanced around the yard, headed over to the built-in barbecue by the pool, and on to the kiva fireplace close by. Dropping down to one of the padded wrought iron chairs by the fireplace, as if to try the experience on for size, he asked, "Does this work?"

With a flip of a switch in the wall of the barbecue, she turned on the flame, sat down opposite him. Wood had built the barbecue, fireplace, pavers and all, because she'd asked for them. And she could count on one hand the times they'd sat out there together. She should have invited him out to do that more.

It just hadn't occurred to her. She'd figured he'd come out if he wanted to. Because she'd been so deeply into her own world that she hadn't even thought to ask about his.

"What about you?" she asked Greg, forcing herself out of her own head. Thinking about him. "Do you have family who need to know about the baby?" She blinked, shivered, lifted her hands to the warmth of the fire. Or... "Do they already know?"

What family did he have? Biological family to the child she couldn't even feel moving inside her yet.

"My parents are in Nevada," he told her, sitting back, an ankle across his knee, seemingly content to hang out. "Both retired. Dad was a plumber. Mom worked in Human Resources for the local school district. No siblings. Five sets of aunts and uncles, all but one younger than my parents. A slew of cousins, but none that close to my age. We all lived in a town of about ten thousand people and yet I mostly only saw my cousins at holiday get-togethers. And you might as well know... I was the quintessential small-town nerd. Not one of the popular guys. Truth be told, I think my younger cousins, two of whom were cheerleaders, were kind of embarrassed to have people know they were related to me."

At first she thought he was kidding. No way could Greg Adams have been unpopular. Nurses all over the hospital practically drooled when he walked into a room now. They tripped over themselves to beat each other to tend to his needs—medically speaking, of course.

But he wasn't smiling. Nor was he frowning, really. He seemed at peace with his past. Maybe even fond of it.

She liked that about him.

And...on to the tense stuff... "Do they know about the baby?"

"Do you *see* them on the doorstep?" He grinned with that one.

She shook her head and he grew serious. "I won't tell them without you and I deciding together that it's time," he told her. "And certainly not before we get our immediate situation worked out."

His words brought a wave of alarm. That made no sense. "It's not worked out?" she asked, upset to know that. "You don't want the suite?"

Maybe she should offer him something to drink. Make him feel more welcome to a potential home instead of letting him feel like he was on trial.

"I want it," he said quickly, and her muscles relaxed a bit. "Hell, I'm already mentally moved in. But that's only the beginning. Where do we go from there? We'll want a pretty firm plan before we bring my mother into the picture. She's going to have questions, and she'll want answers."

He wasn't kidding but didn't seem to be complaining, either. She liked that about him. Even more than she'd lusted after his gorgeous body all those months.

"So, just to be clear, you're going to move in."

"Yes. And I intend to pay rent, too, so I'll need you to come up with an amount."

She hadn't expected him to offer that. In fact, she was about to argue the fact when she realized he was right to make that part of their agreement. She named an amount that was less than what she knew a neighbor was charging for an adult child to live at home but was still not dirt cheap; she said it included utilities, and wasn't surprised when he just nodded, agreeing automatically.

And just like that, she apparently had a new tenant.

"When were you thinking you'd move in?" she asked, a little bit scared at how fast things were progressing. And a little bit excited, too.

Her life really was moving forward. She wasn't

sure she was ready, not that she had any choice in the matter with a baby growing inside her, but she was certain about not wanting to be stagnant anymore.

"I'm off tomorrow," he said. "I'd like to get started then. I already have a lot of things packed. I had a mover lined up for later in the month, to get me to LA. I can arrange with the company to make that a local move. But I'd like to get shelves in the shed, first."

He really did rush right in. In her world of dragging her feet and letting things ride, that adrenaline wasn't a bad thing. Feeling almost...invigorated—a sensation so foreign to her current life she'd almost forgotten what it felt like—she tried to slow herself down.

To focus on the one thing in front of her as she'd taught herself to do, so that the periphery didn't crowd the air out of her lungs.

The one thing. First, her focus had been grieving for her parents. Then Peter. Falling in love. The wedding. Getting him through medical school. Grieving again. Marrying Wood. Learning to walk again. Medical school. Wood leaving. The baby.

The baby. That was the one thing. Except...here was Greg. A person. With feelings. Who made her feel things. Moving in. Temporarily of course, but he wanted to put shelves in the "shed."

"It's not a shed," she said. "It's a workshop." The designation mattered. Wood had found his own survival out in that building. She'd finally figured that out when she'd brought lunch out to him one afternoon and saw how lovingly he was working on Alan's crib. That day had been a no-turning-back moment for her. She'd seen what she'd unwittingly been doing to him. Holding him captive in a life that was going nowhere. Because she'd felt safe there. Content to go nowhere.

"There's already a full wall of shelves. And a built-in workbench. There are drawers from floor to ceiling on one end, full electric..." Her heart cried a little as she thought of the years that Wood had given to her. And knew she couldn't allow herself to use the man seated with her. Wood meant so much to her. And Greg...he was waking things in her...and in so doing, meant more to her than anyone else in her life.

"Would you rather I not use it?"

"Of course I want you to use it!" she said. "I just... want you to be careful, Greg. Don't let me suck you in..."

His grin took some of the sting from her thoughts. "You keep defending your independence as you do and I won't get sucked in," he promised her. "Seriously, Elaina, I feel good about this. We're two intelligent, aware adults who've learned from our mistakes and are heading into an exciting adventure. One that will probably be one of the most remarkable of our lives. Instead of saving lives, we're creating one."

Yes. That comment made her feel more whole than she had since her parents had been killed. As though she had a full life. As much to offer, and to do, as anyone.

And as much accountability as anyone, too. No more letting her get away with things because of all she'd suffered. All she'd been through. No more allowing herself to accept pats on the head instead of kicks in the butt. She was a survivor. Not a victim. And owed society as much as anyone else...

Shivering again, she leaned closer to the fire. And then started to sweat when he asked, "You planning to tell Wood that I'm moving in before I actually do so?"

Greg's question put her back on the hot seat.

She hadn't been on one for so long she wasn't sure how to stay put there. But she knew she must. For the baby's sake.

"You haven't given me much time if you're planning to start the move tomorrow."

"I was going to buy shelves. Now I think I'll just look at the workshop and finish up packing tomorrow. Maybe bring over canned goods and perishables from the kitchen—"

Completely inappropriately, Elaina felt a bit of fire shoot between her legs at his comment, as if mingling their kitchen goods would be akin to how they'd mingled their bodies that had produced the baby that was now mingling them together. She'd shared food with Wood—shopping lists even—for years and never once felt that.

"Yes." She said it abruptly, stopping him mid-stream. "I would like time to speak with Wood and Cassie before you move in. And...maybe you should meet them, too. They're my family. They're going to be hugely involved in this baby's life. And Alan. He and this baby will grow up close, being cousins and all..."

She stopped, realizing that she'd segued to the old plan—where Alan was supposed to be biologically related to the baby she was carrying. Through Peter's sperm.

"I'd be happy to meet them," Greg said. Whether he'd realized her misfire or not, he bridged the gap for her between what she'd planned and what was. At least in that moment. Between the two of them.

She nodded. Assimilating. Trying to catch up with movement in a life that had been stagnant for so long.

There was so much she hadn't realized, hadn't considered, while she'd floated nowhere, personally speaking, at least.

"You think he's going to have a problem with me moving in?" Greg asked, squinting at her over the fire as darkness had begun falling around them. Cloaking them in an intimacy that she didn't find distasteful.

And yet, that closeness threatened everything that

had kept her going for so long, the peaceful nothing-
ness that had become her private life.

He was making her uncomfortable. All of the sudden need to share themselves with each other...and
yet, she didn't want him to leave, either. The fire
was...nice. Comforting. And setting a mood that
could have been romantic had the two of them still
been involved that way.

He was suddenly her biggest danger. And he was
her safest place, too.

When he wasn't supposed to be anything to her
except the father of the child they were going to raise
together.

Somehow.

"Truthfully, I think Wood might be relieved to
have you around," Elaina told Greg what she truly
believed. No platitudes, or niceties.

No more hiding. If she could help it.

Greg burst out in a half chuckle, half cough that
made her frown. "What?" she asked.

"Maybe you don't know as much about men as I
thought you did. The man's your ex-husband. Still
firmly in your life. Clearly he feels some ownership
over you..."

She shook her head. "You don't know Wood.
Family truly is everything to him. More than money,
career...he works to provide for his family, because
the only thing that really completes him is caring

for his family." She needed him to understand. To be okay with Wood in their lives.

"He thinks you're getting ready to have his brother's child."

"He was against that from the beginning," she said with a shrug. "Cassie understood, but Wood thought that I was holding myself back by using Peter's sperm. What he really wanted was for me to wait to fall in love and get married, but when he realized how serious I was about finding love within myself and sharing it outward, not sucking love inward, he thought I should use an anonymous donor."

She'd been the one who'd been adamant about having Peter's child. As though justice could be served...

That option was out of her hands now. The challenge ahead of her was the biggest she was ever going to face. To get to know Greg Adams and not get involved with him, to avoid leaning on him or letting herself become dependent upon him. That was particularly difficult because some of the emotions she felt around him were more compelling than anything she'd ever known.

And the second, but most important part of that, was to bring Greg's child into the world and shower it with the unconditional love she'd been soaking up for so many years.

She had some doubts where the first part was

concerned, but the second, she was all over that one. And ready to get on with it.

Wood thinks Elaina should use an anonymous donor. Sitting at the firepit the man had built, contemplating moving into the home Wood had initially purchased, sleeping in the room he'd slept in—even storing his things in the workshop her ex-husband had built—Greg had to wonder if he wasn't falling more deeply into his own trap than ever before.

Practically speaking, the plan made sense. He had no immediate place to live. He wasn't ready to buy a home until he knew more specifically what his life was going to look like, and he didn't know what kind of space he was going to need or want.

Would he have a child staying with him if he moved out? Need a room for it? Or would he just be visiting Elaina's house?

In which case, having lived in that home himself would make him feel more like part of his child's family.

Staying with Elaina gave him the chance not only to get to know her, to plan with her, but to be present as his baby developed.

He couldn't imagine having been married to Elaina himself and then being happy to have another man move into the life he'd shared with her. He was secretly glad to hear Wood had moved on and was happily married with a family of his own, but couldn't imagine the man wanting him around.

"You really think Wood will be relieved that I'm here?" he asked.

"I'd bet money on it."

Greg would bet money that he should proceed with extreme self-care and observation. He'd already played the second-best fiddle. Been the guy the girl settled for. He'd jumped in with Heather without seeing how deep the water actually was—or how dirty.

With Wendy, he'd jumped in the same exact way.

And here he was, flying off the cliff into unknown waters a third time. Except that this time he knew what he was flying toward. And for whom. His child.

"You wait, he'll be taking you on, too," Elaina was saying. "Any need he knows you have, he'll be there trying to help if he can. In his unassuming, stay-out-of-the-way manner."

She was smiling—a full-out, eyes-glistening-in-the-firelight, hit-him-in-the-gut kind of smile.

While she talked about another man. So...he knew what he was going to do. And what he wasn't going to do, too. And he needed his eyes wide-open to make it happen.

"You sure you're not still in love with him?" The man had been her husband. Yes, she'd married him under extreme circumstances and for practical purposes, but sometimes love grew out of those kinds of situations.

And if Elaina did still have feelings for Wood, all the better for Greg himself. Less chance of him forgetting himself in a weak moment. Less need to guard against those moments.

"I do love him—as a family member. So much. But I was never *in* love with him."

"Because you loved his brother."

"That," she said, cocking her head slightly as she shrugged. "And... Wood has always been a brother to me. He's a hunk, don't get me wrong. Women have been flocking around him ever since I've known him. He just...doesn't do it for me...in that way."

He felt sorry for the guy. Deeply sorry.

And gratified for himself.

Not sure what kind of man that made him, he said, "Yet you lived together as husband and wife. At least for a time."

He couldn't imagine sleeping with someone he wasn't sexually attracted to.

When Elaina shook her head, he was suddenly sitting up at attention. "My marriage to Wood was never consummated."

At first Greg wasn't sure he'd heard her right. Took a second to give himself a mental instant replay. And then another to quit high-fiving himself.

There was nothing to celebrate in her news. He hadn't just been elevated up a step in the rankings.

Nothing had changed. The facts were still their

facts. But in a way he couldn't yet define, those seven words had changed everything.

Greg no longer had a living, breathing man keeping him from Elaina.

His only deterrents were a ghost and his own desire to avoid emotional complications.

Greg was sure that Peter's memory would linger forever.

He was not going to make more of their association than was there. Was not going to rush to find something that didn't exist. Or to make it exist.

His child's best chance at a happy future depended on it.

And Elaina was depending on him to keep his distance, too.

Chapter Eleven

Elaina wasn't unhappy when Greg decided it was time for him to go home. Sitting there talking to him about her lack of sex with Wood, about not being turned on…when he knew more than most exactly what did turn her on, in detail…wasn't the way for them to proceed successfully on their quest to a healthy future for all of them.

He couldn't just be her no-strings-attached lover anymore.

And she couldn't take him to her bed in any other capacity. Too much inside of her prevented that choice.

Still, she couldn't help realizing, as she walked him back through the house toward the garage door, that it was easier having him leave knowing that he was coming back.

To stay.

"I was thinking about getting a dog," she blurted when his backside in those tight jeans got her again. When would she learn to quit looking?

Or at least quit getting herself in positions where she was walking behind him?

"What do you think about dogs?" she continued, focusing on his shoulders and finding them equally distracting. She knew the strength in them as they held her full weight up against the wall of his bedroom as he'd...

No. She couldn't erase the memory. Or the fact that she'd enjoyed the mind-blowing sex she'd had with Greg Adams, but she could most certainly control her thoughts about it.

She was a grown woman. Not a pubescent kid.

"I like dogs." He'd turned, his hand on the doorknob, and she'd been so busy not looking at him she'd almost run into him. Was so close she could practically see the whiskers on his chin move as he spoke.

"I...was thinking about getting a rescue..." she said, taking too long to take a step back.

"With two of us living here, it might be a good time to do so," he said, seemingly completely unaware of how close she was to leaning forward to kiss him goodbye.

And she stepped back. Firmly. "I've narrowed the choice down to eight," she told him.

His brows drew together in that way of his that meant he was interested. "How many did you start with?"

"Eight."

Even his chuckle turned her on. Time for a bubble bath, some peaceful music and bed. Right after she made a call to Cassie and Wood to tell them about the baby and the change in her living situation.

The thought, like a glass of cold water splashed on hot skin, got her back on track just as Greg turned back from the door one more time.

"Dr. Miller mentioned that you've got an appointment next Friday. I'm assuming that includes getting to see the first sonogram?"

The picture produced by an ultrasound...

"It does."

"I'd like to be there."

She'd figured as much. But appreciated that he was talking to her about it. Not just showing up or assuming.

She told him the time but didn't suggest they ride together. Didn't want them to ride together.

She'd be coming from work, and didn't know where he'd be driving from.

It wasn't like she was privy to his schedule.

Though...maybe, with possibly adopting and training a dog and all, they should keep each other apprised. She thought about what it might be like, them knowing each other's whereabouts all the time. Maybe cooking for each other now and then. Eating together.

When he opened the door to leave, she was about to ask him what he thought about sharing grocery bills, when what she wanted was to share something far more intimate. But he headed out to his car, and she thought it better just to get him out of there until she had time to think things through.

It had been a couple of long, emotional days. And weeks.

All she needed was a good night's sleep.

And to remember why she'd broken up with Greg Adams to begin with.

Yeah, she knew she'd enjoy having sex with him again. Very much. She'd missed having those hours in his arms.

But if she gave in to her body's desires, she'd want more, and would eventually probably talk herself into allowing that intimacy regularly, which, along with living together, would mean they were a couple, and she'd be right back where she'd always been. Leaning. Not standing.

She wasn't going to do that to herself, to Greg or to their child.

When Elaina called just after ten the next morning, to ask Greg if he'd mind meeting her for lunch, he was ready to jump in the car and go. But then she told him where she wanted to meet: a law office.

He didn't like the sound of that.

And when he thought about his first reaction, just running off to eagerly do her bidding at her first invitation, he didn't like that much, either.

By the time she'd gotten to her third sentence, letting him know that they were having lunch together in the conference room of Cassie's law office so that everyone could meet before he officially moved in, and to sign a leasing agreement that Cassie thought they should have for the protection of both of them, he had calmed down. Logical. And, he figured himself a semblance of the highly respected professional he was, as he asked the time and address.

So he'd been a little reactive at first. Big things happening in his life.

The man who'd been in a slowly gestating state of mourning over the fact that he couldn't have kids had just found out he was going to be a father.

The mind switch took some getting used to.

He dressed with care. In dark pants, a light short-sleeved shirt and tie, shined shoes, shaved face and hair combed as well as kind of longish natural curl could be, he presented himself to the receptionist at the address he'd been given—an impressive building with privately leased office suites—at the exact time Elaina had mentioned.

Apparently, lunch was being catered—not for

him, but because it happened regularly at Cassie's office—but he was fine to not eat. He wanted the meeting with Elaina's Wood over with.

She'd never even told him what her ex did for a living.

And he'd never asked.

Though he was glad to know that the other man wasn't the competition he'd originally thought he was, it only took one second in the same room with Elaina and Wood for Greg to know what white-hot jealousy felt like.

It was like nothing he'd ever experienced before, that was for sure.

He didn't want to scratch the other man's eyes out. Or smash his face, either. Instead, he stood there, full of envy, knowing that what he wanted more than anything in the world was what Wood already had.

He wanted the Elaina that Wood saw when he spoke in that teasing and knowing tone of voice, wanted to be privy to their life experiences, to understand the pains that, while unspoken, were evident in the looks, the things not being said, the words between the lines.

And he got all of that in "Wood, this is Greg..."

And Wood's standing there in a dusty shirt, mussed hair and blue jeans, handing a baby to a beautiful blonde woman who handed it off to Elaina's wide-open, waiting arms.

"Elaina hasn't told us enough about you, but I'm

glad we finally meet," Wood said, his voice deep, confident and quiet. "I presume you're the doctor she was having lunches with in the cafeteria…"

He hoped to God he was the one.

Wood had known about him?

"Wood saw us together once when he came to see me at work," Elaina said, half over her shoulder, as she crooned to the baby, rocking him slowly, nuzzling his neck.

Already more of a parent than he knew how to be. He'd probably be all businesslike and make the little one cry.

"Like Wood, I'm glad to finally meet you," Cassie said, extending her hand. "And if there's anything you need…you let us know."

He nodded. Hoped he made responses that sounded as appropriate as he thought they did. And couldn't wait to get out of there before he started wanting things he couldn't have.

Before he started spinning visions of himself as a part of their obviously close little family. Fitting in. Helping them, too, anywhere he could.

And forgot that he wasn't jumping in anymore.

Because when he didn't look before he leaped, inevitably, people got hurt.

Because this time, he couldn't afford to rush after what he thought he wanted.

Glancing at Elaina's belly, he knew that everything had changed.

He didn't need to rush. Or push.

He already had what he most wanted. And it was going to be another seven months before he got to do much more than stand on the sidelines and wait.

The lunch meeting with Cassie and Wood was all civilized and positive, as their response had been when she stopped for coffee early that morning, didn't have coffee, and told them she was pregnant. They were so supportive, excited, a tad bit worried about her unusual situation, afraid she'd be hurt and had Elaina yearning for a perfect world. She wanted to believe everyone was deeply happy, feeling real affection, not just surface politeness. Wanted to know that it would last forever. The four adults, baby Alan and the little one she and Greg were adding to the mix.

She and Greg signed a lease agreement. There'd been a second there when Cassie had asked for an end date, but when she'd quickly offered to leave it open-ended, with either party able to terminate the lease with one month's written notice, everyone relaxed again. Chatted.

When there was so much not being said.

No one mentioned Peter. Or the fact that her baby would now not be biologically related to Wood or sweet baby Alan.

The fact that that still mattered to her shook her

a bit. Like she didn't believe Wood and Cassie and Alan were family without the biology?

It had all just been so neat and clean—her plan to atone for her part in Peter's death, something no one knew about. And to become a legitimate part of the only family she had left in the world.

As she went through the next couple of days, the next week, she alternated between feeling more alive than she had in…memory. And struggling not to shut herself off from the world again. To love from afar.

She'd hurt people. What if she hurt Greg? Or the baby?

And she didn't feel worthy of the happiness that was starting to infiltrate little parts of her day…to hang there in a tantalizing little wisp of hope as she opened her eyes each morning. She was afraid to grasp it. Couldn't bear the thought of reaching for it and having it snatched away.

And yet there it was, dogging her steps, daring her to take the chance.

Greg had moved in while she was at work. She'd left an empty garage and returned to find his car there and the door at the end of the hall shut. He'd had the day off.

She'd come home to find a magnetic notepad on the refrigerator, though, and her cupboards stuffed with more food than she'd had in them since Wood left. A note on the pad told her he'd meet her at the ultrasound.

And also had a curious message… "#2." She pondered that on and off for the next couple of days, smiling at how the man seemed to occupy mind space even when he wasn't around. He was doing a couple of night rotations.

She'd had an email from him at work, a response to the most recent scan she'd done on Brooklyn. This was the third week in a row in which the hospital had administered a dose of medicine, instructing its staff and her mother to not give the little girl another dose at home. And the scans were showing the same healthy results. Different from Brooklyn's other scans. When they knew for sure Brooklyn received her medication in the hospital, she was a much happier and emotionally stable child with no stomach issues. When they couldn't prove that she'd received it at home, she struggled.

The next step would be something that Brooklyn's pediatrician and Social Services would determine. Her job was to step away. To accept ultimately not knowing, and having no control over, the end result.

Up until Brooklyn's case, she'd been thankful for that aspect of what she did. Being able to help where she could, offer all of the compassion in her heart, and then…withdrawing.

As she drove to the ultrasound on Friday, she started to see a common theme in her life.

Withdrawal.

Since her parents died, she'd been doing enough to live life, but always taking baby steps backward.

The realization disturbed her. Disappointed her.

Was she wasting the life her parents had given her?

Telling herself the only baby steps she wanted in her life now were the ones the little human being growing inside her would learn to take, she parked and looked for Greg's shiny blue car, spotting it in the far back of the lot.

As though he'd been watching for her, he got out just as she pulled in, and was approaching her car by the time she was out of it. She had to stand there and wait. It was the polite thing to do.

He looked so incredibly good, familiar and sexy and…solid, in his jeans and short-sleeved pullover shirt. Enjoying the sight was a natural part of being alive.

As was the smile on her face as she walked toward him.

She liked him. Had always liked him. There was nothing wrong with that.

"You ready for this?" he asked as he reached her side and they walked toward the door.

Elaina wasn't sure she was ready for anything.

But she wasn't withdrawing from it, either.

She had a baby to live for.

Chapter Twelve

Elaina was a good patient, Greg noted as he stood to the side, watching as she followed the technician's instructions, sliding up on the table, lifting her shirt, lowering her waistband. A lot of doctors weren't good patients—himself included.

The fact that Elaina was didn't surprise him. She was kind and gracious and good at everything she set out to do, from what he could see.

Her home—*their* home, at least for now—wasn't just clean, it also smelled fresh. Good. Like a spring day, not like the antiseptic that greeted him at his office door each day. And the decor, while understated, was warm. Welcoming. Every single piece, from a small collection of decorative angels in various mediums set up on a china hutch, to a painted wooden sign with floral design and words that proclaimed that family lived there, seemed deliberately chosen to embody peace and love. Even the colors, soft oranges, reds, golds, wrapped him in a feeling of acceptance.

Of belonging to something good.

All of which he thought about to distract himself from the sight of smooth skin that he knew tasted slightly salty with a hint of sweet and a belly button he'd slid his tongue into more times than he could count. He got hard just thinking about how putting his tongue there made her hips squirm.

Less than a minute in the room and his penis was standing at attention. In a pair of jeans. Pulling the edge of his shirt as low as it would go, he looked around at the instruments in the room, the monitor. The camera that the technician held. The gel she was squeezing onto Elaina's belly.

And, God help him, thought about the gel Elaina had used to massage him right where he ached at the moment.

He could hear the technician telling them what she'd be doing, was doing, pointing to the monitor, and he had to wonder if she'd checked Elaina's chart and if she knew that she was talking to a radiologist and an MD.

The woman lowered her camera to the gel on Elaina's belly, sliding it around, and suddenly, Greg had no focus at all except the monitor, assessing every single shape of shadow and light. Noting at once that all of the formations were exactly as they should be. After that first bit of confirmation, he glanced at Elaina, meaning to get right back to the screen he was studying, but he couldn't look away from the slight flush on Elaina's cheeks, the uplifted tilt of lips that were trembling, and the glisten in her eyes.

She'd never been more beautiful to him.

And more inaccessible, either.

"I know it's silly, but I'm going to make it my text message notification sound. I'm calling it my heartbeat song." Phone in hand, tapping and thumb-typing, Elaina walked with Greg through the parking lot toward her car, frenetic, needing to pee and unable to slow down. She had to get back to work. But she just couldn't stop listening to the steady rhythm that she and Greg had just heard moments before. One he'd thankfully recorded on his phone and had already sent to her.

She had a heart, other than her own, beating inside of her.

She felt combustible. Ready to explode. With joy. Fear. Awe. Disbelief. She just couldn't come down from that high.

They had photo scans, too. Pictures she could read like a book.

An incredible, perfect, beautiful book.

Grabbing the strip of photos out of the satchel on her shoulder, she held them up, a long string of still shots. "Crazy how these seem to be entirely different from every imaging shot I've ever taken," she said, and then gave them to him. "You want to take them back to the house?" And before giving him a chance to respond, said, "No, wait, I'll keep them here, in my satchel."

She went back to dealing with her phone. Her fingers fumbling as she tried to type. She had her own "Heartbeat Song." There was no going back. No slowing down.

She didn't want to go back or slow down, either.

"It was something, huh?" Greg asked as she reached her car and he didn't branch off to his.

Glancing up from her phone, meeting his gaze for the first time since she'd entered the ultrasound room, she had a reply ready on her lips. It froze. And then evaporated. That golden glint in his eyes... would their baby have it, too?

"Yeah, it was something." She managed to echo his statement back at him. In lieu of the plethora of feelings zooming through her.

Holding her gaze, he nodded. And it was as if he knew what she wasn't saying.

Because he wasn't saying it, either.

They'd walked out side by side. He was right there. Close enough that she could smell his musky scent—a mixture of soap and deodorant—and as their eyes met, she knew what was going to happen.

Their bodies were having a physical conversation of their own. That half-slumberous look in his eye, the way he was studying her lips, and the way her tongue immediately popped out and wet them as she started to lean in. To breathe a huge sigh at the thought of relief from the emotions coursing through her.

Then he stepped back. Blinking. And the man who stared back at her was closed off. A doctor at a bedside. A committee member heading up a table of professionals.

A man who saved lives for a living.

One who'd just saved her from herself.

And she had to be grateful.

No matter how many laps he swam in the pool in the dark and the chill, Greg couldn't get the heat out of his body. A baby was on the way. He'd heard the heartbeat every day for the past three days. Replaying it over and over. And he needed his family in order. Needed to provide.

To *do*.

He'd never been a sit-around-and-wait type of guy. He was always the one who studied puzzles and found the solutions.

But the solution to the puzzle before him seemed to be nonexistent. How did he and Elaina go from being lovers to parents without anything personal growing between them?

How did he learn things about her, become a part of her life, without getting involved?

And yet, for the sake of his child, he had to stay free and clear from anything that could turn bad. And every single time he'd been involved with a woman, it had eventually gone wrong. The sex stuff, he was great at.

More than that...he seemed to have trouble distinguishing between love and lust. Need and want. Forever and for now.

Or, more accurately, he tried to create forever, need and love out of lust, want and for now. And let himself get used up in the process.

And when something like that ended, it didn't leave the type of atmosphere where one could give a child a secure, happy, loving life.

He'd lost count of the number of times he'd swum the length of the pool, something he'd done each of the three nights since the day he'd heard his child's heartbeat. He would get off work at midnight, drive to his parking place in Elaina's garage, avoid looking at the door that led into her suite where she'd told him she'd stay, leaving him the house when he got home, and, instead of showering, opt for a cold swim. After a twelve-hour shift in the ED, he was still thrumming with adrenaline.

But the excess energy wasn't all due to work.

He was adjusting to a life that had drastically changed course. He had his plan. Just had to get through the twists and turns he hadn't foreseen, and those he had, too, to end up where he needed to be in his life.

Dragging himself out of the pool when he figured he'd done enough to acquire a need for sleep—and the ability to get there—Greg wrapped the towel he'd brought out with him around his waist and let himself quietly back inside the dining room door.

He was surprised to see Elaina standing in front of the mounted microwave. She didn't say anything, as though maybe she thought he wouldn't notice her.

Fat chance of that. He could smell that she'd walked through the kitchen hours after she'd been there. Heard her walk through the living room to the kitchen every single morning—with his door shut and white noise ocean sounds playing from his smart speaker.

Unlike him with his rotations, she worked a semi-regular shift. Regular in that she had the same hours every week—semi in that she picked up a lot of extras and adjusted for weekend duty twice a month. She had to be at work early in the morning. And was still in the critical three-month miscarriage portion of her pregnancy. He worried about her overdoing, though, medically, he knew that her working should pose no danger.

"You okay?" he asked, glad for the darkness that

kept his suddenly upright and only loosely covered groin concealed.

"Just getting some decaffeinated tea with lavender—Dr. Miller said that I could have chamomile as long as I watch the strength, don't steep it long and don't do it every night, but there's no danger with lavender, so I'm…um…making some tea with lavender."

All the time he'd known her, he'd only heard her ramble once before. In the parking lot after the ultrasound. Was she struggling as much as he was?

Could they talk about it?

Should they?

Certainly not while he was standing there dripping on her tile floor. Wearing only a towel and loose-fitting trunks that weren't going to keep his body contained if he stood there much longer, adjusting to the gloom, noticing the short silk robe she had on, reminding him exactly what was underneath—or not.

"Are you feeling okay?" He was a doctor and she was carrying his child. He had to know.

"Fine. Just having trouble sleeping and I have to be at work in six hours."

Satisfied, he turned away from her and toward the space that he'd begun to think of as his. As far as he knew, she hadn't even been down that hallway since the day he'd moved in. "Good night," he said, eager to make his escape before he made a mistake.

"I didn't know you were out there…when I came

out. I heard you get home, heard you come in, but thought you were in your room."

He turned halfway back—enough that he could look in her direction, not enough that she could see him head-on. Because the wrong "head" was definitely "on."

"Elaina, this is your home. You're free to move about as you please and certainly don't have to explain yourself to me."

The microwave beeped and she took out her cup. She dropped a tea bag into it and dipped it up and down. "Is this your first night in the pool?"

"No." But it was probably going to be his last.

At least until he could get his severe attraction to her better under control. If he didn't know so well what he was missing...if his body didn't know exactly what hers would do to him...

But it did. And he had to get down that hall and behind his door.

"Can I ask you something?"

Now? He wanted to let out a little whine but said, "Of course." Concentrate. Sutures. Blood. Broken bones.

"What's #2?"

Seriously? She was playing childhood games with him? Number one was pee and...

"On your note," she continued before he completely humiliated himself. "You said #2."

Ahhh. He smiled. "The dog," he said. "I vote for #2 on your list."

Her smile lit up the gloom. He could see a hint of teeth, see the glistening as her lips moved. And turned without thinking. "He's a poodle mix, so no shedding and no dander, in case the baby's allergic. And small enough that we won't have to worry about him knocking the baby over, and it says he's good with kids."

She'd come closer. And was staring downward.

Thinking of broken bones hadn't had enough time to do its job. He'd barely made it to considering a simple fracture before she'd grabbed his attention back.

"And he's only two, so we'll have a lot of good years with him," he continued talking, though he could hear the strain in his voice, and didn't have much hope she'd missed it. "You'll..." he corrected. "*You'll* have a lot of good years with him."

Cup in hand, she'd stopped walking. "You're planning to remain an active part of our child's life," she said softly, sounding more like herself even as he heard himself sounding less and less composed. "So you'll be around him, too. And...thank you. I'll call the shelter in the morning."

So that was it. She could see the evidence of his severe desire for her and she was going to pretend it wasn't there?

"Let me know if you want me to go with you to

eventually pick up the dog," he said, though why she would, he had no idea. He just kind of wanted to go. The dog was going to grow up with his kid.

"We're doing the right thing, Greg. We made the right choices." She hadn't even had a sip of that tea, but appeared to be noticeably calmed by her decision. "It's hard, going from what we were to what we are, but we both need it to be this way."

Her matter-of-fact tone and words did what broken bones had not. His body shrank, settled.

And he knew she was right.

"Sleep well," he told her.

"You, too. And Greg?" He stopped, again—as he figured he was always going to when she called out to him.

"Leave your schedule on the refrigerator and I'll fix up the shelter appointment for a time you can make."

She smiled at him.

He smiled back.

And figured the evening had turned out all right after all.

Strangely enough, Elaina slept well that night. And for several nights after that. Knowing that Greg wanted her, that she wasn't alone in her fight against physical attraction, was a strange kind of comfort.

Having him in the house…even more so.

She knew she couldn't get used to having him

there. It wasn't like he was going to spend the rest of his life down the hall from her, staying celibate. And she had to live solidly on her own feet, not go around feeling good because she had a man in the house again.

But getting her rest was paramount for the baby's well-being, so she allowed herself to feel thankful. Until one Friday night, two weeks after the first ultrasound, when she was suddenly lying wide awake at two in the morning.

In years past, she'd have thought it was Retro waking her, going out through the doggy door that she seldom heard from her suite, but there was still no dog in the house. Number Two had already been adopted by the time she'd called to inquire about him. And she hadn't yet settled on another.

Maya, the shelter volunteer, had suggested that she come in and meet all of the dogs—they were having an adoption day in another couple of weeks—and though she hadn't told Greg about it yet, she figured that the suggestion was a good one. Planned to ask him if he wanted to come along.

She just hadn't really seen much of him in the weeks since.

If he'd told his parents about the pregnancy yet, she didn't know about it. And figured, since there was no sign of his mother, it hadn't happened yet.

Cassie and Wood were getting tidbits of information when she stopped by on her way to work a couple of mornings a week, just to get a hug from Alan, as she'd been doing since the baby's birth. They knew she wasn't having any morning sickness, and that things were going fine with Greg living in the suite at the end of the hall.

And at work, she'd told her administrator that she was pregnant. Her techs knew, too, as she told them she would not perform a couple of procedures until after she gave birth—but she hadn't said who the father was, and no one had asked. If Greg had said anything—and she assumed he'd at least have put in an address change with hospital HR—he hadn't informed her whom he'd told, or what was said.

Funny how, now that they were sharing a house, she saw less of him than after she'd broken up with him.

He was working nights—a shift she knew he had to have volunteered for—and was generally sleeping, or out, when she was about. The times they ran into each other, he asked about her health, looked her over as though she was one of his patients, wondered if she needed anything, and that was it.

Their interaction at work was limited to business, as it had been since their breakup.

To the point that she was beginning to wonder why he was staying with her at all. And she knew that wasn't fair, either. He was there for when the baby started to be active. When she started to get bigger. When she hit the eighteen-week mark and their baby began to hear sounds and would need to become familiar with his voice.

He'd left her a note at the twelve-week mark, on the notepad on the refrigerator—"Past the critical point"—with a check mark and a big smiley face.

She'd taken it down and tucked it in her satchel.

And hadn't looked at it since.

But she knew it was there. Liked having it there.

And there…she heard a noise again. Not the dining room door—not Greg going out or coming from the pool—but…voices. She heard a voice. Higher than Greg's. Female.

In her house.

He had a woman in her house?

She couldn't make out words, or even sound for a bit, and then…there it was again, a faint hint of a female voice.

In her house!

Greg was dating someone.

Heart pounding, she told herself all the reasons why it didn't matter. He had every right to have a relationship with someone else. But instead of finding calm, she wanted to curl up and cry.

Greg was with another woman.

He'd brought another woman to Elaina's house and was doing…

She started to tremble.

Was his tongue leaving wisps of desire down her stomach? And…

Turning over, she pulled the pillow up to cover her ears.

The other woman wouldn't have gotten naked yet, not if Elaina could hear them. It wasn't like he'd be making out in her living room.

Or would he?

Realizing she was behaving like a juvenile, Elaina pulled the pillow off her head. Sat up.

Heard the low rumble of a male voice. Remembered how Greg would keep her engaged during his lovemaking with a softly spoken "You like that?" or "I want to..." or "You want to?" He'd never just moved on her, or with her; he'd talked them through it. Asking her before he did something new. And she'd found herself growing out of who she'd been with Peter, becoming someone more adventurous. Someone who allowed herself to take pleasure.

Silence followed, and it was worse than the hints of voices. Lying back down in the dark, she hurt like she hadn't hurt in a long time. Hurt in a way she'd never hurt before.

Like a woman whose man was being unfaithful to her.

She'd suspected once that Peter was having something on the side with a woman who was in medical school with him. She'd been bothered to the point of finally asking him about it. And when he told her that the woman had offered, but he hadn't wanted to screw up his marriage, she'd been gratified. But never, in all of those moments combined, had she felt anything like the pain she was feeling right now, lying there alone in her bed.

She'd never been a jealous person, but for a few seconds there, she hated the woman in the other room, whoever she was.

She spent another few moments trying to figure out who it was. Someone from work? Had to be... Greg didn't really do a lot outside of the hospital. Not that she knew.

She didn't want to know who it was. Or what they were doing. It had been quiet for a while. Had they gone back to his room? Was he slowly undressing her? Telling her how beautiful each part of her body was to him? With that golden glint lighting up his eyes?

Were her hands running through the sandy curls on his head? Or the ones further down?

Tears pooled in her eyes and Elaina didn't fight them. All those years she'd lived with Wood she'd hoped that he'd bring someone home, that there'd be a woman in his bed occasionally. She'd needed him to live his life—and to feel like their home was home to him.

She'd never thought about what the woman would be getting. And not getting. Until Cassie had come into the picture. She'd had moments of unease then. Maybe even some envy. But she'd been glad for Wood. Why couldn't she be glad for Greg?

There. There it was again. A higher lilt. They were still in the living room.

After all that silence?

Tea. She needed tea.

Could make noise getting up, open her door loudly, slowly, so they'd have plenty of time to make themselves decent. She could apologize, head to the kitchen.

And knowing she was awake, they'd at least vacate the living room, wouldn't they?

She had to be up for work in less than five hours. Even if Greg wasn't in the living room with his lover, she should get some tea.

Getting off the bed, Elaina pulled on her longer silk robe over her nightie, as opposed to the shorter one she usually preferred, tied it around her waist, not trying to be quiet about moving around her room. Just for good measure, she moved the armchair under the window, adjusting it, making noise.

And then she went to the door.

She intended to avoid looking toward the couch as she walked through the back portion of the large living room, toward a light switch.

But the glow in her peripheral vision drew her attention.

"I'm sorry. Did I wake you?" In sweat shorts and a T-shirt, Greg had been lounged in a corner of the couch, his legs stretched out and crossed, but he sat up as he saw her.

Sat up alone, she could see by the soft glow of the accent lighting she'd just switched on—sconces along the wall.

She heard again the voice that had awoken her.

And saw the source.

Not a flesh-and-blood woman.

Not even a young woman.

The voice was coming from the flat screen mounted to the wall.

Chapter Thirteen

"**Y**ou're watching television!" The surprise in Elaina's voice wasn't expected. Greg figured she'd come out because the television had woken her, though he always kept the volume as low as he could and still make out enough of the words to follow whatever meaningless show he had on.

He watched to dumb down his thoughts so he could sleep. To relax.

The sight of her covered from neck to toe in silk had the exact opposite effect. The woman was trying to kill him. A long, slow, painful death.

He stood, clicked off the set. "I'm sorry it woke you." He was not going to get an erection at the sight of her in a robe. Not to full stiffness, anyway. And he truly was regretful. She needed her rest.

"It's okay," she said. "I just came out to get some tea."

But she hadn't moved toward the kitchen.

"I guess I'm just not used to having the TV on in here."

He needed her to move toward the kitchen. He had to pass where she was standing to get to his room. "I have it on every night."

"You do?" She didn't seem to be in any hurry to leave. Greg sat back down. Sweat shorts didn't hide much. He'd had just that one glimpse of her body, had focused on her face since seeing the robe, but this woman did something to him.

It wasn't like he walked around with a hard-on in his pants on a regular basis. Most of the time his mind was so focused on other things that he got no exercise in that region at all. But with Elaina...

"I got in the habit during medical school," he said. "I watch old shows, things that I find mildly entertaining but that take nothing out of me, to quiet my mind and get sleepy."

"But...you watch it out here?"

"Sleep experts tell you that if you struggle to nod off, you should do nothing in your room except sleep, so that your body is trained to know what to do when you go there. Like a dog's Pavlovian response, I guess. I'm not sure how valid the advice is, but it was mandated by someone my parents took me to when I was a kid, and I've just always kept up the practice."

They were supposed to be getting to know each other. He figured this discussion qualified. And got his mind off her body and how badly he wanted to be allowed to touch it again.

"You've always struggled to sleep?" Her head tilt, the compassion in her voice, didn't help him get any sleepier.

"I'm a full-steam-ahead type of guy. But I sleep fine once I wind down."

She'd taken a step, finally. Toward the couch, and him, not the kitchen. "And you've been out here every night since you moved in?"

"Pretty much."

"I had no idea."

"That was the point. I won't watch out here if it's going to keep you awake."

He could always get his flat screen out of the workshop where he'd ended up putting it and set it up somewhere in the office. He wasn't into streaming on his phone—too small a screen for him. He spent his days dealing with small detail. Maybe he'd move the couch in there, too. He'd thought to keep things simple, since he was only likely there for a matter of months. Until the baby and Elaina were separated and he could have his own time with it.

"You're fine," she said. "Tonight's the first night

I've even heard it at all. And if I'd known that's what it was, I'd have fallen right back to sleep."

Interesting. And yet, there she was, saying she needed tea to help her sleep. And the natural conclusion to that was to assume she'd been awake long enough to need help falling back to sleep.

What had she thought the sound was? And how long had she been awake?

She hadn't come out with her phone or any kind of weapon in hand. And there was the robe to consider. So probably not expecting an intruder.

More than that, if she'd thought there was any kind of danger, wouldn't she have just picked up her cell phone and called him?

They might not run into each other all that much, but he *was* in the same building. Right down the hall...

"What did you think it was?" Curiosity got the better of him.

Her lack of immediate response whetted his appetite for an answer. Elaina, other than a couple of incidences of rambling or in his bed, was always calm, controlled. The most disciplined individual he'd ever met. And yet she stood there, fidgeting with her fingers, avoiding his gaze. Finally, chin up, she said, "I thought you had a woman out here."

The idea floored him. A surge of anger followed immediately by incredulity, and then, lagging behind, a shot of...something else.

It was that last that had him saying, "And that bothered you?"

Her nod came after the question. Before he could form a response, she said, "I know it's ridiculous. Of course, you have every right to have a relationship. And to invite anyone you'd like over. This is legally your home. You've signed a lease, you pay rent... and while technically the communal space could be considered off-limits for entertaining, as we're both using it, nothing was specified to that end, so..." She shrugged. "I'm overreacting."

Maybe. And maybe not.

"This is your home, too, Elaina. If you're uncomfortable with anything I'm doing, I'm trusting you to talk to me about it. Otherwise little things become irritating and irritation grows into resentment, and there's nowhere good from there."

He'd tiptoed around Wendy—and watched her tiptoe around him—for too many months for him to not have learned something.

"Thank you."

That could have been the end of it, but when she should have left the room, prepared her tea, taken herself out of his realm, she came over and sat on the other end of the couch, pulling the throw off the back of it and cuddling up in it.

As though they were siblings on Christmas morning or something! She was giving him more credit than was his due if she thought he could sit with her in the middle of the night, both of them half-dressed, and keep himself unaroused.

Sex with her had always driven him wild, but the knowledge that she was pregnant with his child... seemed to have put his desire for her on steroids.

Odd that it didn't seem to be affecting his interest in other women, though. He couldn't even think of anyone he'd have wanted to bring home that night. Let alone done it.

"I was out of line," she said. "Being bothered by the thought of you out here with someone else."

She apparently needed to have this conversation. He couldn't walk away from it. "We haven't talked about seeing other people."

"We aren't seeing each other, and it's not like either of us is signing on to a life of celibacy."

Good point.

"Is there someone you want to date?"

"No! I'm pregnant!" She seemed to think about that for a second while he sat and watched the expressions flit across her face in the night's shadows. "I can't imagine many guys will want to date a woman who's pregnant with another man's child," she said. And then, "And I'm serious about standing on my own."

Good reminder. He was deadly serious about not diving in headfirst and getting stunned by the force of the blow when he hit bottom.

And just as serious about no longer making promises he couldn't keep. He couldn't make Heather love him. Couldn't keep Wendy happy. He'd told them both he'd do both.

Their pain was partially on him for barreling so forcefully ahead, being so sure he could make it all work if they'd just let him show them he could. But they'd also led him along, liking what he was willing to do for them more than they liked him.

And now he didn't hear from either one of them anymore. He didn't even want to imagine a world where he couldn't stay in touch with Elaina.

They couldn't just ignore what was going on between them, though.

"Were you bothered because you thought I had a woman right outside your bedroom door, because I brought her to your house at all or just because I was with another woman?"

She met his gaze head-on. His hard-on got more painful.

"Because you were with a woman at all."

He was glad to hear it. He shouldn't be. But he was.

"I'd feel the same way if you were to have another man in your life."

Her lips tilted upward a bit, like she was holding back a smile. "It's probably dangerous, us feeling this way. I mean, I know I have no right to expect you not to date."

He shook his head, wanting to be open and honest with her, but not wanting to analyze so deeply they got themselves lost.

"The danger lies in not communicating with each other," he said. "I think it's probably pretty natural, with everything going on right now, and the adjustments we're having to make, going from two people who had sex but didn't really know each other, to broken up, to living together as parents-to-be... It's a natural reaction to not want the added complication of other intimate relationships that would directly affect and be affected by what we're doing here."

"You really think that?"

He took a minute to reassess. "Yeah. I know I certainly don't want any more complications added to the mix."

"Me, either."

"So we're good?" He was serious as he looked over at her.

"We're good."

"Then would you mind getting the hell out of here so I can get up and go to bed?"

She didn't look at his crotch. She might or might not know why he chose not to get up with her there.

He figured there were some things best left unsaid.

The night of the television incident was a turning point where Elaina's dealings with Greg were concerned. He was still working nights—getting home a little after midnight most evenings—so she wasn't seeing him all that much, but she felt differently about having him at the house. His initial desire of wanting to be around during her pregnancy still stood and she was fine to have him there. He'd accepted the full-time ED position at Oceanfront, but had decided to put off looking for a house of his own until after the baby was born.

The change wasn't in their situation, but more in how she felt about having him in her space. Knowing she could talk to him honestly, openly, seemed to free up something inside her that had been under lock and key for a very long time.

With no expectations between them, and no past romantic history to speak of, she didn't have to worry about hurting him. Or letting him down.

And she trusted him to listen to her. Not just to hear her words, but to really listen. Just as she listened to him. Because they both had one common goal—to bring their child into a healthy environment, and then to raise it in one.

As another couple of weeks passed, she thought about Greg more and more. Wanting to spend some real time with him, to talk about baby things.

Mostly.

The man's musky scent in her home, his notes on the fridge, his dishes in the dishwasher, the trash disappearing from the can, a soft sound coming from the living room lulling her back to sleep if she happened to wake up in the night were all settling in on her, though she knew, too, that they weren't a permanent part of her new reality.

But this new routine seemed to have a particularly noticeable side effect—she was more turned on by him than ever. To the point of having dreams about the sex they used to share. Only in her dreams, they'd be in a place she didn't recognize. Or his face would suddenly disappear.

She'd wake up hot, needing to feel him inside her, and blanketed in a sense of foreboding that left a shadow on her. She was pretty sure—based on what she'd seen that night he'd come in from the pool, and then again on the night on the couch—that he was suffering some of the same, and that added sparks to the fire. But she was also aware of the sense of regret that would follow if they gave in to the fiery attraction. They had too much at stake to ruin it with lust.

She'd left a note for Greg telling him about the dog adoption day at the shelter in Mission Viejo, and another one mentioning that her sixteen-week check was coming up and asking if he wanted to be there. When he'd replied in the affirmative to both, she scheduled the doctor's appointment on the same day as the adoption day, thinking it would be easier just to go from one to the other.

What it did was have them spending the whole day together. They would go together to these ap-

pointments from her house, as they'd both scheduled the day off.

She'd come out of her suite only long enough to
get her morning tea and toast, taking it back to her
suite to consume while she had a relaxing soak in
the tub and then got ready. And yet she felt his presence. While she lay naked, submerged in warm bubbles, while she was drying off, rubbing every inch
of her skin with the soft fluffy towel, and when she
chose her clothes.

She'd told herself to dress for comfort. And the
black leggings and tight white T-shirt were definitely
that. But they also made her feel…feminine. Attractive.

While her tummy wasn't showing her pregnancy
yet, there was definitely more of a roundness there
than normal for her, and she wanted to show that
off—to the man who'd put it there.

And for once she left her hair down around her
shoulders and down her back. Greg loved her hair.
Thought it silky and lush. Had played with it in any
number of ways…

Truth was, she liked it that way, too, which was
why she'd left it long. It had become habit to keep it
tightly pulled back and out of the way during all of
the months of therapy. And then, so it didn't get in
the way during medical school.

But maybe her hairstyle had all been part of the
hold she'd put on her life…

Shaking her head against the thought, not wanting such a serious intrusion on a day off, she grabbed a pair of gold hoop earrings Wood had given her for Christmas when Peter had still been alive, put them in and slid into her favorite wedge sandals.

Greg was waiting for her in the kitchen. In beige shorts with pockets down the thighs, a black shirt and black slip-ons, he looked like a guy any dog would run up to and adopt. His glance at her, the way he turned abruptly and poured the rest of his coffee down the drain, rinsed the cup, put it in the dishwasher and then reached for his keys...gave her a wonderful sense of being appreciated.

And a reminder that she had a responsibility to the choices they'd made, too. There'd be no flirting. No making more of the day than it was.

"I'll drive," she said, grabbing her keys as she put her satchel over her shoulder. And not to be disrespectful or thinking her desires automatically won out, she added, "Your car, being basically a two-seater, isn't really big enough to bring a pet home, if we do get one today."

Though she'd been approved by the animal shelter, she was trying not to get too excited about the prospect of a dog. Was trying to remain practical in light of the baby coming and the hours they both worked. Didn't want to make a selfish choice.

Though she and Wood had worked a lot of hours

and Retro had been fine. The big dog now acted as both guard and best friend to Alan, too.

Greg fidgeted in the passenger seat a bit on the way to the clinic, as though he didn't know what to do with himself, and she kept her resulting smile to herself. He might not be used to being a passenger, might not be comfortable with it, but he wasn't complaining.

Something she'd grown to count on with him. He was the same way at work. If he saw cause to do something in a way not of his own choosing, he did it with good attitude. Like the Brooklyn situation. He hadn't made accusations. He'd just quietly sought the truth through factual tests and then reported them.

"We need to start talking about the future," she said as she turned off her street. "If you really want to be a part of the baby's life in utero, we'll have to start spending more time together…"

"I've already put in to be back on day shift," he interrupted. "It won't be long now before the baby's moving. And listening…"

Her belly jumped, almost as though the fetus could already hear and was responding, except the sensation was a little lower than where the baby lay growing.

And Greg was talking about maybe having dinner together in the kitchen any night they were both home. "We could set a time to show up, maybe put together a cooking schedule, that kind of thing."

He'd evidently given it a lot of thought. "I was thinking about scheduling time each week to go out to eat, or do other things...you know, like today, going to a pet adoption day..."

Eating together every night: that sounded a lot like family to her. And she and Greg weren't going to be that.

"That's fine," he said. And then... "Eating together every night... I'm still me...still fixated on building something that isn't there."

"It's obviously something you need, Greg. There's nothing wrong with wanting a family. You have to know that."

His nod was easy, the accompanying shrug casual. "I just need to let nature takes its course, to wait for the...what did Heather call it? Wait for the butterfly to alight upon me. I actually do know that, you know..."

"And I actually like that you think like a family man," she told him as she turned into the clinic parking lot. "I put a high value on your overall willingness to do hard work when required for the greater good. And then head home as opposed to always having to be somewhere else. And I know other women who also value that quality in a man."

Because it couldn't be about him and her.

Still, it felt good knowing that about him. Understanding it.

She was getting to really know the man who was father to her child.

And liked what she was learning.

The baby she was carrying was lucky to be coming into the world with Greg as a permanent part of its life.

Chapter Fourteen

The sixteen-week checkup was an uneventful and quick evaluation of Elaina's weight and vitals, along with Dr. Miller listening to the baby's heartbeat, and with an "everything looks good, see you in a month," they were done.

"Just one other thing," Dr. Miller said as Greg got up, eager to leave the small examination room that he felt was overpowering. Three doctors in one room...and a man who was doing exactly what he always did—weaving stories in his mind about the woman who was attached to his life. Trying to make a forever family out of a relationship that was barely a friendship... "If you two want to know the sex of the baby, we have a couple of options. We can do a blood test—with new technology we can generally tell at seven weeks—or we can do another ultrasound and try to see..."

"I don't want to know yet," Elaina said, even as Greg was shaking his head, too.

She glanced at him, smiling, and he smiled back.

As parents, they seemed to be on the same page already.

"You seriously don't want to know the sex of the baby, either?" Elaina asked him while he sat beside her trying to be fine with not being behind the wheel. She was a decent driver. Great. Maybe even better than him—or as good as him—but he just... enjoyed driving.

Not so much riding. He liked being in control of the machine barreling him down the road. Liked being able to control the power in the machine.

Lord knew there was little else in his control at the moment.

"I really don't want to know yet," he told her. And then kept talking. "I don't want the sex of the child to narrow our choices in terms of how we're going to parent. I'd like us to come to agreements about what our lives are going to look like, first, how we're going to co-parent, before we start thinking about nursery colors or names."

"I was thinking purple and yellow for the nursery," Elaina said. "Faith and fun. Wisdom and youthful joy. Which is what some experts say those colors represent or inspire. And even if they don't, I think they're bright and peaceful at the same time. And if it's a girl, Marisol, and if it's a boy, Austin."

Point taken. She was already way ahead of him. Nursery colors and names firmly decided. But... "That's your nursery. Will I have one? More to the point, will I have need of one in my own home? And my parents' names are Wilma and Fred. What if I'd like my child to be named after them?"

She glanced his way as she settled into a lane on the highway and slipped on cruise control. An option on his car that had never been used. "Your parents' names are Fred and Wilma? Like the Flintstones?"

Her grin made him want to nod, just to see her keep smiling. "No, they're Anna and James, but my point is—"

"I get your point and you're right," she said, her expression growing serious. "And I'm sorry I didn't think enough about things from your point of view...exactly why I do not trust myself in a relationship."

"I wasn't criticizing, Elaina. I haven't been spending a lot of time in your point of view, either. How could we expect to when we were both hit with shocking news? I'm just saying...for me...it's time to start making the bigger decisions."

She nodded. Changed lanes. And said, "I'm afraid to have the conversation."

"Why?"

"Because I don't know the answers."

"Maybe we find them together."

Another quick glance in his direction showed him her raised brows. He wasn't sure what they signified.

"Isn't that what co-parenting means? Doing it together?"

"What happens if you want Wilma and I want Marisol?"

"I actually like Marisol, by the way. But in answer to your question, I guess that's where the hard work comes in. We have to be open to hearing each other's opinions, and then weighing them both for the best of the child. I'm sure there'll be times when either side could be right, or neither answer is better or worse, and then we'll have to learn to compromise. And maybe have an argument or two. Get a bit miffed at each other. But because we both love the baby so much, we'll find a way to work it out on a case-by-case basis."

She didn't quite smile, but he was getting used to seeing the slight upward tilt of her lips, the relaxing of her features. And liking it.

"Okay, so if you're okay with Marisol if it's a girl, which is my choice, then maybe you get to choose the name if it's a boy. And since we don't know either way, the agreement is fair."

Her willingness to give him his fair say made him feel good. And he had no ideas for boys' names.

Not Gregory. He didn't want a namesake, to give the kid any idea that he had to follow in his footsteps. But...

"Can I have some time to think about it?"

"Of course." Traffic was light. He could play with names while they drove. Instead, he instinctively pressed his foot to the floor as red taillights shone in succession in front of them, signaling a massive slowdown. But she had the brake pedal, not him.

Pumped it well. Slowed the car without any jerks, or extra wear on the brakes.

As he sat there, feeling a bit useless, it occurred to him that she'd just given him an example of shared parenting. They'd made a decision to discuss their child's future and to respect each other's opinions.

It wasn't going to be easy. Wasn't always going to look as he envisioned it.

But he was determined to make it work.

Elaina knew the second she saw Beldon that he was the one. Two years old. A poodle mix with unusual black-and-white coloring. And much bigger than the ten or twelve pounds she wanted. The dog was easily thirty pounds. He was housetrained. Had been in a home with five kids since his birth—and then had been left behind when the family moved.

What got her, though, was the way, when she and Greg approached his temporary, makeshift cage, he sat down, looked up at her, held her gaze and stuck his paw through the fencing.

"He's obviously the one," Greg said before she could even find a voice. So she nodded. And while she knelt down to speak to the dog, asking him how he was and if he wanted to come home with her, Greg was already off finding the volunteer who could get them through the adoption process. She'd already filled out an online application, had been approved. Had all the necessities at home. There was still paperwork to do.

And money to pay.

Different dogs, different adoption fees. She had no idea how much Beldon cost. And didn't care. She'd planned to donate extra anyway. Because of all of the animals she couldn't take home with her.

"It's going to be an hour or so before we can take him," Greg said, rejoining her. He reached out a hand to the dog, and Beldon licked his palm. Just once. A greeting, not a meal. "They suggested we get some lunch," he said. "They'll be taking Beldon back, getting him ready to go…"

She didn't want to leave the sweet guy, even for a second, but nodded. "We're coming right back," she told him, her tone dead serious. Hoping that he understood. "You're not alone anymore." When she stood up, Greg had the most peculiar look on his face. Like he'd seen something that both frightened and intrigued him.

"What?"

"That's what it's all about, isn't it?" he asked, walking with her toward the door of the shelter. "Both of us... We just don't want to be alone."

Maybe. She couldn't let him convince her to stray off course. "I'd rather be alone than hurt anyone by not being able to give them the love they need." Peter had needed something different from what she could give him. She'd fought him. And he'd been so upset by her outburst that he hadn't seen what was coming right at him.

She'd seen. She'd screamed. But it hadn't been soon enough...

Blinking away the blinding memory of oncoming silver glints, she walked next door to a family-owned café, slid into the booth of the window seat they were shown and picked up her menu.

"There are many ways to not be alone," she said, when she realized she should have been making a meal choice. She hadn't even seen what the place served. Didn't really care. As long as it was healthy for the baby. "Many ways we can love..."

"And there's danger here, with you and me, because in one sense, we both want the same thing, and that wanting brings out characteristics in us that lead to relationships that don't work."

Sitting across from her, Greg picked up his menu, at least appearing to be studying it, while she sat there with her mouth open. Here she'd been getting all defensive inside, bracing herself to not fall back into her old ways, and he hadn't been providing her the means, after all.

He understood.

And more, made her feel almost...normal. God, it had been so long since she'd felt normal. Ever since her parents had been killed, leaving her a college sophomore all alone in the world...

All alone.

There were those words again.

She hadn't been alone. She'd had Peter. And Wood. Neither had felt like family as her parents had.

But Greg did?

"The wanting, though...needing to have people in your life...that's human nature," she said slowly, not needing her menu to hide behind.

"Yep."

They each had their personal issues. They had a baby to raise. And they had each other's backs.

It wasn't perfect. It wasn't the family life she'd always wanted.

But she was glad he was sitting there across from her.

That he wanted to be a part of his child's life.

Glad that he was the father of her baby.

And a bit ashamed that she felt that way.

Because where did that leave her with Peter's memory—and the child they were supposed to have had?

* * *

"Why didn't you want to know the sex of the baby?" Greg finished his club sandwich, sat back and couldn't get enough of looking at his companion.

She fascinated him. Losing her parents...her husband...the fight she waged to get herself out of that wheelchair... Even without seeing her medical records, having seen the extent and placement of her scars, he knew that the percentages had not been in her favor. Knew the pain she had to have endured, day after day, week after week...

And there she was, still trying to do better.

She'd nearly finished the chicken salad and pineapple sandwich she'd ordered, having looked at her watch every ten minutes or so. The shelter was clearly going to get one hour. Not a second more.

"Kind of like you, I want our decisions made before we know the sex of the baby, but for a different reason." Her downward glance seemed almost embarrassed, but she looked back up almost immediately and told him, "Knowing the gender makes it all more real, makes the baby seem more concrete, and... I want to know if our co-parenting is sharing things together, or separately, before we get that news. It seems like one of those moments that will live on forever, and I don't want it spoiled by awkwardness."

Emotional reasons—not logical ones. This part of Elaina, this woman sitting across from him, had never shared his bed. He couldn't help wondering, even though their time together had been phenomenal, how much greater it could be to have all of her.

"Just judging from my own experience growing up, I think, the baby would benefit from having its parents celebrating together," he said. "I had a friend whose folks were divorced and didn't get along, and he was always having to choose who to call first, who to invite...always worrying that if they were both there, like at the science fair, did he approach one or the other first. If they'd simply been able to walk in together..."

"I like that. A lot. Walking in together."

"Maybe, where the baby's concerned, we're a united front," he said aloud something that he hadn't allowed himself to envision fully previously. The call wasn't only his to make. And he didn't want it to be solely his.

She nodded. "We'll need to take each instance as it comes, but overall, we're in this together."

In it together. It was all he'd ever really wanted.

And the woman he'd found it with was counting on him to not ask her to marry him. Or to even try to engage in a personal intimate relationship.

Life's ironies were sometimes cruel.

Elaina was outside with Beldon that evening, just before dark, sitting at the pool and watching the dog trip over himself in his eagerness to explore the yard. He'd been out to the shed a number of times, and over to explore the house Wood had built for Retro, who'd never used it.

Whatever dissatisfaction Retro had found with Wood's handiwork, Beldon didn't seem to share it. He went in and came back out again. Went back in, turned around and came out. He was like a little kid, eager to explore his world with none of the fear that life inevitably taught.

Beldon had learned a hard lesson already. He'd loved and been abandoned. And yet was clearly open and keen to taking on another home, another life. She'd been warned, while sitting on the floor with the dog as she signed papers, to expect some nervousness when she first introduced him to his new home. Apparently Beldon hadn't understood the message.

Greg had taken off almost as soon as they'd arrived home. Headed to the beach. Coming from Nevada, he had seen a lot of the desert, he'd told her once, and couldn't seem to get enough of the ocean.

She missed him. Wished he'd stayed home to watch Beldon acclimate.

But understood, too, that while her child was his child, and that they'd share, her dog was hers. Hers and the baby's.

It was all so confusing.

"I bought some steaks for dinner. You want to join me?"

Turning, she saw the subject of her thoughts walking toward her from the house. She hadn't heard him come out. But then, she had been listening to the rock waterfall flowing, emptying into one end of the pool.

Steaks. For dinner. The two of them. Together.

"I'd like to talk to you," he added.

Which somehow changed the invitation?

"Sure, I can make a salad," she told him, and before either of them could make a big deal out of a shared meal, she went inside to do just that.

Make the salad.

And a big deal out of the shared meal.

It wasn't a date. She didn't want it to be a date.

But she was looking forward to sitting outside with Greg again. Using the grill and enjoying the pool that had been built for a family, but never used by one before.

The summer California evening was just right for being outside. Warm, but not hot. If she'd been alone, she'd have gone swimming. Didn't think it was a great idea with Greg right there.

Didn't think it would be good for her if he decided to join her.

Just seeing his body in shorts and a tight-fitting polo shirt on those shoulders brought back memories from another life.

Another person.

She wasn't that shut-down woman anymore…

"I wanted to discuss my access to the baby after it's born." Standing by the grill, with tongs in hand, Greg glanced over at her. His tone was conversational. His stance was not.

He could have been saluting someone with those tongs, as stiffly as he stood.

She didn't want to discuss his topic. It was one she'd been particularly avoiding.

He'd mentioned a nursery earlier. And she didn't think he'd been talking about hers.

"You'll have legal visitation rights," she said now. "That's a given in the state of California." Reminding herself that just that afternoon they'd decided they were parenting as a united front, together, remembering how right that had seemed, how glad she'd been, she walked over to lean against the L-shaped sink portion of the outdoor kitchen. Watched him flip steaks. Bent down to get herself a bottle of cold water out of the little refrigerator she'd been keeping stocked since he'd been in her home and she'd known he was using the pool.

She got a bottle of it for him, too. Set it on the counter by the grill.

Because they were doing it together.

"DNA paternity testing established your legal rights," she said, although she knew he was as privy to that information as she was. He'd wasted no time after that day's conversation to put them to the test.

And if she was going to make this work, to avoid an attraction to him ruining everything, she had to keep the conversation strictly professional.

He knew she didn't want her child to have two homes—a fact she'd stated when he thought the child wasn't his. When he'd shown no interest in being a part of the baby's life. It seemed forever ago—when it had only been a couple of months.

And she knew he wasn't asking about his legal rights. "I'd like us to have one set of rules to serve as solid boundaries against decision-making, so that as he or she traverses the world, there's a solid set of understandings to guide him. Or her. Responsibilities, expectations, rewards and punishments should be unchanging from parent to parent."

"You're okay, then, with the baby staying with me sometimes during the week and on at least two weekends a month?"

Of course, she wasn't. But she had to be.

She wanted her baby to have its father in its life. To know and love Greg. To have Greg's love and care. His supervision. And his energy, too.

His fairness.

His ability to listen openly and have an ear to understanding.

She knew she had to tell him she was okay with it, but no words came out.

"Let me ask you this." He jumped into the silence. "If you could take our situation and write the future, what would your script look like?"

She looked over at him. Still didn't answer.

"Just gut thinking, what would it be?" he asked.

"That you'd stay in your suite and we'd both parent the baby in the same home."

The words had come out so quickly. As though they'd been hanging there waiting for a chance to be said. And yet…as badly as she wanted to know he wasn't leaving, the solution left her empty, as well.

"But that's exactly what I did to Wood," she quickly added. "I let my needs keep him in that suite and left him no room for a life of his own."

"Funny, for a guy who had no chance for a life of his own, he's sure doing a good job having the one he created."

Greg's tone held no humor. His direct look into her eyes held challenge.

What was he…

"Tell me I'm wrong," he said. "So, you want me to believe Wood never went out on dates? Never slept with another woman? The whole time the two of you shared this house? Because as I recall, you told me early on in our association that Wood had his own life, just as you had yours."

"Well, yes, he did… I mean, I didn't know who he was with, or even when exactly, but I know he dated. And some nights he didn't get home until the early morning hours. It wasn't like we sat around and talked about our sex lives. Other than to acknowledge that we were free to have them…"

She uncapped her water. "Don't try and talk me out of what I know I did, Greg. The only way for me to go forward is to be aware, to take accountability… to make certain that I don't repeat past mistakes…"

Like arguing with the driver when you were a passenger in a car. Or in any other way distract him.

She'd yet to ride with Greg in his car. The time would come. Could even be when she was in labor. Which would be a distraction.

And something she'd think about at another time.

"I'm not trying to talk you into or out of anything," he said, frowning as he flipped the steaks again. "I'm trying to help us both see beyond our emotional albatross and find facts. And as I look at Wood, I don't see a man who was held hostage by you or anyone else. It seems to me that he was here because this is where he wanted to be. And that you gave him something he needed, too."

She wanted to see that. Wanted so badly to know that her selfishness hadn't hurt Wood. Of course he'd told her, more than once, quite adamantly, that it hadn't. But that was his way—making her way easier. And her way…was to what? Sabotage herself? To not let herself be happy? Because, for some reason, she didn't deem herself worthy of true joy?

Or just didn't believe she could ever feel it again.

"If nothing else, his choices led him to be free when Cassie came so unexpectedly into his life."

There was that.

"And when she did, he didn't let you stop him from pursuing whatever life had to show them."

And there was that, too.

Taking a long sip of water, she watched as he cut open a thick piece of meat and checked the color of the middle.

"Where exactly are you going with all of this?"

"Just that...for now... I'd like to put off house hunting...and continue to rent my suite from you. I'd like to be here for middle-of-the-night feedings, to trade off with you, taking whatever shifts work for us, so that you can get some sleep when you need it. I want to be here to see the baby's first steps, to know if it spits peas out, to watch it around Beldon to make certain that thirty pounds of dog and fifteen pounds of baby don't get tangled up."

It could happen when he was at work. He couldn't watch over the baby every second of the day. And meeting his gaze, she knew he knew that, too.

And that he was struggling to find his own healthy space.

He wanted what she wanted? To remain in the suite indefinitely?

"I thought you thought Beldon was the right choice," she said, homing in on the reference to the thirty-pound dog getting tangled up with the fifteen-pound baby. Knowing she was avoiding the issue in doing so.

"I do."

As if he'd heard his name—and he very probably had—Beldon came running over, slowing as he walked up to Greg at the grill, his nose in the air.

When Greg reached down, scratching the dog behind his ears, telling him that he'd have to wait until they were done eating to get a bite, Elaina fell a little bit in love.

With Greg's parenting skills...right?

"You haven't said what you think about my taking you up on your gut suggestion." He was looking at her, not the dog who still stood beside him, looking expectantly up at the grill.

"I'm scared to death that we might be building something that's going to be difficult to get out of."

"Then rest assured that I'm a grown man with a mind of my own. And down the road, when I meet a woman and need more space, I'll feel completely free to buy myself a house."

When he met a woman. Not *if.* The distinction was huge. Brought a huge pang of...whatever it was she'd been feeling in the bed that night she thought he had a woman in her living room. She wanted to cry. And that little word choice, when not if, gave her the freedom to say, "Then feel free to stay as long as you'd like." She gave the permission, hoping that she was finding a life that fitted her—as unorthodox as it was.

She wanted joy. She wasn't going to settle for thinking she didn't deserve it. Not anymore.

Chapter Fifteen

Greg called his parents on his way to the hospital Sunday morning, thinking he'd make it quick and simple, and ended up pulling off the road to deal with the questions coming at him. He had over an hour before he was on shift, and he wanted his parents to know what was going on.

Elaina was starting her fifth month and he didn't feel right putting off telling them any longer.

Didn't want to put it off any longer now that he and Elaina had a solid plan. Truth be told, he was excited about his life for the first time in a very long while. No, it wasn't ideal. But nothing ever was. Ideals were just fantasies that people built because they didn't know any better.

Reality was what you made out of what life gave you.

His mom wanted to make more of that moment than it was. Half an hour into what turned into a video call, after he'd answered both of his parents' questions, assuring them that he was happy, that while yes, he acknowledged his situation with Elaina was out of the ordinary, it was working for them and was best for the baby.

"And if there comes a time when it doesn't work for us, I'll buy a house close by."

"You should have your own place, son," his father said, but with a knowing tone in his voice. His dad loved kids, and he loved Greg. He'd known how devastating it had been for Greg when he'd found out he was infertile and Wendy wouldn't consider adoption. "It's a secure investment."

"I can always buy a place and rent it out."

"You don't get the tax break if it's a rental…"

And so it went. As always, his parents jumped right into every aspect of his life that they knew about. He loved them dearly. And they drove him nuts.

Just as he might drive his own child nuts someday. What a glorious thought. He was going to have an adult child in his future.

"What do Elaina's parents think of all this? You living in her home, but not marrying her?"

"I'm renting a suite at the opposite end of her house that, for years, was occupied by her brother-in-law, Mom. I told you that. And Elaina's parents were killed when she was in college. In a car accident." And he figured it didn't hurt for them to know. "She was an only child. She married her college sweetheart and then lost him in a car accident, as well. Only that time she was in the car, was left paralyzed. With help from her brother-in-law, she managed to handle that, as well. With a well of determination I can only stand in awe of, she made herself walk again, and to look at her now, you wouldn't even know she'd ever been hurt."

To look at her, you wouldn't know. But to know her... Elaina had been so badly hurt... Greg wasn't sure she'd ever completely recover. Wasn't sure someone who'd been through all she had could allow herself to let go of the barriers that protected what was left of her ability to love.

"It sounds like you love her," his mother said, her words soft now, and powerful. His defenses shot up.

"Don't make more than there is, Ma. I care about her. But it's not like that. We're sharing parenting, living on the same premises. We aren't committed to each other. We're committed to the baby."

That had to be clear. Period. They didn't have to like his choices, but he expected their acceptance of the terms.

And as they hung up, his parents made it very clear to him that he had their complete support. And a fervent desire to visit him and meet Elaina. He put them off with a promise that he'd talk to Elaina about a possible trip to Nevada sometime in the near future. And hoped that would be enough to get them to stay put for a bit. Things were still so new with him and Elaina, felt too fragile, to think about having company just yet.

Kind of like having a newborn, he figured as he finally pulled into his reserved parking spot at work. You wanted everyone to love your baby. You wanted your child to know everyone who cared about it. You just didn't want everyone descending on you the first day you brought that new fragile life home from the hospital. It needed time to grow, to gain some weight, build an immune system and antibodies, before being exposed to the outside world.

Shaking his head at the somewhat goofy thought, Greg was smiling as he walked into work.

He wasn't smiling a few hours later as he closed the door of his office with his phone at his ear.

He'd been about to head to the cafeteria to pick up some lunch when he'd seen an incoming call. He hadn't recognized the number, but he'd known the exchange—it had been his for most of his life. Someone was calling from his rather small hometown.

Not his parents. Or anyone else who'd come up on his speed dial.

"Hello?" he asked, having spent the morning dealing with the emergencies that had befallen other people. Some serious. Some not so much so.

"Greg?"

Glad that he was behind his closed office door as he recognized the voice, Greg strode to the window. "Wendy?" The ocean beckoned. Reminding him that life ebbed and flowed. Even when relationships and dreams died.

"I just ran into your mom at the store," she said. "She told me you're going to be a father!"

He hadn't known Wendy had moved back to his hometown. Hadn't asked. Hadn't cared.

Last he'd known, she was working maternity at a hospital in Vegas, having quit her job at the hospital where they'd met after the divorce. Maybe she was just visiting...

"I am." He didn't see that it was any business of hers. But maybe it felt good for her to know that though she'd deemed him broken and therefore of no use to her, he was all in one piece after all.

"Listen, Greg, I've been meaning to call you for some time. I think about it, and you, a lot. I just... kept hoping you'd come home and I could, you know, do it in person."

Do what? Remind him what a fool he'd been, giving her and their marriage his total focus, his heart and soul, all of his energy, only to be told that he wasn't enough to make her happy?

She had to have biological children of her own to be happy, she'd said. All she'd ever wanted was to feel her own baby growing inside her. To birth it and be a mother.

And she hadn't been open to considering donor sperm and fertilization options. The idea of another man's child growing inside her hadn't thrilled Greg, but he'd been willing to deal with it, to give her what she'd needed. And he'd have taken on that child as his own in all ways. He had no doubts about that.

"This is really hard..." She paused as her voice dropped. In years past, he'd have softened at that tone, knelt down in front of her if she'd been seated, taken her hand, pledged to her that he'd do whatever he could...no way he could see himself doing that with Elaina. She'd never allow that. Not from him, or anyone.

"I...made a huge mistake, Greg," she said, and started to cry. "I'm...s-so sorry. This is what I didn't want...to do." The words came out partly as a soft wail.

Compassion came, hung there, didn't entirely possess him. "You're fine," he told her. She had no reason to apologize for tears. Or for anything else that had happened, either, he realized as he stood there. She'd been honest with him. Had needed something different from what he could give.

He was the one who'd been so determined to push for what he thought was best—saving their marriage at all costs. And as he stood there, he wasn't even sure why he'd pushed so hard. It wasn't like he'd missed Wendy horribly after she'd left. He'd missed being married. He'd missed having his future stretching before him in the way he'd envisioned.

He hadn't missed feeling like he was damaged goods.

And if she'd loved him, really loved him, wouldn't she have done something about that? At least tried to help him feel better about his infertility, rather than making it all about her?

"I…never should have left you, Greg. I was immature, thinking only of myself… I hate that I did that."

"It's good that you did," he said, his brow clearing as he looked out at the body of water that carried massive energy to and from the shore every day. "We were traveling in separate directions and you saw that first."

"No, that's just it. It's you I still love, Greg. I've been out there, seen what there is to see. I've dated some great guys. Heck, I've been married and had a child. But… I couldn't make it work. He's not you."

Right. Him, now that she knew he could father a child?

"I might be too late, now that you're having a child with someone else, but I swear, Greg, I was going to call six months ago, when I transferred back here. It's why I came home. I didn't know you'd moved on."

She could have checked the hospital roster, though it sounded as though she'd only missed him by a matter of months.

"I heard about that woman who died…"

He nodded. Thought of Brooklyn, who he'd heard was doing better now that her mother understood that she had to take the medication. That it wasn't a choice.

He'd never be able to make up for the mistake of another, never be able to bring back that patient who'd died while trusting him to make her well. But he could spend his days saving lives.

And know that he'd done all he could do.

"I moved back ready to tell you that I'll adopt, I'll consider in vitro, whatever you want or need…"

Eighteen months ago he would probably have been heading to his car at those words, ready to drive across the desert. Ask her to meet him halfway, go to Vegas with him and retie the knot.

As he stood there in his office, all he felt was relief that he knew better. Knew *more*. Settling for the fantasy, the picture of what you thought you wanted, wasn't living.

Finding what made your heart throb…deep inside, not just from blood coursing through it…figuring out a way to stay where it throbbed…no matter if it fitted your picture or not…walking into the unknown with anticipation… That was real life.

Wendy wanted to move to Marie Cove. To buy a house with him. To take on co-parenting with him during the times he had visitation. And having a child of their own, too. She went on about having his sperm paired with her eggs in a petri dish, as many times as it took, for one to swim on over. Or adopting if that didn't work.

He listened because that was what he did. Listening, understanding, trying to do what he could to make another feel better...

It wasn't him being used. Being too much.

It was the best part of him.

The trait that made him a good doctor. Would make him a good dad, too.

And maybe, if he got lucky, it would make him into a lifelong friend to the mother of his child.

A woman he loved.

His mother had said so. He should have known to heed her words.

He hadn't, before now.

But talking to Wendy...to the woman he'd once thought he wanted to spend the rest of his life with, listening to her promise him everything he'd ever thought he wanted—even being willing to make a traditional home for him and the baby he had coming—he realized something he could no longer deny.

He already had what he wanted.

Maybe not in the way he'd write it if he was in charge of a script. But loving someone meant accepting them as they were.

He didn't say as much to Wendy. Just let her know, as kindly as he could, that while he very much appreciated her call, he'd moved on.

And as they both hung up, he didn't suggest that they stay in touch.

His time with her had taught him a lesson in his life. One that had, perhaps, prepared him to meet the love of his life.

Elaina wasn't what he'd originally envisioned as his true love. A woman who apparently couldn't allow herself to commit to a man other than her beloved Peter.

Greg would never be more than second best to him. A stand-in was the one thing he'd said he'd never be again.

She cared about Greg. He'd even go so far as to let himself believe that she loved him some. It might go somewhere someday.

Her ability to give intimate love might never fly again.

Either way, he wasn't going anywhere.

By conscious choice, knowing the inherent dangers in opening up to her, he was finally right where he was going to stay.

For as long as he and she both wanted him there.

Elaina hurried out of her room Thursday night of the following week, Beldon trotting along happily beside her, as she headed toward Greg's end of the house.

They'd driven into Mission Viejo to look at nursery furniture on Tuesday after work, in Greg's car,

meaning Elaina was a passenger. In a very small
car. While she'd been fighting car accident anxiety most of the way there and back, she was pretty
sure Greg hadn't been aware of the struggle. She
wasn't ashamed of how she felt, someone who'd almost died in a car accident, who'd lost her husband
in one, could be prone to bouts of riding anxiety in a
small vehicle that felt as though it would be crushed
to smithereens in a battle with most of the vehicles
sharing the road with them. But Greg would want to
do something to help, and the fight within her own
mind was something only she could resolve.

He'd asked if she minded one more stop on the
way back to the freeway, which, of course, she
hadn't, and she'd been more than a little moved that
he'd wanted her to take a look at a new SUV he'd
been looking at, wondering what she thought. When
she'd told him she loved it, he'd made arrangements
on the spot to trade in his little sportscar for the
much larger, nine-passenger, midnight blue metal-
lic luxury vehicle.

They were scheduled to shop for groceries together after work on Friday. Other than that, she'd
seen him only at work. They'd had lunch together
once, as they used to do back when they were coworkers with benefits. And the talk had remained as
neutral as it had always been at the hospital. If anyone
had anything to say about Elaina being pregnant and

Greg staying in town, they were respectful enough not to say it to the two of them.

At that moment, as she turned on the light and sped up toward his door, she didn't care what anyone thought about anymore.

She'd just come in from dinner with some friends she'd known since medical school. Had told them about the pregnancy she could still camouflage with loose clothing but didn't want to hide. And her stomach was rumbling. But not with food.

"Greg!" She had to get to him. Didn't know how much longer the sensation would last...

"What?" His door flew open before she'd connected her fist with the door and she almost fell into the room.

"Feel this!" Grabbing his hand, she placed it on her stomach, held it just above the lateral left portion of her bladder. Beldon lay down by the door as though used to owners who thought stomachs were amazing. With her hand covering his, she put a little pressure on her stomach and waited, looking at Greg's face. Waiting to see his expression.

Hoping...

And realized, too late, that he was standing there in a pair of black cotton boxer briefs. And nothing else.

With his hand pressed to the fabric of the short silk nightie she'd just pulled over her head.

There was no movement from within her uterus.

"I felt the baby move..." She was looking up at him—couldn't make herself pull her gaze away from the golden glint in those intelligent green eyes—and didn't recognize herself at all. The composure, the discipline that had seen her through so many years... that had saved her life and dealt with the pain as her legs learned to walk again...where were they now?

"It was...soft, kind of tickly...nothing I've ever felt before..." Her throat dry, she wanted him to share in the experience, too. "Kind of like a bubble that popped, and then...more."

His palm was hot on top of the thin piece of silk covering her. Radiating heat through her abdomen. And below.

The baby hadn't moved since she'd entered the hallway. Elaina meant to drop her hand, to back up, but stood there instead, soaking up the intensity in his gaze.

He hadn't said a word, though she was certain he'd cataloged every one of hers. And when she felt a nudge against the thigh that was almost leaning up against him, she couldn't pretend that she didn't know what was happening.

He wanted her.

She'd seen his arousal previously, but this time it was different. It wasn't just the physical proof. It was a sense, a knowing. Prompted by physical evidence and confirmed by what she read in his slumberous eyes.

Her body responded, as it had quickly learned to do when she saw that look. It fired up, moistened instantly, readying for what she knew was coming—an appeasement to the great hunger he raised in her.

Her lips lifted, met with his, instinctively. Moving as they knew to do with him. Mating in the way their mouths had taught each other. Openly, wetly, tongue to tongue.

Whimpering at the ecstasy of fulfillment after so much unabated hunger, she leaned in, lifted her arms to drape them around his neck, clung to him.

Felt his answering passion, which was almost desperate, as his arms wrapped around her, holding her to him in an iron grasp. He devoured her lips and she took from him. He filled her up and she gave all she had.

It was different, holding, being held, in the home that was her sanctuary. And yet…it was heartbreakingly familiar, too.

She'd missed his touch. Too much.

Missed having the right to touch him, too.

He groaned and the aching sound flowed through her, finding an answering need inside of her that only he could raise. And she thought of the baby moving…

She felt him slow down just as reality dawned on her. Whether Greg felt her withdrawal, or she'd been reacting to his, she didn't know. He didn't step away. Didn't abandon her. She kept herself pushed up against him, her pelvis putting pressure against what had to be a seriously uncomfortable hardness, as she continued to hold him.

To ease them both back to the choices they'd made because they knew they were the right ones for their future.

"I'm sorry," she whispered at his shoulder.

"Don't be," he replied, his head bent so that his chin lightly scraped the back of her neck as he spoke. "I'm not."

She had to let go. And feared that when she did, he'd be gone. Honestly wanting him to leave if that was what he needed.

"We aren't going to be able to make this work, are we?"

He straightened, still holding her, but moving his lower body away from hers. "I think we just did," he said.

Hope flared in spite of her recognizing its foolishness.

"This baby needs you in its life as a full-time father," she whispered, wishing she could wrap her long dark hair around her and hide. She also admitted, "And I can't stand the thought of losing your friendship."

"Neither of you are going to lose me," he said, sounding so sure of himself as he took a gentle hold on her shoulders and bent until she was looking him in the eye. "And did you hear what you just said?"

He was smiling, so she thought back over her words. Repeated them...

"There..." he interrupted. "*Friendship*. You said *friendship*. You know what that means, don't you?"

She knew what it meant to her, but had to stay silent to keep her tears from falling.

"We're in a relationship!" he told her. "You and me. It might be platonic, and it's not a marriage, but it's a friendship. And when I think about everything I could have with you, friendship is number one, Elaina. It means that nothing else gets in the way of us having each other's backs."

So she'd been wrong. Staying silent hadn't stopped the tears. They pooled and dropped to her cheeks as she stood there, smiling at him.

Wanting to believe him.

Wanting so badly to believe.

And determining that she'd try with all of her might.

For her baby's sake. For Greg's.

And for her own, too.

She was coming back to life.

Chapter Sixteen

Greg knew that the real problem preventing him and Elaina from ever having more than a friendship was the memory of Peter Alexander. Knew, too, that he'd never be able to compete with a dead man.

Didn't even want to.

If he was going to go up against anyone for anything, he wanted all competitors present there of their own accord, and on an equal playing field.

He'd never been much of a competitor, anyway. He liked to read. To study. To figure out perplexing puzzles.

And he liked Elaina Alexander more than he'd ever liked anything or anyone in his life.

He hadn't been sure she'd want to keep their grocery shopping plans for Friday after work, not after they'd nearly lost their minds in his room only hours before, but he was glad to see her car pull up the drive just a few minutes after he'd arrived home to change. Living with the admission that he was in love with her, he was relieved as hell, was more like it. He'd looked for her at work that day, but during the only break he'd had, she'd been with a patient.

"I wasn't sure you'd still want to shop with me," she said as she climbed into the front seat of his new big SUV, having changed out of her scrubs into a dark, tie-dyed tank sundress. She'd redone her ponytail, too, leaving her shoulders bare. With the humid eighty-degree temperature that day, he understood her need to be cool. Comfortable. He could have done without seeing those shoulders, though, so soon after having buried his head in them.

"We have to eat," he told her a second later than he probably should have. She surely knew he'd been thinking of something else.

And smart as she was, or more accurately, as well as she knew him, she'd probably know what he'd been thinking about, too.

"And the way to handle what happened last night is to face it head-on," he hastily said. "If we pretend it didn't happen, it's just going to lie in wait, and get us again."

She nodded. "You must have been...uncomfortable..."

"I took care of it." She could make of that what she liked, but he hoped she was picturing him with his hand active—and wanting it to have been hers—since he'd been picturing the hand as hers.

"For what it's worth, I didn't," she replied pragmatically.

So much for her sharing his lustful solution. He needed to face it head-on, but wasn't so fond of being hit on the head with it.

"For future reference, can we keep that kind of information to ourselves? Unless of course you want us both to share every time we have…um…difficult nights?"

She chuckled. "You're going to hold me to the fire, aren't you, Adams? Making sure that I don't require anything of you that isn't also required of me."

"Would you have it any other way?"

"No."

They rode in silence for a couple of minutes and, laying her head back on the seat, she sighed, looking more relaxed than he'd seen her outside of his bed immediately after sex.

"You're certainly a different passenger than I had riding with me to Mission Viejo earlier in the week," he said, wanting her to see that they really could get through the tough times. Less than twenty-four hours since they'd almost made a horrible mistake, and there she was, comfortable going grocery shopping with him.

"I feel safer in the bigger car," she told him. "And safer when I'm the driver."

And he felt like an A-class idiot.

He'd been all over what it had to have taken her to recover from paralysis. And to deal with the death of the love of her life in a vehicle.

He'd failed to process that she'd been a passenger in a fatal car accident. No one forgot something like that. He saw too many incidents of post-traumatic stress in his line of work.

"Were you conscious?" he asked, wanting her to know that she didn't have to be alone with whatever horrors were stored in her mind. "After the crash?"

She nodded. And then said, "And it's not that I don't want you to talk about it, but can we please just keep the conversation easy while we're on the road?"

Note taken. She needed his attention fully on his driving. Not on her.

As did anyone else driving within his vicinity.

Elaina might think she didn't have enough to offer, might think she did all the taking, but Greg knew differently.

Even if he hadn't been in love with her, even if she never returned his love in the same way, in her quiet, unassuming way, she was giving him a much fuller awareness of everything around him. Making his world more alive.

How could a man not stick around for that?

* * *

Pushing her cart out to his car, Elaina was happier than she'd been in a long, long time. Peacefully so. With anticipation for the future lingering around the periphery of her mind. She'd grasp at it and it would fade, but if she didn't pay attention, it would flit around again.

She loaded her groceries and Greg loaded his—on opposite sides of the huge space in the back. "We're probably wasting money here," he said, closing the hatch.

"I supposed we could figure out a monthly average and include it in the rent," she allowed hesitantly, waiting for her mind to come up with some reason why it wasn't a good idea. Or some stab of guilt to poke her from the inside out.

Pulling her seat belt down, fitting the clasp into the holder, she let it go when she did feel a sudden stab from the inside out.

"What's wrong?" Greg, instantly attentive as her seat belt snapped back, turned toward her.

"Nothing," she told him, afraid to move this time, lest her little one freeze again. "Put your hand on my stomach," she said. "Right where I put it last night."

"The baby's moving?" He glanced at her, and then at her belly, as though he expected the child to just pop right up and say hello.

"Yes," she said softly, not wanting her voice to distract her little one from exercising.

Placing his hand gently right where she'd helped him place it the night before, Greg applied a very slight pressure. And sat completely still.

Reminding her of a time she'd seen him with his stethoscope on a patient's chest, counting heartbeats. He looked like he was concentrating that completely. Was intensely focused.

The baby moved again, more strongly. Greg's face blanked. As though he was in shock. She watched him, waiting for him to glance up at her. Waiting for his smile.

He didn't look up. He just kept staring at his hand on her belly, his eyes moist. Then welling. And tears dripped slowly down his face.

Elaina, unable to hold back her own tears, thanked whatever fates whose bad side she'd been on for so long, for allowing her to give Greg this gift.

"I think maybe it's time to find out the gender of the baby." They'd put away their groceries and Greg made the comment to her as he returned from putting the toothpaste he'd purchased away in his bathroom. She was standing at the sliding glass door in the dining room, watching Beldon out in the yard, and as he spoke, she opened the door and walked outside, leaving the door open.

Because she was coming right back in? Or as an invitation to follow her?

Greg took it as invitation. "Unless you don't want

to," he amended his statement, plopping down in a chair on the patio right outside the door. There were two padded chairs and a love seat there, with a wrought iron table. He'd never seen any of it used.

She laughed as Beldon came running over to her and sat, his whole body seeming to wiggle with his tail. When she didn't pet him or hand down a treat, he jumped up on her.

"Down," Greg said, kindly but with the firmness that told everyone at work to do as he said at once. And then realized that he'd just rushed right into something that wasn't his business.

"Down," Elaina repeated, taking the dog's paws off from her belly and lowering them to the ground. "I shouldn't have butted in."

Sitting down opposite him, Elaina called Beldon to her and started petting him. "Of course, you should have," she said. "You're going to be here indefinitely, and he's part of the household. The way I see it, we're co-parenting him, too. Although the responsibility of Beldon is all mine, I'm not shoving that off onto you…"

He hadn't thought for a second that she was.

"It actually worked, huh?" she asked, smiling again as she looked at him. "You're right, he needs to know that he can't jump up. Most particularly after the baby comes. I just wasn't thinking about that…"

"What were you thinking about?"

"Finding out the sex of the baby."

Ah. Curious, he asked, "What do you think about it?"

She shook her head. Which made him need to know even more. He waited.

"I want to know," she said. "It's time. I get that..."

He nodded, not following.

"Right now..." Putting both of her hands on her belly, she continued, "This is just the beginning. We have a heartbeat and movement. It's a safe happy place to be...and not much else to think about..."

Or worry about. Greg stood up, reached a hand down to her, and when she hesitated, shook his hand a bit. "Come on, walk with me," he said.

Warmth flooded his entire being as she put her hand in his and stood, walked with him across the yard to the shed, Beldon trotting along beside them as though certain that he'd been included in the invitation.

Taking a key out of his pocket, he opened the door and stepped aside, showing her, on the workbench side of the building, the beginnings of a new project.

"You work with wood?" she asked, sounding shocked enough that he could have been offended. Except that her shock was valid.

"I've never tried before," he told her. "But you've talked so much about the great work Wood does and so... I called him and asked if he'd mind giving me a hand in making a crib for the baby."

They'd looked at furniture. Hadn't landed on any crib that seemed like...the one.

"You called Wood." She stared at him, and by the blank expression on her face, he couldn't tell if he'd upset her or not.

So he just continued on with what was. "I did. And he's come over a couple of times while you weren't here, to help me get started. I'm doing the legs," he said. They were the most basic. "And I'm on my seventh one."

"The crib's going to have seven legs?"

"Five are in the trash."

Elaina glanced toward the two good stems he had sitting on the worktable, with the router he'd recently learned to use, and said, "You think you'll have it done in time?"

Practically speaking, the question had merit. "I know I wouldn't if I was doing it myself," he told her. "Wood's making the majority of it at his place. I've been there once, and then he set me up here with the legs."

"Wood's making us a crib?" Her eyes lit up at that one. And after having seen her ex-husband's abilities, the bedroom and nursery furniture in his and Cassie's home, Greg understood Elaina's excitement.

"We're making it *together*," he told her. Because he had a point to make. "When you talked about Wood making Alan's furniture, it made me want to do the same for my baby. I'm a doctor, good with my hands and doing math. I'm great at figuring out puzzles and putting things together…but I don't know the first thing about woodworking. What tools to use for what. How they work. The glues, the types of woods…yet I couldn't get that idea of a finished crib, handmade, with my work in it, out of my head. Maybe I wasn't going to be living where the crib would live, but even more so if I wasn't, I was jazzed by the idea that my child would sleep in a crib I'd helped make…"

She was looking silently from him to the workbench with those two spindles of wood, while Beldon went back out to run in the yard.

"I might not end up doing much of it," he said. "I might not ever get the legs right. But I'm happy if all I do is sit and think about how cool it would be. If I let fear of the unknown stop me finding out, I'll miss a whole bunch of experiences along the way."

Her gaze turned on him, not in a particularly friendly way. "You think I'm letting fear stop me from moving forward? Because let me tell you…"

"…I think you could let fear rob you of enjoying every step of the way," he interrupted her. "And I think you're so set on doing it all on your own that you don't factor in the Woods in your life. Wood being one of them. But there's Cassie. And me. Among others. Yeah, the more the baby grows, the more we find out, the more real it all becomes, but… You want to know the sex of the child. And yet you're holding back…"

"When I should be moving forward, enjoying every step, no matter what it brings?"

Spoken by a woman who'd walked more incredibly painful steps than he'd ever fully grasp. Her words stopped him.

"You're right, Greg." The soft tone had him looking up at her. "I need to let myself enjoy more. To reach for more." She was looking at him in a way he recognized from their previous situation and his body lit up.

And then she reached for one of the crib legs. "This is actually pretty good," she said, sounding impressed.

"I thought so, too, but it hasn't passed Wood's inspection yet. I have to tell you, Wood isn't going to let anything less than perfect on that crib."

"I can't believe he's making us a crib!"

"I can't believe you didn't know he would," Greg said. "When I talked to him about it, he'd acted kind of hurt that you hadn't already talked to him about what you wanted. Apparently you weren't shy about asking for the bedroom set he made you." He hadn't known until then that Wood had furnished Elaina's suite.

Elaina's hands ran slowly, almost lovingly, along the sanded edge of a crib leg. "That was a while back…"

"To hear him tell it, that bedroom set saved his life."

She turned back to him. "What are you talking about?"

"That's up for him to tell you, but I gather that he was on some thin ice after Peter died. And felt that, with his lack of education, there was little he could do for you, except give you a home that welcomed you, a bed to sleep in that pleased you, landscaping that spoke to you..."

Her eyes teared and Greg had to fight not to reach out for her as he said, "You were so determined to fight on your own, as I think you had to be to survive. Yet you welcomed him into your life, built a home with him, which neither of you would have had without the other, from what I can see. You did as much for him as he did for you, Elaina..."

She nodded, rubbing the leg of the crib again, caressing it, and Greg knew his first bout of jealousy of an inanimate object.

"Once we know the baby's gender, it will all be more real," he said softly. "We'll be loving on a deeper level as the baby takes on an identity. Maybe our worries will grow, too, but so will the joy."

She nodded. Smiled. But he saw a tear slide down the side of her face that was visible to him, knew that he'd pushed as far as he should.

"This was supposed to be a surprise, by the way,"

he said, picking up the second good leg. "My idea, not Wood's, so we can let him know you know."

Elaina glanced up as she took the leg she'd been fondling into both hands. "It seems too good to be true...the way this is all working out. It makes me afraid of what could be around the corner."

"I know." And he understood why. There was no denying that she'd suffered more than a lot of people. Had memories of horror locked away in her brain. No taking away the shock of tragedy from her emotional instincts. "Just know that I'll be there...and others will be there with you. Around every corner."

If she got that he was telling her he loved her, so be it.

If not, then that was okay, too. He didn't want to give her more than she was ready to handle. And wasn't ready to know if she didn't return his feelings.

One step at a time.

For both of them.

Chapter Seventeen

Elaina was in the kitchen that weekend, making a cup of tea, when Greg came in from the shed. Now that he was no longer hiding his project, he'd spent most evenings after work outside. Sometimes Beldon was with him, sometimes not.

Sometimes she had to shake herself to put it all together. How could it be that she was experiencing some of the things she'd enjoyed with Wood—watching him working wood in the shed and seeing a dog in the yard—and yet experiencing them in a whole new way?

A much fuller, more alive way?

Greg had said that much of the life she and Wood had shared had been of her own making. And that she'd saved Wood as much as he'd saved her. More and more, she was beginning to see truth in that belief. But still, she feared every good thing that was happening.

She wanted the baby. Didn't doubt her ability to love it. To give it a happy life.

And yet…she couldn't accept the possibility that her own life could be happy, as well. It was like she had a mental roadblock she just couldn't get around.

Watching Greg come into the kitchen just then, she felt the pang of her inner battle worse than ever. He wanted her. She wanted so badly to give him what he wanted. To try to make him happy. Sexually. Emotionally. For life.

And yet…to do so…felt wrong. Even the thought of it brought forth feelings of immense guilt. She fought them. Fought with herself. Was fighting for her personal emotional freedom and right to feel utter joy. But couldn't figure out how to win the battle.

"I've chosen a name if it's a boy," Greg announced, sending a spiral of emotion through her. Anticipation. Excitement. An instinctive hold on both.

They had an ultrasound scheduled the following morning. And if that didn't reveal the gender of the child, they would have a blood test done at the same time.

Greg hadn't said another word about finding out the gender after their talk in the shed. She was the one who'd made the decision. Who'd pushed to have it done.

Because she did want to be fully alive.

To that end, she looked up from the cup of micro-waved water into which she'd just dropped a tea bag. "What is it?" she asked, trying not to notice how sexy he looked in the jeans and white undershirt he'd adopted as his woodworking attire. She didn't even care about the sawdust that clung to the material and would soon be leaving a little trail down the hallway.

If Greg noticed, he'd vacuum it up. If he didn't, she would.

If she were a different woman, she'd be rubbing herself against him and getting some of that saw-dust on herself.

"Peter," he said, leaning back against the counter as he spoke. "You wanted to honor your husband, and Wood, and I want that, too," he said. His gaze was direct, clear.

And easy. Convincing her that he was speaking the complete truth.

Where her heart should have flared, it wilted.

No.

The word came to her mind clearly. With no ex-planation.

And no hint at its origin.

She waited a second, searched for the reply she wanted to give, an expression of how much Greg's choice meant to her, opened her mouth and heard "no" again. Out loud.

She'd given him the right to choose the boy's name, no stipulations added. He got to choose.

Frowning, he glanced at her, toward the tea bag she was bobbing and then back at her. Her peripheral vision caught the movement. She'd yet to look at him directly.

Not since she'd heard her deceased husband's name come off his lips.

"You'd planned for Peter to be the father," Greg said. "You were having yourself inseminated with his sperm when you found out I'd already managed by some act of supreme fate to perform the job first. It's right that Peter be remembered here. That he have a place in this family, and in your life. I feel good about the choice. My son, if that's what we're having, will have a namesake to look up to. And maybe even more of a reason to bond with Wood—as his brother's namesake."

Elaina sipped from her tea. Burnt her lip, her tongue, and didn't care. She sipped a second time. Put the cup down, shook her head. "No."

Still shaking her head, Elaina walked out of the kitchen, her tea still on the counter. She wrapped her arms around her middle, went to the living room and sat in the darkness, feeling at home there. Too at home there. Her world had been dark for so long.

Dark felt normal.

But the life she was building for her baby...that was going to be filled with light. She wouldn't have it any other way...and while she'd loved Peter, memories of him were tinged with sadness and frustration. And guilt.

"What's going on?" Greg sat beside her. Not touching her, but...there. She moved farther away. Didn't want to feel his heat, to be so aware of him. He belonged in the light, with the child they'd unknowingly created.

There was no mistake about that baby's creation. She knew that as well as she knew that life came with no guarantees, that bad things happened to good people, that there was nothing you could ever do to make sure bad didn't happen.

She'd made a very real choice to wake up. To give instead of take. She'd put her intentions out into the universe. And the response had been a baby with Greg instead of with Peter.

Because with the baby, there would be light.

"I don't want this baby to forever wear a reminder of my tragedy." The words came and she approved them. They were ample, without spilling any more darkness.

In a room where she couldn't see well enough to make out more than shadowy outlines of features.

"Peter's life, the things he did when he was alive, weren't tragic."

"He lived life exactly as he wanted to live it." She could say that with conviction.

"And that's a bad thing?"

"It can be. When those around you are made to continuously sacrifice so that you can have things exactly as you want them." Doom settled around her. She knew she'd made a mistake the second the words escaped. Why had they suddenly refused to be held back?

"Are we talking about you now?" Greg sounded truly perplexed.

"I somehow became what he'd been…" Why hadn't she seen that? Was she talking out loud? She most certainly wasn't having a conversation with Greg. She knew he was there. Felt his presence. Knew she had to keep herself separate and apart from it.

"All those years, Wood sacrificed, and Peter let him. Wood was smarter than Peter even. He could have been anything he wanted to be. Before he quit school, he was already getting scholarship opportunities. For sports *and* for academics. He turned it all down to finish raising Peter. Who, by the way, didn't get any major scholarships. Not because he didn't try. He just didn't win them. And that was fine, because he worked harder than most.

"But when he graduated high school, rather than insisting that it was Wood's turn, going to work before college so that Wood could have a chance to finish his own education, Peter just kept taking from his older brother. He never once encouraged Wood to do more. Never even asked what his brother might have wanted for his own life if their mother hadn't been killed.

"And after we married...he did the same with me. He loved me. He brought me things I wanted. Gave me a home and family. But all of those things served him, too. Which isn't bad. It's the way it's supposed to be..." What was wrong with her? She didn't usually ramble. Didn't go on and on.

"I loved him, but he was my past. This child is my future. I want to move on."

So badly she wanted to move on. Move away from... Greg could have been there. Or not. There was only silence, and she couldn't stand it any longer.

"Two people, filling each other's needs. That's how it's supposed to work," she said, but not sounding at all like the self she knew. She was acting like a ghost. Some creature that didn't really exist, emitting words that had always been there, lingering, but not meant to be spoken.

Or heard. Not even by her own mind's ear.

Peter had given her life after her parents had been killed. Without him...

And he'd been good to her. Loved her. Brought her gifts she'd truly wanted.

Been gentle in his dealings with her. And he'd been good to Wood, too. But in return, he'd expected both her and Wood to support him unconditionally. Peter hadn't even considered Wood's dreams—or her own. Peter had made Elaina feel obligated to him. Unlike the unconditional love she'd known with her parents, his had seem to come at a price. Like she was forever in his debt. And while she still cared for him, and was grateful for all he'd done for her, she didn't owe him her future. She never had.

She'd been thinking, talking silently to herself, but heard a voice and realized she was talking out loud.

She watched it all happening, her on the couch, Greg somewhere there, words flying everywhere... Like a horror movie, a nightmare, she could see it all and couldn't stop it.

There was roaring in her ears. A loud surf encasing her head in cotton. She was in a battle for herself. Breaking free from the misconceptions her mind had taken on, probably, in part, of her own accord, but from Peter's confidence and strong personality, as well. She couldn't hear Greg move; she couldn't breathe.

"I tried to encourage Wood to do more...and he was so used to Peter taking that Wood somehow took my encouragement to mean that I thought he wasn't enough. I...it kills me to think he ever thought I thought that... That I hurt him..." Emotion welled. She wasn't sure what to do with it.

There was too much to let out. Too many tears to cry.

And too much to keep boxed in any longer.

She couldn't grasp her own happiness. She'd lost the right when she'd hurt the two men who'd saved her from near death. Those two men who were the only living family she'd had.

"I was responsible for the accident," she blurted out. "It's because of me that Peter's dead. I took from Wood the one thing he loved more than anything else in the world. And I took away everything Peter had worked for. And no one knows."

The words were said.

Her truth had been exposed.

And she was done being a prisoner. For better or worse, her most horrible truth was free.

Greg just reached up and flipped the switch on the tableside lamp. The light infused the room in a soft glow that reached over to Elaina's side of the couch, illuminating one side of her face and casting shadow on the other.

There were tears wetting her beautiful features, but they weren't streaming, engulfing her. They just welled slowly over her eyes, dripped down her cheeks. The expression in her eyes seemed to have no beginning and no end. A part of her that had always been there, but that he could only now see.

Her ponytail, as neat as usual, seemed stark, unkind, as though expecting too much of someone who was weary from having to hold it all up, so perfectly, for so long.

She didn't react to the light. Didn't turn to look at him. Or turn away, either.

And he knew they weren't done.

He couldn't leave her in the tragic place she was occupying. There was more. There had to be more to this story.

Not for him. Not even for their baby.

But for the sweet spirit that she was.

Elaina would see that their baby was happy. She'd tend to it. Shower it with affection and discipline, too.

She'd even do everything she could to give Greg anything that was in her power to give.

But unless something changed about the way she dealt with her tragic past and her grief, she'd never be able to give either of them the only thing they really needed from her—her whole self. Heart and soul. All of her. Open to all of them. To whatever life had to offer any of them.

"Tell me about the accident."

She'd put it out there and he'd bet his life it was the first time she'd ever even really talked about it. He had a feeling she hadn't said a word about this before. Not to a counselor. Not to Wood. Or her friends. She'd put it out there to him. Trusted him with it for some reason. He had to help her manage this memory.

"Peter had achieved his goals, the list of things

we'd said we would accomplish before I went to medical school. I'd taken all of the mandatory courses. Had even put in the clinical hours. I wanted to be a doctor as badly as he did. But he'd felt strongly about going first, because once I started having kids, I wouldn't be able to take on him in school, too. I would support the household first, taking care of household details, the bills, fixes, cleaning, shopping...so he could focus fully on school. And then he'd support us for the rest of his life."

From what she'd said earlier about Peter's scholastic career, he translated the most recent insight into meaning that in order for Peter to successfully master med school, he'd had to be able to focus on nothing else. Having been to medical school himself, Greg could see that.

"That day, the accident... I'd just been accepted to medical school, was so ready to begin my turn. He'd just been awarded his license, had a new practice he was starting with some others, and my time had come."

Relieved that she'd recognized that she had a time of her own, Greg made himself sit still, leaning back on his side of the couch as though he was in any way relaxed. He readied himself to listen to what she had to say. Listen so that he could understand her. Not so that he could change her.

If she ever wanted to make any changes in her life, she'd have to do it herself. First, because he knew she wouldn't let it be any other way. And second, because he knew that unless any maturation came from within, it wasn't real. And though personal developments could last for years, it could also unravel at any moment—any particular point of stress.

"Except that, from Peter's perspective, my time hadn't come yet. Or rather, it had, but what 'my time' was to entail had changed—to fit *his* needs. He told me he was giving me the world. A lovely home. A life in which I would never need to go to work and do the bidding of any boss. To stress over classes or tests or deadlines. He'd worked so hard for so many years and was ready to enjoy the fruits of his labors, not have to go to work, and help out at home, too. He told me that I didn't need to go to school or get a degree that our family didn't even need me to have."

Greg's skin tightened as he grew hot. And then cold. Sometimes a clearer vision wasn't pretty. Or even palatable.

"He wanted to start a family."

Greg almost stopped her. Could see at least somewhat the explosion that was to come. He didn't know about the actual crash that took Peter Alexander's life, but he knew all he wanted to know.

And still sat quietly. Because he wasn't listening for himself.

And more than what he wanted, what he needed— the desire to be a real friend to Elaina—was holding him silent.

"He wanted to be young enough, after the kids left for college, for us to learn to sail and spend a year on a yacht, to travel all over the world, maybe do some volunteer work in countries where medical attention isn't as readily available as it is in the United States..."

The more she talked, the more his heart sank. If Peter had been evil, perhaps Elaina would have better hope of ever getting herself to the other side of guilt. But Peter Alexander had apparently had some great qualities. Enough so that they masked his innate narcissism. Not that he was in any position to diagnose a dead man. Nor would he ever do so out loud. But the picture was so clear to him that it wouldn't disappear, either. Peter had consistently neglected Elaina's needs in favor of his own. Instinctively, Greg knew that he'd never make the same mistakes. Elaina and their child would be his world.

"He wanted me to put off my own medical school until after we'd had the kids. And I suddenly knew that when that time came, he'd have me put it off again, then, too. Putting if off while he was in school was a given—we needed money coming in. But when he passed the boards and used kids as a means to stall me, I knew he didn't see me as a doctor at all. He never had."

Greg had reached the same conclusion. Didn't make a sound.

"In the car that day, I told him that I was going to

medical school. He'd brought the subject up first. But I was glad he was driving when I had to tell him, so that he couldn't go off on me as badly. That way, he wouldn't be able to give me his full attention. But he did. He raised his voice to me in a way I'd never heard. Told me that medical school just was not an option. That he was not going to support me through it because our family didn't need it."

Oh, God.

"I screamed back at him." Tears still fell slowly. Intermittently. He wanted to wipe them away, to kiss them, to hold her until she exorcised every negative emotion and she could start over.

But he knew better. Life didn't work that way.

Talking about a traumatic event was good. Probably even miraculous, given what had happened to Elaina. But even that wouldn't be a miracle cure.

"I'd never screamed like that at anyone before," she said, her voice soft, her tone questioning. As though, even then, she couldn't believe how she'd sounded to herself in the car that day.

"I told him that I wanted a divorce…"

Her tears came swiftly then. Accompanied by broken sobs. "In a spur-of-the-moment conversation, I was willing to throw away the only family I had for what *I* wanted…"

Yep. He'd known it wasn't going to be good. Or miraculous.

And he knew she had to finish explaining why

she was so afraid of being selfish, of taking care of her own needs. Which was the only reason he wasn't hauling her up into his arms and showing her that she wasn't alone right then. Promising her that she'd never be alone again.

It wasn't a promise she'd be able to believe.

"And that's why he was staring at me in complete disbelief, in utter shock, when another car, driving in the wrong lane, suddenly veered toward us. I screamed again, trying to alert him and get him to look at the road, but it apparently only sounded like more of the same to him. He glanced up. He saw the car. The look on his face... He turned the wheel sharply, putting his side of the car more completely in front of the other car. And protecting me... I'll never forget that look on his face. He knew he was likely going to die.

"And I think, in that split second, he chose to die, because my remark about divorce had done him in..."

"You don't know that."

"No, I don't. And there's no way I ever will, for sure. But I knew Peter..."

"And loved him for all you were worth for many years." And ever since her husband's death there'd apparently never been any voice but her own condemning one, talking to her about what really happened that day.

Maybe she hadn't allowed there to be one. She

was alive and Peter was not. Her last words to him hadn't been what she'd ever choose them to be.

But his death didn't wipe away the damage some of his actions had done. It didn't wipe away his own culpability in the fight they'd had that day. Greg wasn't into damning a dead man—a man with what sounded like some great qualities. But he'd be tempted to deck the guy one if he showed up alive in that moment.

And something occurred to him. "Maybe Peter made the choice he did, sparing you, because in those last seconds, he'd wanted to give his life for yours. He knew you had more to do, because he knew he'd robbed you of any chance to live your dreams, too, being married to him."

She sniffled. Wiped her nose with a tissue she'd pulled out of the end table drawer beside her.

"Maybe you honor that choice by doing what you've been saying you're ready to do—living fully again. Otherwise, what was his sacrifice for?"

"Maybe."

He heard the word. And heard the lack of conviction in her tone, too.

Elaina had been living too long in her silent pool of guilt to suddenly swim to shore and climb out. He fully understood that. The demons there with her were set on robbing her of a future life.

He could only hope that her talking to him was one

step forward, like she was calling out from within the pool. Letting someone know she was there.

So she had a light toward which to swim.

He hoped against hope that he and the baby would be that light.

Chapter Eighteen

The baby wasn't positioned in a way that made gender detection possible, they discovered the next day. For all of her angst about finding out whether she was having a boy or a girl, Elaina was hugely disappointed when the ultrasound didn't give them an answer.

Whatever Greg was feeling, he didn't say. He'd sat with her the night before until she'd fallen asleep sitting up on the couch after her confession. And when she'd woken, he'd still been there, dozing. She'd stood, thinking she wouldn't wake him, but he'd stirred awake, as well, and with a "Get some sleep," he'd given her a light brush of his lips on her brow and headed down the hall toward his suite.

He'd left her...feeling as though she was enough. For the first time in a long, long while. He'd left her, but not really. He'd given her space she needed to work things out in her own mind, to come to terms with what she'd told him. With the perspective he'd added to what had been a one-sided mental rhetoric for far too long. But he hadn't gone away. He'd merely walked down the hall.

He'd been gone by the time she came out to make her tea that morning, and had come into the clinic just as they were being called back to the ultrasound.

From down in the darkness, she wondered if he was avoiding her. Didn't blame him. But there was a shimmer of light now, too, deep down inside. It wasn't all bad anymore. Maybe she'd let out some bad and made room for some good. Maybe she'd let it in when she'd cracked the night before.

Maybe, she'd let him in.

Either way, she didn't really think he was avoiding her so much as giving her time to process.

She cleaned off her belly, pulled her scrub top down, got off that table and submitted to the blood test that would tell them most definitively the gender of their baby.

Greg, also in blue scrubs, was waiting for her in the lobby. "You want to have lunch in the cafeteria?" His gaze was warm. A little distant, or maybe hesitant, but still warm.

More than bedside manner.

She cataloged every nuance.

He didn't seem to be turned off by what she'd told him. And strangely, she wasn't embarrassed for having fallen apart on him.

Such an oddity, considering her usual reticence and need for privacy. But she'd changed, at least a little bit. And left room for more.

"Yes," she answered his lunch question after a few seconds of silence. "I apologize for last night," she added, as they walked out toward their cars. And before he could tell her no apology was necessary, or thank her for giving one, she continued, "But... thank you...for hanging out with me."

"I wanted to be there."

Such a simple truth. More for her to think about.

He wasn't asking questions. Didn't seem to be placing judgment. And now that her truths were out, they didn't seem as life-threatening. For a second, she caught a glimpse of what her life might look like from his perspective.

And could still breathe.

"So...we're good?" she asked as they reached her car. He didn't have questions? Advice? Recommendations? Diagnoses?

"We're always good, Elaina," he told her. "I'm the guy who jumps in and stays until I'm no longer wanted around."

He was only half joking. And she felt another pang as she considered his self-concern when they'd first talked about him renting the suite from her. He didn't want to push himself in where he didn't fit.

And her, with her propensity for leaning on the guy that was there...but maybe that habit within her had grown with Peter's manipulation. Maybe he'd needed her that way. Maybe they'd have worked things out, worked long term. Maybe not. But she'd given him her all. Tried to be the wife he needed. And fought for herself, too. Just as Greg was fighting for what he needed?

Because people were supposed to need things from each other. And, to be healthy or find joy, they needed to ask for things, too...

"I've come to accept that I'm that guy," Greg said, sobering completely as he stood at her car door, meeting her gaze. "And I'm okay with that. I'll be here until you no longer need me."

She couldn't imagine that ever happening. The thought came to her out of nowhere. Somehow, Greg completely felt a part of her.

The realization panicked her. And brought a curious sense of more, too.

"Unless you meet the woman of your dreams and want to get married." She grasped at a safety straw, but said it mockingly now. She'd overplayed that card and now it was done. There was no going back.

"Even then," he said, still peering directly into her soul. "I'm here. Father to the child we created. And your friend."

She wanted so much more than friendship from him. And was afraid to trust herself not to hurt him. Knowing that your actions could devastate someone, because you meant so much to them...

Like her parents' sudden deaths had devastated her.

And her cry for a divorce had devastated Peter...

Greg knew. And seemed to take for granted that she was handling the situation.

She knew she was handling it. She'd been in and out of counseling. Would go back if the current situation seemed to demand it. Mostly therapy just helped her figure things out.

She was working diligently on that already. And was still standing the morning after. Still competent.

"I'm here for you, too," she said, and wanted to snatch the words back immediately. Afraid of what they could mean, what she could be promising, what need he might have that she didn't yet know about.

Afraid she'd let him down.

And still, she was glad she'd said them. The night before, when she'd seen him sleeping there, perched awkwardly on the end of the couch, her entire being had swelled with compassion. With a strong compulsion to take care of him. To get him comfortable so he'd be rested in the morning.

She needed to get to work. To get out of herself and focus completely on others. People she could help from afar, whose parameters in terms of need of her were clearly identified.

"I'll see you at noon, then," Greg was saying, and she smiled at him as she gave him her "okay."

Her heart got jumbled some more when he smiled back.

Greg was just coming out of a patient cubicle, pulling off his gloves, when he saw Elaina enter the ER a couple of days later.

The emergency surgery he'd just done—making a small but critical cut into the eyelid of a teenager to relieve pressure off the optic nerve so he wouldn't lose his sight due to swelling—had gone well. The football player's words of thanks were still ringing in his ears, which could have something to do with the surge of good mood that filled him at the sight of the mother of his child walking toward him.

The intense look on her face—not bad, not good, just…fervent—had him pulling her into an empty cubicle at the end of the row, pulling closed the curtain at the front of the three-walled exam space.

"What's up?"

"It's a girl!" Her mouth remained…impassive but the glow in her eyes matched the jubilant tone in her voice.

She grabbed his hand, pulling it to the slight mound of belly covered by her white doctor's coat.

Keeping her hand on top of his on her stomach, she said, "Daddy, meet Marisol..."

Daddy.

Marisol.

It hit him like the downward slope of the very tallest roller coaster. All at once. No stopping it. Exhilarating. And his stomach flew upward into his chest—it was frightening, too.

"I'm going to have a daughter." Who'd have thought? Who'd ever have thought?

A little girl was going to climb up into his lap, put her tiny arms around him and know that he'd protect her.

Or, or...ask him to read to her.

And put sticky lips against his cheek.

The wet drip of a tear on his hand had him glancing quickly up at Elaina. "I'm so glad I can give this to you," she said, so serious. "I don't know why it's me, or now, or you, but I'm glad, Greg. I'll be a good mother to her..."

"You're going to be a great mother," he said softly, keeping his hand with hers over their baby, while with his free hand he gently cupped Elaina's head beneath her swaying ponytail. "And I'm glad it's you," he told her. "If I could choose all the women I've known in my life, you'd still be it."

Her eyes glistened and she gave him a wobbly smile. "Marisol," she half chuckled. "Oh my God, I can't wait to see her..."

And she was scared. He saw the fear in her gaze.

Just as he knew that whether Elaina ever overcame her fears enough to let herself fully engage, or not, whether they were close friends, lovers, roommates or just co-parents, he'd be right beside her, raising their child.

And the rest...whether or not they'd be partners in life or in bed...time would either bring that to him, or it wouldn't.

No amount of jumping in, pushing or action on his part was going to make a damned bit of difference.

He'd finally figured out life's little secret.

There were some things you just couldn't make happen.

You did all you could do, and then just had to trust.

Over the next weeks, Elaina fell in love with Marisol with an intensity she couldn't control. There was no option. No ability to take her usual step back. Her daughter was alive inside her. With her every second. Growing beneath her heart. Living off her very breath.

She lay in the dark in her room, scared to death. Knowing that something could happen to the baby or to her at any time. And yet...she lay there smiling, too.

She'd never known love could feel so...good in an

all-encompassing way. That happiness could flourish in a way that made it stronger than anything fear could dish out.

Or maybe she had. When she'd been a kid. But she had blocked the best memories of the good feeling in order to survive after her parents had been taken from her.

She'd been an immature college sophomore all alone in the world with a life insurance policy that would barely keep her in school. If she worked, too.

The hard work had been good for her. She didn't begrudge it.

And she didn't begrudge working to help put Peter through medical school, either. There were a lot of times she'd wanted to stay home when he needed to go out. Times she'd have gone to the beach on a Saturday and he'd needed the stimulation of a game or hiking. She'd have liked colored lights on their Christmas tree. To own a home, even if it was a smaller starter home.

So many, many things she'd wished for back then. If she'd ever been able to choose, to have her way over his when they didn't agree...

Something Greg insisted on giving her even when she wasn't cognizant enough to ask for it.

A couple of weeks after her late-night talk with Greg, Elaina was on her way to the grocery store on Saturday when she made a detour. She'd left Greg at home in the shed, working on crib spindles. He'd mastered the four legs to Wood's satisfaction and her onetime brother-in-law, ex-husband and family member had promoted him to spindle maker.

Peter was still occupying a portion of her mind. She couldn't make a move without him there, in her thoughts. And so, almost in desperation, she went to see him. It had been over a year since she'd visited his grave.

She didn't have so much a conscious thought that she didn't want to go as a resistance inside her to being there. Still, her car took the turns by rote. She knew where to turn without any thought to where she was. In the first year after the accident, she'd had Wood bring her to the cemetery. Just as he'd brought her from the hospital in a wheelchair to attend Peter's funeral.

And the years after that...she'd gone on her own. Sometimes twice in a day. But with weeks in between visits.

Trying to find herself in their togetherness, and in not being a part of him.

To take honest accountability.

To grieve.

That day, though, she wasn't sure why she was there. Just that she had to be.

She'd told Greg their secret.

And as she parked, walked the short distance on the cement sidewalk and then through the grass to his grave, Elaina kept her hands in the pockets of her long black cardigan sweater, not caring about the recently watered grass wetting the bottoms of her jeans or the tips of her toes exposed by her sandals. She hadn't dressed for a trek across the lawn.

She'd asked for the placement of one of the cemetery's little cement benches across from the headstone years before. Sat down on the cold stone.

And still didn't know why she was there.

To introduce him to Marisol? Tell him that she was having a baby girl? And that it wasn't his?

That she was glad it was Greg's? And that, while she would have never meant to hurt him, she wasn't sorry she was glad that Greg was her baby's father?

Time passed. She had no idea how much. Memories of her years with Peter played out. Some were great, some were not. From pleasure to tension, peace to stress, happy and not so much. The time, on the anniversary of her parents' deaths, he'd brought her a beautiful frame full of pictures with her and them, to remind her of all the good that had come before.

The love that existed still…just like her love and Peter's would never leave.

She needed to get that frame out. To hang it on a wall in her home. Marisol should know her grandparents.

"I didn't want to divorce you…" The words came out. She hadn't been thinking them. Yet, there they were, falling at Peter's feet. Bones that were beneath the ground, but still there.

"I never would have." The truth was there.

And what if she'd met Greg at the hospital with her husband still alive, in the same way she had after Peter's death?

She might have been attracted to Greg—seemed pretty doubtful that whatever was between them wouldn't have been there—but she knew in her heart that she wouldn't have acted on it.

Knew it with her baby right there, inside her, with secret powers to see all truths. She wasn't going to lie to her child. Which meant she couldn't lie to herself.

Even by omission. But Peter *had* died, and she was attracted to Greg, and she was having his baby.

"I didn't mean those words..." Her voice broke and she started to cry again. Bent over herself, she sobbed. So afraid. And so...still there. Still alive.

Giving life now.

"Since the moment I sat in that car with you and knew you were gone... I promised myself that I'd never, ever speak out of pure emotion again. That I'd hold my tongue. Watch my words, and I have, Peter. I swear to God, I have. But..."

And there was the crux of it. But...what?

"But emotion is a part of life and you're ready to start living it again."

The words came from behind her. A voice so dear to her for so many years.

One she trusted.

And needed to hear.

Chapter Nineteen

"How'd you know I was here?" Elaina didn't have to look up to know that Wood's blue-eyed expression would hold concern. Or that the jeans he'd have on would be worn. That his shirt would be collared and probably denim.

"Greg said you'd been gone a lot longer than a grocery-store run would take. He was worried. Told me that you'd been talking about Peter…"

"Did he tell you what I said?" She glanced over, her face stiff with cried tears, a tissue balled up in her fist. She wasn't even sure she cared if Greg had told her secrets. Maybe the world needed to know.

"What do you think?"

She shook her head.

"I figured you were here," Wood said then. "Offered to tell him how to get here. He suggested that maybe it was better that I come."

"I'd have been fine on my own. Either of you could have called. I'd have answered."

Sitting beside her on the bench, Wood said, "It's time, Elaina."

And he was there to help. Just as he always had been. As he always would be. Alive or passed on.

Because family wasn't always biological. The bond was one deeper than science.

"He didn't really want me to go to medical school."

"I know."

She looked over at him, mouth hanging slightly open. "You knew?"

"He told me."

Of course, he would have. Peter had always told Wood things. He just didn't do anything he didn't want to do. Anything that didn't suit him.

"I balked at agreeing with Peter."

"I'd hoped you would."

"You did?" She made the statement. Confirming she'd heard him. Belief lagged behind.

"I knew how much it meant to you. I hoped you'd be strong enough to stand up to him."

She couldn't make sense of what he was saying. Wood had adored Peter. Given him everything. Supported him in every endeavor.

"My brother did many good things in his life," Wood said. "He worked hard. He felt true compassion. He was gentle. And he also, always, put himself first. It's just the way it was, from the time he was born. Peter only saw the world around him if his own needs had been met—and if the viewing device met his needs."

Now that she understood. Completely. Peter putting himself first. And only seeing the world, situations, her, from his own perspective.

"Being a doctor was perfect for him," Wood continued. "He could learn the science. Master the skill. The job was important. Respected. He'd be in charge. All things that made him feel good about himself. And because he felt good about himself, he made a great intern and resident. Because his compassion was genuine. He *did* care. But he had to come first."

Always.

In everything.

"I think you had to live with him to really see that." She could barely speak through the lump in her throat. Felt as though she was a ghost, right there with her deceased husband. And yet, felt alive, too. More than she had in a very long time. She was breaking free from Peter's manipulation.

Wood didn't respond. He'd never been a man of many words.

"He never encouraged you to reach for your own dreams," she said. It was the one thing she could see clearly. The way Peter had minimized Wood—Peter had done the same to her. She realized that now. But it had been so much harder for her to see.

"You did encourage me," Wood said. She was so glad he understood that—glad they'd had the conversation they had about it one day, shortly after he and Cassie had been married.

"I love him still," she said, needing total honesty. She'd never be completely free of the guilt. And probably shouldn't be. It gave her greater understanding. Greater compassion. A need to look at life from perspectives other than her own.

"I know. Me, too."

"And he loved us."

"Absolutely."

She took a deep, shaky breath. Let it out, her hands shaping Marisol. Guarding and protecting her.

"It's time to set yourself free, sis."

Her eyes filled again at the nickname he used to call her, back when Peter had been alive.

"I never want to lose you as family."

And that was the only reason she'd wanted to have Peter's baby. The truth was bald. Not pretty.

"That's up to you. I signed on as your brother for life when I witnessed your marriage to Peter. You know that. Cassie knew it, too, before we agreed to marry. She loves you."

She nodded.

"Okay, well, I'm going to go..."

That was so Wood. He'd say what he had to say and head out. And she loved him so much like the brother he would always be.

"Tell Greg I'll be a little while longer?"

"Yep." With a nod, and a tap to her shoulder, he walked back the way he'd come.

Taking the ghost she'd been with him.

Greg stood directly under the shower spray, water sluicing over his head, to his shoulders and down his body, when he thought he heard something in the other room. With a quick glance, he noted Beldon was right where he'd left him, lying just outside the shower door.

Thinking the dog had left the room and come back, he turned his back, closed his eyes, lifted his face and continued to allow himself to soak up one of the sensual pleasures he was at liberty to enjoy. Warm water pounding down on naked skin. Relaxing muscles that were far too tense after every workshop venture. He enjoyed the activity. Even more than he'd figured he might. But Marisol's crib…he wouldn't accept even the most minor flaw…

The shower door opened. Eyes flying open to a deluge of water, Greg started to turn, arm raised and ready to fight, only to hear, "Steady there, sailor. I come in peace."

Sailor.

Oh my God. He'd once dared Elaina to try to send

his ship out to sea... They'd been in the shower after a particularly energetic bit of lovemaking and he'd been certain she couldn't get him turned on again so soon.

She'd made him into a sailor that night. And several other times, as well.

As his mind was still processing the words, the reality of her voice inside his opened shower door, she slid fully behind him. Her hands began moving over his back. Down his sides.

The door shut behind her. Whether on its own or with her aid, he had no idea. He just knew that his neglected penis was not missing one second of what was transpiring.

And—oh, God—things were transpiring. A hard round ball pressed up against his lower back as Elaina's fingers slid around him to find his belly button, and then travel upward, tangling in the hair of his chest. Moving on to his nipples. With hands desperately plastered to the tile of the shower wall, Greg leaned a bit forward, spreading his legs as he did so.

If she wanted something from him, she'd tell him so.

This part of "them," he had down pat.

And so did she.

Slim, feminine fingers slid down his torso, finding the bush of hair at the apex of his thighs, and then moved lower. Closing around him with just the right amount of pressure to drive him out of all rational thought. He moved within her fingers, some idea lingering about being inside her, bringing her with him, but didn't have a chance to focus on it as he exploded, almost immediately, in her hand.

She'd been gone most of the afternoon. And for months, too.

For a few brief moments, as he recovered, he allowed the water to wash over them, allowed himself to savor the feel of her warmth against his back.

Until there was a very definite complaint. Or call for acknowledgment at any rate, from a tiny body part with a big punch right to his kidney.

And he noticed the water had started to go cold.

"We need to talk." Elaina spoke the words into his back before she let him go, and he nodded. Turned off the water. Reached for towels and handed her one.

Then got hard all over again when he saw her naked body, quite pregnant with his child, in his shower with him.

He'd seen her belly during the ultrasound, but the whole picture…was something his imagination hadn't drawn nearly as perfectly as the real thing. He had no breath, standing there looking at her.

So beautiful. Just so beautiful.

She covered herself up with the towel he'd handed her. Started to dry off, still covered. And he heard again the ominous words she'd stated just seconds before.

We need to talk.

Very little good ever came from those words beginning a conversation.

And while the sex they'd just shared had been wonderful, it did nothing to reassure him.

Quite the opposite, in fact.

Sex was what they did when there was nothing else between them.

All he had in the bathroom was a pair of thin cotton pajama bottoms and a T-shirt. He pulled them on and left her to redon the clothes he saw thrown over the edge of the bathtub on the opposite side of the room.

The noise he'd heard earlier. The poodle had to have known she'd been there, but he had not given anything away.

"Thanks, buddy," he said dryly to the dog, who'd moved from the shower rug to the bed at some point.

He could hear Elaina dressing—pictured the jeans and loose-fitting cotton top, covered by the calf-length cardigan she'd left in that afternoon. Running a hand through wet hair that he hadn't taken the time to comb, he paced back and forth from the end of the bed to the chair and table under the window, and back again.

He'd leave if she asked him to. Immediately. Move out in the morning. He'd even understand if she told him that the sex had been a fond farewell.

He'd give her whatever space she needed.

He had no choice there. And no desire to do anything where she was concerned that was directly contrary to what she needed.

But he was not going to turn his back on her. Or Marisol.

Back and forth he walked. Repeating what he knew to be his deepest truths. He might be getting ready to lose a piece of his life, but he'd found himself in the process of loving Elaina Alexander.

And for that he'd be forever grateful.

"I'm sorry." Her words stopped him in his tracks. She stood at the bathroom door, sandals on, ponytail perfectly intact even while wet.

And his heart sank.

Still, he stood there. Listening. Ready.

Loving someone, standing by them, wasn't just easy, or fun, or happy. He hadn't lightly made his promise to always be there for her. He'd meant the words.

Still meant them.

If she needed him to jump out, he'd jump.

And knew that if he needed her to video-call him every night he wasn't putting Marisol to bed, she'd do so. Because their promises to each other worked both ways. She'd do everything in her power to give him what he needed.

She just couldn't be anyone but who she was...

"Sorry for what?" he asked, when she just stood there, seemingly unable to express what she had to say.

"For coming in here...into your space...without

permission…with you in the shower…and then… touching you like I did."

He wasn't sorry. Not in the least. Hell, he'd gotten the best end of the deal, to be sure. But… "Why did you do it?"

He needed to know.

"Because when I got home and couldn't find you…your SUV was here but you weren't… I glanced down the hall, saw your bedroom door open, called out, you didn't answer, and you weren't in the shed. And then I saw Beldon run into your room and followed him, heard the shower and…" She shrugged. "I just was so glad…and… I've missed your body so much."

She shook her head as her words trailed off.

None of which told him what she'd actually come to say.

"Why were you looking for me?"

She shook her head again, looking at him. Looking different, somehow. Her eyes more alert, open wider, and her chin tilted up higher.

She looked…determined. Something he'd only seen at the hospital, explaining why a scan read she'd done was absolutely accurate and needed to be acted upon.

She'd been right, too.

"I think… I don't know… I'm not good at just doing what I want to do for someone, without consultation and agreement…"

He breathed his first sigh of relief since his orgasm.

"Okay, so let's consult."

"I've already...kind of...moved forward..."

And relief left the premises. Still, he stood there. "Moved forward how?"

"I got us plane tickets. To Las Vegas."

For the first time since she'd invaded his shower, he started to question if she was okay. To worry about her.

"We've never talked about going to Las Vegas." Yes, he'd grown up an hour and a half from there. And Vegas was the closest national airport. But...

"I know." She stood there, nodding, her belly hardly looking pregnant beneath the top, with the sweater wrapped around her edges.

"When were you planning on going?"

"Whenever we're ready. Both of us. The tickets are open-ended."

Something about her, an energy, the way she was kind of wiggling on her feet like she had to pee, but not really...finally got through to him. Actually traveled across the room and entered his body was more like it. His nerves started to buzz.

Maybe just coming back to full life after the orgasm...

"I want to marry you, Greg. If you'd been out in the shed, or come when I called, you'd have found me perfectly rational and kneeling in the kitchen with a pair of wedding rings in my hands..."

She'd come home to propose to him?

It was then that he noticed the two little black boxes on his dresser, by the door. He hadn't made it that far in his pacing. Wasn't sure he could make it over there then, with the way his heart was pounding.

He sat on the end of the bed. Ridiculous. Stood up. And walked slowly toward her, holding her gaze the whole time. Waiting for her to blink. To look away. To shut down on him.

When they were toe to toe, she was still gazing straight into his eyes. Into his soul, felt more like it. "Will you marry me, Greg? I love you so much. More than that, I'm in love *with* you. I know now that that's why I broke up with you before, and why I wanted you to live here, and why I was so glad that you're the father of my baby, and why I couldn't let myself love you before I came to terms with my past."

His heart soared. His body soared. And his mind was mostly blank. "Why you couldn't let yourself love me?"

"Because it's so much easier to go through life without having to worry about hurting someone, about doing something that ruins their dreams...or ends their life. Because I was afraid to love and lose again. Because life isn't perfect and love comes with no guarantees and recovery is so damned hard. And because if you don't let yourself love, you've already lost. And that's worse than death."

"You aren't responsible for Peter's death." He

hadn't said the words the night she'd given him the chance. And had been doubting that choice ever since.

"I know," she said. "The drunk driver is. And Peter started the conversation. He wouldn't let the matter go. And I engaged because I didn't want to get home and then have the conversation with him standing over me, convincing me once again to give in to him. For the good of our family."

He lifted a hand to the side of her face. Just needing to touch her. To feel her skin. Her warmth and softness. "You not being who you are, just giving in, doing what you need to do—that's not good for your family."

She covered his hand with her own, holding his fingers against her. "I know that now, too. Thanks to you."

"To me? I said nothing...there was so much I could have said, and I sat there like..."

"Like a man who loves me enough to know what I need," Elaina interrupted him. "I had to come to the answers on my own. But you're the one who sat with me, Greg. Not just that night, but all the nights we spent in your bed, letting love grow without any expectations on me, without any pressure...and then... moving in here...still without ever once pushing me further than I was ready to go."

"Because you were giving me what I most needed," he told her. He wasn't a saint, like she seemed to be making him out to be.

"Because I love you, too," she said softly, her eyes glistening again. "Because that's what healthy love does… It lets you hear your partner's needs without losing sight of your own, and together you find a way to fit together in the best possible way."

"And the sex is great, too." He said the words with a grin on his face, but with a voice heavy with emotion and a hint of moisture tickling the corners of his eyes, too.

"You haven't answered my question."

"Yes, I have," he said. "I wed myself to you the first time I took you to my bed and found a goddess who moved me more than any other woman ever had. When I had lunch with you and felt…uplifted just to hear you talk. The day you told me you were pregnant with my child and I didn't believe you. And the day we found out you were right. Yes, I love you, and I'll marry you, Elaina Alexander. Whenever you're ready. In Las Vegas. Or anywhere. And I'll renew my vows every single day from now through eternity, on this earth, or beyond."

She reached up and kissed him then, open mouth, her tongue knowing exactly how to fit with his. Her arms slid around his neck, his around her waist, and… Marisol kicked.

"I can see our daughter has your strength."

"I only hope she has your patience," Elaina said, kissing him again. "And your wisdom." The words were punctuated by another kiss, her eyes half-lowered, telling him what she needed. He took his time to undress her, touching her where he knew she liked most, how she liked most, and slid into her right there at the end of the bed, laying her on her back, with him still standing.

He went at her speed, angled himself how she liked it and cried out with her as they both reached their climaxes, one just after the other. He was ready to head to Vegas right then.

"Let's go tonight," he said boldly.

"Go where?"

"To Vegas. You said whenever..."

"But..."

He put a finger to her lips. "Not to get married, though I'm ready for that, too. Just to get away, me and you, a couple who's just admitted they're spending the rest of their lives together."

It wasn't until Beldon nosed his leg that he realized they couldn't just run off like two kids with no responsibility.

"Beldon," he said, half to the dog, but seriously concerned, too. No kennel was going to be open after five on a Saturday night, not in Marie Cove... And they weren't those people, the ones who could just throw all caution to the wind.

"We can drop him off at Wood and Cassie's," Elaina told him. "I've heard that Retro would welcome a playmate."

"You call them, and the airline, and I'll get a room."

And he had to add, "It's too soon for a wedding tonight, but I'm hoping for one before our daughter is born."

Her smile, minus any sign of fear or doubt, earned her another very long kiss.

"First, how about another shower, as soon as we get to our room tonight?" she asked when they came up for air.

"I can agree to that plan. And this time you stand under the water...in front of me...so I can see every inch that I'm touching..."

Elaina shimmied up against him as well as her belly would allow, grinning, and then sobered.

"I'll always have your back, Greg." He knew by the deeply serious look in her eye that she was talking about the shower...and not.

"And I'll always have yours."

As doctors, as people who'd suffered, they both knew that there were many things they couldn't control, but they'd just made a promise they could keep—for themselves and their family. Forever.

* * * * *

MILLS & BOON

Coming next month

ITALIAN ESCAPE WITH THE CEO
Nina Milne

'What's wrong?'

'Nothing. Just keep talking. But I think we've been spotted.' Out of the corner of her peripheral vision, she saw someone point at their pod, camera in hand. 'We *have* been spotted.' Her mind went into overdrive, on automatic she appraised the scene. Champagne, private pod, the whole thing shrieked of date night. This was the perfect set up for a launch of their relationship, discovered by accident, it would reek of authenticity.

Instinct took over; and leaning over she kissed him; her intent had been a simple quick featherlight brush of the lips but she hadn't bargained for her body's reaction. Or his. Because it wasn't enough, the sheer giddy sensation whirled her head. After a first startled second where he froze, he turned his body, raised his hands and cupped her face in his hands, the firm cool grasp made her catch her breath.

Then he deepened the kiss, slowly languorously as if they had all the time in the world and Ava forgot where she was; forgot everything except this heady moment in time where nothing mattered except the sweet sensations that glided through her whole body. Then all too soon it was over, the wheel literally stopped turning and Ava realised they were near the top.

As she pulled away she caught sight of his expression, knew it mirrored her own. Shell shock, surprise. All wrong screamed the one bit of her brain that was still in gear. Pull this together. Seamlessly she pulled a smile to her lips and whispered. 'Don't look surprised.' Knew that a photo like that splashed on social media would give away too much.

To her relief Liam got it instantly, leant forward to hide his expression, looked as though he were whispering sweet nothings in her ear and then he moved away to pick up the champagne bottle to top up their glasses, a smile of sorts on his lips.

Ava focused on breathing, sipped the champagne, wished it were the bubbles that were swirling her head rather than the aftermath of the kiss. 'Sorry. I reacted on instinct – I saw an opportunity to make this look real and I took it without thinking.'

'There's no need to apologise – you took me by surprise that's all.' With an obvious effort he cleared his throat, brought his voice to a normal tone. 'What do you think will happen now?'

Continue reading
ITALIAN ESCAPE WITH THE CEO
Nina Milne

Available next month
www.millsandboon.co.uk

COMING SOON!

We really hope you enjoyed reading this book. If you're looking for more romance, be sure to head to the shops when new books are available on

Thursday 21st January

LET'S TALK
Romance

For exclusive extracts, competitions
and special offers, find us online:

f facebook.com/millsandboon

𝕏 @MillsandBoon

⬡ @MillsandBoonUK

Get in touch on 01413 063232

For all the latest titles coming soon, visit
millsandboon.co.uk/nextmonth

MILLS & BOON

THE HEART OF ROMANCE

A ROMANCE FOR EVERY KIND OF READER

MODERN

Prepare to be swept off your feet by sophisticated, sexy and seductive heroes, in some of the world's most glamourous and romantic locations, where power and passion collide.
8 stories per month.

HISTORICAL

Escape with historical heroes from time gone by. Whether your passion is for wicked Regency Rakes, muscled Vikings or rugged Highlanders, awaken the romance of the past.
6 stories per month.

MEDICAL

Set your pulse racing with dedicated, delectable doctors in the high-pressure world of medicine, where emotions run high and passion, comfort and love are the best medicine.
6 stories per month.

True Love

Celebrate true love with tender stories of heartfelt romance, fro the rush of falling in love to the joy a new baby can bring, and a focus on the emotional heart of a relationship.
8 stories per month.

Desire

Indulge in secrets and scandal, intense drama and plenty of sizz hot action with powerful and passionate heroes who have it all: wealth, status, good looks…everything but the right woman.
6 stories per month.

HEROES

Experience all the excitement of a gripping thriller, with an inte romance at its heart. Resourceful, true-to-life women and strong fearless men face danger and desire - a killer combination!
8 stories per month.

DARE

Sensual love stories featuring smart, sassy heroines you'd want a best friend, and compelling intense heroes who are worthy of th
4 stories per month.

To see which titles are coming soon, please visit
millsandboon.co.uk/nextmonth

JOIN US ON SOCIAL MEDIA!

Stay up to date with our latest releases, author
news and gossip, special offers and discounts, and
all the behind-the-scenes action
from Mills & Boon...

 millsandboon

 millsandboonuk

 millsandboon

't might just be true love...

Set your pulses racing with Medical, for undeniable frissons in the high-pressure world of medicine, where emotions run high and passion, comfort and love are the best medicine.